SAY SO

BESTSELLING AUTHOR OF IN THE GRAY

B.B. REID

ALSO BY B.B. REID

Standalone
Lilac
The Wrong Blue Eyes
In the Gray
Say So

Men of the Wilds
Crucible
Chrysalis

Broken Love Series
Fear Me
Fear You
Fear Us
Breaking Love
Fearless

Stolen Duet
The Bandit
The Knight

When Rivals Play Series
The Peer and the Puppet
The Moth and the Flame
Evermore
The Punk and the Plaything
The Prince and the Pawn

For those afraid of the fall but who leap anyway.

PLAYLIST

Girls Need Love - Summer Walker
Best Friend – Saweetie ft. Doja Cat
Nights like This – Kehlani & Ty Dolla Sign
Shit – SZA
Ante Up Remix – M.O.P (ft. Busta Rhymes)
Suddenly – Billy Ocean
Soft Girl Era – Ari Lennox
Trick'n – Mullage ft. T.I.
Doin' It – LL Cool J
Nobody Gets Me – SZA
Haunted – Beyoncé
Lover Girl – Meg thee Stallion
Yeah, I Said It - Rihanna
Best Friend – Young Thug

CONTENT WARNING

You can stop shaking in your boots now, silly. I'm not gon' traumatize you…this time.

This book contains:

- Kidnapping
- Light Stalking
- Excessive mutilation in the name of love.
- Vegans

ACT I

THE BRIDE

CHAPTER ONE

COBY

I NEVER IMAGINED THE SUN WOULD BE SHINING THE DAY I learned that heartbreak was the most deafening sound I'd never heard. It arrived silently like the wind until you were ready for it to pass through you.

But it's been hours since my epiphany.

It was nighttime now.

I stared up at the full moon peeking out from behind gray clouds, wondering how I got here. I thought I'd felt the worst of this pain when I became an orphan at fifteen, but as bad as losing my parents was, somehow this woe felt worse. Walking away from someone you loved, someone who was still alive for you to touch and hold and see, was unbearable. Time heals all wounds, but what about the ones that were free to keep tearing themselves open? Even now, far from the source, my anguish echoed through me as I bypassed the long line outside the Diamond Lounge.

The upscale club straddled the boundary line between the high-end and low-rent district, sitting on the corner of the busy street where it attracted patrons of all types—young professionals, grad students, influencers, scammers, singles, couples, and friend groups. Business was booming for my older brother's club, but the pride I normally felt was dulled by the agony that sent me running to him for comfort in the first place. As if to rub salt in the wound, a fresh wave of tears fell just as I reached the door where two bouncers were checking IDs.

"Hey, Dre," I said to the friendly bouncer as I cut the line wrapped around the corner, pissing off all the people who were waiting. I ignored the sound of their mad asses kissing their teeth and grumbling and focused on sounding like I wasn't two seconds from falling apart. "Is Shaun here?" I hadn't even tried to call him because Hunter's relentlessness forced me to turn off my phone after I stormed out in the middle of our fight.

"Nah, you just missed him," Dre answered. "He left for the night about ten minutes ago."

"Already?" I asked, feeling dumfounded as I looked around. The club was busy even on a Thursday night, so it made no sense for Roshaun to leave this early in the night I'm sure they needed all hands on deck this for crowd. "Why?"

Dre glanced up from the ID he was checking with a flashlight before shrugging and waving the group of girls inside. They were still talking shit, but I paid those bitches with their beauty store bundles and ashy heels no mind. "I don't keep that man's business in my back pocket, but you know your brother, Coby."

Meaning, Roshaun found someone to screw and ditched work early to play rather than get this money. Why my brother started his own business when he had no work ethic was beyond me. The new manager he hired to run his club was probably ready to quit, just like the last two. Roshaun always piled too much on them because his priorities were fucking, spending money, making money, his car, and then me in that order.

"Okay, then," I said with a sniffle as I turned to go. "I guess I'll see you later."

I didn't make it more than a step before Dre laid a gentle hand on my arm. "I don't know about that, girl. You seem like you're going through it. I don't know if I feel right about letting you leave."

I had trouble meeting his gaze as I lied. "I'll be all right."

Dre made a frustrated sound. "Just…just go inside and wait while I try to get a hold of your brother."

It was unlikely that Roshaun would have answered for me anyway since our relationship was rocky at best, but if Dre called, there was a chance my brother would answer. It was sad but true. I thought about it for a moment longer before also realizing I had nowhere else to go. I could go home, but Hunter was there, and she was the last person I wanted to see right now. Exhaling heavily, I accepted Dre's invitation with a faint nod.

He muttered something to the other bouncer before escorting me inside.

The club had two floors, each with a bar. There were mirrors along the walls and chandeliers in the ceiling. The white flowers, which appeared purple under the LED lights decorated the fluted pillars around the club. The sparse crowd in the lounge section upstairs was surprising for such a busy night. The stairs were even blocked off by a red velvet rope, and at the top stood a stone-faced guard who definitely didn't belong to the club.

Someone high-profile was in the building.

Dre didn't seem to care as he bypassed the downstairs bar and led me over to the glowing spiral stairs. I watched him unhook the rope before placing a hand on my lower back when I hesitated. While he led me upstairs, I tried once again to convince Dre that I was fine, but the gentle giant wasn't convinced. Before I could insist, the bodyguard placed a hand out to stop us from going any further once we reached the top.

"Let us through," Dre ordered through gritted teeth.

"No more girls."

"She's not here for your boss. She's another VIP guest."

"*No more girls,*" the bodyguard barked as if Dre hadn't spoken.

Dre's massive chest puffed out, and I almost palmed my forehead. "Look, you can let us through, or I can call Mr. Perry and let him know how his *guests* are treating his little sister."

Another guard walked over at that moment to investigate, and

I felt my cheeks warm as the commotion drew more gazes and the whispering started. The guards spoke low to one another before the nosy one walked away again. I tracked his path with my gaze as he made a beeline for the bar that was also being guarded by a wall of bodyguards. They parted to let him through, and I barely got a glimpse of a lone man sitting at the end of the bar before the gap quickly closed again.

It made me wonder who their employer could be that his men were out-ranking my brother's bouncers. Dre was practically seething, which means whoever the VIP was has been a problem all night.

Ohhhh booooy.

Forgetting my aching heart, I rolled my eyes at the dick measuring.

A moment later, the guard was already returning. I was prepared to be turned away when he waved his hand instead. "Boss said to let her through."

Dre lifted a brow while I fought my anxiety. I wasn't even dressed for the club, so I felt self-conscious enough in my skin-tight jeans and off-the-shoulder crop top.

"I need to search her," the stair guard said before we could pass.

Dre started to argue, but I shook my head and held out my arms for the guard to pat me down. He then looked inside my oversized crossbody purse that I got from a thrift store before confiscating the pocket knife that Hunter made me carry around. "I'm gonna need that back when I leave," I warned.

The guard said nothing as he straightened and waved me through.

I forced myself to put one foot in front of the other and let Dre escort me over to the end of the bar where there were far fewer people. Everyone seemed to have gravitated toward the opposite corner where Mr. VIP sat. I was careful not to look around or make eye contact with anyone as I sat.

Dre distracted me by wiping away the tears that hadn't dried with a cocktail napkin. After I gave him a tremulous smile in thanks, the sweet bouncer ordered me the sluttiest drink on the menu and a plate of their only vegan option. Once he was sure I wasn't going to fall apart, Dre fist-bumped me before quickly leaving.

As I watched him muscle his way back to the stairs, I had a fleeting moment of regret for turning him down when he asked me out. Now he was happily married with a baby on the way, and I was single yet again thanks to Hunter.

Who am I kidding, though? She would have run Dre off too, so it wouldn't have mattered.

To say my bestie was possessive was an understatement, and I was guilty of the same. But that was before we broke a cardinal rule that threatened everything. Hunter tried to turn back time, and when I told her it was too late, she said we had to try. It wasn't the first time one of our relationships crashed and burned so that our friendship could endure. I was just foolish enough to believe this time was different.

When my food and cocktail arrived, I ignored the former since my stomach felt like it had been shredded. I quickly downed the strong drink, hoping to numb the shitty feeling, but it didn't work and brought a fresh wave of tears. I was still fighting them back and *losing* when the hairs on my arms suddenly rose. Forgetting the drama my arrival caused earlier, my head shot up so I could find the source of the eerie feeling and immediately my gaze clashed with another across the long length of the bar. Time slowed as I choked on the sight of the fine as fuck man lounging in a relaxed pose against the back of the bar stool.

He seemed to have been watching me for quite some time because he didn't startle or look away now that he'd been caught. In front of him was a portfolio, which he ignored along with a drink and a basket of wings. His dark brown skin glowed under the purple LED lights around the bar, but he was slightly turned so the half of his face that wasn't exposed cast his features in shadow.

It made him look like a demon.

I searched and searched, but it was the only flaw I could find.

Those high cheekbones and chiseled jawline looked like they had never even borne a single pimple. His jet-black hair was cut into a low fade, heavily moisturized, and meticulously brushed. The crisp white button-up shirt he wore underneath his blue pin-stripe vest pulled tautly against his muscles and had me choking on my damn tongue.

I thought maybe it was a coincidence that our gazes happened to meet, so I waited a beat and then two more, but he never looked away. The VIP guest who had commandeered my brother's club openly watched me as if he weren't at all concerned over the repercussions of making me uneasy. He studied me like one would a horse before they rode it.

Okay, it wasn't the best analogy, but I didn't know how else to describe the intent and possession in his eyes. A man who looked like *that*, who wore his obscene wealth like a second skin, and reeked of too much power certainly had his options.

Could a nobody like me truly be the focus of his attention?

I blinked away my tears to clear my blurry vision, and he seemed to finally notice them, though his calm expression didn't change. He had no reason to care that I was upset. He merely found my tears fascinating.

It was unnerving the way he watched me because I couldn't read his thoughts, and secretly I wanted him to love what he saw. I craved his approval, and that bothered the shit out of me, especially when I just swore off love forever.

I huffed my frustration when a full minute passed and he continued watching me as if I were both fascinating to him yet still too unremarkable to act on it.

What the fuck was his problem?

I silently communicated with my eyes that I wasn't in the mood and that he should fuck right off.

Finally, the relaxed expression on his handsome face shifted, and the slow smile he unleashed on me at my attitude was indulgent—as if he found my anger cute. Unwillingly, my frown melted away while confusion and desire prickled my flushed skin. I thought maybe his smile was an invitation—not that I'd accept it—until he suddenly looked away, dismissing me to address the scowling man standing over his shoulder. They whispered back and forth, and it seemed the mystery man had forgotten all about me, until the grump he was speaking to suddenly flicked his gaze in my direction, then looked away and nodded at whatever Mr. VIP was saying.

I knew without a shred of doubt that they were discussing me. In what detail and to what end, I didn't know.

But I did care—enough to consider going over there and asking him what was so fucking funny. I fantasized about slapping him too, but that thought was swiftly swept away when the bodyguard straightened, and I caught sight of the gun resting on his waist.

Weapons weren't allowed in my brother's club.

The man he was guarding must have had some serious pull if my arrogant brother bent the rules for him.

That's when I finally took a real good look at my surroundings for the first time and noticed everything amiss. Among the droves of scantily-clad women were the obvious bodyguards. The ones who resembled Secret Service agents in their suits and neutral, non-threatening stances that weren't fooling anyone.

And then there were the ones you weren't supposed to see...

The true muscle, who at first glance blended with the other club goers. It was their constant vigilance and quiet menace that gave them away, and I counted at least thirty sprinkled around the club. They lingered around the exits, watching everyone who came and went. They inserted themselves onto the dance floor below, standing like immovable pillars amongst the writhing bodies. They were even posted at both bars, but they didn't order drinks or converse with anyone. Even the sections were occupied by the secret assassins.

Anyone stupid enough to try the man sitting at the other end of the bar wouldn't see the trap until it was too late.

When the hidden guards weren't scanning the building for threats, their focus gravitated like a magnet toward the mystery man whose lure was unrivaled and the scowling man standing over his shoulder, who I concluded must command them.

It was possible I had it all wrong, though.

Either these men were here with Mr. VIP, or they were here *for* him.

Feeling like I'd fallen into a snake pit, I didn't think twice before I eased to my feet with my heart in my throat. I quickly threw down some cash to cover my tab before I eased away from the bar. I was hoping my departure went unnoticed, but when I greedily stole one last look, I found *him* watching me again.

He didn't look amused or relaxed anymore.

His body was coiled tight, and the emotion coming from him wrapped itself around my throat like an invisible collar. He looked like he wanted to give chase but was fighting himself. I didn't want to be here when he decided, so I severed the connection and quickened my steps toward the stairs.

This time, I didn't look back as I fled the club.

It wasn't until I was safely in my car and heading back to my apartment, where I knew Hunter was waiting for me, that I started to feel a little silly for running. He was probably just a celebrity or some crypto bro who hired all that muscle to feel important.

Shaking my head, I parked my car once I reached home and then tiptoed inside the dark apartment that I shared with my best friend. I didn't let myself breathe until I spotted Hunter lying on the couch. She was fast asleep with her cell phone clutched in her hand. I didn't even think about it as I grabbed the blanket tossed over the back of the couch and covered her with it.

When she didn't stir, I let myself watch her for a little while until I felt the crushing weight of my sorrow return. I had no idea where we stood after our fight. Hunter and I met when we were fifteen. Our souls have been tied from that first moment.

She was my best friend. My twin flame. The yang to my yin.

I'd rather lose myself than be without her, so if pretending is what Hunter needed to go on, then so be it.

Quietly, I wrote my capitulation in a note and placed it where she would find it easily in the morning. I then kissed her soft cheek before leaving the living room. Locked inside my room, I filled the tub with water and tossed in one of my bath bombs before shedding my clothes and sinking into the hot water. Usually, I read to pass the time, but I couldn't focus beyond replaying the events of tonight in my head. Once I started nodding off, I used the last of my energy to drag myself out of the tub before drying off, and then I dressed in sleep shorts and a matching camisole.

Once I slid into bed and shut my eyes, I sobbed into my pillow to muffle the sound.

In the midst of my undoing, the man from the club suddenly invaded my mind, and I shut my eyes against it, but that only sharpened the image.

That's when my shitty-ass memory finally whispered a name, and I sat up with a terrified gasp.

I knew him.

And I didn't just know his name. I'd seen him once before. Three years ago, shortly after my brother opened his club.

With any luck, I'll never have to see the heir to the Fola again.

CHAPTER TWO

COBY

Two years later...

"WILL YOU HURRY UP?" I URGED MY BEST FRIEND.

"Bitch, I'm trying," Hunter huffed back as she shoved and yanked on the old-ass window of the apartment we were attempting to break into. "I think this shit is stuck."

Our window didn't even lock, so it was a good thing we didn't have a ground-floor apartment like our landlord, Luther. I bounced anxiously on my toes while keeping an eye out for other tenants and Luther. Luckily, most of the street lights around our apartment building no longer fucking worked, so we were at least partially concealed to anyone who happened to pass by.

And then there was the fog.

Sunny days were rare in Black Veil. My great aunt used to say that there was too much sin, so God had turned his back on us like Babylon. A month later, she retired to Florida, and I never saw her again. The old bitch never called and didn't seem to give a shit if Roshaun and I were still alive or not, so on a good day, it felt like my brother was the only family I had left. On a worse day, it felt as if I had no family at all since my relationship with my brother was rocky at best. Still, my Aunt Pat might have been on to something.

After all, Black Veil belonged to the *Fola*.

Or as everyone who wasn't *made* called the infamous crime family—the Blood mafia.

The corruption and crime that ran rampant in this city all led back to them. If you were selling ass, the *Fola* was taking a cut. If you specialized in street pharmacy, they supplied the pills and potions. And if you wanted to settle a feud the old-fashioned way, the mafia was the only way you were getting your hands on the hardware. Even legitimate businesses like my brother's had fallen under their heel.

It was even rumored that the Kilpatrick family founded Black Veil when they immigrated from Ireland before the Prohibition era, but anyone with access to a textbook knew that couldn't be true.

The Fola hadn't *founded* Black Veil. They *seized* it.

Their influence and might had grown so much that the government had pretty much given up trying to do anything about them. And Black Veil had been living in a dark cloud ever since—like an obscure island covered by never-ending fog, except we weren't hidden at all.

We'd been abandoned.

We even had our own Tower of Babel, where the rich and powerful gathered to show the poor that they were gods amongst mortals. And guess who owned the deed to all of that decadence?

Malcolm Kilpatrick—the boss of the Fola.

Although everyone knew it was his son who was truly running things.

I turned my gaze toward the glittering onyx tower in the center of the city. Only a few blocks separated me from it, and yet it felt a world away. The highest three floors of the penthouse were cloaked in clouds and fog, casting its resident in obscurity. Did they feel safe and secure hidden away from the rest of the world, or were they lonely?

Some days, Black Veil felt dreary and grim. On nights like this, it was as if I were trapped in a noir film. Considering the overwhelming crime rate—including the one happening right now—it was pretty astute of me.

Hunter and I just paid our rent despite the heat in our unit being broken again for the fourth time in two months. Luther kept hiring his cousin to fix it because the labor was cheap, but that fake-ass handyman couldn't seem to get it working for longer than a day or two. To make matters worse, we'd heard his cousin got pinched for running scams and was currently locked up at county.

Luther promised to hire someone else to fix our heat, but it's been two weeks, and each time we pressed him about it, he'd give us the run-around. And now Hunter and I were running up our electric bill using the open oven to heat our apartment on top of the cheap space heaters we had running around the clock. It was a good thing our apartment wasn't large to begin with.

To solve our Luther problem, Hunter had the bright idea of withholding our rent until he fixed the heat, but all it had gotten us was the threat of eviction and a hefty late fee tacked on to the two grand we owed him.

Luckily, we always paid in cash.

Luther had quickly left after collecting our rent, but we knew he'd be back soon, and since he was nothing if not predictable, he wouldn't be alone. We lived only a block away from the red light district, Luther's favorite haunt, and a creep like him wasn't picky, so we didn't have a lot of time.

"Got it!" Hunter finally said before shoving it up the rest of the way and quickly scrambling inside. My short arms hurried to catch the window before it could slam down on her spine, and then Hunter tumbled inside the apartment with a yelp and a curse. Something inside crashed to the floor and shattered.

"Are you okay?" I asked while rising to the tips of my toes and trying my best to peer inside the dark apartment.

There was a lengthy pause, and then she grumbled, "Yeah." Hunter stood to hold the window ajar while I heaved myself up and over the sill. I was even less graceful climbing inside, ending in a heap at Hunter's feet. "You okay?" she whispered after letting go of the window and helping me stand. Her dark brown eyes were full of concern as she waited for a sign that I'd hurt myself.

"Yeah. I'm fine. You?"

I didn't wait for her answer as I pulled away from her soft touch under the guise of looking around the cluttered apartment.

"I'm good," she answered. I could feel her gaze on me.

Nodding absently, I wrinkled my nose at the smell of musty ass and feet and sighed. "How the hell are we supposed to find our rent money in all of this? We should just call the Department of Public Health on his ass."

"That won't get our heat fixed," Hunter reminded me as she peered around the apartment through the holes in her light pink ski mask. Since we were partners in crime, I was wearing a similar one, except mine was a dark pink. I didn't even know why we bothered since everyone in our neighborhood knew everyone. If Luther walked through that door, he'd definitely recognize us. According to him, we'd been nothing but trouble since we moved in, so he was looking for any excuse to kick us out.

I tiptoed over to the tiny kitchen table by the front door, cringing at the sticky sound the dirty floor made under my feet. On the table were several containers of days-old takeout, mail, and papers scattered everywhere, a few empty liquor bottles, an overflowing ashtray, and a gray lockbox with a black handle.

"Hey, Hunt..." I called out as I came to a stop in front of the box. Hunter immediately moved from the side table drawer she had been searching to inspect the box with me.

"That's got to be it," she said with a huff while I tried to pry open the box. "See any keys anywhere?"

"You mean the ones he always has on?" I retorted dryly after giving up.

"Well..." Hunter placed her hands on her wide hips. The thick black leggings she wore were stretched taut over her generous curves. "How are we going to get our rent money?"

"We could—" I was cut off by the sound of a key being inserted into the front door's lock.

Hunter's eyes widened under the mask at the same time mine

did. "Shit!" she whisper-yelled. We scrambled for a place to hide. I tried to duck behind the curtains, but Hunter grabbed my hand and yanked me behind the couch, which is arguably the worst hiding place ever. "What the hell is he doing home?"

"Trying to get his crusty dick sucked?" I whispered back as I peered around the end of the couch.

Hunter didn't reply because the door opened a moment later. Luther, with his receding hairline, ambled inside and flipped the switch next to the door, flooding the apartment with light. Charlotte, an escort we recognized, entered behind him. She wore a cropped purple metallic puffy coat, a mini skirt, and five-inch red heels. Her blonde wig was lifting, but neither one of them cared as they made small talk. Luther headed into the small galley kitchen while Charlotte lit a cigarette. She'd probably need a whole pack in order to fuck that troll. Luther didn't offer Charlotte a drink as he pulled a beer for himself from the kitchen and popped the top on the edge of the counter.

I could feel Hunter behind me as I waited for an opening to escape. The window was only a few feet away, but the open-space apartment didn't allow for much coverage.

Finally, after haggling over the price because the creepy piece of shit thought thirty bucks for a blow job was too high, the two moved into the bedroom. I didn't dare move from my spot until the door shut firmly behind them.

Sighing, I rose from the filthy floor, ignoring my crawling skin as I tried not to think about the last time it was cleaned. "Let's get out of here."

"Not without our rent money."

"What the fuck—Hunter!" But she was already disappearing down the hallway toward the bedroom.

I didn't think twice about following her, but then she held her hand up for me to wait before opening Luther's bedroom door a crack and disappearing inside. The sounds that briefly escaped before the door shut once more made me more than happy to oblige.

Regardless, I was giving Hunter exactly sixty seconds before I came in after her.

It only took forty-nine before the door opened again and Hunter slipped out.

"What happened? Did you get it?" I asked as we moved swiftly and quietly away from the bedroom. Luther and Charlotte were full-on fucking now, the sounds following us down the hall.

Hunter opened her gloved hand with a smirk and showed me the key ring. "Got it."

"Okay, good. Let's get the money and go then."

We reached the front room, and Hunter tried to stick a key into the lock box, but it didn't fit, so she tried another and another. There were over thirty on the large silver ring.

Suddenly, the sounds of sex ceased, and I felt my heart kick into gear as my ears picked up Charlotte and Luther moving around.

"Hunter, hurry!"

"Shit, shit, shit, shit." She stuck two more keys into the lock, but none of them worked.

"Wait, those are all apartment keys," I told her. And then I plucked a square key with green rubber around the head from the loop. "Try this one." Hunter stuck it into the lock and turned it just as the bedroom door opened down the hall. As soon as we heard the lock disengage, Hunter snatched open the box, and I grabbed the envelope full of cash on top with our apartment number on it. As soon as my hand was clear, Hunter started to close the box, but I stopped her. "Wait!" I whisper-yelled. "We can't just take ours. Luther will know we did it."

"I don't give a fuck what he knows," Hunter replied coldly. "I care about what he can prove."

She closed the lock box just as we heard two sets of footsteps coming down the hall. "Go! Go! Go!" Hunter and I made a mad dash for the door, no longer caring if we were heard as long as we weren't seen.

"Hey!" I heard Luther shout just as Hunter threw open the front door. "Who's there?"

Hunter ran out of the apartment first with me on her heels, but I couldn't help looking over my shoulder once we were free. Charlotte entered the front room, and our eyes met briefly before Hunter grabbed my hand and tugged me from my view.

Together, we flew up the stairs and didn't stop until we reached the fourth floor. Once we were behind the safety of our locked apartment, we collapsed on the ground. For a minute, there was only the sound of our heavy breathing before Hunter started laughing, triggering my own.

Snatching off my ski mask, I wheezed out, "I can't believe I let you talk me into that. Bitch, we're going to jail."

Hunter removed her ski mask, revealing dark brown skin, a round face, upturned eyes, and full lips. She had a small scar along her jaw that her bitch-ass father gave her when she was younger, but other than that...flawless. Hunter was stunning and at times, so much so that it hurt to look at her. "Maybe. But at least we got bail money now." Hunter held up the envelope with our rent money crumpled in her fist.

"Good," I said as I sat up. "Let's call JD and get our fucking heat fixed."

"You call him," Hunter said with a groan as she rose to her feet and stretched. "I need to shower. I got a shift tonight." Her shirt rose a little from the movement, and my gaze got stuck on her belly button before I forced myself to look away. Hunter's thick hourglass figure squeezed inside those leggings made me feel like I was no better than a man, especially when I was the opposite of her in almost every way. I was short, skinny, and pale, but Hunter never hesitated to tell me how pretty I am. Sometimes, I'd even catch her staring, but she'd brush it off by telling me something stupid like my eyelashes were crooked, or I had a booger in my nose. I rose to my feet while Hunter finished her stretch, and then she looked at me hopefully. "Are you coming?"

Our codependence meant that whenever one of us was scheduled to work a separate shift, the other would tag along and hang around until it was over.

"Not tonight," I answered. "If I miss another Pilates class, Sheema's going to give my spot away, and you know no one else in the city is as cheap as her."

"Fine." Hunter feigned a wounded look. "You'd rather torture yourself than spend time with your bestie. I see how it is."

Rolling my eyes at Hunter's dramatics, I freed my phone from my pocket while Hunter went to her room to get ready. After arranging an appointment with the handyman, I retreated to my own room and lay down since I had a couple of hours before class started.

Our apartment was small and sparsely furnished with mostly second-hand items, but it was also the birthplace of some of my favorite memories. Like Hunter and I buying our first Christmas tree and each claiming a side to decorate. We had both chosen pink ornaments since we shared a favorite color, but Hunter had forgotten to use hooks and had simply shoved the thick branches through the tiny holes, making the ornaments appear lopsided and the branches stiff. My side hadn't come out much better because I'd forgotten to decorate higher than eye level, leaving the top and bottom of the tree barren.

And for our birthdays every year, we baked each other a cake and talked about all the places we'd visit once we had the money.

I was beginning to nod off when Hunter suddenly burst into my room. My eyes flew open, and I lifted my head to see her storming in naked and dripping water. I frowned despite feeling like I'd swallowed my tongue as I watched her storm into my tiny bathroom. "What's wrong?" I asked as I got out of bed and followed her into the en suite.

She was pumping some of my lotion into her hand when she met my gaze in the mirror. "Nothing. I forgot to go to the store."

"Well, don't forget to hit those elbows this time. You don't want to look like you've been praying in flour again."

"Bitch, fuck you," Hunter retorted with a chuckle while I cackled. "What did JD say?"

"He said he can swing by in a couple of days to look at it, but if new parts are needed, it might take longer."

Hunter only nodded as she massaged the lotion into her skin. I stood there awkwardly for another moment, and feeling my presence, Hunter's gaze flicked toward the mirror again, and I could see the question in her eyes. At that same moment, there was a knock on the front door, so I used it as an excuse to flee the room.

It wasn't until it was too late and I was already opening the door that I remembered it could be Luther coming to demand the money back, but instead, it was Charlotte. She was standing there with a lit cigarette caught between two fingers and her other hand resting on her hip. Her wig had slipped back another couple of inches, showing the cap and frizzy braids underneath.

"What are you doing here?" I asked.

"Hey, to you too," she returned dryly. I didn't respond and just waited for her to get to the reason she was standing at my damn door. Picking up on my silence, Charlotte rolled her eyes. "I just thought you should know that Luther is on to you. He's already noticed the missing rent money."

"What missing rent money?"

"The one you and Hunter took. Yours, I'm assuming."

"I don't know what you're talking about."

"Cut the bullshit, Coby. I saw you in Luther's apartment. You know I did."

I scratched my scalp like I was truly confused. "It sound like you be smoking more than tobacco because I don't know what you're talking about—like I fucking said."

"Look," Charlotte huffed before stabbing out her cigarette and then flicking it away. "I want half of whatever you took, or I'll tell Luther what I know."

"And I already told you—" It was all I got out before I was nudged aside and a shadow blew past me.

A fully dressed and *furious* Hunter stepped into the dimly lit hallway, and I didn't see the Sig she was clutching until it was too late. "Hoe, tell it to me since you want to talk so fucking bad." Hunter was seething while Charlotte made a terrified sound as my hot-headed best friend pressed the muzzle of her gun against Charlotte's cracked, cum-stained lips. "What do you know?" Hunter nudged her when she didn't speak.

"N-nothing."

"You sure? But you were so fucking eager to yap a moment ago."

"I don't know nothing!" Charlotte screamed.

"I fucking thought so." Hunter took a step back and waved her away with the gun. "Beat it, dummy."

Charlotte fled down the stairs, but neither of us moved until the echo of her footsteps faded completely. Only then did Hunter storm back into the apartment, tossing her gun on the counter, which I frowned at before shutting the door behind us.

"You shouldn't have done that," I scolded while Hunter finished wrapping long dark hair in a neat top knot. "I had it under control."

Hunter threw back her head and sighed because it's an argument we've had many times before. She was as fiercely protective of me as I was of her. "I know you did."

"What if she goes to the police and tells them you threatened her?"

Hunter snorted. "She won't. Them Birch street three-o-fours stay away from the cops on principle."

I shook my head and muttered, "If you say so." Don't get me wrong. It's not that I'm ungrateful that she had my back, but Hunter's shoot-first, ask-questions-never approach to everything had me constantly afraid of losing her. I wouldn't survive being separated from her, and I don't think Hunter would either, so I tried another tactic to get my best friend to see reason. "Charlotte said Luther knows we took our rent money."

Hunter shrugged like I knew she would. "So? We got our receipt proving we paid it. What happens to the money after that is his fucking problem."

Luckily, our landlord was too cheap to install security cameras, and he'd be too embarrassed to call the police and have his business in the streets, so there was nothing he could do about it.

"Okay, fine."

"Cool," Hunter replied immediately before hugging me tight. "Stop worrying so much. We'll be fine, okay?" For some reason, all I felt from her vow was the crushing weight of guilt. "I'll see you later."

I squeezed her back as if it would be the last time. We were dramatic like that whenever we were forced to part, even for a little while. "See you later."

Perched precariously on the bar stool of the Diamond Lounge, I pretended to be in my own world as I sipped my cocktail and swayed to the music playing inside the nightclub.

I'd lied to Hunter.

I didn't go to Pilates at all.

Instead, I snuck inside my brother's club while he was away so that I could be eye fucked across the long length of the marble bar. It's been a few weeks since I got the timing right, so imagine my delight and sudden disquiet when I walked inside the Diamond Lounge an hour ago to see the man I'd been fantasizing about for two years sitting in his usual spot.

I'm going to talk to him, I vowed silently. I resisted the urge to fuss with my appearance to ensure that I was up to par. I promised myself that if he came tonight, I would finally shoot my shot, and there he was. It's the only way I'll ever know if the burning looks and slow sweeps of appraisal exchanged across the glittering surface of the marble-top bar for the last two years meant something. For my sanity, I had to put an end to this longing that's been plaguing me for years. Sink or brick—tonight, I'm giving my crush no choice but to claim me now or let me go forever.

From the moment I first saw him, I've had eyes and thoughts for no one else, and the dry spell that came from it had me ready to hump a wall. Hunter's been calling me Miss Coochie Cobweb.

The nightclub was upscale, so even though my crush had forgone his usual suit, he was still mouthwatering in a fitted black shirt buttoned only halfway and an understated but no doubt pricey watch on his wrist.

His identity was no mystery to me, though. In fact, it was the reason I stayed away.

Ocean Kilpatrick was a foolish, terrible dream.

The man had more blood on his hands than God.

Hunter would have me committed for even daring to fantasize about a man like that. What would she do if she knew I've been sneaking here at least one night a week for the last one hundred and four weeks with the hope of living them out one day?

The thirty feet or so separating me from Ocean was the closest I ever allowed myself to get in the five years since I first saw him. I was twenty the first time, but my brother had been adamant that I stay far away from the underboss. The second time was two years ago on the night when it felt like my world had been yanked from under my feet. That night had been the end of a chapter I never thought I'd close and the start of my obsession with the bloodthirsty prince of crime.

I couldn't say why I'd come back to the club the next night looking for him, especially after fleeing in terror, but once I had a taste of Ocean's attention, I became addicted. I couldn't help wanting more of that thrilling feeling if I tried.

Most of the time, seeking him out proved fruitless.

But on the nights it didn't...

We never spoke. Not once.

No matter how many times I offered myself up on a platter for him to feast on, he never made a move. He would just openly eye fuck me and then ignore me until I felt stupid and left, only for my dumb ass to spin the block once the sting of his rejection wore off. I've never been thirsty, so I didn't know why I kept torturing myself. All I knew was that I was playing with fire, but it was the promise of the burn that kept me coming back.

It didn't matter what I wore or what I did, though. The asshole never took a bite.

A year ago, I even tried making Ocean jealous, but I quickly regretted it when the man I'd chosen found himself grabbed out of nowhere and thrown out of the club. It was the first time I'd almost broken character to curse Ocean out, but the look on his face that night warned me not to fuck with him, and my scary ass took heed and never tried it again.

I stared despondently at my drink as I felt the familiar doubt creeping in.

Was it all in my head?

"Girls Need Love" by Summer Walker was a dull roar to the deafening drum of my heart. I wanted to look and see for myself if it was real and not imagined—that I was indeed the focus of Ocean Kilpatrick—but I was too much of a coward. I had used up all of my bravery coming here tonight. I'd lost count of how many nights I snuck to see him without Hunter or my brother learning about it. They didn't see eye to eye on much, but they'd both lose their shit if they knew.

One way or another, this game of ours had to end.

So go over there, the horny devil on my shoulder whispered. *Talk to him. He's only a man.*

But like every night that I've given in to temptation and sought him out, something always held me back from actually going for it.

Could I handle him? I wasn't so sure.

Could he handle me? I wasn't sure of that either. Not when the other half of me—the part I loved more than anything—was sure to run him off like all the others.

And how long are you going to keep allowing Hunter *to dictate your love life, hmm?*

Groaning, I raised my hand to request another drink, but it was gone quicker than the first, so I ordered another and then a third. I'd actually worn all white tonight as if it would make a difference. My dress had a deep plunging V in the center and was tight enough to accentuate what little curves I had. The heels I'd borrowed from Hunter, even though her feet were bigger than mine. The white thigh-high boots made me feel sexy and confident enough that I actually believed I could accomplish my mission tonight.

There was only one problem.

I hadn't counted on the foreboding in the air. It curled inside my gut, filling me with tension and not the kind that made my thighs quiver.

Something was *wrong*.

Tonight, everyone had gathered on my end of the bar as if they could sense Ocean's dark mood as well. He was surrounded by his usual armed bodyguards who didn't so much as twitch as they stood with their backs to him, clocking every one who came and went or ventured too closely. Only one of the men from his security team ever spoke directly to him, but even he mostly left Ocean alone, standing a little further away than usual.

It's been two years, and I still haven't learned the scowling bodyguard's name. He was rougher around the edges than Ocean's polished, almost aristocratic presence, but he was handsome with a closely shaven beard, a long jagged scar over his left eye, and dark eyes. I didn't notice much else about him, though. I only had eyes for his charge.

Fury rode Ocean's thick brows and the sculpted line of his jaw while he reviewed the paperwork in front of him before barking something to his head of security. The man nodded and swiftly departed, only to return moments later with a familiar face frozen in terror.

It was the exact opposite of how I usually felt, being the sole focus of Ocean Kilpatrick's attention.

Ocean and I wore twin expressions, but for different reasons, as

I watched him question Brandon, who answered quickly. What the hell could Ocean want with my brother's club manager?

Their exchange went on for a while before Ocean suddenly looked my way as if he had just remembered I was here. Before I could feel some type of way or pretend I wasn't attempting to eavesdrop, he turned his head to bark an order.

Immediately, Brandon was seized and dragged away by two of his guards. As soon as he was gone, Ocean calmly took one last sip of his drink as if nothing was amiss before rising to his feet. He was so goddamn tall that my kitty purred at the sight of him. Ocean's dark gaze flicked toward me in that moment—too fast for me to erase the desire from my expression and I stopped breathing when he actually paused. For the first time in two years, we stared openly at each other rather than the covert glances we exchanged when we thought the other wasn't paying attention.

He looked…

Fuck.

He looked like he wanted to snatch me up and drag me away like Brandon before he shook his head and spat a vicious curse, abruptly severing the moment and departing with a twitching jaw.

It was the first time he'd ever left the club before me.

I was still reeling from seeing Ocean casually kidnap someone with hundreds of witnesses around when a shadow fell over me, and I looked up to see the head of Ocean's security standing there.

"Coby Perry," he greeted, as if it were a fact and not a question. He knew who I was, and I knew who he worked for. There was no sense in pretending.

"Yes?"

"Mr. Kilpatrick would like you to know that it's time for you to go home now."

My belly immediately sank. "Excuse me?" All I could do was blink in befuddlement since this wasn't our usual game.

Ocean and I *never* acknowledged one another, even though we both knew I had a crush. He and my brother did business together, but I didn't know the extent of it. Roshaun refused to tell me, only ever saying it was safer if I didn't know. Either way, getting involved with my brother's business partner and a made member of the *Fola* would have been a mistake for many reasons.

"Ocean's retired for the night and requests that you do the same." When I didn't move and only stared, the grump lifted an impatient brow. "We can escort you home if you'd like?"

What the actual fuck? "No. No, that's okay. Um…thanks for letting me know." Rolling my eyes, I turned away and considered ordering another drink.

Who the fuck did Ocean think he was ordering me around like that?

Expecting the guard dog to leave now that his message had been relayed, I scrolled on my phone for a few minutes, but he continued to stand there until it became more than clear that he wasn't moving until I did. Feeling like every eye in the club was on me in that moment, I reluctantly left my seat with a grumble and gritted my teeth when Ocean's bodyguard trailed me out of the club.

Outside, I immediately looked around for Ocean, but he and poor Brandon were nowhere to be found. The walk to my car felt long, and by the time we reached it, I was feeling reckless, so I spun around to address the silent bodyguard. "Where did your boss take Brandon?" I demanded.

The man didn't react other than to slide his hands into his pockets and answer vaguely. "Somewhere quiet to talk."

"What the hell does that mean?"

The bodyguard shook his head. "It's best if you don't know."

"What does Ocean want with him?"

"It's best if you don't know," he echoed.

Realizing that I wasn't going to get any real answers out of the man, I shook my head while the past two years played by in my mind like a shameful PowerPoint highlighting all my terrible decisions. "What's your name?" I softly requested while staring at but not truly seeing the passing traffic.

I could feel the bodyguard staring at my profile for a long while, and I thought maybe the question was too personal before he surprised me. "Abel."

"Abel," I said, testing his name. It was nice. "Please tell your boss that I don't take orders from him and that I don't appreciate being toyed with. I thought…" I closed my eyes and inhaled deeply before letting it all go. "I thought he was interested in me," I confessed honestly and pathetically. "Clearly, I was wrong. You can also tell him that I'm not coming back. I'm done with this charade." The man searched my gaze for a moment, probably trying to assess my seriousness, before dipping his head in a polite nod. "Thanks. Goodbye."

Abel didn't return the farewell as he shut my car door for me. As I drove off, I glanced in the rearview mirror to see a phone plastered to his ear, already relaying my message to his Boss as he watched me drive off.

It didn't matter.

I meant what I said.

CHAPTER THREE

COBY

A week later, I found myself back at the Diamond Lounge. It was a Friday night, so the club was packed, but for the first time, I prayed that Ocean wouldn't show his face. I wasn't here for him anyway.

Roshaun texted me an hour ago, saying he needed to talk to me and had asked—damn near begged—me to come here. Hunter and I had already been getting ready to go out, so I agreed even though Hunter had plenty to say about my dropping everything for my brother.

She wasn't wrong, but I could never turn my back on Roshaun—no matter how much he secretly resented me or how many times he pushed me away. Besides, I had my own reasons for coming.

"Look at those bitches," Hunter grumbled beside me. "You'd think that man's dick was covered in bread crumbs the way the birds are flocking."

My heart thumped inside my chest, and I followed her gaze in a panic toward the sections above us. It was packed to capacity, but a moment later, I was sighing my relief when the DJ shouted out Fat Pack. He was a local rapper who had recently signed a huge deal with Making Waves music group, and it seemed as if the whole city came out to celebrate with him. It was rumored that the record label was owned by the *Fola,* but no one's ever been brave enough to point the finger and confirm it.

Hunter loved Fat Pack's music, so once she learned he'd be here, it was much easier to convince her to come with me, even though she had good reason not to. According to her, Roshaun, who sacrificed everything to raise me after our parents died, was a snake in the grass. Nothing I said in his defense would change her mind.

And their beef wasn't one-sided either.

Roshaun thought Hunter was bad news, and while not even Hunter would disagree, my brother failed to realize that I was just as bad.

Hunter and I were two parts of a whole.

We shared everything, including our penchant for trouble.

Roshaun had only been a few years older than I was now when he tragically went from being my big brother to sole guardian. He never got to properly grieve our parents because of his determination to be strong for me. Hunter said I didn't owe him shit, but I couldn't see it any other way.

I caught her eyeing the VIP again and was about to ask if she wanted to go up there when my phone vibrated in my hand. When I glanced at the screen, I saw that it was a text from my brother.

> **Shaun: Where r u?**

I sighed as I unlocked my phone and texted back.

> **Coby: Downstairs w/ Hunter.**

> **Shaun: Meet me outside. Use the private entrance and come alone.**

I wrinkled my nose at his request and sent another text, pressing my brother for more details to distract myself from Hunter dancing with our neighbor, Gary. After five minutes passed with no response, I rolled my eyes and decided to get this over with. I had my reasons for accepting Roshaun's olive branch, since the last time we'd spoken ended with us not speaking for months.

Despite our age gap, we actually used to be close before our parents died, but I wasn't so sure we could ever go back because of how much he hated my other half.

"My brother wants to talk," I shouted over the music to Hunter.

She immediately straightened and dismissed Gary without a word. "I'll come with you."

Overhearing, Gary sucked his teeth and stormed off.

He'd been trying to get with Hunter for years, and a half-hearted dance was the closest he'd ever gotten.

I'd laugh if I weren't terrified of what her rejection might lead to. Hunter had more restraining orders than bodies. Her presence was a siren call to any man who ventured too close, and sometimes they didn't handle her refusal to grant them access very well.

I was just glad I didn't share her effect on men.

I wasn't ugly even by the most hating bitch's stretch of the imagination, but Hunter had a natural sex appeal that I didn't share. She exuded it even when she wasn't trying. The girl could brick a dick in her sleep.

But it came with its own challenges too—such as her penchant for attracting stalkers.

Hunter had an obsession with guns and knives. She literally had an armory stashed in our apartment, so she could more than handle herself, but I still worried for her.

I shook my head at her offer, making her eye me like I've bumped my head and forgotten our bestie code. We'd both burn the world down before leaving the other behind.

"He said to come alone."

Hunter pursed her painted lips in disapproval but didn't argue. Unlike Roshaun, Hunter never tried to come between us despite her personal feelings.

"Wish me luck?" I said playfully to ease her worry.

"Your brother's the one who'll need it if he doesn't cough up your money. We'll just jump his ass until he does," Hunter said, completely serious. "You know I've been dying to cut him."

I chuckled before kissing her cheek. "And that's why you're my bitch."

She hooked her pinky with mine like always before one of us made our usual vow. "Ride or die, sis."

We kept our fingers locked as I slowly walked away until that last moment when we were forced to let go. My stomach felt like it was caving in from the heavy dose of foreboding filling it. I looked over my shoulder to see if Hunter felt the same. She was still watching me, looking like she wanted to stop me, so I knew she felt it, too.

I forced myself to keep going because I'd rehearsed this moment a thousand times, and I wasn't backing down. It wasn't easy asking someone for half a million dollars, but I just had to do it—like ripping off a Band-Aid. Tonight, I suppose, was as good as any. Maybe Shaun would be in a good mood, and I wouldn't be subjected to another lecture about how I'm too young to be trusted with so much money.

Our parents had left us both a small inheritance after they died. Roshaun had used his half as seed money to start his club with the help of an angel investor. Since I had been a minor when our parents died, the other half had been placed in a trust controlled by Shaun until I turned twenty-five.

My twenty-fifth birthday had passed nearly a year ago, and I had yet to see a penny. Hunter had been urging me for months to say something, but I'd been reluctant, knowing my brother would see it as a sign of distrust.

I ran my sweaty palms down the front of my green sequin corset once I reached the back of the club and the hallway that led to the alley. It mostly went unused because it was meant for the celebrities Shaun paid to appear at his club. Most of them preferred to use the front entrance to be seen and photographed for the blogs. Instead, only members of the *Fola* put it to use, but they—*he*—didn't make an appearance very often.

My steps faltered when I noticed a stoic man armed and dressed in a black suit, blocking the entrance. After two years of pining for their leader, I was now able to spot one of his goons from a mile away, so I spun on my heels without a moment's hesitation and headed in the opposite direction.

Maybe I could find another way around.

"This way, Ms. Perry," the man called out before I could take more than a few steps away.

Stopping in my tracks, I slowly turned with my heart racing and my skin flushing. "What did you say?" He wordlessly beckoned me forward, but my feet refused to move. Had Abel not given Ocean my message? "Sorry, no, I can't," I said while trying to sound like I wasn't losing my shit. "I'm looking for my brother.

The hair on my arms rose when the goon nodded. "This way," he repeated.

Oh shit.

Roshaun, what the fuck did you do?

"Oh…okay, thanks." I hurried past, my unease growing when his shadow fell over me immediately after. Peering over my shoulder, I clutched my mace a little harder as I scurried along when I noticed the giant following at a carefully measured distance. I once again considered slipping past him to run back to Hunter.

My phone vibrated in my hand again, and I knew it was Shaun. I didn't know what had his boxers in a bunch tonight, but I was not in the mood. Sighing, I quickened my steps as I followed the short hallway all the way down to the end. I could already feel the cold air outside bleeding through the walls of the club as I grew closer to the exit. I picked up my pace, praying my brother was in one piece.

The goon's footsteps seemed to thunder behind me, and I knew it was all in my head, but I still rushed to press on the bar that should have released the catch, but it seemed to be stuck. I slammed my hands on it repeatedly until it finally gave, and I stumbled into the alley. It was small, with only a couple of dumpsters on either side and a single lane for traffic.

At the moment, it was filled with a line of black SUVs and a small army lined up like toy soldiers. None of them reacted to me charging through the door, and that dreaded feeling that this was all for me returned swiftly.

"Oh, um. Sorry." I wasn't about to turn myself into a witness, so I kept my eyes on the ground as I tried to back through the door again, only to find my way blocked by my giant shadow. "Excuse me," I said with a huff to the goon.

He didn't move or respond as he magically turned into a statue once more.

I was getting ready to make a fucking scene when a wet cough and a groan had me glancing over my shoulder to the one happening in the alley.

That's when my legs nearly buckled from beneath me.

My brother was kneeling on the ground in a pool of his own blood. He was clutching his ribs with snot dripping from his nose and a wet crotch. "What the fuck? *Shaun?*"

Hearing my voice, his head shot up, and I could see from here that his eyes were swollen. "Coby—" He released another cough that had me taking a protective step toward him. "You're here." *Cough. Cough.* "Good."

Good?

I rushed to help him but was arrested by the sight of a hand wearing black leather gloves curling around my brother's shoulder. It squeezed a warning meant for me while Shaun winced and groaned.

Seeing my brother in pain did the trick and brought me to a screeching halt before I could get too close. Instantly, I recognized the pull demanding my attention, but I couldn't. Looking away from my brother for even a second felt a lot like the morning I woke up and found out that my parents had died in a car crash. Bile rose in my throat from the fear of Shaun disappearing, but I knew I had no choice if I wanted to save him.

And when I met familiar dark eyes, I was shattered with the betrayal of seeing the man I fooled myself into thinking I wanted to marry standing over my brother like an owner would a dog on a leash.

And now that day would *never* come because Ocean had chosen another path—to stand between my only family and me. Already, I could feel the illusion slipping further away.

Usually, Ocean wore tailored suits.

Tonight, he dressed for war.

And his eyes…

I should be used to them watching me, studying me, slowly breaking me down with the promise of someday. One day, he'd put down the drink he always nursed for the sake of the ruse. He'd hold my gaze forever instead of watching me in secret, and then he'd walk down the long length of the bar and take me home with him.

I'm such a fucking idiot.

Shoving my disappointment away, I dismissed Ocean and focused on my brother instead. "Shaun, what did you do? What's going on?" Everything about my brother's posture was wrong. His light brown skin was even paler now, and he was hunched over and sweating profusely. Roshaun looked moments from death.

"Coby, I need you to…" He grunted and inhaled deeply, but the simple act cost him dearly. "I need you to listen to me very carefully. It's important that you don't…" My worry quadrupled when he seemed to search for the right word and then settled on, "Resist."

Like a magnet, my gaze flew to Ocean as I did the exact opposite. "What the fuck happened to my brother?" I snapped. Fuck my stupid romantic heart. And fuck Ocean too. For my brother, I'd take on the heir to the mafia. Shaun had given so much for me already.

"His ribs are broken," Ocean stated bluntly and without feeling.

His ribs are broken, my mind echoed to me. It was the first time he'd ever spoken directly to me, and those were the words fate had chosen.

The dominating force of Ocean's steady gaze took every ounce of will not to drop my own in submission. "I'm no doctor, but I think he might have punctured a lung, too." My brother was dying a foot away, and all I could think of was how smooth and cultured Ocean's voice sounded.

Shaking my head, I lifted my phone, then dialed 911 without replying.

No one stopped me. Ocean even looked…amused.

"Hi, yes," I greeted when the dispatcher answered. I kept my gaze on Ocean while he casually slid his hands into his pockets and cocked his head. "Could you please send an ambulance to The Diamond Lounge? My brother, Roshaun Perry, he…" My gaze flicked toward Ocean, who lifted his brows as he waited for my answer. "He fell and broke his ribs."

I hung up.

"Good girl."

"Fuck you," I snapped, ignoring the way my cheeks warmed at his words. "I don't know what my brother did to upset you, and I don't care." Gathering my courage, I moved toward Shaun. "The ambulance will be here any minute. I suggest you get the fuck on."

"Our business hasn't concluded, Coby."

"Your business with Roshaun is none of my concern. My brother is the only thing I care about, and *we're leaving.*"

Without regard for Ocean's personal space or the serious don't-fuck-with-me vibes he was giving, I wedged myself between them and crouched to help Shaun. It wasn't easy in heels or with my petite stature, so when I rose with my brother under my arm, I stumbled a little trying to support his weight. Shaun looked moments from passing out, but then he made a sound of protest when we stumbled forward, and I realized too late that it was a warning.

My brother was yanked from my arms and thrown to the ground, leaving him open to vicious kicks while I screamed at them to stop. Arms immediately closed around me the moment I tried to intervene, and I was lifted and pulled away from the violence while I kicked and screamed.

"I see that listening isn't your strong suit," Ocean whispered while he carried me away. "My business is with *you, mo aingeal*[1]."

---

1   My angel.

If not for Ocean holding me, I would have collapsed to the ground. "Pleeeease. Let me go," I sobbed.

"I tried that," he whispered so fiercely to me that I felt my body relax against my will, "but you kept coming back, Coby. What did you think would happen?"

A chill as I've never felt before washed over me, and then I was kicking and clawing again while Ocean simply tightened his hold. I weighed a measly hundred and five pounds, and he easily weighed double that, but still, he let me fight.

If his body was a wall of rock and stone, I was the furious sea crashing against it.

Neither would bend to the other, but at the moment, one clearly had the upper hand.

"Stoop!" I screamed until my throat was ravaged—as if I hadn't daydreamed about this man holding me just like this since the start. I was short with toned arms and legs and some curves, but I was no match for Ocean's brute strength, and I wasn't no damn *Karate Kid*.

Even if I could disarm him, Ocean seemed crazy as hell. I'd probably have to dodge bullets to get away from him.

If only Hunter was here.

She'd gladly shoot Ocean in the face, fine or not.

"Stop this shit," Ocean ordered when he realized my corset was slipping down and I was close to flashing my breasts to everyone in the alley.

I didn't care, I just threw my head back.

Satisfaction and pain rippled through me simultaneously when the back of my skull connected with his nose. Ocean's grunt was my cue right before his arms loosened, and I dropped to the ground just barely managing to land on my feet. I whirled around to face him and saw blood leaking out of his nose.

Good.

I hope it was broken.

Ocean touched his nose and nodded with carefully banked fury when he saw red on his fingertips. He was still staring at them when his other hand suddenly whipped out, and he grabbed me by my throat. There was no time to react before he dragged me forward and ignored my cries while he wiped his fingers across my face, marking me with his blood. "*Tugaimid onóir don fhuil²*," he rumbled deeply. Ocean's gaze was less patient when he added in English, "Now you are mine."

The sound of sirens suddenly rent the air.

Ocean calmly set me back on my feet, but I was too shaken to react to the emergency lights I spotted from the street. Feeling Ocean's blood drying into my skin, I walked unsteadily back over to my brother and collapsed to my knees once I reached him. Gravel sliced into my bare skin, but I was numb to it all.

My mind had already accepted that there was no way out of this.

"Shaun…" I touched his shoulder gently, careful not to jostle him. "Roshaun!" I screamed, losing it a little when I tapped his face and he didn't respond. "Wake up! Please wake up! Shaun!"

I thought about checking his pulse, but I didn't know how, so I stared at my brother's chest rising and falling faintly.

Roshaun was alive, but for how much longer?

The back door of the club burst open, and two paramedics hurried through with a gurney. A grateful sob broke free as I leaned over and kissed my brother's cheek. "You're going to be okay," I whispered. "Just hang on for me, please."

"Mr. Kilpatrick," the first paramedic greeted. "Did you call for assistance?"

"No," I corrected on a shaky breath as I rose to my feet. "I did." Ignoring me, the paramedics continued regarding Ocean as if waiting for permission. "Why are y'all just standing there?" I screamed. "Fucking help him!"

The second paramedic shifted uncomfortably but still made no move to save Roshaun. "Mr. Kilpatrick?"

Mouth agape, I too turned to Ocean.

_____

2   We honor the blood.

He was leaning against the Denali now with his hands in the pockets of his hoodie as if he had all the time in the world.

"Would you like us to help the gentlemen?"

Ocean shrugged while staring at me. "That depends on the lady."

"Yes, I want you to help him," I rushed to answer before those weirdos could ask me. I knew the Fola ruled the city, but corruption this deep left nothing but a crushing hopelessness.

"We'll get to that. First, we need to talk," Ocean dictated calmly. The paramedics stayed put while my brother lay dying at my feet. There was a sarcastic tilt to his smile when he said, "I think it's about time we did that, don't you?"

"I don't want to talk to you," I confessed hoarsely. Hard to believe there was a time I wanted nothing more.

Ocean was unmoved, though. He was as rigid as my growing hatred of him. "The sooner you listen, the sooner your brother can receive medical attention."

Inhaling deeply, I closed my eyes as I shook my head.

I couldn't lose Shaun. I couldn't.

Other than Hunter, he was all I had. Truthfully, I barely remembered our parents, and that was enough guilt for me. "Ju-just hurry the hell up and tell me what you want," I snapped once I'd regained some of my calm.

I swear his goons shifted nervously at the tone I directed toward his boss. Abel, on the other hand, stood patiently at the helm as if confident that Ocean wouldn't actually hurt me. I wasn't so sure about that when Ocean rolled his shoulders as if the physical strain to keep from living up to his reputation had already taken its toll.

"Your brother owes me a debt," he announced as he slowly closed the distance between us, "and I fully expect to be paid, Coby."

I forced myself to take a calming breath, but all that did was give me a nose full of his rich scent. "What does that have to do with me?"

A few more minutes and Hunter would come looking for me.

But the realization came with panic at the thought of Hunter being hurt because of me, and all I could do was hope she stayed in the club where it was safe.

"Your brother couldn't pay."

Money. Of course, he wanted money. That's probably all he ever wanted from me. Just how long has my brother been in debt to him? "I-I have some savings, but it's locked in a trust. I can get to it, but only if my brother is alive. Whatever he owes you, I'll pay back every penny, but I—"

"Three million, one hundred and forty-seven thousand, six hundred and three dollars and sixty-six cents," Ocean announced before I could finish. My mouth snapped shut with a loud click of my teeth. He stood before me now, his expression patient but stern, as I slowly came to terms with the fact that there was no way out of this. "And that doesn't include interest."

"Stole..." I echoed with a punch of breath.

Had Roshaun really been stupid enough to *steal* from the fucking *mafia*?

How was this my life right now?

I didn't realize I'd voiced the question until Ocean answered it.

"I own fifty-one percent of this club. Your brother has been skimming from the profits since its inception."

My knees were knocking by the time Ocean was done. *Roshaun, you stupid fucking waste of our parents' DNA!*

I swear to God, I was going to kill his ass once I was done saving his life.

In full-fledged denial, my deep-rooted sense of loyalty had me shaking my head. "He wouldn't do that."

Ocean volleyed calmly, "He would, and he did, Coby."

Hunter's warnings about my brother being a low-down dirty snake were staring me right in the face now. "Okay, I get that, but... what does this have to do with me?" I was starting to sound like a broken record.

Ocean's gaze was unflinching as he stared me down. "Your brother has nothing else I want."

Later, I might be embarrassed by my gasp, but luckily, it was small enough that it had only been heard by the two of us.

Our little secret.

Ocean ran his tongue over his teeth as he stared at my lips like he'd heard my thoughts and shared them, or…he wanted to kiss me.

"I don't have that much right now, but if you just give me some time," I begged earnestly, "I will pay you back."

"Yeah?" Ocean licked his sexy-ass lips this time, and before I could remind myself that he'd lured me here to get at my brother, my gaze eagerly followed the path his tongue took. "Tell me how, *mo aingeal*?"

"I can work for you."

To my surprise, he nodded immediately in agreement. "Those were my thoughts exactly. There's a position in my organization that I think you'd be perfect for, and it just opened up."

Hope bloomed in my chest as I took an unconscious step forward. "What is it?" I asked.

Did it really matter? I'd do anything to save Roshaun.

"We can discuss that later," Ocean said after glancing at his watch. I didn't even recognize the fucking brand, but the price tag could probably buy a house. "Right now, I need you to get in the truck for me, baby."

My belly dipped. "What?" The wind picked up, so I wrapped my arms around myself. I'd barely noticed the frigid temperature until now. "Why do I have to go with you if I'm just going to work for you? Can't I just come by your office in the morning?"

As soon as I voiced the question, I knew it sounded ridiculous. Did mob bosses even have offices? Technically, Ocean was the underboss. He was second in command to his father, who was the actual Boss, but everyone knew who was truly running things.

Ocean didn't respond right away. Instead, he reached behind him and removed his hoodie. I didn't catch on to his intention until he stepped forward. Eyes widening, I stepped back, but he kept coming. When he grew tired of the cat and mouse, he grabbed a fistful of my corset and yanked me forward before forcing the hoodie over my head.

"You didn't have to do that," I whispered as soon as my head popped through the hole. I was drowning in the incredibly soft material—drowning in *him*. Ocean smelled *diviiiine*.

"We're not done with our discussion," he said, ignoring my gratitude, "and I've been exposed for too long."

"Can't you just email me?" I asked as I backed away again.

Ocean dragged me right back and said, "Get used to being near me, Coby. The position you'll be filling requires constant and close contact. I'll be your only company until I'm sure you're loyal. Now get in the fucking truck."

"I—"

"Get…in the fucking…truck." His order was delivered with enough dominance to make my nipples painfully hard. "I don't like repeating myself."

Gulping, I reminded myself that my brother was slowly dying a few feet away. Hunter would tell my silly ass to get a damn grip. Ocean was fine and rich, but not kill-my-brother-and-get-away-with-it fine and rich.

"I'm just trying to understand," I pleaded. No way I was going anywhere with him without the assurance that he wasn't going to dump my ass in the sound later.

Ocean suddenly pulled me close until I was wrapped in his strength and his heat. "No harm will come to you," he promised with a kiss to my cheek. My thong immediately dampened. "But until the debt is paid, you belong to the Fola, and unless I decide otherwise, you are *mine*." There was a thoughtful pause, and then he added, "But I wouldn't count on that last part happening." My belly dipped. "Come willingly, and your brother lives," Ocean warned. "Fight me, and he dies." I peered up at him to find him watching me. "And then I take you anyway."

"Those aren't *choices*," I argued. "That's like telling me to choose between a cage and a cell."

Ocean pinched my chin, and then he stared at my lips. "One has the potential of being comfier and more enjoyable than the other, *mo aingeal.*"

"How generous."

"No." I gasped at his tightening grip when I tried to look away. "The first lesson you'll learn about me is that I'm a greedy motherfucker and I always get what I want in the end." Without warning, Ocean lifted me into his arms and carried me over to the Denali. The back door was already open as one of the goons stood sentry by the taillight.

"Wait!" I screamed when Ocean tried to dump me inside the truck. To my surprise, he actually paused. "My brother?"

One nod from Ocean and the paramedics rushed forward.

I felt helpless and sick as I watched them load my brother up on the gurney before carting him back inside the club.

I should be going with him.

Once the paramedics disappeared with my brother, Ocean lifted a brow expectantly. Knowing there was no more reason to stall, I finally submitted to his will, and Ocean exhaled softly like he was relieved before carefully placing me inside. My ass and thighs immediately sank into the rich leather while Ocean took the time to buckle my seatbelt. Our gazes met once more when he was done, and I found it impossible to breathe with his face only a few inches from mine. His pupils were completely blown while he stared at my lips again.

Instinctively, I knew he wanted to kiss me.

And…to my woe…I still wanted that too. My fingers slowly uncurled from where they were clenched around the hem of my shorts, and then I was reaching for him when he suddenly swore in that language again and jerked free of the Denali.

I jumped a little when he slammed the back door closed, and then I watched as he spoke to Abel. Two of his men climbed into the front seats while the rest dispersed, blending into the shadows before disappearing entirely.

It wasn't long before the back door opened again, and I

questioned the immediate relief I felt when Ocean joined me inside. The driver wasted no time backing the Denali out of the alley as if he knew Ocean was eager to get me locked away for no one to find me.

I was still fighting the panic those thoughts brought on when the back door to the club flew open again.

Ocean's security went on high alert, so did I when I recognized that metallic silver dress wrapped around plush curves. My heart skipped a beat when Hunter stepped into the light, her stunning features twisted with confusion and concern as she frantically searched the alley for me.

The Denali had nearly reached the main road when she finally spotted us. The headlights were on full beam, so I knew she was blinded while everyone inside the vehicle could see her clearly. I could tell by her posture that she was already imagining the worst. Hunter must have noticed Roshaun being rushed through the club by paramedics and that I wasn't with him.

I was so focused on Hunter that I was startled by the sound of Ocean's voice breaking through. "Who is she?" His gaze was locked on Hunter through the windshield, but his tone was cold with a growl building in the back of his throat like he sensed someone hunting in his territory.

"No one," I lied. *Go back inside, Hunter. Go back. Please go back.*

Instead of heeding my silent plea, I watched as she lifted her phone and tapped the screen while keeping her gaze locked on the Denali.

Hunter was the other half of me.

The sun to my moon.

I knew she could sense me nearby just as I could sense her soul crying out for me.

Please go back, Hunter. Please.

Placing the phone to her ear as she fearlessly strutted towards us, her generous hips swayed with every stride. A second later, my phone rang. Somehow, I'd forgotten that I still had it. It was weird that Ocean hadn't thought to take it away. I'm sure kidnapping was a regular occurrence for him.

Needing to hear Hunter's voice if only for the last time, I was still at war over whether to answer when my phone was deftly plucked from my hand. I watched helplessly as Ocean studied the screen.

On it was a provocative photo of Hunter posing in a thong bikini on the beach. Her long hair was wind-blown, and her round ass was in full view as she peered over her shoulder at the camera with an alluring smile.

It wasn't even the most damning evidence that I'd lied.

It was that I'd saved her contact name as Mine.

Ocean stared at the screen for longer than was decent. I closed my eyes and inhaled deeply to fight the jealousy that made me want to snatch my phone back, and when I opened them, I found him watching me curiously.

"How *cute*," he remarked sarcastically. "But right now, I think it's time we discussed my rules." Hunter hung up and immediately began calling again. Ocean didn't bother checking the screen this time. We both knew it could only be her. "Rule number one—lie to me again and the deal is off. That means I find your bitch-ass brother and rid him of his existence. Now let's try again. Who. Is. She?"

"My roommate," I said honestly while still downplaying what she was to me. Hunter was so much more, but I'd be a fool to give him another pawn to use against me. "She has nothing to do with this."

The Denali finished reversing out of the alley and slowly turned until we were on the main road facing the flow of traffic.

"That's for me to decide. Is she going to be a problem?"

"No," I lied again. My best friend was definitely going to be a problem because she wouldn't stop looking until she found me, and while God might forgive Ocean, Hunter sure as fuck wouldn't.

"Can she track this phone?"

This time, I didn't lie. It was easy to ignore my one shot at being rescued when it meant protecting Hunter. "Yes."

"Stop the truck." Ocean rolled down his window before we were even stationary. I thought he would chuck my phone through it, but he didn't.

Instead, he powered it off and then tucked it inside his pocket before leaning back until he was out of sight with his long arm stretched along the back of the seat, his fingers within grabbing distance of my throat in case I tried anything.

I realized too late the reason why.

The bastard was giving Hunter an unobstructed view of me.

And it took her no time at all to spot me. Hunter's voice was full of alarm when she shouted my name and began sprinting toward the truck.

"Hunter!" I yelled, leaping toward the open window as if I might dive through it. Ocean immediately seized my throat, his fingers a hot possessive collar around my neck as he pressed me back against the seat and kept me there. Even now, I could hear the rapid click of Hunter's heels as she sprinted for the truck.

God, she was fast, even in heels.

Hunter ran track in high school and for a semester in college to stay in shape before we both dropped out after freshman year. She'd only gone because I wanted to give it a try, but when I realized it wasn't for me, we dropped out and worked odd jobs to make ends meet, living our best broke bitch life.

It never mattered.

Since we lived together and had no plans to ever separate, we always felt like we had everything already. The only time I ever questioned if it was true was two years ago, the night I met Ocean.

He rolled up the window just as Hunter reached the SUV. She slammed her fist over and over against the glass while screaming at him to let me go, but Ocean paid her no mind as he waited for my reaction.

It was as if he already knew the truth I buried deep, but I told myself there was no way he could.

"Stop," I begged as my eyes welled with fresh tears. "This is hurting her. It's hurting *me*. Please just stop." Tormenting us both like this, knowing we might never see each other again, was more than I could bear.

Ocean's fingers immediately relaxed around my throat, and while it could be my imagination, I could have sworn there was remorse in his brown eyes. "Drive," he ordered his goon.

The Denali sped from the curb, and I couldn't help turning in my seat to get one last glimpse of Hunter. My sore eyes widened a moment later when I saw that crazy bitch reach inside her clutch.

Goddamn it, Hunter!

I threw myself onto the SUV's floor and folded my body into a ball.

"The fuck are you—"

The muted sound of something hitting the rear windshield repeatedly interrupted Ocean before he could finish. To my horror, I realized Hunter was close to emptying the clip, but the glass remained intact.

Bulletproof.

The goddamn truck was bulletproof.

"Drive faster before she catches on and shoots out the fucking tires!" Ocean shouted.

The driver slammed on the gas.

My body was thrown into the door when he turned down another street on two wheels. Once the truck was righted, I carefully crawled back into my seat, buckled in, and then put my head in my hands.

"Why do I get the feeling that you lied to me again?"

Carefully packing away my rage, I sealed it in an air-tight box that I would only open again when it was useful. "What?" I croaked. My voice sounded tired even to my own ears.

"You said your friend wouldn't be a problem, but that's clearly not true."

"Because she's going to be a problem for *you*, not me."

It was quiet for a long time before Ocean responded. "I sincerely hope you're wrong, Coby. For her sake."

My head shot up, and I glared at the underboss of the Fola like I had a death wish. "Did you just threaten my fucking friend?"

"Our deal doesn't include *Hunter.*"

"Please just…tell me what you want from me? What is this job you want me to do?"

Ocean took his sweet fucking time answering, and I had just begun to give up thinking that he would when he said, "My father is ready to step down and let me take over as head of the family."

"Congratulations," I offered dryly.

Ignoring my sarcasm, he went on. "A standing tradition must be fulfilled before it can be made official."

"What is this tradition?" I forced myself to ask. I didn't give one solid fuck.

"I have to marry." There was no emotion in his tone whatsoever, and all I could do was pray for that unlucky girl. Whoever she was. "And if I want to stay in power, children must follow."

Stiffening, my heart beat a panicky drum. "I'm not sure how I can help you with that other than to recommend a good dating app."

Ocean smiled and thought it was a gorgeous sight, but it was a little too sharp and devious for my liking. Still, I found my attention caught by the divots below his cheeks.

Dimples.

This murderous lunatic actually had *dimples*—deep, distracting ones that made all of his other arresting features fade into the background.

"That won't be necessary, Coby. I've already found my wife."

I had two opposing reactions to that news—warm relief because, for a second, I thought he was going to say he intended to marry *me* and bitter jealousy at the girl who robbed me of my fantasy.

"So who's the blushing bride-to-be?" I asked when the silence became awkward enough. Maybe the bitch didn't have friends, and he wanted me to be her maid-of-honor or something.

But there was no way that would pay off a three-million-dollar debt. It was more likely he'd ask me to be their nanny, surrogate, or something.

I almost begged him to just kill me now.

Ocean's dark gaze held mine for so long that I felt myself falling into his trance again. It truly felt like I was floating higher and higher until his answer dropkicked me back down to Earth.

"I'm looking at her."

CHAPTER FOUR

OCEAN

A S TEMPTING AS IT WAS TO TUCK HER FAR AWAY FROM here, I didn't take Coby to Glamis. My family's estate was outside of the city, and while it would have been like throwing her in the sea without a life raft, it wasn't the only reason she wouldn't be safe there. Coby was my choice, but she wasn't my father's, and that made her a threat to everything, but I didn't give a fuck. I'd never wanted anyone or anything as badly as I did this brave girl.

My angel.

But as she wasted no time showing me the moment I pissed her off, her halo had a dark side too, and now I craved her even more. I was used to getting my way, which meant I never hesitated to stamp out any resistance to my will. It was second nature to me, and I never lost sleep over it.

But I had no desire to trample my future wife.

I wanted to keep her safe, spoil her, love her, and fuck her little ass through a mattress the moment she got over me nearly killing her brother.

We arrived at the apartment I kept in the city whenever my pops didn't need me by his side. Glainne Tower's pinnacle was a sprawling three-story penthouse with panoramic views of the sound and every luxury my future wife would ever need. I made sure of it, knowing that it would be her prison before it became her home.

The driver stopped in front of the building where Wayne, the doorman and a sleeper agent of mine, waited. Wayne's position in the Fola was unknown to everyone, including my father. Everyone except Abel and me. I had many clandestine operatives planted in and out of Black Veil, living normal lives and earning fair wages from respectable jobs while receiving an untraceable, generous stipend from me for their ears and eyes.

I climbed out of the Denali, followed by Abel, my head of security. Doors from the trailing SUVs quietly opened and closed as the rest of my security team formed a protective radius around me.

Coby, my bride-to-be, remained passed out inside the Denali.

Shortly after leaving the club, she'd fallen asleep curled against the door and as far away from me as she could get. We'd spent an hour making a loop around the city to shake off any tails because no matter how true the rumors or how many monikers the streets attached to me, there was always a motherfucker dumb enough to try me. My mind unwillingly conjured the image of the beauty at the club before I shoved it inside a box labeled 'Don't fucking think about it' and closed the lid tight.

"That went well," he said, even though his perpetual scowl said otherwise. The motherfucker stayed in a bad mood, so I didn't press the issue.

"Yeah," I grumbled, "a little *too* well." What was the catch? What had I missed? I couldn't stop thinking about it from the moment I had Coby inside my truck.

Quiet as it was kept, it pissed me the fuck off how quickly Roshaun had given up his sister to save his own skin. I already planned to kill him in due time, but an easy death would not do. Besides, my patience had rewarded me with something I valued more than money and a lot quicker, too.

For two years, I fought with myself over the decision to make Coby mine.

I could tell she was a good girl—soft, wide-eyed, sheltered, and a little spoiled. This life—*my* life—would be hard on her even with me shielding her from the worst of it.

I thought I'd seen the last of her two years ago when she ran away from me. I *prayed* for it. But then she came back, and she kept returning, offering herself up to me like a gift—bow and all. It was like trapping a gazelle in a cage with a hungry lion and asking for it not be devoured. Except Coby was the one with the lock and key, refusing to leave until I did the opposite.

It wasn't until she tried to give what was mine to that poor unfortunate soul who would have to find a way to beat his dick without thumbs now that I decided to make her mine.

Her brother stealing from me was a complication I hadn't anticipated. Roshaun started off small, but then the dummy got bold.

Greedy.

Seeing the bigger picture, I purposely turned a blind eye to it, letting him dig his grave deeper while unwittingly tightening the leash around his sister's neck before moving in to collect the only payment I desired.

Money was nothing to me. I've never been without it.

Lust was also a feeling I've grown bored with.

There was only one thing left that I hadn't tried to make life less dull, and that was falling for a tiny thing with a big heart. I had no fucking clue if it was even possible for someone like me, but I was going to fucking try.

Little did Coby know, her response tonight had only cemented my decision to keep her. The alternative would have been murdering her brother in front of her and then leaving no witnesses.

"So how long before your pops tries to kill the bride-to-be?" Abel asked a little too knowingly.

"Why would he do that?" I returned despite knowing the answer. Not long. "He wants me to marry." I shrugged despite the urge for me to head to my family's estate and slit my father's throat in his sleep before he has the chance to even breathe Coby's air.

"He wanted you to marry someone *he* chose," Abel reminded me. "You know he had that deal with Chicago."

"Arturo is dead, Angel is fresh out of prison, and from what I hear, their new Knight is lacking the required appendage for my father to do business."

"Okay, play dumb," Abel said with a shake of his head. "Just make sure you keep a close eye on your girl in case you're wrong, which…*you are*. We both know your pops will kill her out of spite."

"No one is touching my wife."

"Your wife, huh?" Abel smirked at the possession in my tone, but one of the reasons he was my head of security was because he never missed a thing—including my interest in Roshaun's sister.

"The friend is going to be a problem," Abel said after checking his vibrating phone. "I put Kellan on her tail after we left the lounge. He just checked in." Looking up from his phone, Abel studied my expression, trying to measure my mood. "She already tried to file a report."

A vision of the temptress clad in silver from the club flashes in my mind before I dismiss it. Dismiss her.

Hunter was Coby's past. I was her future.

"Then everything is going according to plan," I returned, mentally moving all the pieces on the chessboard before regarding my head of security again. "Who do we have at that precinct?"

"Only Kaplan, but he's vice."

Fuck. "Get me someone."

"Already on it."

Hunter Parrish can search all she wants. The only thing she'll find is a dead end. Coby was keeping her cards close to her chest, but so was I, and I knew more than she thought.

Pulling my gun free, I ejected the clip and emptied the magazine. I then cleared the chamber before slapping the empty mag back inside and sticking my gun back in my waist. Anyone even passively familiar with guns would know that it was empty, but I knew, thanks to Coby's need to use social media like a diary, that she was uneasy with them.

Wordlessly, I handed the discarded bullets to Abel before turning back to the Denali and opening the door.

Coby didn't stir as I reached inside and carefully lifted her into my arms. She was light as a fucking feather, and I found myself staring down at her sleeping face when she nestled her tear-stained cheek against my shoulder. Her glossy lips were parted, allowing soft sounds to escape while her long lashes hid her eyes from me. A short copper curl was draped over her forehead, and I wanted so badly to wrap my finger around it.

Nodding to Wayne as I passed, I carried my bride inside the building with Abel close on my heels. The building was quiet, save for the sound of one of the night janitors pushing a mop across the lobby floor. As the owner of Glainne, I had a file of all the tower's employees, so I didn't spare him more than a passing glance as I carried my prize to my private elevator.

Abel scanned the key card, and the black, ornate doors, surrounded by white marble, opened. Abel and I stepped inside, and the doors shut firmly behind us before jolting into motion. It was a long and uninterrupted ride up to the fortieth floor, and Coby didn't so much as twitch through it all, so I finally allowed myself to relax.

That's when the strangest fucking thing happened.

The elevator slowed, stopped, and then announced our arrival with a chime.

Coby's eyes flew open just as the doors parted. Feeling my hands all over her, her confused gaze slowly met mine. I was searching for the right words to put her mind at ease when it all came rushing back, and a horrified gasp left her lips. She pushed away from my shoulder and then hauled off, slapping the ever-loving shit out of me.

Caught off guard, I could do nothing as this damn girl

jumped out of my fucking arms, stumbled to the ground when she lost her balance, and then shot back to her feet before darting inside my apartment as fast as her heels would allow.

I watched, dumfounded and pissed the fuck off with ringing ears and a burning cheek as Coby quickly disappeared from the darkened foyer and out of sight.

CHAPTER FIVE

OCEAN

ABEL WAS BENT OVER, CLUTCHING HIS STOMACH, AND howling louder than the wind outside. The windows were tinted to look black from the outside, but I could still see the city clearly from here. If we'd been at Glamis, where my entire family gathered like members of a royal court, his loud ass would have woken everyone, but here at Glainne, it was just us.

Exactly how I fucking liked it.

A few of my cousins owned apartments in the tower, but I only trusted a couple of them around Coby.

Regardless, my mom and pops were out of the country celebrating their anniversary. They'd be back in a couple of weeks, which meant I had less than a month to make Coby understand that she'd be living on a knife's edge from here on. If my father had witnessed Coby slapping me, he would have executed her on the spot. Unwavering obedience and fear were law under Malcolm Kilpatrick's reign.

"Aye," Abel struggled to get out between laughs. "Ole girl said I don't know what you *thought* was about to happen, but not today, partna'!" More roaring from Abel followed as I seriously considered shooting my head of security. "Bruh, I think I saw a little spit fly when she slapped you, real talk." Noticing my glare, Abel straightened and wiped the tears from his eyes before shaking his head. "I don't know why you're standing there mugging me. On my life, you better go get her ass before you never see her again. We ain't at Glamis, but this apartment is still a maze. She's already skinny as hell. By the time you find her little ass, you'll be marrying a damn corpse."

Responding with only a grunt, I walked off, the sound of Abel's laughter following me as I pulled out my phone and used the security feed to track down my wife. After flipping through countless screens, I finally found her wandering one of the dead-end halls on the second floor.

I watched as she reached the end of the dark hall and then whirled around with panic all over her beautiful face that told me she was already lost. Tiptoeing back the way she came, she eventually noticed a cracked door sandwiched between two statues. There was only a moment of indecision before she hurried inside for the only semblance of safety she could find, as trapped prey often do.

Closing the app, I pocketed my phone.

A few minutes later, I strolled inside the library, and I didn't bother to hide the fact that I was on her ass.

"Coby," I called out calmly.

It took a minute more before she tiptoed from behind one of the massive twenty-foot shelves. I didn't miss the pepper spray she had clutched in her hand as she timidly came into view.

"I don't want to marry you," she confessed quietly.

Rolling my shoulders to chase away my rising aggravation, I turned and leaned against the wall. The moon was shining through the paneled windows on my left, creating moonbeams across the twenty feet of marble floor between us. Coby hovered in the shadows on the edge of the moonlight, but I'd know the gentle curve of her silhouette anywhere.

Physically, she wasn't my usual type, but my dick, head, and heart didn't seem to notice.

I'd spent years wanting her from across a dark club. And even if I'd done the right thing and left her alone to marry some simp and have *his* babies instead, she would have still been mine. Unfortunately for her, I was too damn selfish to let anyone else have her. "I know."

"I want to go home."

"I know that too," I said while my tone conveyed that I wasn't going to do anything about it.

Coby scowled at me from her side of the moonbeam, and the light that captured her glare made her brown eyes glow a little. Cute. "Hunter won't let you keep me," she whispered into the dark like a warning.

Pushing against the wall, I stalked her across the darkened library while Coby stumbled backward until her back was pressed against the bookcases I had built for her. I wondered if she noticed that all the shelves were empty, waiting for her to fill them.

Towering over her, I two-handed one of the shelves high above her head while staring down at her. Because of our height difference, her head was tipped so far back that I could see the strain it cost her lovely neck to hold my gaze. "Would that be the girl you claim is just a roommate?"

"She is my roommate."

"Oh, is that all?" I drawled sarcastically. A roommate wouldn't have emptied the clip and tried to turn my car into Swiss cheese, but okay.

Coby had no idea who the fuck she was dealing with. I've never been a slouch—not in school, business, life, and now in love. Whenever I brought someone onto my team, I vetted them thoroughly to ensure my grass remained free of snakes. It meant I knew all of her secrets—even the ones she hoped to forget.

"No," Coby stunned me by admitting proudly. "Hunter's my best friend, which means when she kills you, I'll help her bury the body. For you we'll dig a shallow grave so stray dogs can gnaw on what's left of you."

"Oh, I see," I mused out loud. "You draw strength from Hunter."

Coby was visibly perturbed. Was it because I'd seen through her so easily or that I didn't give a fuck about her empty threats? "We both do," she admitted. "Which is why you need to let me go. Hunter needs me."

I moved in closer, drawing a gasp from her lips when she felt the long length of my body pressed against her much slighter one. "And what if I need you?"

"You don't even know me."

"You're right," I agreed without missing a beat. I skimmed my lips over her throat, feeling her struggling to swallow as I smiled against her perfumed skin. "Let's fix that."

"I-I can't love you," she blurted. "It's not possible. What you did to my brother—"

The wood underneath my palms groaned from my tightening grip, so I forced myself to take a breath. I knew this would happen. I knew Roshaun would be a setback as well as a catalyst for my carefully laid plans. Still, hearing Coby say she couldn't love me made me want to find whatever hospital he's laid up in and put a bullet in him.

"I'm okay with that," I lied. "I don't need your heart. The rest of you will do for now." Wrapping my arm around her waist, I pulled her into my body. Coby's hands flew to my chest, but she didn't push me away as she stared up at me. "We could be friends," I told her. "Really good friends."

Her gaze immediately narrowed. "Friends?" Coby practically growled the word with a curl of her lip, and it took everything in me not to smile. "You asked me to marry you. Actually, you didn't ask. You pretty much ordered me to marry you, and now you want to be friends. Boy, bye."

"Coby—"

"Stop saying my name," she snapped before shoving me. "You don't know me like that."

"What would you like me to call you, *mo aingeal*?" Coby swayed toward me until her fingers were curling in my shirt, and the smile I'd been holding back suddenly broke free. "Oh, I see."

Panic flared in her brown eyes, but it was too late to hide her reaction. "No! No. I mean…no. C-Coby's fine."

"Let's go." Stepping away and taking her hand, I pulled her with me toward the door. She stumbled on the first few steps as she tried to match my hurried strides, so I slowed down.

"Where are we going?" she asked once we left the library.

"To bed. I have a proposal for you, but we can discuss that in the morning. I'm tired as fuck."

Coby immediately tried to snatch her hand away, but I gripped her harder. "I'm not fucking you."

"I didn't ask you to." I was too fucking exhausted from torturing her brother to fuck anyway. Peeking down at my bride-to-be, I bit back a laugh when I saw her roll her eyes at her failed attempt to get a rise out of me.

Coby had always struck me as quiet and sweet, and while I suspected those qualities were still true, I was thoroughly enjoying this hidden side of her. I didn't want a meek wife who'd roll over and play dead when I told her to.

Finding the stairs to the third floor, I led her up them before she spoke again.

"You really live here?" Her wide brown eyes openly took in the opulence with unbridled awe. I'm sure the shitty apartment building she lived in left much to be desired.

"Last I checked," I responded as I led her down another hall with my hand on her elbow to steer and keep her standing. Every other step, she was tripping over her feet in order to drink in every detail. I almost said fuck it and considered carrying her, but I didn't want the taste slapped out of my mouth again, so I wisely reconsidered.

Finally, we stopped in front of closed double doors, and I peeked over my shoulder at Coby waiting patiently, if not a little anxiously. "I'll give you a tour in the morning," I offered as I scanned my key card and prayed she didn't ask about it as I held open one of the doors.

Coby immediately lifted her chin as she passed by me. "Don't bother. I'm going home in the morning," she replied stubbornly.

Glancing at the ceiling for patience, I shook my head and stepped inside, letting the door close behind me with a beep of the locking mechanism. "If you say so, sweetheart."

She tossed a glare at me over her shoulder while walking ahead. I took the moment to admire the way her small hips swayed in those tight ass shorts she was wearing. Even if I hadn't planned to snatch her tonight, I would have once the tail who's been following her sent me the surveillance photo. My hoodie that she still wore drowned her, but it was the way she walked so confidently in those heels that had me rethinking my promise not to touch her tonight.

Mesmerized by her, it took me a little longer than I liked to realize she'd stopped walking in the center of the room and had gone quiet. She was looking around the bedroom, taking in the decor and furnishings.

Paneled windows dressed with pink chenille drapes. Baroque moldings along the ceilings and carved into the walls that were painted a pink so light it appeared white at first glance. An arched, gold antique mirror above the lit fireplace. A cozy reading lounge tucked into the corner next to it with two pink upholstered chaises—one curved and the other round—with a plush rug underneath them for her soft feet to curl into. There was a white vanity desk with gold trim and curved legs. A rare tea set I had imported from France sat on the small dining table by the windows so Coby could enjoy the sunrise in the mornings, since her suite faced east. There was even a small Juliet balcony with Pembroke balusters above the doors to her two-story closet. And then there was the bed with a high tufted headboard and a curved footboard, piled high with pink and champagne-colored bedding. The fringed rug beneath was woven with gold, silver, and pearls and cost more than I ever cared to admit. When Coby spotted it, her brown eyes glittering under the three-tiered chandelier directly above her, I decided the obscene seven-figure price tag was worth it.

"I must have imagined your bedroom a hundred times," she said softly while looking around the room in both awe and agony. "But I got to admit this isn't even close to what I pictured."

"Disappointed?" I asked rather than put her out of her misery by correcting her. My teeth sank into my bottom lip to keep from laughing when she kept side-eying the hell out of me.

"No, it's…it's beautiful. You might not believe me, but I've always dreamed of having an apartment just like this. I even made a Pinterest board," she said with a weak chuckle.

I know.

I wasn't one for social apps, but I always did my homework, and I was shamelessly *thorough.* Luckily, Coby seemed addicted to social media, giving me an unobstructed insight into my future wife without her being aware.

"So what's the problem?" I questioned teasingly.

"I guess I didn't realize we had so much in common," she grumbled.

"Mhm," I hummed.

Exhaling heavily, Coby squeezed her eyes closed and then opened them again before whirling toward me. "Ocean, please tell me you have a daughter or a sister who stays here," she begged, whimpering.

"Sorry. No kids and no sister." Coby's gaze widened before letting out another distressed whimper, and I burst out laughing. "The room is not mine, *you brat.* It's yours."

"Mine?" Her head snapped back. "But where do you sleep?"

"I have a suite on the west side of the second floor. The sunsets are amazing if you ever want to pay me a visit."

Coby, who was unused to wondering how her emotions could be used against her, didn't bother hiding her hurt feelings. "You want me to marry you, but you don't want me to sleep in your bed?"

Pushing away from the door because I couldn't stand how far away she was from me, I took her chin in my hand and tilted her head back to see a sheen in her brown eyes.

"I want more than just you in my bed, *mo aingeal.* I want to hold you in my bed, fuck you in my bed, tie you to my bed so that you can never leave it, and if I'm being real, I wanted to raze this room to the ground the moment it was completed because I knew it meant I would have to wait a little while longer."

"Wait? Wait for what?"

"For you to accept that you're mine. I know you feel some type of way about what I did to your brother, and I'm not going to say I'm sorry because I'd do it again. I don't like that it's pushed you away from me, though. Just when I finally let myself get close."

"Ocean…" I stopped breathing as I waited for her to tell me that I was wrong. That she wasn't holding the situation with her brother against me, and that she was ready. Instead, she said, "Thank you for the room."

I stared into her eyes for a little while longer before I kissed her forehead and forced myself to back away toward the door. "You're welcome."

CHAPTER SIX

COBY

THE DOOR CLOSED BEHIND OCEAN AGAIN WITH A BEEP THAT had me immediately rushing over to it to test the handle. I yanked repeatedly, but it wouldn't budge.

Locked.

Finding the square black pad on the wall next to the door, I stared at the green light indicating it was armed and punched the door. "Ocean! Ocean, I know you hear me, you psycho! Let me out!" I punched and kicked the door, but no matter how much noise I made, silence always answered back.

Defeated, I turned and leaned against the double doors and took another look around the room.

A princess palace.

Ocean had gifted me one of my wildest dreams as a clever disguise to hide what this room truly represented.

A pretty prison.

It wasn't a show of wealth but rather a flex of how closely he was paying attention and his willingness to give me my heart's desires if only I looked past all the red flags warning me to run the other way.

I'd be a fool to fall for it, but tell my foolish heart that.

I'd already spotted the cameras that he hadn't bothered to hide and wondered if he was watching me now. I extended my middle finger toward the camera above the fireplace and went in search of the bathroom.

Instead, I found myself inside a walk-in closet that made me squeal internally. It was so large that calling it a closet was the understatement of the year. It was easily the size of my apartment. The second thing I noticed was that the decor matched the bedroom. The third was that it was empty and waiting to be filled. There were two levels with curving stairs that led to the second floor, but I was too exhausted and wary of falling into Ocean's glittery trap to explore, so I resumed my search of the bathroom.

I discovered it adjacent to the closet through a connecting door and found it as grandiose as the closet and bedroom. The clawfoot tub with gold baroque feet stole the show, and I had the fleeting thought that even if Ocean changed his mind about marrying me tomorrow, before I had the chance to soak in that gorgeous tub, he'd have to drag me out kicking and screaming.

Unlike the closet, the bathroom was fully stocked with products I didn't recognize, and that discovery brought immense relief. Ocean already knowing the exact brand of toothpaste or toilet paper I used would have felt a little too intrusive.

Reluctantly, I fell into my usual routine because it was the best chance I had of sorting my thoughts and coming up with a game plan.

If Ocean thought I was marrying him after he showed his ass tonight, the motherfucker was delusional.

I couldn't call Hunter because he had my phone.

I couldn't escape while locked inside this room—the nail in the coffin where I'd laid my fantasies to rest.

My best chance of getting out was finding my way *in*—past Ocean's defenses. It wasn't until I shed Ocean's hoodie and the rest of my clothes, and I was up to my neck in warm water and fragrant bubbles with my head resting comfortably on the engraved satin pillow, that my mind began to form a plan. Once the groundwork was laid and I was confident it would work, I stood and stepped out of the tub. As soon as I began dripping water everywhere, I realized that I had nothing to wear.

I briefly wondered if it was his plan to get an early glimpse of the goods until I spotted a robe hanging on the back of the door. I preferred to wear as little as possible to bed, but it would have to do.

I had trouble containing my excitement once I left the bathroom and saw the bed again, but since I knew he might be watching, I kept my expression neutral. There was a mountain of throw pillows on the bed, but I didn't bother removing any of them as I settled in the center of the bed surrounded by them. And most importantly, *hidden* by them.

It was nestled in that cocoon of pillows that I closed my eyes and said a prayer for Hunter and my brother.

I've had weird mornings, but nothing beat the one after I was stolen by the mafia and ordered to marry the underboss. It started when I woke up sprawled on top of a bed that wasn't mine, surrounded by extravagance meant to tame me. The sash on my robe had slipped free of its knot, so my bare breasts and belly were exposed to the sunrise-lit room as I lay on my back. It wouldn't be that bad if it weren't for the fact that I was also drooling with my mouth wide open.

Guilt immediately consumed me when I thought about Hunter and the night she must have had. She wouldn't have slept at all, and here I was sleeping a little too well. Grumbling to myself, I stretched my body like a cat and pried bleary eyes open. I blinked to clear them and take in my new prison now that it was morning. My survey was interrupted by an unexpected surprise.

"Ahh!" A startled squeak left me once I realized I wasn't alone. I scrambled to collect myself, and in my hurry, I ended up getting tangled in the sheets that silkworms—boiled alive in their cocoons before they could turn into moths—died to make and tumbled over the side of the bed, landing in a heap of pillows, blankets, and my own shame.

At least he couldn't see me now.

As I lay there, wishing the floor would open the hell up and swallow me, the awkward silence seemed to stretch on forever before he spoke. "You good?"

Peeling myself off the floor without responding, I only made it as far as sitting on my now sore butt as I stared across the rumpled bed at Ocean sitting at the small dining table. It was only a few feet from the bedside, and he had his phone in his hand, ignoring the untouched feast splayed out before him. He was also dressed for the day in one of his suits that made my mouth water. It was a light gray, minus the jacket, which was folded over the back of his chair. His vest and dress accentuated his chest and arms.

"Why are you in here, Ocean?" I croaked.

His gaze silently roamed me for a moment before he returned calmly, "I asked you a question, *mo aingeal*."

Because he cared, or was it to assert his dominance? I decided I didn't want to know the answer because one threatened my plans and the other would only push me to act rashly. "I'm fine."

Ocean nodded with satisfaction and then gestured toward the table, where a small feast awaited. "Good. Come eat."

Holding my robe together, I stood on shaky legs and slowly rounded the bed like a stray that didn't know whether to trust the offering of food but was desperate enough to risk it.

Besides, there was nowhere to run. One glance at the door told me that it was still locked because Ocean was much too smart to let down his guard.

At least...not until I gave him a reason to.

That's how I found myself sitting across from Ocean, sharing small talk and breakfast with the creeping suspicion that this was my new normal. I could run from it, hide from it, but there was no shielding myself from him. Whatever secrets, thoughts, and pieces of myself I didn't give away over the hour-long meal, he saw anyway, and it hadn't even been a day. I'd been dreaming of what it'd be like to be Ocean's girl for so long that it disturbed me how little it mattered that the reality was a lot more terrifying than I'd imagined.

I *still wanted* him.

But I loved my brother, and I missed Hunter.

Ocean had taken them both from me, and for that, I vowed never let him have a single day's peace so long as he kept me from them.

I was sipping my tea from the gorgeous china when I heard a beep at the door. Two uniformed women entered. They wore simple black dresses with a white trim around the short sleeves and collar. I sat up a little straighter at their sudden appearance, a plea on the tip of my tongue, but the cold burn of Ocean watching me so closely silenced my cry for help.

The staff quickly cleared the table and then departed, leaving only a roaring in my ears that dulled when Ocean spoke.

"Someone will come by later to take your measurements," he announced without preamble.

"Measurements for what?"

"Clothes to start. Your wedding gown for the other."

My belly sank. "Already?" I gasped.

Hearing the rising fear in my tone, Ocean reached for me, but I shrank away and felt my heart shrivel a little at the denied contact. Ocean clenched his jaw at the rejection but said nothing. "Yes, Coby. The wedding will happen quickly, so there's no time to waste. We need to get you fitted for a gown and a wardrobe, among other things. These will have to do for now."

As if on cue, the same ladies entered again, this time carrying shopping bags. They set them by my feet before making a quiet but speedy exit once more. "We can shop for the rest of your wardrobe later."

"I don't want to go shopping," I told him as I set my tea cup down. It had gone cold a long while ago, but I kept sipping at it to keep from saying all the things I wanted. I was especially sour this morning since Hunter and I always made and ate breakfast together. Always. "I have clothes at home."

"Mention that apartment again, and I'll burn it to the ground, wife."

"I'm not your wife," I snapped back.

"Not yet, no," he said with a smirk that made me want to slap his ass. "But you will be, and there's nothing you can do about it."

Want to bet?

I conveyed the challenge with my eyes since I knew better than to open my mouth. Of course, he paid me no mind as he resumed handling business on his phone.

Was it business or bitches?

Ugh! I forgot I wasn't supposed to care.

But Ocean showed no signs of remembering that I was even here as he switched to a burner phone to make and answer calls before going back to his main phone.

"I'm ready to hear your proposal now," I announced when I couldn't stand his eyes and focus elsewhere a second longer.

Ocean set his phone down immediately and gave me his full attention, as if he had been waiting for me to demand it. My eyes narrowed suspiciously as I wondered if he'd been ignoring me on purpose or because he was secretly and quietly struggling with this sudden and gaping hole between us as much as I was.

"Is that so?"

"Yes." Clearing my throat, I tried not to fidget under the intensity of his gaze.

But it wasn't just that.

Ocean—as I'd learned—wasn't easy to rattle, which left me feeling paradoxically safe and anxious. He was always so poised and cultured. He spoke like someone who had received an expensive education and moved like someone used to being in charge. He'd seen more, done more, and I was beginning to question if I could really outsmart him. "I already know you want me to marry you and...g-give you a-a s-son."

"Preferably more than one," he corrected with an easy and charming smile.

The back of my neck grew hot.

More than one?

This fool hadn't said anything about getting pregnant more than once!

"I have no control over that. You get what you get."

Ocean shrugged, and with a languid, scorching, possessive sweep of his brown eyes, he casually yanked the metaphorical rug out from under me when he cooed, "More reason for us to keep trying, *mo aingeal.*" *Oh lord.* The heat was spreading, rushing down my body and slipping between my legs. "And if you're hellbent on our marriage not being permanent, the sooner we get started, the sooner you can be free."

"What do you mean?"

Ocean bit into his bottom lip, and I almost came right then. "I'll tell you on one condition."

"Don't play with me," I warned as if I could actually do shit about it.

Ocean scooted his chair back and turned in his seat. "Come here. Come to me."

I shifted to hide the fact that I almost sprang to my feet in a knee-jerk reaction. "I can hear you just fine right here."

"But I can *touch you* much better if you were over here." My fingers curled around the arms of my chair to keep from embarrassing myself again. Nothing ever seemed to get past Ocean, though, his gaze briefly dropping to my hands. I quickly loosened my grip, which seemed to frustrate him. "You don't need to hide from me," he said with a slight growl. "I have no intention of using your feelings against you, and nothing will happen that you don't want. You have my word."

"I believe you. I mean…" It felt like a betrayal of my brother, but it was for him that I purposely lowered my lashes in a show of bashfulness and said softly. "I don't think you'll hurt me."

"What a good fucking girl you are."

Something burst inside of me, like a long-dormant volcano finally waking up. Silence fell between us again while Ocean watched me squirm and patiently waited for me to make a decision. I didn't have to fake the uncertainty in my movements as I rose from my seat or the shaky steps I took toward him until I was in grabbing distance. Despite his teasing, Ocean made no move to touch me, and it took me a few agonizing seconds to understand why.

He was proving that I was safe with him, but I also had a point to prove—to myself.

I could play the game and win.

Inhaling deeply, I lowered myself into his lap.

I was still wearing the robe and nothing else, so there was almost nothing keeping him from discovering my hot, dripping pussy.

The possessive hand he immediately placed on my thigh once I was settled told me he wasn't unaware of my aroused state. This close, I could feel how tightly coiled he was, and something in me purred knowing he wasn't unaffected either. My fingers idly toyed with the terry-cloth sash while I waited for him to do what he promised.

I waited for him to touch me.

"Ocean," I whimpered when he seemed to be taking his sweet fucking time.

"What's up?" he asked, his deep voice an erotic rumble.

"You said you were going to touch me."

"Did I?"

I hit him.

I punched the heir to the *Fola*'s arm because I was sick of Ocean amusing himself at my expense. "*Yes*," I growled.

Ocean chuckled and kissed my shoulder before sobering. The immediate shift made me nervous as he regarded me with a serious expression. "Maybe I want you to kiss me."

"What? Why?"

I was no blushing, fainting virgin, but this fine specimen of a man staring me down and telling me to perform for him had me losing a few G points.

"Because last night took a turn I hadn't planned on and I need to know that when I fuck you, it's because you want it."

"Oh." I guess he had a point.

"Yeah...*oh*."

I frowned as my mind immediately began jumping two or three steps ahead. "And after I kiss you? What then?"

"Then I'll tell you how we turn this hostage situation into a business arrangement that benefits us both."

My hesitation made no sense and at the same time made perfect sense. I'd fantasized about this man for years, and now that I had him, I was falling back. In my defense, none of my fantasies had started with Ocean nearly killing my brother and trapping me. It sort of shattered the romantic view I had of him.

I'm not naive.

I'd known Ocean was a menace, but I'd chosen to ignore that fatal flaw until the danger hit a little too close to home. Now I was forced to face it, but Ocean wasn't giving me any space or time to process it.

Unlike my brother and Hunter, I was a straight-up square. All of my exes were, too, which was probably what made it so easy for Hunter to run them off. Keeping it a buck, I had no fucking clue how to handle a man like Ocean.

"You've got me twisted in a goddamn knot and have since I first saw you, so I wouldn't worry too much about it," he replied, making me realize I'd spoken my deepest fears out loud. Ocean bit those succulent lips to keep from laughing at me, but it didn't matter.

I wanted to die.

"Oh, God," I groaned, hiding my face in my hands.

Suddenly, I could hear Hunter of all people in my head, telling me to step my pussy up, kiss this fine-ass man, and stop being so damn scary.

Fuck it.

I fisted his vest and surged forward like this was my first time kissing anyone. Our lips fused together without warning, but Ocean was more than ready for it. He didn't waste any time taking over, and I quickly found myself racing to match his energy.

Every fear, score, fantasy, and reservation I ever had about this man melted away with one kiss that shattered them all. I forgot to fear him, hate him…I forgot I should want him dead.

He controlled the kiss, leading me where he wanted me, setting the pace and the pressure, and showing me exactly how he liked it.

Ocean was the teacher, and I was his student.

I hadn't expected him to be so gentle and patient. I hadn't expected me to be so eager to please.

When he suddenly ripped open my robe as if he were about to take me right here and now, I arched my back to give him better access. The cool air was a balm to my flushed skin, but it teased my aching nipples to painfully hard points.

Ocean didn't think twice about taking the offering. He twisted me in his lap until my legs were on either side of him and then placed a possessive palm against my chest, his large hand dwarfing me as he pressed me back against the table's edge.

Our gazes remained locked as he leaned forward to lick a slow, hot path up my sternum. There was a bead of sweat near my collarbone that Ocean claimed before kissing the inner curves of my breasts. My nipples were next to receive his attention, and it opened the floodgates of desire that I swore to myself were bolted.

It wasn't long before he kissed a path back to my mouth.

It was for Hunter, my brother, and a little for me that when Ocean fed me his tongue, I answered with mine. As fucked up as it was, I secretly liked that Ocean had gone to such lengths to have me when he could have had anyone.

I wasn't stupid.

I knew this wasn't love.

It was lust.

It was infatuation—on my part at least.

Perhaps for Ocean, marrying me was simply convenient, but he'd already given me more passion than any man. None of my ain't-shit exes ever made me feel even a tenth of this. Like they would rewrite the stars to be mine, carve out a piece of themselves just to make room for me, and find me in every lifetime.

That is the way Ocean kissed me.

What he made sure I could feel with each press of his mouth against mine.

"Mmh," Ocean moaned as he finally pulled away. My lips were swollen and numb, and I was panting for breath I couldn't quite catch. "Real sweet, baby. Real sweet. The next time you kiss me, do it just like that."

A little indignant and self-conscious from his words, I wiped my mouth of our shared spittle. We'd gotten a little carried away. "I know how to kiss, Ocean."

"But you've never kissed anyone the way you just kissed me, have you?" I shook my head before I could even consider denying. Ocean pecked me one last time. "And you never will."

I didn't have shit to say to that, so I nodded and tried to recall what we were discussing before.

I wanted him to fuck me.

No, that wasn't it.

But I wasn't wearing panties, and all he had in the way was a belt, a zipper, and his boxers. It'd be so easy, so quick. A few seconds, and he could be stretching me out. I could feel his thick dick trapped between my ass cheeks, and I gave a teasing wriggle.

Ocean groaned, his body shuddering against me from the restraint it took to keep from taking more than a kiss. "Shit, Coby," he grumbled. "Why are you fucking with me?"

"Because as it turns out, I don't like you very much," I said while grinding my ass on him. "You're not who I thought you were."

Ocean's dark chuckle as he clutched my hips and matched my rhythm. "Ditto," he returned as we dry humped one another. "At least, one of us can say they're not disappointed."

He moved to kiss me again, so I gripped his jaw firmly to stop him. "The proposal?"

"Five years," he blurted with his gaze stuck on my lips. "Give me five years."

My smile fell as my brows pinched curiously. "Of what?"

I already knew he wanted to marry me, but it felt like he was asking for more.

"Us," he said, confirming my suspicions. "Marriage. You." He slid his hands up my thighs until they circled my waist. I liked his hands on me more than I should. "Be my wife for five years and never want for anything ever again. I'll even pay whatever the fuck you want for every year we're together. When the five years are up, you can divorce my ass." Another one of those infuriating smirks appeared. "If you want to."

Never before had I ever thought I'd agree to a relationship with a guaranteed expiration date. I was an incurable romantic, always dreaming of forever. Then again, I'd never met a man like Ocean Kilpatrick and knew that I never would again.

It was that gut feeling and the sharp pang of regret already settling there that made me say, "If I marry you, I have conditions of my own."

"I'd be disappointed if you didn't." He held me tighter and kissed my shoulder. "What are your conditions?"

"Hunter." Ocean merely raised a brow as if he wasn't shocked that she was a condition, just surprised that she was my first. "I want to see her. I can only imagine what she's thinking and how scared she is. I won't do that to her. I need her to know that I'm okay."

Ocean considered me for a very long time before he finally said, "You may see her." My heart leapt at the thought of being with my best friend again. "After the wedding." It plunged again.

I didn't even try to hide my panic. I let it pour from me in crushing waves. "I can't get married without her, Ocean. If you say I have to, then my answer is no. And I don't just want her at the wedding. I want her to be my maid of honor. You're asking for a lot. I can't do it without her." Squaring my shoulders, I stared down the heir of the Fola while attempting to bend him to my will. "Hunter is non-negotiable."

Ocean stared at me for a long, long while, and just when I thought he'd refuse or threaten me, something like pride entered his eyes, and he shrugged. "If you want Hunter at the wedding, you'll have her. I'll make sure she has a front-row seat. Anything else?"

"My brother lives."

Ocean's answer came even quicker than my agreement to marry him. "Absolutely the fuck not."

"Then my answer is no."

"Coby—"

"No!"

"Who the fuck you shouting at?" he barked back.

Goosebumps rippled over my skin, but I refused to back down. I owed Roshaun that much. "I can't be with the man who took my brother from this world. I don't know what made you decide marrying me was worth three million dollars, but I do know it doesn't matter. Nothing good that lives inside of me will survive if you kill him. It's him or me, Ocean. It's that simple."

"Then I choose you," he decided so easily and quickly that it made me blink.

"Just like that?" I peered up at him in disbelief. "You really won't kill him?"

"As long as he does nothing to threaten your safety again, he can keep breathing, and *that* is non-negotiable."

"Oh," I said while feeling a flush spread over my chest. "I don't know. I thought—" Lowering my head, I shook it, unable to finish the thought.

Ocean tipped my chin up a moment later. "Never underestimate how much I want you, Coby. I'd agree to almost anything to have you. Name your price. I'll gladly pay it."

My nipples hardened as I gulped—two warring reactions to the understanding that Ocean was leaving me no room or reason to deny him. I felt trapped, and I craved the feeling as much as I loathed it. Hunter would say I was crazy, but she wasn't here to talk me out of it. "Okay."

"Perfect," he purred. This man was too damn smooth. "Now that we're on the same page, what would you like to do, my sexy and darling bride?" Lowering his head, he gently kissed each of my knuckles, and I shivered in response. I was beginning to love the little ways he doted on me almost as much as I craved his overbearing dominance. "I could give you that tour I promised, or we could fall back in bed and fuck all day. I've got my preference, but the choice is yours. We have some time."

Ignoring the way my pussy throbbed at that second suggestion, I asked, "Time until what?"

He stared at me for an uncomfortable amount of time before he answered reluctantly, "Until I introduce you to the family."

"Already?" I snatched my hand away before he could feel the nervous tremble, while my gaze flew to the bedroom door as if his family would come bursting through it at any moment. I hadn't thought about the fact that I'd have to meet his family. What were they like? What if they didn't like me? What if I didn't like them? "Can't it wait?"

"We're getting married, baby," he reminded me while reclaiming my hand. I was in his lap, but he still couldn't seem to stop touching me.

I almost asked if I could just meet his people at the wedding, but he was already shaking his head, answering my unspoken question. "Fine."

This time, he nipped my fingers, making me yelp. "Don't be a brat." Ocean sat back in his seat and seemed content just to stare at me. I nervously retied my robe just to give my hands something to do, and his gaze dipped down briefly before returning to mine again.

"Don't you have mafia business to do?" I grumbled before I became completely undone.

Ocean chuckled as he rested his cheek on his propped fist and swung his knee back and forth. I could feel the muscles in his thigh flexing with each movement. "Mafia business, Coby?"

"Yeah, like ordering hits on people, having meetings in smoky restaurants with dark lighting, and shoot-outs in a black town car."

Ocean merely raised a brow. "My name is Antonio Montana," I imitated Al Pacino's accent from *Scarface*. "And you? What you call yourself?" The brown in Ocean's eyes lightened as if I were a wonder to him, so I blurted, "Skrrt skrrt."

Ocean lost his composure, tossing his head back and exposing his Adam's apple to me as he laughed even harder this time. I quickly clapped a hand over my mouth to muffle my giggles.

I made the underboss of the *Fola* laugh.

I could only admit to myself that I liked this newfound power of mine. He looked so normal and younger when he smiled. And I realized with an aching heart that he probably didn't get to do it often.

The second most powerful man in the city had no one to make him smile.

It made my heart hurt.

"Yeah, you watch too much TV," he said after his laughter subsided.

"Actually, I prefer to read."

Ocean nodded like this wasn't news to him, and then seemed to catch himself when I narrowed my gaze. "What do you like to read?" he asked while looking guilty as hell.

"You mean you *don't* already know, stalker?"

"I do," he said while looking bashful and ashamed for the first time, "but I want you to tell me anyway."

"I like poetry," I answered, since it was my favorite. "I used to write them in middle school, but I stopped."

"Why?"

"My parents died."

Ocean didn't outwardly react other than to pull me closer. "I'm sorry."

My nose began to tingle, so I shook my head before I could yield to sorrow I'd convinced myself I was past. "It's okay."

"What else do you like to read?"

"Romance. The smuttier, the better," I said proudly.

Ocean grinned. "What else?"

"Sci-fi, lit fic, women's fiction, mystery…"

"So everything."

"No." I frowned. "I can't read horror or thriller."

"Why not?"

I blinked. "It's scary."

"Makes sense," Ocean said while biting back a grin.

"Now will you tell me what you do?"

Ocean winced as if he were hoping to avoid talking about himself. It probably had something to do with my saying he wasn't what I expected. I hadn't meant to make him think I was disappointed, but I won't pretend my brother hadn't become a wedge between us. It was up to him how permanent it would be. If he kept his promise and left my brother alone, I could maybe start to forgive him.

"It's safer if you don't know the specifics," Ocean answered, "but for your information, I haven't needed to get my hands dirty in a long time. It's risky for me to show my face too often. Having men I trust to handle the streets for me is imperative."

"Like that guy who's always with you? The one with the eye problem?"

Ocean gripped my chin suddenly, and my lips parted on a silent gasp, but then he seemed to wrangle his darkest impulses, sweeping his thumb gently across my bottom lip instead. "Who was eyeing you, sweetheart?"

I gulped. Ocean tried to keep his tone casual and curious, but I knew better. Or at least, I was beginning to. There was jealousy, possession, and murder brewing behind his eyes, which meant someone was about to die.

"Not like that," I clarified quickly. "I just mean he looks like he's in desperate need of a vacation."

Ocean snorted and relaxed again. "Abel."

"He's your friend?"

Ocean flashed a condescending smile, as if to say he found me adorable. "He's my head of security. Abel watches my back, trains my men, and advises me when I need it, but our relationship is purely business."

"Sounds like a friend," I mumbled.

"It's better if I don't blur those lines. If I let our relationship get personal, I won't be able to wield him effectively."

"Will our marriage be that cold?" I blurted before I could rethink pissing off someone whose moniker was the Bloodthirsty Prince.

"It doesn't have to be." Ocean's gaze searched mine for some sign that I might want that. As courting goes, this was far from romantic and yet...I still felt like I had landed in a dream.

"What makes me different?"

"To start? I'm not fucking Abel."

Right... Moving on.

"So um..." I looked down at my lap as I twisted my fingers.

"So?" Ocean prompted when too long passed without another word from me.

"You said I'm yours."

"That's right," he said without hesitation or doubt.

"Okay." Another long silence passed, but this time Ocean was content to let me squirm. *Just say it. Don't be a pussy.* "Does that mean you're mine?" I blurted in a rush. "Do I get to call you my man?"

It took me getting played a couple of times to learn that men staking their claim didn't always go both ways. In fact, it was often one-sided when it came to loyalty and ownership. I'd find myself locked down—heart and body—to a man who had community dick.

I didn't realize how wildly my heart was pounding while waiting for Ocean to crush it until he surged forward and kissed me again, forcing my mouth open for his tongue. I was reaching for the buttons on his vest when I broke the connection to warn against my lips, "Unless you want a lot of people to die, you fucking better call me your man."

I was still panting for breath and still fighting not to tear off his clothes when I forced myself to ask instead, "Why would people die?"

Ocean nuzzled my nose with the tip of his own before pecking my lips so softly it only made me crave him more. "Because I'm cranky and bloodthirsty when heartbroken, so what's it going to be? You gon' break my heart, baby?" Feeling a range of emotions that were competing to undo me, I could only shake my head while holding onto his shoulders for something to ground me. Ocean flashed a beautiful smile, but it was sharp and dangerous. "Then we have nothing to worry about, do we?"

"N-no?"

"I didn't think so. Now let's go see your library."

I froze. "My what?"

CHAPTER SEVEN

COBY

ONCE I WAS DRESSED IN THE NEW CLOTHES OCEAN procured for me—a plaid brown, pink, and cream pleated hemp skirt with a cream chenille sweater, flesh-toned tencel tights, and thick socks that reached my knees along with the pink ribbon that I tied under my clothes and around my waist today—he took me back to the room I'd hidden in last night. Until the moment I stepped inside the now sunlit room, I assumed I'd misheard him.

A library.

Ocean had a library.

No. *I* had a library. He'd said it was mine, and there was no mistaking that once I saw inside.

Last night, I'd been too traumatized to react to the stunning architectural art that was now my room, but today I had no such reservations. Letting out a screech loud enough to make my fiancé wince, I let go of his hand and ran to anything that caught my eye while Ocean droned on about everything the room had to offer.

As if it were an extension of my princess palace, the interior of the library was highly ornamental—baroque, airy, pink, and white. Directly across from the door, across the short expanse of marble floor, was a paneled window reaching at least twenty feet high, if not more. I could see the sound below and the sun kissing the gently lapping waves. In front of the window was a weeping cherry tree about eight to ten feet tall. I assumed it was fake until I faintly touched one of the pink petals and discovered it was real. The soil was set inside a stone enclosure for watering. There were arched alcoves along both walls that housed empty bookshelves, and more on the upper levels, which had curved Juliet balconies like the one in my bedroom.

The seating area in the center of the room looked cozy, and I was pleased to find the stylish sofas as comfy as they looked.

Spotting the winding stairs tucked discreetly away, I squealed again and eagerly ran up them, ignoring Ocean's warning to be careful. The mezzanine level connected both sides of the room, and even though there weren't any books yet to marvel over, I couldn't help holding out my hand as I passed, imagining my fingers brushing across all kinds of spines.

Moving over to stand at one of the Juliet balconies, I was unaware of the huge grin on my face until I noticed Ocean with his phone raised, snapping a picture.

"Wait, I wasn't ready!" I screamed. I was never good at being photographed by others. Hunter was the only one I trusted because I knew she'd never let me take a bad photo. A candid of me just sounded horrifying, especially when someone who looked like *him* with eyes that could see.

Ocean studied the picture and then tapped a few buttons before tucking his phone inside his pocket. "It's perfect. Now, come down here and thank me for your gift, wife."

He didn't have to tell me twice.

I skipped down the stairs, which only seemed to piss him off if the glower was anything to go by. As I approached, I smiled, and that seemed to soften him a little, so by the time I was standing in front of him, most of his scowl was gone.

His irritation didn't stop him from lifting me off my feet, and it didn't stop me from wrapping my legs around his waist. "You're testing me, Coby."

"You like it."

Ocean made a noncommittal sound before using his hold on

my butt to lift me higher and knock me off balance. The move jostled me forward, and somehow my lips found his.

Okay, fine. I kissed him.

And Ocean kissed me back—like he owned me, like I was the only thing he's ever wanted and now he had me. He kissed me in my dream library right under the skylight he had installed so that I could see the stars while I walked through worlds. I didn't want to fall for this crazy-ass man, but it was starting to feel like I wouldn't be able to help it.

"Thank you," I said once he stopped kissing me and set me back on my feet.

"Ain't shit."

"It is to me. I never knew how sweet you are," I said as I caressed his cheek. "And generous."

Ocean laughed at that while nuzzling my palm. "Other people would disagree."

"Mmh…that's okay. Call me selfish, but I want this side of you only for me."

"Then that's the way it will be. Come on."

"Where are we going?" I asked as he tugged me toward the door.

"We're doing the rest of the tour."

I took one last look at the library before following Ocean out. I could see it and enjoy it whenever I wanted, and that felt… amazing. "I feel like I'm taking over your home," I whispered a little guiltily.

Ocean stared down at me unflinchingly as we traveled the hall towards the stairs. "It's your home now too, *mo aingeal*." When he reached out to brush his fingers down my arm, I couldn't help falling into him. "Take as much as you want. I can think of no better person to give everything I have."

"You mean that?"

"Of course."

I eyed him skeptically. "You barely know me."

"I know enough," he returned.

It was a good thing his focus was ahead of him, not on me, because I didn't want him to know how easily he made me melt.

It took almost an hour to do the full tour. The penthouse was huge—so big that calling it an apartment didn't feel right. I've certainly never known an apartment to have its own ballroom. Ocean showed it to me, along with the gym, the pool, and the rooftop terrace. The rest of the apartment was a blur of extravagance until he finally showed me his room.

"It's nice," I said as I walked around. The room's dark interior screamed masculinity, and the massive bed beckoned me as I ran a finger over the heavily starched bedding. "Not as pretty as mine," I teased, "but it suits you and it…smells like you."

The scent of his cologne lingered in the air along with the smell of freshly washed sheets. His staff was incredibly discreet and swift. Not once did we see any of them during the tour. It felt like we were blissfully alone even though we weren't.

"I'm glad you approve," he said as he leaned against the wall by the door.

I didn't respond as I walked over to his nightstand and boldly opened the drawer to see what he kept inside.

Nothing.

Not even a box of condoms.

Thinking maybe I guessed his side of the bed wrong, I walked to the other side and found the same thing. Nothing at all.

Tossing a frustrated glance at Ocean, who was watching me with his fist covering his mouth to hide his grin, I hurried over to the double doors and found the closet with only a few suits hanging inside. No box of secrets or even a junk drawer.

His bathroom was just as cold and sterile, so when I emerged crestfallen, Ocean noticed immediately.

"I don't understand," I said so softly that I'm surprised he heard me.

"Why don't you tell me what you're looking for, and maybe I can help."

"You!"

"I'm right here," he barked while throwing out his hands.

"No! I mean everything that makes you who you are. There's nothing here. You seem to know everything about me down to my wildest dreams, but the only thing I know about you is that you're dangerous. You don't—" I paused with a hiccup when the answer dawned on me with the crushing weight of a sledgehammer. "You don't really live here, do you?"

"Yes, Coby. But only when necessary."

"Then why am I here if this isn't your home?"

"Because where I live most of the time isn't safe for you. At least until after the wedding."

"Tell me why," I demanded. When he hesitated to answer, my mind formed a conclusion of its own that my mouth didn't hesitate to share. "Let me guess…it's where you keep your other bitch?"

Ocean pushed off the wall and closed the distance so quickly I barely had time to do more than stumble back. "Is that the kind of man you take me for?"

"I don't know, stalker. You know everything about me, but I don't know shit about you."

"Then *ask*."

"Okay, what's your favorite color?" I asked just to be a smart ass.

"Red," he answered without missing a beat. "What else?"

"F-favorite TV show?" I stumbled to ask.

"I don't watch TV."

"Favorite book?"

"I don't read."

"Why?"

"I don't have time, Coby. Anything else?"

"But you're here with me now," I argued. "You've been here all morning showing me around."

"I made time."

"Okaaaay," I drawled, starting to feel like a bitch. "What's your favorite memory?"

"The day I saw you."

"Okay, Mr. Smooth. Be for real."

"I am, *mo aingeal*." His phone started going off, but he paid it no mind as he waited for me to interrogate him some. "Anything else you want to know?"

"Just one…why can't I go home with you?"

"Because my father will kill you, and even though he needs to die, I'm not willing to use you as bait."

Ocean's phone started going off again, so he ripped his phone out of his pocket and checked the screen. When his gaze lifted, they were so cold and dark, I knew…

Someone was about to die.

I didn't think for one second that it was me, but when he took my arm and led me out of his room, his touch was far less gentle than before. Abel was in the hall, armed to the teeth and waiting for him when we stepped out. He trailed us at a distance as Ocean and I made our way back up to the third floor.

"Ocean?" I whispered once we reached my cage and he deposited me inside. The muscle in his jaw was beating a steady rhythm. "Is everything okay?"

"I'll be back as soon as I can. You'll be safe here," he said. The assurance only made me feel less so—not because I didn't believe it, but because he felt compelled to give it.

"Do I have a choice?" I snapped as I yanked my arm away from him. "You're locking me in. *Again*."

Ocean hesitated before turning away to leave and tossing over his shoulder. "The door's not locked, wife."

He made a swift retreat, and I was left alone trying to answer one question.

What the hell was going on?

CHAPTER EIGHT

OCEAN

"OCEAN! MY BABY," MY MOTHER GREETED WARMLY AS SHE hurried to me on the tarmac of the private airfield. Euphemia Kilpatrick was *tiny*, instantly reminding me of Coby, who was only a couple of inches taller. Dutifully, I leaned down so my mother could kiss my cheek and then wipe away the lipstick she left behind before gifting me with a warm smile. While I knew she was genuinely happy to see me, the tightness around her eyes told me the real truth.

My father was a few paces behind, shaking hands with the pilot and the crew. Appearances were all that mattered to him next to power. I didn't realize I was clenching my teeth until my mother caressed my jaw with her thumb. A silent but gentle reminder of how dangerous it was to show Malcolm Kilpatrick what I was thinking.

"How are you, son? Have you been sleeping? Eating?"

"A little," I lied as I smiled down at her. "How was your vacation?"

"It was nice," she lied. "You didn't have to come, you know." Another lie. "Your father and I could have seen ourselves home."

Behind me was Abel and the rest of my personal guard, and further behind them was a motorcade of armored cars waiting to escort my parents back to Glamis. They had gone to Santorini to celebrate their anniversary and were supposed to be gone for a month, but my father had cut their vacation short, and no one knew why. He

hadn't even bothered to warn me until they'd already landed. I had
to scramble my men and haul ass to the airfield to ensure my mom
was protected from my father's enemies. And mine.

"Then I would have had to wait a day to see my second favorite girl."

My mom looked confused, and I hid my smile until she caught
my meaning. Her expression brightened. "Oh, your *second*, huh? I
know she must be special. When do I get to meet her?"

My gaze moved over her shoulder to the imposing figure heading this way. "Soon," I told my mother, and she didn't press for more
when my father came to stand by her side.

Malcolm Kilpatrick was a tree trunk of a man with medium-dark
skin, a bald head, a salt-and-pepper beard, a patch over his left eye,
and a vacancy in the other.

"Son, you're here," he said by way of greeting. It was as good as
I was going to get. "Good. Let's go. We have a problem."

My father walked off and climbed into a Bentley Mulsanne, leaving my mother behind.

I escorted her to another and put my personal guard, including Abel, on her before joining my father in the back of the Bentley.
Neither of us spoke until the motorcade started moving, heading
north toward the outskirts of Black Veil.

"I received word that another one of our stables has been raided."

"And that was enough to cut your vacation short? I could have
handled it."

"And who would have handled you?"

Smiling sharply as if laughing at my father wasn't as dangerous
as drawing on him, I said, "I wasn't aware that was an option."

"Balfour tells me that you defied my orders and skipped the
sit-down."

"Something came up."

"What could have been more important than your future and
the future of this family?"

"What's even odder than having your father pick out the woman you're going to fuck for the rest of your life is that the woman you'll be fucking is your cousin. Keeping it a buck, I think it's fucking hilarious that you thought I'd go along with that shit."

"She's your third cousin."

I stared down my father—the Boss of the *Fola*—with nothing but pure disgust. "Is that supposed to mean something to me?"

"The blood's diluted."

It wasn't. Not even close.

But then I realized what my father said, or rather what he didn't say.

Enough...

Someone who wasn't a sociopath might have said the blood was diluted *enough*, but my father has always been careful with his words, which meant these unveiled his true and far more sinister intentions.

"I'm not doing it."

"Have you forgotten who you're talking to?"

"So then kill me," I said to my father. "Kill me and let Julius take over because I'm not marrying Niamh. I won't do it to her, and I sure as hell won't let you do it to me. I can choose my own wife."

The *Fola* was made up of three families—the Kilpatrick, the Balfour-Young, and the Torrance. It went back to the start of my great-grandfather's original crew. They called themselves the Brothers of Rory, and each wanted an equal piece of the pie, so James did to his sisters what my father is attempting to do to Niamh. What he already did to Priscilla. And what he'll eventually do to Chiara.

"That's not how this goes," my father, the traditionalist, responded. "If you want me to abdicate my throne, if you want to be Boss, you will marry who I fucking tell you."

Or option B: I could kill him.

And little did he know, it was my option A.

"What do you want to do about the raids?" I asked. "Black knows something. We need to question him more thoroughly."

Michael Black was an old-school pimp who had been chased

out of Chicago for reasons unknown, but my father wouldn't listen, which only made me distrust the man even more.

There was only one explanation for why my father wouldn't listen to reason. Black had something on him.

"Black works for us."

I rolled my eyes toward the roof of the SUV. My father's ego was so great that he believed fear was enough to keep everyone loyal. It was a mistake that would cost him in the end. I'd make sure of it.

"He's also the one in charge of the girls. If someone's coming at us, why just the stables? Why not the weapons depot? The shipments? The traps? The gambling spots? Why always the one piece of business we entrusted with the shadiest motherfucker we know? Have you considered that whoever is doing this is after him and not us?"

"It has crossed my mind."

"So why don't you do anything about it?"

"Because there are bigger things at play here."

"What does Black have on you?" I asked because I didn't like mincing words.

"What makes you think a peon like Michael Black could ever have something on me and live to threaten me with it?"

"Then let me send him packing."

"No."

"Why the fuck not?"

"Because Black's useful. He gets the job done, and he doesn't ask questions. Can you do the same? Find out what is happening to my stables and end it."

The rest of the ride to Glamis, my family's sprawling estate north of Black Veil, passed in stony silence. On the outskirts of the city, the motorcade broke up, going in four different directions to confuse any tails. When the twenty-five-thousand-square-foot home sitting on thirty acres of land came into view, I felt nothing.

JJ, my grandfather, decided it was safer for his family to live far out of reach of his enemies but close enough for him to keep an eye on his interests, so he bought this land deep in suburbia once my great-grandfather stepped down. What started as a simple cabin sitting on miles of land stretching in each direction had been replaced by a rustic palace—an oasis. Each generation had added on a new wing as more of our family immigrated here over the years, and I knew I would be no different.

To my father, it was the seat of his power. The crown jewel of the Kilpatrick wealth. It was the walls behind which he decided who lived or died, who got money, and who became made.

To my mother and me, it was where we learned to hide in plain sight, shield our emotions, diminish who we were so that there was less of him to trample. It was how my mother taught me to survive him, but I haven't been down with that shit in a long time. I started pushing back when I was fourteen, but it didn't last. Once my father realized he was losing control of me, he started using my mom to re-tighten the leash. And after all he'd done to her, even if my father turned into a saint tomorrow, we were long past forgiveness now.

Once I reached the city, my first stop was to the raided flesh den under Black's command.

"What the hell happened here?" I looked around at the destruction and the executed corpses of the men meant to protect it. I saw as much as the gas mask I'd been forced to wear allowed. Whoever was behind this hadn't been simply looking to rob the place.

This was personal.

Fumes from the toxic gas covering the walls, floor, and furniture had made habitation of the underground hideaway impossible.

"What happened? Look around!" Evan, the *captean* of the Balfour-Young family, shouted. "This is the fourth fucking hit this month! Someone's been razing our houses."

"I can see that," I bit out. "What I want to know is why?"

"We don't know that yet. The person behind this only ever asks for one thing."

"Black," I answered with a nod. "Where is he? He should be here cleaning this up."

Evan scowled as if only just realizing it. "Don't know. Haven't seen him in a few days. Maybe whoever's looking for him finally found him."

"If they had, they wouldn't have done this." I gestured around the restored historic hotel that was once abandoned and now served as one of Black Veil's stables and a safe harbor for girls with no other options. "What about the girls? Are they good?"

"The whores are fine." Evan waved me off as if their well-being was of little importance. The girls who worked the flesh dens did it as much for our benefit as their own and had only asked for one thing besides fair wage—protection. "They're spooked but ain't hurt. Except…"

"Spit it out," I barked.

"I don't know what those bitches are complaining about. Whoever is doing this isn't concerned with some whores. They haven't touched a hair on their heads, but the girls are talking about quitting if we can't guarantee their safety. Don't worry, I'll—"

I spun toward Evan and wrapped my hand around his thick throat. He had about fifty pounds on me and little brains to go with his brawn, but he wasn't a complete idiot. He knew for whom and when to bare his belly.

"So guarantee it," I ordered. Evan tried to speak, but I tightened my grip until his words became garbled. "This is your division. Your responsibility. Keep the girls happy and deal with the person behind these attacks, or I'll find someone who will, *captean*."

Evan had inherited his position just as I had, but only one of us had bothered trying to earn it before and after the fact. The Balfour family had descended from Titus Young, one of the founding members of the Brothers of Rory. Titus married one of my great-great-grandfather's sisters and assumed the Balfour name to become made.

I let go of his worthless scion and ignored Evan's glare as I took one last look around the destroyed parlor before leaving the underground brothel.

I made a few pit stops before returning to the penthouse after dark. There was music playing when I entered, and the change from the silence I had become accustomed to was jarring enough that I didn't notice Coby standing at the window in the open-space living room. Her back was to me as she stared at the city below, her hands and forehead pressed against the cool glass.

"You have a lot of faith in that window," I said as I shed my coat and tossed it over the back of the couch.

The elevator would have alerted her to my return, so Coby wasn't surprised to see me when she turned away from the window. "I always wondered what the view looked like from up here," she confessed. "You can see everything."

"I'm glad you found a way to keep yourself entertained."

Coby didn't respond, and I didn't wait for one as I entered the kitchen. I already knew she was about to curse my ass out, so I ate from the picked-over charcuterie board my private chef prepared while I patiently waited for my baby to speak her mind.

It didn't take long.

"I agreed to marry you, but let's be clear about one thing. It doesn't mean you won't need to earn me. I'm not a puppy. You can't just keep me locked up in here to wait for you to come home. Try that shit again and I'll...I'll—"

I couldn't resist the urge to touch her, so I grabbed her hand and gently pulled her closer until she was trapped between me and the counter. I kissed along her jaw as I pawed her lower back, her slight frame in my arms reminding me how easily I could break her. "What will you do, *mo aingeal*?"

I grunted when Coby's nails dug into my chest—a testament of how easily she could break me, too. "I'll smother you in your sleep."

"Damn, okay."

"I'm serious."

Sighing, I lifted her onto the counter and kissed the palms of her hands. "My shit isn't in order, Coby." I saw the question in her eyes when she blinked in confusion at me. "It may not seem like it, but taking you was an impulsive decision. Your brother wasn't the only one to force my hand."

"But my room…the library—"

"Moments of weakness," I whispered and then shrugged. "A man can dream."

"It sounds like you were just lying to yourself."

I chuckled at Coby calling me out. "Maybe."

Coby did that thing she does whenever she's trying to decide whether to speak her mind. Her teeth sank into her bottom lip, and then she pouted before drawing a deep breath. "You dream about making me happy?"

"There's a lot I want, Coby. None more than you, but there are things that I have to do first before that can happen. Things that will keep you safe." I kissed her knuckles.

"Like killing people?"

"Yeah."

"I don't know if I want anyone dying just so I can marry you. Maybe we should slow down and date for a little while or something. You're going through an awful lot of trouble when you barely even know me."

Sidestepping that bullshit she was spitting, I replied, "It wouldn't be just for that. There were many reasons before you."

"Who do you have to kill?" I shook my head rather than answer, and Coby seemed to accept my reasons without knowing them. "I just don't see the reason I have to stay locked in here like a prisoner. No one even knows we're getting married. Why can't I go home?"

"Because you're my wife. Your home is with me." Coby looked like she wanted to kick me in the face. "It won't be like this forever. I know I don't have the right to ask you for anything considering how shit went down, but I need you to be patient with me."

"Okay. I can do that." I didn't react because that shit was too easy. "But I want to see Hunter," Coby demanded. "I don't want to wait for the wedding. I want to see her right now."

A staring contest ensued, and though I didn't make a habit of underestimating anyone, Coby somehow managed to surprise me left and fucking right because she didn't back down. She looked ready to tell me to go to hell, but I had more than enough reasons why I didn't want Hunter Parrish anywhere near my wife. The problem was that Coby's little ass thought I was fucking stupid.

"That wasn't part of our deal," I reminded her as I dragged her off the counter and set Coby on her feet.

"Well, maybe I want to renegotiate."

"I promise you don't," I warned as I steered her from the kitchen with my hand on her spine.

Coby stumbled a little, twisting around to glare at me. "What's that supposed to mean?"

Palming the sides of her face, I kissed her lips firmly and smirked when she melted against me. "You're trying my patience, sweetheart," I whispered. "Keep walking before I lose my composure."

"I'm not afraid of you," she retorted with a frown.

"I know," I said with a smirk. "Why do you think my dick is this hard?"

Coby's eyes flew to my crotch before they widened. With a gasp, she turned around and tried to scurry away, but my hand on her nape didn't let her get far. Grabbing one of the shopping bags I brought in with me, I steered Coby upstairs and through the open double doors. The maids must have just finished cleaning because the cavernous room smelled of fresh linen and lemons while the marble floor gleamed with our reflections.

I couldn't see my baby's face, but I felt the tension trapped under my fingers leave her at being back in here.

"I still can't believe you did this," she said in awe as she stared around the library like she was seeing it for the first time. Her soft voice echoed a little, reminding me that it was still waiting to be filled. "This must have cost a fortune. What if I said no to marrying you?" she asked curiously.

She wouldn't have said no.

"Then you would have been a well-entertained, long-term, involuntary house guest. And the library would still be yours."

"You mean your prisoner."

"Call it whatever you want, *mo aingeal*, but you would be alive. Safe. Protected. My father is going to find out what your brother did. This is the only way I can protect you. At least for now."

Coby's confusion at that last part had me releasing her and setting the bag on the coffee table. Her gaze fell on it, and when she recognized the logo from the local bookstore she frequented, I knew all questions about my father had vanished.

I watched her internal struggle over keeping her attitude or finding out what was inside before her addiction spurred her forward. Squeezing by me when I refused to make space, I held in my laugh as she gave me the stank eye before lowering to sit on her heels and eagerly pulling out the stack of books.

"I thought we might christen your library," I said as I took a seat on the couch next to her spot on the floor. One of the staff arrived like clockwork with a tray bearing a single drink. I took it and sipped from the glass while Coby oohed and aahed over the pretty covers.

"I've read some of these books," Coby whispered as she fingered one of them open. "They're my favorites. How did you know?"

"I have my ways," I said as I leaned against the back of the couch.

"More internet stalking?" Coby asked with her gaze fixed on a random page.

"I prefer sleuthing." Picking up one from the stack, I ignored Coby wrinkling her nose at me and flipped it over to read the back.

I only read a couple of sentences before the weight of her gaze drew mine away from the book. "What?"

"Nothing. You just think you're so smooth," she said with a giggle.

"Smooth ain't got shit to do with it. I just know you even though your pretty ass wants to believe I don't." I pinched Coby's cheek, and she blushed before turning away. Quietly, I knocked back my drink before standing and grabbing the rest of the books. "I'm hungry as shit. Come on. Let's find somewhere to put these so I can feed you." Coby's eyes were glowing as I helped her to her feet before grabbing the books and walking over to the closest book-case. "This looks like the motherfucking spot right here," I said, hyping her up. "What you think?"

"Mmmh...yes, that's good." Taking the first book from the stack, I started to put it on a shelf in the middle when she yelled, "No, wait!" Pausing with a book mid-air, I raised a brow. "Maybe we should put them over there." She pointed to the bookcase by the weeping cherry tree, and I followed her over to it. Peeping that this wasn't going to be as simple as I thought, I handed her the book and let her choose a shelf. "There," she said with a bright grin aimed at me after putting it in its place. I nodded my approval and tried to hand her a second book, but she frowned at it, then at the bookcase, before taking it and hurrying to another bookcase on the opposite side.

Coby placed the book on a shelf only to decide a second later that she didn't like it there either, grumbling something about the lighting and the color gray before finding another shelf. It went on like that for another fifteen minutes until she finally picked a spot.

Two goddamn hours later, we finally had all twelve of the books shelved while I was thanking God I hadn't bought more.

Apparently, Coby wanted them all categorized by the books she *really* loved and the ones she only sort of liked, then by genre, and finally by color. I made the mistake of asking her what she was going to do with the books she hadn't read yet, and a look of horror crossed her expression before she started studying the shelves again with a different eye. It took another twenty minutes before she designated a shelf for unread books that she may never read and unread books she'd definitely maybe read. I almost cussed her ass out until Coby suddenly turned and threw her arms around my neck. I was trapped by my own astonishment as she peppered my face with kisses. Just as I was considering bending her over the back of the couch, Coby placed a final kiss on my lips and stepped back.

"What was that for?" I asked to keep from snatching her back.

Coby only grinned harder, looking sweet as fuck. "Best evil fiancé daddy ever," she answered with a twinkle in her eye.

I was still imagining her coming on my dick when her title for me finally clicked. *A what?*

CHAPTER NINE

COBY

OCEAN WAS STILL TRYING TO FIGURE OUT HOW TO REACT when I felt this burn in my belly that shifted forms and snaked between my thighs the closer I stepped to him until I pressed my body against his again. My hands trembled as they clutched his muscled arms. I didn't know how to do this.

Seduce.

I was very much used to being chased, but Ocean seemed cool with taking things slow, and I was becoming less fucking grateful by the hour. I wanted to be mad at him for hurting my brother, and I was definitely pissed at him for taking me from Hunter, but my pussy admittedly didn't care about any of that shit.

It wasn't like I couldn't walk and chew gum at the same time. I could still hate his ass for ruining the fairytale and still get a nut or two out of him.

But no.

It would just be me being delusional all over again because reducing what I felt to something as fleeting as an orgasm wouldn't be true to my heart. And my heart wanted *him*.

Ocean's gaze sharpened to a laser point focused on me when he felt my body once again pressed against him.

"I was thinking," I said with false confidence as I pushed his suit jacket off his shoulders. It fell to the floor with a soft thud. "I-I never showed you how I like to be kissed."

Ocean's grip on me tightened, and then he pulled me closer. "Think carefully about what you're saying to me, Coby."

Thinking about Hunter and what she would do, I decided to do more than that. "I want you to kiss me…" Grabbing his hand, my heart thundered inside my chest as Ocean let me guide him between my thighs. Long fingers breached my tights, skating briefly over bare skin and an engorged clit before tunneling between swollen lips trapped by damp cotton. "Here." I stopped breathing at the same time his breath shuddered out of him. "Kiss me here."

Ocean's lips slammed against mine, and then we were moving backward until I cried out when my back struck the edge of the nearest bookcase. Ocean crowded me a moment later, his lips devouring while his hands groped and demanded I yield to him. Coming up for air, he turned me to face the bookcase, and then I felt his hard body press against my back. Ocean was a fucking furnace, and all I wanted to do was let him melt me into a puddle.

"Where is it today?" he demanded with a growl aimed at my ear. "The ribbon, *mo aingeal*. Where is it?"

"M-my waist."

I felt his weight leave me as he backed away a little and yanked at his tie until it was loose around his neck. "Show me."

With a whimper, I raised the hem of my pleated skirt until the thick material was bunched underneath my breasts. The knot in the bow I'd tied this morning was nestled inside the dip in my spine, while the dark pink tails of the ribbon fell across the top of my butt. "D-do you like it?"

"Fuck, Coby. Why are you so fucking sexy, huh?"

I didn't get a chance to respond before my tights were yanked down my legs. They cleared my feet with little effort and disappeared with a careless toss across the room. Ocean had even less patience with my panties, choosing to tear them off with a vicious yank that left an enflamed strip across my flesh. The satin ribbon teased the bare crack of my ass, making Ocean curse under his breath.

"This ass is mine," he said with repeated slaps across my butt. "This pussy is mine." Lewdly, he forced his hand between my thighs and cupped me while whispering in my ear. "What else is mine, sweetheart?"

His tone sounded a little threatening, and I thought about everything I learned about Ocean in the short time since he took me. Ocean was generous but possessive, patient and yet demanding, and dominant in a way that made me feel safe rather than suffocated. And for it, a man like him would demand no less than my absolute surrender.

"Me," I answered breathlessly. "I'm yours."

Ocean's only response was to grab the underside of my thigh and lift my leg until my right foot rested high on one of the empty shelves. He opened me up for him and then sank to his knees with a groan. My nails dug into the wood, and a soft moan escaped me when I felt his teeth graze the skin above where a small pink bow was tattooed on my left ass cheek. There was a larger one on my right thigh like a garter belt, but all thoughts of tattoos fled when I felt the first hot lash of his tongue a moment later. It became devastatingly clear within the first few moments of his head between my thighs that Ocean was no novice to eating pussy. It took him no time at all to uncover what I liked—the right pressure and speed, when to pull back so that I wouldn't come before he was ready.

And the sounds he made as he licked and slurped and took.

My body shuddered against the bookcase, but when I tried to move my hips and chase that feeling to the end, Ocean reached up and gripped my nape firmly as he feasted. My cheek was trapped against the shelf as I shook, cried, gasped, and moaned.

Meanwhile, Ocean was oblivious to my sweet woes as he uttered cruel and filthy things to me.

"Look at you making a mess on my face."

"Pretty little pussy gonna purr for me."

"*Lift your leg for me, sweet girl. More, more…*"

"Ocean, pleeeease," I begged as my toes curled to the point of pain. My arm was hooked underneath my propped-up leg as I opened myself up more for him. "I want to come."

The bastard stopped fucking with my clit long enough to say, "But I'm not done eating."

Fuck that. I came anyway, twitching uncontrollably until I was spent and slumped against the bookshelf while Ocean laughed at me with his face pressed against my thigh. "You surprised me," I said once I caught my breath.

"How did I do that?"

"I thought you were one of those pretty boys who think they're too good to eat pussy."

Ocean lifted his head and kissed my thigh. "You were testing me?"

"Not really." I shrugged. "But it was still a nice surprise."

Ocean stood and fixed my skirt before turning me around and kissing me. His nasty ass made sure to feed me his tongue so I could taste myself and rose onto the tips of my toes so he could get a better angle.

"Keep on, *mo aingeal,*" he warned. "And I'll fuck you through the wall."

Not quite ready for that, I backed away and bumped into the shelf, sending the one book on it tumbling over the side. It was an embarrassing display that didn't go unnoticed by the finest man alive. Maybe it was the orgasm talking, but I chose not to dwell on it. Ocean had made it more than clear he wanted me, and he didn't seem like the type to be easily swayed. He gallantly rescued my book from the floor and re-shelved it while I thought of something to say.

"Thanks for the books and the um…other thing."

"When you're ready for more, just say the word," he whispered.

Wait… books or orgasms?

I didn't ask out of fear that it might lead to more, and Ocean didn't seem interested in clarifying as he took my hand and pulled me from the library. We traveled up to the third floor and through the door that led to the rooftop terrace. A bar took up most of the space, but there were couches and loungers around the lit fire pit and a covered area with a dining table laden with food.

And candles.

There were candles everywhere—scattered on the floor and on every surface. Music played from some hidden speakers. "Yeah, I Said It" by Rihanna set the mood, but the cherry on top was the largest bouquet of red roses I'd ever seen. I could barely wrap my arm around the bundle.

Something cracked open inside of my belly. Something warm and fluttery that took my breath away. Fortunately, Ocean excused himself only to return five minutes later looking like a million dollars while I was still disheveled.

I pouted while he pulled out a chair for me and kissed my cheek once I was seated. He then sat next to me at the head of the table. Out of habit, I glanced at the empty chair in front of me. Hunter would always sit across from me so that I could see her making faces at my choice of food.

As if he read my mind, Ocean murmured, "You're going to have to explain this vegan food to me and why you torture yourself with it."

Thoughts of Hunter fled as he poured white wine into a glass for me. I never really got into drinking the stuff, but for the sake of appearing more sophisticated than I was, I accepted the offering.

"It's not torture." I giggled. "It's good for you. Good for your temple and your soul."

Ocean spooned some black beans and rice onto my plate, along with some spicy jerk tofu. He then topped it with mango, pickled onions, avocado, and cilantro. "My soul?"

"Yes." I shifted nervously in my seat because I couldn't figure out why I found Ocean doing something as simple as filling a plate so damn sexy. Like everything else, he was just so damn efficient at it, knowing just how much food to give me and arranging it all in a way that made my mouth water. The sleeves of his dress shirt were rolled up, and the veins in his forearms became a constant distraction as I tried to remember what we were discussing. "No innocent animals had to die so that we may live."

"What about carnivorous animals? Should they only eat plants, too?"

Used to the same arguments, I shook my head with a sigh. "They don't have the capacity to know any better. We do."

"Hmm," Ocean hummed as he began making his own plate.

"You don't have to eat vegan food just because I do." I gave a tasting sip of my wine. It was light and crisp and a little dry, but also fruity. I immediately took a second, larger sip. "I already tried that with Hunter, and she told me to go to hell." Ocean's unreadable gaze flicked to me, and I shrugged with a small, fond smile. "She doesn't pull any punches," I told him. "Ever."

To my utter shock and dismay, Ocean gently demanded, "Tell me about her. Your Hunter."

"She's my best friend," I said matter-of-factly as if those two little words could encompass everything she is and has been to me. "We sort of grew up together, but we didn't meet until we were fifteen during grief counseling. A-after my parents died."

"Hunter lost someone, too?"

"Not really. Her mom died, but that bitch abandoned Hunter long before that. The counseling wasn't her choice or mine, but we found each other because of it and promised we'd always be together no matter what."

"A family of your own never entered either of your minds?"

I stared Ocean in the eye and repeated, "No matter what."

Ocean held my gaze as he abandoned his food and slowly sat back in his chair. I realized with a phantom kick to the gut that I may have just thrown down some kind of gauntlet. At least that's how it would seem to a man like Ocean. "Is that right?"

I swallowed back the urge to take it all back and squared my shoulders instead. Hunter was the other half of my soul. I wasn't whole without her. We were good and evil. The sky and the ground.

We were light and darkness. The sun and the moon. One could not exist without the other.

But it didn't mean we were fated either.

Because Hunter and I were loss and love too. One could not exist without the other.

We could never be separated, but we could never truly be together either.

"Yes," I said, the word tasting like ash and doom on my tongue. I plucked my wine glass from the table and took a healthy gulp to wash it all away.

"Aight then. You think she'd want to live with us?"

The glass slipped from my fingers. The remaining wine quickly stained the crisp white tablecloth as the goblet hit the table with a thud, rolled, and disappeared over the edge. "Wh-what?"

Before he could answer, one of the staff appeared out of thin air and cleared away the broken glass before disappearing into the shadows again.

"We've got plenty of room," Ocean went on as if nothing had happened. "But if she prefers her own space, it ain't nothing for me to set her up in one of the apartments in the building." He shrugged.

Oh. I thought...

It didn't matter.

I waited for my heart to slow to a normal rate before I spoke. "She'd probably like that. I'd have to talk to her first," I said, unable to keep the hope that I'd see her again from my voice. "Get her to accept our marriage."

"Is there an alternative?" Ocean asked me with an arched brow and an edge to his tone that told me to tread carefully.

Yes. She kills you.

If it were anyone else, I wouldn't believe they could kill Ocean. But Hunter could—even if it killed her too. Obviously, I didn't want to lose either of them so handling this *delicately* was imperative. Ocean was already so possessive of me, and that shit wouldn't go well with Hunter at all. And he was already off to the worst start in history. Turning this around would take a miracle, but I would find a way because I couldn't be without Ocean either. Hunter was my soulmate, but Ocean had the key to my heart, and I wasn't about to rescue it from him anytime soon.

"No," I answered finally. "There's no alternative." I sighed. "Look, Hunter won't like that we're together after what happened, but she'll understand. I'll make her."

It felt like a betrayal of my best friend to admit that I wouldn't let Hunter run him away—not this one, not this time. But if I were being real, I knew damn well Ocean would never allow himself to be run off either. Ocean wouldn't back down, but neither would Hunter.

Suddenly, I had this premonition that shit was about to get real fucking messy.

After dinner, Ocean took me to my room, kissed me, and told me goodnight before leaving. I soaked in a steaming bath until my skin started to prune, then got ready for bed before slipping my feet into the giant, fluffy slippers that made me smile as I left the room and went downstairs. I was feeling too restless to sleep, so I made myself chamomile tea before wandering around the lower level and eventually finding myself standing in front of the grand piano by one of the many windows.

Was it for show, or did he really play?

I used the question as an excuse to seek out Ocean. His room was on the same floor as my library, so I stopped in there to grab a book—the same one that had fallen to the floor after I came harder than I ever had. And when I closed my eyes, I could still feel his mouth on me.

Hence, the restlessness.

Ocean was asleep on his back when I let myself inside his room. I felt nervous treading where I hadn't been invited, but it didn't stop me from tiptoeing forward until I stood by his bed. Setting my book on the nightstand, I freed my feet from my slippers and climbed onto the bed. Ocean stirred as I threw a leg over his torso before settling my weight on his lap.

"Coby," he mumbled with his eyes closed. His hands had no trouble finding my hips, though. "What are you doing?"

"I can't sleep." I sipped my tea loudly as I admired the way his dark lashes framed the top of his cheeks. His chest was bare, but I couldn't see what he was wearing underneath the blanket.

"Why can't you sleep?"

Setting my tea on the nightstand, I slid off Ocean's body until I was lying half on the bed and half on him. "I don't know. I'm just worried," I said as I lay my cheek on his chest. His strong arms immediately wrapped around my back and nearly swallowed me whole. Ocean's chest was so damn warm, I felt like kicking the unnecessary covers away as I melted into his warmth.

"Worried about what?"

"That you're love bombing me."

Ocean shifted, his chin dipping to his chest to look down at me. I peered up at him, and the worry sitting in my gut like a stone eased a little at the angry look in his eyes. "You want me to fall back?"

Panic speared my chest, and I couldn't take a breath as I shook my head. "No."

Sighing, Ocean tipped his head back and closed his eyes again. "It will be okay, Coby. You just have to trust in love."

Before I could ask what the hell that even meant, his ass had fallen asleep again.

CHAPTER TEN

COBY

GLUG. GLUG. GLUG. GLUG. GLUG. GLUG.
Sluuuuuuuurp.

I lifted my head with a gasp and inhaled deeply as I stroked and admired the hard dick I gripped in my palm. A deep groan rumbled from Ocean's chest when I licked a slow path up the thick shaft while holding his gaze. It was early morning, and I've been his captive bride for two weeks now. I can't really say what brought on my need to taste him, but when I woke up next to him yet again, I was suddenly faced with my heart's deepest desire, and so I asked myself one question.

What the fuck was I waiting for?

Ocean had still been asleep when I had my epiphany, so I'd found myself reaching for him before I could lose my nerve, and that's how we ended up here. I was folded in half in the middle of the bed with my thighs trapped against my chest and two of Ocean's long fingers tunneling in and out of my pussy. His strong thighs hovered near my head while I snaked my neck back and forth, mouth stretched wide for that dick.

"Fuck, baby. Shit. Just like that." He was hovering above me on his knees, and his eyes were low as he watched me suck him off. "Greedy girl and her wet ass pussy."

Whimpering, my eyes rolled back as I tightened around his

fingers. I was getting ready to come up for air again and beg him to fuck me when someone started pounding on his bedroom door as if they were seconds from knocking it down.

"Ocean! Ocean, open up! I know she's in there!"

What. The. Fuck? I quickly released him from my mouth, my gaze bouncing between him and the door as I angrily swiped the back of my hand over my mouth. I almost spat in that bastard's face until I remembered that, though he wasn't loud about it, the man was crazy as fuck.

Ocean, on the other hand, didn't seem bothered by the demanding knocks and instead sucked his teeth and tried to stick his dick back in my mouth. I felt so damn stupid for even trusting him enough to let that thing get anywhere near. He tapped my lips with it, and I snapped my teeth at him. "Stop fucking playing with me. Why did you stop?"

"You don't hear that?"

"Ignore it, *mo aingeal.* She'll go away."

She? My stomach sank at the confirmation of another woman. I knew this no-good-cheating-slime-ball-bucket-head-ass bastard was too good to be true. I scrambled to sit up, fighting off the tangle of blankets and sheets as I threw myself at him.

"What the—Coby, stop!" he screamed when I bit his ass. I was still locked on like a pitbull when he managed to stand from the bed with me wrapped around him. He tried to pry me off him, but I just bit down harder. "Ahhh shit! Coby, I think you drawing blood!"

Suddenly, my head was yanked back with such force that it blinded me. I was tossed away, landing on the bed a little too hard and bouncing off over the other side. I tasted blood when I hit the floor, but I knew it wasn't mine.

When I stood, Ocean was clutching his shoulder. When he pulled his hand away to inspect his palm, it was covered in crimson. "*Tugaimid onóir don fhuil*[3]." His eyes rose to meet mine. "That's the

---

3   We honor the blood.

second time you've made me bleed, *mo aingeal*. Keep it up, and I'll return the favor."

"Did you just threaten me?"

"I would never hurt you, but you're killing me, sweet girl. Don't look at me like that. It ain't what you think."

I ignored the prickling in my eyes and the insistent knocks and forced myself to meet his gaze. "What the fuck do I think, Ocean?"

He traveled around the bed, devotion carved into his beautiful face as his fingers made a collar around my throat. "That it's someone I'm fucking. I don't want to fuck anyone but you."

The pounding on the door grew louder. "You can't hide her forever. Let us in!" another squeaking voice demanded.

"Shut your lying ass up," I grumbled and pushed away from Ocean when I remembered that I was naked and about to be jumped. I couldn't fight for shit, so this was bad.

Huffing, I grabbed my new bamboo robe. It was another gorgeous gift Ocean provided, like a magician pulling a rabbit out of a hat, after I admitted the reason I stopped sleeping in my bed. Because baby moths died so that my bedsheets could be pretty. Ocean bought me the robe as an apology for the oversight, but made no attempt to address the sheets. Every morning, I peeked inside my girly and gorgeous room after the maids were done cleaning and changing the bed, only to find that the sheets had returned.

I quickly pulled on my robe and tied the sash tightly. "How did they even get in here? Shouldn't you have guards or something?"

Now that I was covered up, Ocean ignored me and stalked to the door. He snatched it open, but only enough to speak to the callers without them seeing me.

Hmm…definitely suspicious.

"What the fuck do you two want?"

Um…okay.

Ocean had doted on me so much, I'd almost forgotten how cold he could be.

Whoever was on the other side of the door responded, but they spoke too low for me to hear what was said.

"So your nosy asses couldn't wait until family dinner?" he returned with a teasing note to his voice. "I was about to get some pussy."

My face became red hot. "No, you weren't!" I yelled at his back.

"First of all, *ew*," one of the voices on the other side said. "Second of all, move out of the way, fool."

Ocean was grinning when he stepped back in time to keep from getting smacked in the face with the door as it was shoved open. Two women with perfect hair and makeup and dripping in designer clothing strutted inside on a cloud of perfume and old money. They sure as hell didn't look like they came to brawl, so I felt myself relaxing a little while keeping my guard up as I eyed the mysterious women warily.

What the hell was going on?

The two women noticed me right away but didn't react. The shorter one with shoulder-length dreads and a small gold hoop in her right nostril smiled politely while the taller one took her time looking me over before coming to the conclusion that she wasn't impressed.

Rubbing the back of my neck, I mumbled, "Lord, give me strength."

"As you can see, we weren't expecting company."

"Well, hurry up and introduce us, and then we'll get out of your hair," the taller one ordered dismissively. Her tone made my brows rise.

Ocean glanced back at me and then sighed as he held out his hand to me. "Come here."

I dutifully went to him, and it wasn't until I saw the approval in his eyes that I realized I did it without hesitation. Ocean took my hand and tucked me into his side before returning his attention to the smiling women. They were watching the exchange like they were witnessing some new wonder.

"Sweetheart, these are my cousins, Chiara and Priscilla," he introduced.

I waved a hand and greeted dryly, "Hey."

Ocean—still peeping my unease and frustration at being am-bushed by his family—squeezed my hip in reprimand before con-tinuing. "Chi. Pri. This is my baby. Coby."

"You're bleeding," Priscilla dryly informed her cousin. Her gaze flicked to me, so I boldly licked his blood from my lips like I was a vampire, and then lifted a brow that said, *Yeah, I did it. Fuck are you gon' do about it?*

"Sorry for interrupting," Chiara rushed to break the tension. "We just couldn't wait to meet you. Ocean never brings anyone home. We wanted to see what was up."

"Well, that's good to know," I said while finally offering the cous-ins a real smile. "This apartment is beautiful. I'd hate to make him burn it down."

"Burn it do—" Chiara's eyes lit up with humor. "Oh, I like her."

"Why am I not surprised that Ocean likes 'em crazy?" Priscilla asked with a shake of her head. "That's good. You'll fit right in."

I wasn't so sure about that, but I kept my feelings close to the chest and chuckled with no real humor. "So when you say you're re-lated, do you mean play cousins or real cousins?"

Priscilla smirked, and I could see the first sign of respect grow-ing in her eyes. "Real, though distant. We share great-great grandpar-ents, so that makes us third cousins, but our mothers and Malcolm grew up together like siblings."

"Malcolm?" I directed at Ocean.

"My father," he supplied. Leaning down to sweep his lips across my hairline, he whispered, "You'll never have to meet him."

"Oh." I gulped, my voice cracking when I added, "O-okay."

"The whole family has been talking about Ocean's new girl. Who she is, what she looks like, where she came from…" Priscilla gave both of us pointed looks before adding, "And why she's here…"

"How the fuck they find out?"

"Come on, cuz," Priscilla said. "You have your spies and your dad has his. You know how it is. Do you really need to ask?"

The muscle in Ocean's jaw ticked furiously. The cousins waited for him to fill in the blanks, but he just stared at them until I cleared my throat and attempted to plow through the ice. "So, do you guys live in the building?"

"Oh, no," Chiara said. "The city can be too much sometimes, and not all of us can live under armed guards twenty-four-seven like our big cuz. Most of the family lives closer to Glamis."

Chiara looked closer to my age—maybe even a little younger—while Priscilla looked closer to Ocean's age. There were other differences between Ocean's cousins that were hard to ignore. Priscilla was tall and thin, while Chiara was short with a little more curve. Both of them had Ocean's dark eyes, though their skin was a fairer brown than his but not as pale as mine. Chiara was the warmer of the two—soft spoken and quick to smile. Priscilla was more reserved and observant, taking everything in quietly and rarely chiming in. Although that could just be because she was clearly a bitch.

"Uh…Glamis?"

"I guess we don't have to ask how you two have been spending your time because it clearly wasn't talking," Priscilla scolded. "Glamis is the seat of our family," she explained with an impatient sigh and a hint of loathing for both me and the Kilpatrick family estate. "It's where the Boss and his family stay, but we've all called it home at one point or another."

"Anyway, now that you're here," Ocean intervened before I could check her ass. "I have a job for you two." He walked over to his wallet on the dresser and plucked a black credit card from it before returning to the door, where his cousins still stood. "Coby had to leave everything behind when she moved in with me. She needs a new wardrobe and all of the other bullshit y'all spend my money on. You think you can handle that?"

"Shopping!" Chiara squealed before snatching the card from Ocean's fingers. "I can't believe you're crazy enough to trust us with the black card. Ooh! Coby should come with us. We can have a girls' day and get to know her better."

"Nah," Ocean said.

"Why not?" Priscilla challenged.

"Because I said so."

Oh, boy. Feeling Ocean's dominance rolling off him in waves, I rubbed my nape nervously. Priscilla must have too because she backed down with a roll of her eyes and one last glance at me before spinning on her high heels and leaving the room. Priscilla didn't seem to care one way or another if I came, but Chiara seemed genuinely disappointed as she turned and reluctantly left, too.

"There," Ocean said with a panty-melting grin directed at me like he was proud of himself. "That should keep their nosy asses out of my business for a while."

"What was that about? Why couldn't I go with them?"

Ocean was halfway to the ensuite when he paused and regarded me with a raised brow. "You wanted to?"

"Not really. But I'm curious why you didn't want me to."

Ocean didn't respond right away, turning to disappear inside the bathroom, so I followed him. "I don't really have the men to spare right now."

"Okay…and?" Ocean didn't respond as he pulled out the first aid kit and sloppily patched himself up. "You think I'll run, don't you?"

He simply stared at me through the mirror as he wrapped his shoulder. His dark eyes warned me to drop it before he moved away from the sink to turn on the shower. After shoving down his sweats, he stepped under the cold spray. He must have really wanted to avoid a fight because he didn't even wait for the water to turn warm. For a few seconds, I was distracted watching the water sluice over his dark skin as he washed himself with a thick bar of soap.

It took too long for me to realize Ocean still hadn't answered me.

He turned his back on me to continue showering. I narrowed my gaze on his strong back and tried not to be distracted by the way the muscles bunched and flexed as he moved.

Ocean still didn't trust me.

Did I trust him?

Maybe a little, but not blindly. At least…not yet. And not in the way I trusted Hunter.

If she told me to wander blindfolded into rush hour traffic and that I'd make it unscathed, I wouldn't think twice about throwing myself into danger.

I wasn't there with Ocean yet, but I would like to be.

"Your cousins seem afraid of you," I said, changing the subject. "Is there a reason why?"

Besides the obvious…

Ocean's attention finally returned to me, and then he beckoned me inside the enormous shower. I only hesitated half a second—worried that he'd distract me from the answers I wanted—before I untied the sash on my robe and let it fall to the heated floor.

The water was warm by the time I stepped inside, but not to my liking, so I turned one of the many matte black knobs on the wall before facing Ocean, whose expression was pensive as he drew me close. I didn't even notice the sponge in his hand until he tugged on my wrist to lift my arm out in front of me.

"They're not afraid because of something I've done," he explained as he slowly ran the lathered sponge up my arm and back down again. "They're afraid of what I could do once I have the power. Priscilla is…protective of Chiara. The two of them try to stay on my good side so that I'm not tempted to marry Chi off to the first abusive asshole who offers me the slightest advantage."

"Why would they think you'd do that?"

"Because it's what my father did to Priscilla. And what our great-grandfather did to his sisters—Priscilla and Chiara's great-grandmothers." Ocean flinched suddenly, but before I could ask what was wrong, he flinched again. "Argh. Shit."

"Wha–"

"Argh! Argh!" He yelled while leaping to the other side of the shower, where he huddled in the corner out of range of the water pouring down like a rainfall. Ocean and I stared at each other with matching confused expressions when I continued to stand under the water while steam quickly rose around us, fogging up the glass wall.

I placed my hands on my hips. "What is wrong with you?"

"You don't feel that?" he yelled.

"Feel what?"

"That water is scalding, Coby! The fuck are you trying to do? Give me third-degree burns?"

Rolling my eyes, I spun on my heels and quickly turned the knob until it was halfway between where he had it and where I wanted it. "Better?"

Ocean held out his hand to test the water, and I choked back a laugh as he returned to me. I didn't want him thinking I did it on purpose, so I schooled my expression into a concerned one, and he smirked before letting out a laugh of his own and shaking his head.

"So your family is like old school, old school," I remarked, picking up where he left off. I was even less convinced of how well I'd fit in with his family if they were still doing arranged marriages.

"It's not about tradition. It's about power. It's about control." Ocean moved on to washing my neck. There was a deep furrow between his brows, telling me he wanted to say more but wasn't sure he should.

"Please continue," I whispered, wanting to know more about Ocean's family, and what I was getting myself into.

His gaze flew up to meet mine, and he seemed to understand what I was asking.

"Once James got a taste of it," he said as he started washing my other arm, "there was nothing he wasn't willing to do to keep it. My great-grandfather and his younger brother, Rory, left Ireland after Rory was caught having an affair with a married woman. When the husband confronted Rory in a bar and nearly killed him, James stepped in and saved his brother. What they didn't know was that the man they killed was the nephew of a gang lord, who put a price on their heads. Nowhere was safe, so they fled to America."

I inhaled when Ocean paused to dip the sponge between my legs.

And I say again…a girl could get used to this.

He seemed to need to take care of me—like he was proving something to himself—and I couldn't help but wonder why.

"A few months later, James found his brother beaten and lynched, and he knew that he would need someone watching his back if he wanted survive, so he put together a crew. They called themselves the Brothers of Rory. At first, their aim was freedom, but they realized there was no such thing without money. They didn't just need to survive. They needed to *thrive*. It was the Prohibition era, and while Black folks could own property and businesses, it wasn't that simple—shit, it still ain't—so James and his crew found their fortune in speakeasies. That evolved into smuggling, illegal gambling, prostitution…the list goes on. The Brothers of Rory became more than just a brotherhood trying to survive. They became an organization attracting attention—good and bad—and as their riches grew, so did the distrust among the founding members. The leaders didn't trust that James wouldn't eventually get greedy and cut them out since he was so big on blood ties, family, and building a legacy. My great-grandfather became a powerhouse, but he was far from invincible, and he knew it. Everything he'd built was being threatened, so he concocted a plan. The Brothers of Rory had been born from the loss of his brother—his blood—so he believed that bringing blood in was the only way to ease the tensions within the crew."

Ocean inhaled deeply as if he wasn't proud of whatever part of the story came next. It was even more evident when he stopped washing my stomach to turn me until I was facing away from him.

"As I told you, James had two unmarried sisters—Davina and Frances. He lured them over here with the promise of a better life and forced them to marry his partners. James also married and promised his partners that once children were born of their unions, their induction would become permanent—irreversible even by him."

"And did they have children?"

Ocean nodded. "Many, but they still didn't trust James, so his partners wanted to ensure they had backups if one of their children were to meet an untimely death."

"How moving."

"Once the first of the new generation was born, the Brothers of Rory became known as the Fola. Or as the streets like to unofficially call us—the Blood mafia. The only way in or out was to spill blood or give it—an offering only the Boss could accept."

"Blood In, Blood Out," I uttered, reciting the *Fola's* chilling motto. I'd always wondered what it meant.

"Exactly," Ocean confirmed.

"Well, that's a relief." Ocean turned me to face him and then lifted his brows in question. "Honestly, I thought it meant you all stood in a circle, slitting your palms and pouring your blood in a golden chalice before taking turns drinking it."

Ocean barked out a laugh and then slapped my ass so hard it stung. "No, smart ass."

"My second theory was that you all sacrificed some poor virgin and drunk their blood." I paused, my gaze narrowing as I eyed him. "I'm not a virgin, by the way. I got rid of that when I was sixteen, so…"

Ocean just stared at me.

"Sorry," I mumbled nervously, resting my hands on his shoulders. "You were saying?"

He brushed my lips with his before continuing, "In keeping with the tradition that started with the original crew, to lead the family, the chosen heir had to marry and bear children. Blood in. My family's grown from a lone immigrant to a small gang to a powerful syndicate, but not much else has changed in the last ninety-six years."

"But with you, it will be different?" I ask, feeling a spark of hope bloom in my chest. I was also reeling a little with the knowledge that the Fola was almost a century old.

"I hope so."

"That's where I come in?"

He nodded and nuzzled my shoulder. "That's where you come

in. My father is getting old, and I've already taken over most of his responsibilities, but he's still the Boss. His word supersedes all. Including mine. I have to be careful. If my father catches wind of what I plan, he could still choose someone else, and then none of us will be safe."

I was quiet for a while as I pondered everything he told me before nodding. "My brother stealing from you... is that the only reason you chose me?"

"You are the reason I chose you."

"Because you want to fuck me."

"Hell yeah."

I wasn't adept enough at masking my feelings to keep my disappointment from showing on my face.

Ocean suddenly dipped the sponge between my legs, and my sorrow was quickly muddled with desire as he gripped my chin with his other hand. "But I have a feeling that if I took you against the wall right now, I still wouldn't be free of you."

The sheer agony and want pouring from his gravelly tone made me shudder.

"I can get sex anywhere, sweetheart." He squeezed my chin harder when I stubbornly tried to look away. "But I could search this entire universe and never find another you. My world is...cold and lonely, Coby. Every conversation is a game. Every encounter is a power play. And I'm no better. It was all I knew, but then I met you." He gave me an adorably crooked smile. "Sort of."

For years, all Ocean and I had were prolonged looks and secret longing, and the knowledge that we could never have more because he was in business with my brother, and I would cut off my own arm before I did anything to jeopardize Roshaun's dream.

"I saw how warm you were, and how much you cared for your brother more than yourself. I saw how you gave without expecting anything in return. The world should be bowing at your feet, Coby Perry, but instead, you're constantly overlooked and shoved aside. I promised myself I'd change that if I ever had the chance. If you ever let me in, I wouldn't be the center of your world. You'd be the center of mine. I would worship you."

"You want to…worship me?"

"More than anything. Give me five years to prove it. If I fail to measure up, you can leave my ass and walk away a wealthy woman."

"Will I be safe?"

"No, Coby." My previous dread swiftly returned in the wake of his brutal honesty. "I won't lie to you. You will never be safe from the moment you are mine." He took my chin in his hand when my nervous gaze shifted to the side. "Look at me." My eyes flew back to his. "I will die before I let anyone harm you."

I…believed him.

I didn't tell him, though, and Ocean didn't press the issue. He finished cleaning me, and then we left the shower. I wandered out of the bathroom after brushing my teeth while Ocean pulled out his electric shaver. Against my will, I found myself eyeing the closed bedroom door. The battle with my curiosity was short-lived, ending the moment I heard the quiet buzz of the shaver.

As I wandered over to the door, I kept sneaking glances over my shoulder like Ocean might materialize and drag me back by my hair. My hand was trembling by the time I reached the door and curled my fingers around the sleek handle.

A surprised puff of breath escaped me when I pushed down on the lever, and the handle actually turned.

Now that freedom was staring me in the face, my heart began to race, and I was once again reminded of how insane it would be for me to marry Ocean.

I barely knew him.

He was dangerous.

He nearly killed my brother.

And the things his family would expect of him once he ascended…

He said he would be different, but what if power changed him? What if one day, he sold our daughter for territory or riches? What if his feelings for me changed, and the man I was falling for disappeared altogether?

My panic overcame me, and I snatched open the door, wondering in the back of my mind whether it was carelessness or cockiness that had persuaded Ocean to leave it unlocked.

I didn't get a chance to find out because the hallway wasn't empty.

Abel was standing guard.

Or maybe he was waiting for Ocean. Sentry duty seemed a little below his pay grade. The stoic bodyguard took one look at me and raised a brow.

My breath caught in my throat, and I quickly slammed the door closed, cringing when I realized Ocean would have definitely heard it.

I was on edge by the time he came out of the bathroom, but Ocean paid me no mind as he disappeared inside the closet and re-emerged dressed in dark-wash jeans, a plain black shirt, and a long, hooded fur overcoat.

"Is that real?"

He looked down at himself in confusion and then back at me. "What?"

"The fur."

"It was a gift from Priscilla and Chiara, so...most likely."

"You do know they breed and force animals to live in horrible conditions and then subject them to even crueler deaths for their pelts, don't you?"

Ocean raised a brow. "I do now."

"You can't wear it, Ocean." I crossed my arms and held his stare. "Poor baby rabbits were murdered so you could look good."

"It's mink, actually, but I see your point." Ocean shook his head and went back inside the closet. When he returned, he was wearing a different coat without fur. My belly fluttered with warmth as he came to stand before me. "Better, baby girl?"

I nodded, my chin dipping so I could hide the fact that I was blushing. Ocean wasn't having it, though. He lifted my chin and made me look him in the eye.

Adoration.

That's what I saw in his eyes.

"I'll make sure the fur is sold, and the proceeds are donated to an animal rights foundation of your choice." Ocean brushed his lips across mine before saying fuck it and forcing them to part.

His kiss was just like all the rest.

Demanding.

Drugging.

By the time he let me up for air, all I wanted to do was bend over so he could give me backshots for days.

I really hated his self-control.

CHAPTER ELEVEN

OCEAN

"WAIT, WHERE ARE YOU GOING?" COBY ASKED IN A PANIC as she followed me to the door. She looked like she'd been run over by a train if that train was *me*.

Coby Perry was the most beautiful woman I'd ever seen, but I liked this look on her too—disheveled, dazed, a little traumatized, and looking like she'd been ridden hard, even though I'd mostly kept my hands to myself.

She'd never looked more like mine than she did right now.

As for the reason I haven't fucked her yet, I had to be sure that when she fucked me back, it was because she wanted to and not because she thought she had to for her survival. She was vulnerable right now and afraid of the unknown. I was a patient man and didn't want to ruin what could be thinking with my dick.

"As much as I'd love to stay in that bed with you and *not* fuck, I need to work," I answered as I stopped by the dresser to grab my phone, gun, and key card.

"Oh. Can I come?"

"No," I denied while holding in my laugh. I've been doing a lot of that since I stole her for myself. I expected tears, but she's funnier than I expected. Easily adapted. A survivor. "You cannot come. I'll see you for dinner, baby."

I glanced over my shoulder when she didn't respond and saw

her sitting on my bed now with her knees pulled to her chest and her kissable mouth in a pretty pout. It all felt pretty calculated, and I had to dig my feet in and stand my ground. It killed me sometimes how easily she'd gotten me wrapped around her finger.

It's even crazier how quickly her little ass went from demanding I take her home every five minutes to wanting to be under me all the time. I'm not going to lie and say I didn't like it. If I could wave a magic wand and create a bubble for just the two of us, I would. But I had to get to the money, so I could blow it all spoiling her rotten.

"Don't look so sad, pretty girl. I'm going to go get Hunter. That's what you want, isn't it?"

"Wait…what?" Coby scrambled to leave the bed while I made a beeline for the door. "Don't you think I should be there?"

"No."

"Hunter isn't just going to come with you. You need me there. I'm the only one who can convince her!"

"Yes, she will, just like you'll do what the fuck I said and sit yo' ass still until I come back."

"But Hunter doesn't *do* what she's told. She'd sooner shoot you in the face."

I swung around so quickly she almost crashed into my chest. "Even if it means never seeing you again?"

Coby fell silent, and I could see uncertainty and fear flicker across her face—the uncertainty that Hunter couldn't be reasoned with and the fear of never seeing her friend again if she can't. I took advantage of her doubt and tossed her on my shoulder before marching her back to the bed. She didn't fight me because she was still worrying about her friend, who was already becoming annoying as fuck. "Don't trip, baby girl. I promise I won't take no for an answer."

It was the wrong thing to say. My vow only gave her fear a new direction, and I glimpsed the panic in her eyes before I turned and damn near sprinted for the door.

"Ocean! I swear to God you better not hurt her! Ocean!" she screamed at my back.

I heard her running after me just as I slipped from the room. My bedroom door slammed behind me, and I quickly swiped my card over the pad just as Coby collided with the door. The beep and flashing red light confirmed it was locked. Knowing she'd eventually end up in my bed (I didn't think it would happen this soon), I'd had the same lock installed on mine because while I might be gone for this girl, I couldn't turn off the part of me that always thought three steps ahead. I hadn't intended to lock her into today, but it only took one mention of *Hunter* to bring us back to square one.

Even now, Coby's fists banged on the other side as she cursed me out. "Let me out, you psycho bastard, so I can fucking kill you!"

"I'll miss you too, sweetheart."

"Fuck you!"

Already eager to return to Coby, I was grinning as I walked away, but Abel wasn't when I reached the end of the hall and saw him waiting outside the wing's double doors. His phone was plastered to his ear, but he quickly hung up with a curse and fell in step beside me.

"What's up?" I asked as I steered us toward the housekeeper's office. If Hunter was going to stay with us for an undetermined time, she'd need somewhere comfortable to stay.

"We got a problem. Your pops called a meeting, but he wouldn't say why."

And just like that, my smile and excitement fled as I recalled the warning my cousins had brought under the guise of petty gossip. "I know why."

Pulling out my phone, I quickly sent Priscilla a message before leaving the apartment.

Hunter Parrish would just have to wait.

"The fuck yo ass do now?" my cousin Keefe leaned over to whisper as only the *Fola*'s leadership—the *capteans*, my uncle Tyrone, and I sat around the conference table in my father's study at Glamis. We were all waiting for my fucking pops to finish taking a shit. The only sound was the hammering and drilling in one of the rooms my mother was having redecorated.

A bridal suite, I was told.

For Niamh.

"I found her," I said simply as I ignored the migraine forming and kept one eye on the room. Most of the men present were of the blood, but that didn't make us family. Abel, along with everyone else's personal guard, waited outside but within shouting distance in case someone (me) decided on a whim to paint these dark walls red.

"Who?"

"My wife."

"Shiiiiit," Keefe croaked as he leaned back in his chair and rubbed his head in agitation.

It was possible we wouldn't leave this room alive if my father somehow found out that I wasn't just reluctant to marry his choice, but that I'd gone out of my way to find my own. The look Keefe and I shared expressed exactly what we both thought of my father's trifling ass.

The only ones who weren't apprehensive about the impromptu meeting were Tyrone and Evan. The latter wore a sneer directed at me while the former seemed resigned to his entire day going to hell.

Tyrone was my father's *comhairleoir*[4]. Other than my mother and me, no one else was closer to the Boss than he was. Tyrone liked to think of himself as important. Indispensable. In actuality, Tyrone was a wannabe politician, a sometimes lawyer, and a glorified secretary. He was also my mother's younger brother, who sold her to my father in order to become made. Shitty-ass siblings were something Coby and my mother had in common.

Evan's bitch ass was the only one of my cousins I didn't trust because he believed he should be the next Boss instead of me. To keep me in line, my father let Evan's dumb ass believe he could really

4   Advisor

choose him over me, but the truth is that Malcolm would rather slaughter our entire family and progenerate a whole new line than concede the throne to someone else's seed. My father believed our empire was his right as a direct descendant of James, but that kind of thinking is exactly what could lead to a civil war within the Fola. Luckily, my father knew better than to make his feelings known. The Kilpatricks have been in power since the start, but the Balfour-Young and the Torrances were just itching for a reason to take it from us.

Finally, the door to the study opened, and we all stood in deference as my father entered the room. The largest of us all, he towered over everyone as he walked to the head of the table and took a seat. I sat on his right while Tyrone sat on his left.

On my side of the table were all of the caps secretly loyal to me. On Tyron's side were all of the ones loyal to my father.

Every seat around the table was occupied, and yet my side was fuller.

It brought a grin that made the other shift nervously, especially when my father took notice.

"Something you want to share with the class, son?"

"They wouldn't get it."

"Then let us get on with business. Have you figured out who's been raiding my dens, or have you been preoccupied with other matters?"

Dodging that obvious trap, I stated needlessly, "I'm your second in command. When am I *not* preoccupied?"

My father slammed his fist on the table and roared, "Answer the question!"

"Black is still in hiding, but I have people looking for him."

"Those were not your directives. Michael Black is my concern, not yours."

"You expect me to find the person hunting him with one hand tied behind my back?"

"I expect you to follow orders and set an example."

This could have been an email, I thought with a sigh. Drumming my fingers on the arm of my chair, I looked around the table at all the heavy expressions before regarding my father again. "Is there a reason you called us all here today?"

Several people shifted nervously in their seats.

No one else would dare tell the Boss of the Fola to get to the fucking point.

My father sat back in his chair, caressing his beard as he studied me. I could see him weighing the words he wanted to say in his head. Even though he was Boss, he still had appearances to keep. He had to maintain the semblance of control even though it was slipping by the day.

And for now, I had to maintain the pretense of obedience.

"I've been informed by our accountant that a significant sum of money has seemingly vanished." On cue, the door opened, and Angus stepped inside. It seems the amount of revenue reported does not match what we received." *Damn. I wasn't expecting Roshaun's treachery to be discovered so soon. I was hoping for a few more weeks.* "Luckily, we were able to successfully trace these discrepancies back to one of your ventures. A nightclub called The Diamond Lounge."

"Yeah, I know about that shit, and I've taken care of it."

"What I want to know is how it escaped your notice for so long?"

"It didn't. I was aware of what Perry was doing. Almost from the start."

"So you allowed this peon to steal from us?" Tyrone butted in with a look of horror. His weak-ass chin was starting to piss me off.

"Was there an advantage we're all unaware of?" my father questioned.

"Yes. But the benefit was mine alone."

Tyrone and my father shared a long look. "Then I expect every penny to be repaid from your personal accounts," my father dictated.

"Of course. It's already being handled."

"And the man responsible? He's dead, I assume?"

I paused at that since lying would be a deadly mistake, but so would telling the truth. I didn't give a fuck if Roshaun lived or died.

His sister, unfortunately, did. "Dead-ish," I supplied with a noncommittal rock of my head.

"What the fuck does that mean?"

"It means I'm not done playing with my food. I'm sending a message. Killing him too quickly won't get my point across."

"And is that the only reason?"

I took the time to sip my drink before answering. "What other reason would there be?" Staring at him over the rim of my glass, I silently dared him with my eyes to call me out.

Filled with too much ego to play the long game, my father played right into my hands. "Is his sister not your guest at Glainne right now?"

"I wouldn't call her a guest," I retorted honestly and yet duplicitously. After all, Coby was the queen of my castle, not a fucking guest. "As I said..." I set my glass on the table with an audible *thunk*. "I'm sending a message. Coby Perry is mine until I'm done collecting interest."

It was all I could do not to outwardly revolt when something like pride and approval filled my father's eyes. "Very well. Do with the girl what you will, but do it *quickly*. I want this shit handled before anyone else gets any grand ideas."

"And now for the other matter, " Tyrone said. "We've set a new date for your marriage to Niamh. Given your recent and troubling objections, we've decided to move up the wedding to prevent any further disruptions. The ceremony will take place exactly two months from now."

Knowing my father was incredibly literal, it was easy to calculate the date he had in mind.

Silently, I swore, but it made no difference. A second later, I threw my glass at the wall in front of me. Unfortunately, Tyrone's reflexes were better than I gave him credit for, which pissed me off even more, especially when I knew this was his doing.

"And you all agree with this shit?" I shouted at the silent table. "No one finds it fucking weird that *she's our fucking cousin*? This is the twenty-first fucking century. Even James knew better." I directed that last part at my father, who idolized the father of the *Fola*. Still, no one at the table said a word or stood up for Niamh, who was only eighteen fucking years old. She regularly babysat for the men around this table, helped a few of them study to get their GED, always remembered everyone's birthday, patched our wounds when one of us took a bullet or a knife, and always showed love no matter what. "No, of course not," I said with open disdain. "Fucking pussies would rather cower under my father's heel than risk being trampled by it."

Or maybe they were all just hoping my father would disown me and pick one of them.

"Are you done, son?"

Shoving away from my chair, I stood. I've known since I was a kid that my father wasn't sane, but he was so much worse than having a few screws loose because morals and madness were not mutually exclusive. A man with no conscience was infinitely more dangerous. "Yeah, I'm fucking done. Plan all you want, but I ain't marrying Niamh."

My father shoved to his feet as well. "You will do as you're told!"

The crystals in the chandelier above the table shook at the end of his roar. The men around the table looked at each other nervously. The room my mother was having renovated was right above us. One of the contractors probably dropped something, but my father *capteans* couldn't see through their fear, so instead of reaching for reason, the trembling chandelier added to the imagined omnipotence of my father.

I palmed my face.

I'm surrounded by weak and idiotic sycophants.

Not for long.

"Aye, I can't lie. I think Ocean's right," Diontay said hesitantly. I forgot all about my father as I watched Dion lean forward to meet the gaze of everyone at the table. "I'm not down with this inbreeding shit. Y'all might be able to look away because it ain't you, but I'm not dumb enough to believe it will stop with Ocean and Niamh."

Wrinkling his nose, he sat back in his chair and freed a blunt from his pocket. "There's a planet full of bitches just itching to fill that spot," he said as he lit up. "I know we all about blood ties and shit, but this is taking it too far." Meeting my gaze, he nodded.

A heavy weight gradually lifted from my shoulders as pride and appreciation burrowed into my chest. Dion was our youngest *captean*. He was loyal, hungry, and smart as hell. He oversaw our weapons caches as well as the distribution and shipments in and out of Black Veil. Among all the *Fola's capteans*, Diontay's division was the largest. He had more soldiers under his direct command than even me because if anyone ever got their hands on just *one* of our armories, it would be an all-out war.

Fortunately, he was sitting on my side of the table, but that was by design since he had his position because of me. My father was power hungry, but he lacked vision and didn't trust the younger generation. That's where I came in. I gave them power, a voice, and a bigger slice of the pie. In return, they made sure that when I inevitably went to war with my father, I would win.

"Sorry, Unc. I'm with Diontay and Ocean on this one," Keefe said. There were murmurs and faint nods of agreement all around.

Without a word of warning, my father pulled his gun and fired.

"Aargh!" Diontay flew back in his chair, hitting the floor while a chorus of shouts and curses rang out around us. My cousins all reached for their guns out of self-preservation, but one look from me had them pulling their hands away and relaxing in their chairs again.

"Diontay!" Rodney, his father, shot out of his seat and over to his bleeding son, who was clutching his shoulder. Seeing Dion still alive, Rodney looked down the table at my father with eyes full of rage. "You shot my fucking son! You could have killed him!"

"It was a shame that I didn't," my father stated coldly. "Anyone else want to express their objections?" The room fell silent again. Only Dion's pained grunts could be heard as he writhed on the floor. "I didn't fucking think so." My father regarded me with a look that said if he had a spare heir, I'd be fertilizing my mother's garden. "Son…

do not think for one second that I will not put you down if you prove useless to me. For your mother's sake, I'll give you until *la Nollaige*[5] to understand who runs this shit. Now get the fuck out of my sight. You're all dismissed."

Chairs scraped the floor as everyone pushed away from the table and left. Rodney helped his son out of the room, leaving only my father and me. I didn't have shit to say to his ass though. I was busy wondering what the fuck I was going to do now.

Two months...

Christmas.

I had until the day of my wedding to decide how I wanted to become the next Boss of the *Fola*—if I wanted to honor tradition (or my father's sick version of it) or start a war.

Well then...I guess I was getting married in two months.

I just prayed Coby would forgive me.

It wasn't until we reached the city that I realized Kellan missed his check-in. I fished my burner out of my pocket and called him, but the line rang so long I thought it might go to voicemail (which wasn't allowed to ever happen). Finally, it stopped, and a voice that didn't belong to my newest associate answered.

"Hi," the soft voice greeted. I was surprised to find it was a woman on the other end, and my anger reappeared when I assumed Kellan was off getting some pussy when he was supposed to be watching Hunter. "Kellan can't come to the phone right now," she informed me cheerily. "He's currently nursing his head and his ego, but I can take a message." I was too fucking stunned at the audacity of this soon-to-be-dead bitch to respond, so her playful tone quickly hardened into a pissed one. "Look, pervert, if you're not going to talk, I'm hanging up. I got shit to do."

5   Christmas Day

I actually heard the faint sound of metal scraping against metal, something being slapped into place, and then the unmistakable sound of a gun being cocked.

Intrigued, I moved over to one of the lounge chairs to sit and put my feet up. "Who is this?" I asked even though I suspected the answer already. A smile was already playing on my lips. Remembering my bride waiting for me back at home, I let it fall.

"Me?" the voice teased. I heard a door open and slam closed in her background. She was on the move, but where? And where the fuck was Kellan? "I'm the new owner of this phone. Who are you?"

"The former owner of this phone," I informed through gritted teeth. My amusement with *Hunter* was fading fast. Abel turned in his seat at the front of the Denali, a questioning look on his face, and I mouthed Kellan. He immediately turned in his seat and gave the order to drive to Coby's old apartment.

"Well, that's impossible since you sound nothing like the handsy bastard I lifted it from."

My voice dropped to a dangerous rumble as I asked, "Kellan touched you?"

The other end of the line grew quiet, and I realized my tone must have thrown her off.

Shit, it was scaring *me*.

Hunter recovered faster and said, "Yup! You should really try teaching your goons some manners. I had to squeeze his balls, literally and then figuratively, but I think he's getting the message. You're welcome."

Chuckling, I rubbed my brow as I was once again forced to move the pieces on my chessboard. "I underestimated you, Hunter."

"People tend to do that." She didn't pretend to be at all surprised that I knew exactly who she was. "So here's the deal…" I heard beeping in the background as she spoke, and I lost the battle with my honor as I pulled out my actual phone and tapped into the security feed from the hidden cameras. I never allowed myself to look at the feed until now.

What I saw sent the blood in my veins rushing to my dick.

Hunter was standing in the middle of the room, wearing only a glittery fucking thong and nothing else except the kunai strapped to her thigh. Her back was to the camera, but her round, perky breasts jiggled with every movement as she slowly braided her long hair into a single plait at the back of her skull. When she was done, the tail swept the top of that fat ass. My gaze was glued to it as she bent over to grab something from the bed. I grabbed my dick with a hard grip when it jerked in my jeans. *Don't even fucking think about it.*

It took me far too long to look away and notice the bed.

At her feet, poking out from underneath the bed was a heavy, long, flat safe that had already been emptied. On top of the bed were two large Sigs, a pink subcompact Ruger, one Glock, a goddamn switch, a pump action shotgun, three serrated hunting knives, more throwing knives, several boxes of ammo, a fucking hand grenade, and a sniper rifle.

Hunter made peanuts and had a record, which included at least one felony obtained when she was fourteen. There was only one answer for who could have supplied her with that much hardware.

Us.

The *Fola.*

Fucking Dion.

If he were standing right in front of me, I would have shot his other shoulder.

"I know you're the one who took my Yin," Hunter said as she moved over to the dresser and started to dress. "I don't know why, and I don't really give a fuck. You're going to give her back in one piece, and it's going to be now."

"Don't leave me in suspense when you've worked so hard to intrigue me, Hunter. What will you do if I don't?" I challenged.

"I'm sure you can fill in the blanks." Dressed now in skin-tight black pants, a matching long-sleeve shirt, and a bulletproof vest, Hunter grabbed a box of ammo and an extra mag and began loading the clip.

"Do you even know who you're threatening?" I asked out of curiosity.

"Should it matter?"

"No," I said after a long silence. My respect for Hunter Parrish was foolishly growing. Now that Coby was mine, I could understand Hunter's reckless desire to go to war to get her back. I'd do the same, which is why I said, "It sure as fuck wouldn't matter to me."

On the screen, I could see Hunter pause a moment before she resumed sliding bullets into her magazine. "I'm glad we understand each other."

"Hunter, I think we're far from understanding each other. Stand down. This is your last warning."

Ignoring me, she strapped one holster around her thigh and another around her waist. "And this is my warning," she said as she shoved one of the Sigs into the holster. "You have an hour to return my friend. By the end of that hour, I'll be on your doorstep, shooting anything that moves."

Grinning widely, I cooed, "Show me yours, and I'll show you mine. And Hunter?"

"What?" Her movements grew increasingly agitated.

"I promise mine are bigger."

Unafraid and strapped for war, Hunter snorted. "Okay, I hear you. I guess we'll just have to pull them out and see."

"I'm looking forward to it." I ended the call and the video feed.

Abel turned around in his seat again, but I paid him no mind as I stared out the window while deep in thought.

I'd found Coby's warnings cute before, but now I wondered if she'd just been playing along and hiding her friend up her sleeve this entire time. Eager to find out, I slid over in the backseat and pressed my gun to Paul, my driver's skull. "Hurry the fuck up and get to that apartment," I barked. "You have seven minutes before I splatter your thoughts on the windshield."

Paul punched the gas and got us there in six, but when Abel kicked in the door, I stepped inside the girls' apartment and discovered that we were too late.

Hunter was long gone.

CHAPTER TWELVE

COBY

"WHAT DO YOU THINK OF THIS ONE?" I TURNED AWAY from the pink cherry blossom Oscar de la Renta dress I was inspecting with a ridiculous ten-thousand-dollar price tag to see Chiara holding up another dress from the same designer, this one was rose gold with hand-cut mirrored panels, a large ivory rose motif, and a layered A-line skirt that was full and sure to twirl with every movement. It was a dress fit for a princess.

The problem was that I didn't belong in this world. It's not that I resented the idea of living a soft life, but it didn't feel right without Hunter. Even now, I couldn't stop thinking about her. Ocean said he was going to get her, but I knew it wouldn't be as simple as extending the invitation.

Someone was going to get hurt.

"It's beautiful," I forced myself to say as I admired the way it glittered under the store lights. Ocean had apparently changed his mind about my going shopping with his cousins, and shortly after he left, they returned and told me I was spending the day with them. The armed escort that tailed us everywhere, though, made it clear that I was still under lock and key.

"Eek! Good. I checked the tag and double-checked with the sales associate. Absolutely *no* cute little woodland animals were harmed in the making of this gorgeous couture. We thought you could wear it at the reception after the wedding," Chiara suggested excitedly.

My eyes widened because I just knew they weren't suggesting I buy it. "Chiara, you can't be serious. That dress must cost a fortune."

"Girl, do you know who your man is?" She rolled her eyes. "Please, this is chump change to him." Spinning around, she handed the dress to the sales associate standing by and told her we'd take it.

"Chiara!"

"Sorry, cousin-in-law, but we have orders." She strutted away to join Priscilla by the shoes.

I couldn't lie. The dress was fire, but it was going to be the only thing I bought.

Five hours and over a dozen stores and countless bad decisions later, I had just sat down to a late lunch with Chiara and Priscilla when a dark-skinned girl who was tall, chic, and svelte entered the restaurant. She drew a lot of eyes immediately as she spoke with the hostess. A white collar peeked out from the top of her short black dress with double-breasted gold buttons. Her long black overcoat nearly swayed around her knee-high boots as she moved. It was a sophisticated look for someone so young, but she wore it with confidence.

I had to give the girl her props. She was bad as hell, and she was headed this way.

"Hey, y'all," the girl greeted as she sat across from me in the seat next to Priscilla. "Sorry, I'm late. My man was tripping again."

"It's cool." Priscilla waved her off as she studied the menu without lifting her gaze. "We just sat down ourselves."

The girl nodded and removed her beret. I watched her finger-comb her wig, which fell into soft, long, jet black waves cascading down her back, before her gaze finally fell on me. "Shit!" she shrieked, causing me to glance behind me. "Where are my manners? You must be Coby! I'm Niamh. It's so nice to meet Ocean's girlfriend."

"Fiancée," I corrected automatically before I even knew the urge was there. I didn't bother to take it back or apologize, though, since it was the truth. Niamh was a good sport about it. She seemed genuinely surprised, then confusedly relieved, telling me she'd been innocently unaware and wasn't trying to be funny. You never knew with some bitches, even family.

"Really? Oh, my God! Congrats! Priscilla and Chiara didn't tell me how gorgeous you are."

"She aight," Priscilla said.

"I know you ain't talking with them ashy knuckles." I rolled my eyes, and the cousins all snickered.

"Hell yeah. You gon' fit right in with us. So are you and Ocean really getting married?" I didn't miss her quick glance at my bare ring finger.

I asked Ocean why he didn't have an engagement ring for me, but all he said was that it was almost ready, so I nodded at Niamh with a close-mouthed smile while my stomach twisted nervously. The engagement and moving in with Ocean had happened so fast. It still didn't feel real most of the time.

I'm pretty sure it was the guilt over my brother being hospitalized because of my fiancé that wouldn't allow me to fully accept it in my heart. I said a silent prayer that Roshaun was okay and that he would forgive me for the things I'd have to do to keep him alive.

I was still mid-prayer when seemingly out of nowhere, Niamh started sobbing at my confirmation, which had me side-eyeing her ass while Priscilla and Chiara consoled her. "See, I told you everything would be all right," Priscilla said gently as she rubbed the girl's back. "Ocean would never let anything happen to you."

Chiara, who had reached across the table to hold Niamh's hand, glanced my way and smiled apologetically when she noticed me staring but didn't offer an explanation.

Okay then.

"Sorry," Niamh said once she collected herself. "I'm happy for Ocean. I really am. It's just…stupid family drama."

I nodded and was grateful when the waitress came over to take our orders because I wasn't buying Niamh's story for one moment. I still had fun at brunch, which we mostly spent talking about the wedding that I hadn't even thought to start planning. Niamh turned out to be really sweet and funny. Priscilla was as dry as ever, but she was surprisingly the first to volunteer her help with the wedding plans. She was the only one at the table who was married, but when I asked about her husband, she rolled her eyes and mumbled that he wasn't worth discussing. Chiara was a whole vibe with tea for days about everyone in their family. She had a way of telling a story that made me deeply invested, even though I didn't know who anyone was.

After brunch, we went shopping again, but only visited a couple of stores before Priscilla announced that her feet were killing her.

The driver took us back to Glainne, and the four of us headed up while Ocean's guards trailed us with my shopping bags in tow. There were *a lot*. The cousins helped me put everything away inside my enormous closet, which made even Priscilla, Chiara, and Niamh gasp when they entered.

"Girl, what kind of pussy you towing that got my cousin tricking like this?"

"Bitch, please," I said with a snicker as I dodged Chiara's question and hung up my seventy-thousand-dollar wedding reception dress that was still wrapped in a heavy garment bag.

Ocean and I hadn't fucked yet, but we were getting close and…I couldn't fucking wait.

The anticipation of his weight on top of me and that dick inside me made me smile, but I didn't want his cousins to think I was a weirdo, so I brushed all thoughts of fucking aside.

The cousins kept me company for a few more hours. We ate the dinner the chef prepared and were talking about heading downstairs to the bar for drinks when Priscilla's husband—whose name I learned was Tory—started blowing up her phone. Priscilla and Tory had three kids together, which she happily showed me pictures of on her phone, but I was starting to wonder about their marriage. Priscilla didn't seem happy, and that made me sadder than it should have. I hardly knew her.

"Oh! I almost forgot," Chiara said as I was walking them to the elevator. "Here." She handed me a heavy, black metal credit card. "It's Ocean's. Tell him we said thanks and give him a kiss for us, please."

"Okay, boo. Thanks for today. I had fun."

"Me too!' Chiara hugged me tightly before dashing into the elevator like the apartment was on fire. "Call us when you're ready to shop for your wedding dress!" she yelled just before the doors closed and the elevator descended.

I went back to my room to relax for a little while, but instead ended up going through all the receipts of everything I bought today with Ocean's money. I started to mentally tally the total until I had a number.

"Oh, my God," I softly wailed as I quietly freaked out. "I spent half a million dollars. How the *fuck* am I going to explain that to Ocean?"

Now I knew why Priscilla, Niamh, and Chiara were so quick to rush out of here. They'd each only purchased a single item for themselves—a diamond necklace for Priscilla, a Birkin bag for Chiara that made her smile softly when the sale associate told her she was allowed to buy one (I didn't get it), and a pair of strappy heels for Niamh that cost the price of a used car—but the receipts for their items weren't here, meaning I'd racked up the five hundred thousand bill on my own.

"Shit, shit, shit! Maybe I can take it all back."

I stared at Ocean's credit card like it was evil before shoving it under my pillow out of sight.

This was all Ocean's cousins' fault.

They kept showing me pretty things, and after a while, I just nodded along and stopped looking at the price tags because they made me sick to my stomach.

Needing to take my mind off the impending huge fight I was going to have later, I decided to throw on one of my new bathing suits and try out the heated indoor pool. Again, I couldn't help but feel the crushing weight of my loneliness as I thought about the time Hunter and I both called out sick from work and drove for twenty hours down to Miami because she wanted to go to the beach. It was one of my favorite memories. I had even let the bitch talk me into parasailing.

A moment later, I was sobbing quietly with my head resting against the edge of the pool.

I missed Hunter, but I wanted her to be safe. I wanted my brother to live. I had to find a way to go on without them both, but I didn't know how. It was much easier when I wasn't left alone—when Ocean was here to distract and tempt and dote on me.

God, I missed him right now.

My body began to rock as the water lapped against the pool wall, and, startled, I turned to find the source of the motion: a fully clothed Ocean striding through the water toward me.

"Ocean! Your suit!"

"Fuck this suit," he said with a slight growl. "What's the matter?"

"Nothing," I rushed to say.

Ocean looked far from convinced as he pulled me into him. "You were crying, Coby. What happened? My cousins do something?"

"No, of course not," I said with a sniffle. "I had a great time."

Ocean exhaled and rubbed a hand down my back. The feel of him was so strong and soothing that I couldn't help but close my eyes. "Why won't you tell me why you were crying?"

"Just homesick. That's all." Unconsciously, I rubbed my snotty nose on his tie before realizing what I'd done and cringing as I peered up at him. "Sorry."

Ocean's only response was to dip his head expectantly. I eagerly rose onto my toes and let him kiss me until all feelings of hopelessness faded. "Come on," he said, pulling away when I started to rub myself against him.

It was only then that I noticed we weren't alone. Abel stood sentry by the door with his gaze locked straight ahead. I looked to the right and the left of him, as well as behind, but there was no one else in the pool room.

"Where's Hunter?" I asked after Ocean climbed out of the pool and then helped me out. "Did you find her?"

"Actually, she found me," he answered cryptically.

I frowned at that even as my heart sped up. "Is she here?"

"No. She escaped before I could reach her."

"Oh." A confusing mix of relief and disappointment rushed me at once. I wanted to see Hunter, but I didn't want her forced into anything. Ocean didn't seem too hellbent on asking permission.

"I'm sorry, *mo aingeal.*"

Waving him off, I grabbed my towel from one of the loungers and wrapped it around myself. "How was your day?"

He rocked his head. "Could have gone better, but it's ending with you, so I won't complain," he said as he lifted my hand and kissed it.

We went to the second floor to his room to shower, and after we climbed out, I steered the conversation back to Hunter. "So how did she sound?"

"Who?" he asked distractedly as he trimmed his beard.

"Hunter. Did she sound okay?"

Ocean's gaze flicked to mine in the mirror before he returned to his grooming. "I don't know her, Coby, so it's not for me to say, but she sounded fine." He shrugged.

"Hmm," I hummed. "What did she say?"

"She wanted to know where you were."

"And what did you say?"

This time, when his gaze found mine in the mirror, he held it. "I told her that you were being well taken care of."

"And?"

"She threatened to kill me."

I felt a smile tugging at my lips and fought to hide it. "Yeah, that's Hunter."

"Let me ask you something," Ocean said as he turned the clippers off. My stomach sank at the tone of his voice. He didn't sound angry. He sounded suspicious.

"Okay..." I feigned nonchalance by shrugging.

"You think she could?"

"What?"

Ocean's gaze narrowed in the mirror. "Do you think she'd be able to kill me, Coby? It's a simple question."

"I think…I think she'd give it everything she had, but I truly don't know if she'd succeed or not."

He continued to stare at me. "Would you want her to?"

"What? No, of course not!"

"I'm just asking. If your friend gives me no choice, it may come down to her life or mine, so I'm wondering which life you'd prefer."

"Both."

"That may not be an option, Coby."

"You're wrong," I said firmly as I snatched up my wide-tooth comb and started roughly working it through my short natural curls. "It's the *only* option. You won't hurt her. I won't let her hurt you."

After detangling my hair, I ran some product through my freshly washed hair to reset the curls, then yanked on my new pink satin bonnet.

Ocean must have noticed that I was becoming increasingly agitated because he pulled me into him and wrapped his arms around my chest as he stared at our reflection over my shoulder. "I'm sorry, sweetheart." I blushed when he kissed the side of my neck. "I didn't mean to upset you."

"Ocean, you can probably buy me the world if you choose to, but just know that the greatest gift you can ever give me is Hunter. She's more than just my best friend. She's my sister. Hunter's my heart. Only you have the key, but she's *it*. Do you understand what I'm telling you?"

"I think I do," he said with another kiss pressed to my shoulder this time. "I promise I will never let any harm come to your heart."

"Thank you," I said earnestly. "Are you hungry? Your chef cooked."

"*Our* chef cooked and yes. I'm starving, baby. You gon' feed me?"

"Okay," I agreed breathlessly.

Ocean and I went downstairs to the kitchen, where I made his plate, then sat on his lap at the dining table while he ate. He asked me about my day, so I filled him in on my time with his cousins, and he listened attentively until he was done eating. I took the empty plate to the kitchen, washed it, and stored it while he went into the living room with a single drink to watch a recording of tonight's game.

"Ocean?"

Eyes still on the game, he said, "What's up?" He was really into it, leaning forward with his forearms resting on his knees while he shouted at the TV.

"I have to tell you something."

Ocean must have heard something in my tone because he reluctantly tore his gaze away from the TV to see me standing well out of reach and wringing my hands. "All right, what's up? What do you need to tell me?"

"I may have overdone it when I went shopping with Chi and 'nem today."

Ocean licked his sexy ass lips as he studied me. "Overdone it? What does that mean?"

"I spent a lot of money today."

Intrigued, he paused the game and leaned back on the couch. "How much is a lot?"

"Half a million dollars."

"What?" His brows snapped down. "Run that back. You spent how much?"

The anger in his eyes made it obvious that the question was rhetorical, so I gulped and shook my head. "I am so sorry. Of course, we can take all of the stuff back."

"Take it back? Nah, you won't be taking shit back. Why are you crying, *mo aingeal*?"

"B-because…I spent all your money!" I sobbed with my hands covering my eyes.

Ocean suddenly tipped back his head and started laughing his ass off. He laughed so hard, he started clutching his stomach and talking about how he can't breathe.

"It's not funny!" I said, fighting off a laugh of my own. "Why are you laughing?"

"Because you funny, girl. Come here."

Needing comfort—even if it came from that asshole—I shuffled over to him and let him pull me into his lap. He wrapped his muscular arms around me, and I immediately felt better. "Stop crying, baby. If anything, you underdid it. I specifically told my hard-of-hearing cousins not to bring you back until you spent at least twice that."

"What?" I turned my head to look at him over my shoulder. "Why?"

He thumbed away a new tear before saying, "Why not?"

"It's too much. I don't need all of that stuff, Ocean. I just need you." *And Hunter.* "The library was more than enough." I haven't even slept in my room since that first night, making it a waste, but I loved my library. I couldn't bring myself to regret the trouble he went through to make it for me.

"I disagree. You deserve the world, and I don't care if I have to search our entire galaxy to find the perfect one. I'm going to do all that I can." Not knowing what to say to that, I gnawed on my lip, and his gaze dipped before he pulled it free from my teeth. "Okay?"

I nodded. "Okay." *Whew, Lord.* I felt so much better. Enough to say, "Ocean?"

"What's up?"

I nervously twirled the ribbon tied around my wrist today. "There was a necklace I saw today that made me think of Hunter. She doesn't have anything that nice, and she *should.* Hunter's the best person I know." Staring down at my lap, I said. "I know she'd really like it." Too nervous to ask the question, I took the coward's way out and fell silent before I could.

Ever able to read my mind, Ocean said, "And you want to buy it for her?"

I nodded and held back tears that were welling. "Would that be okay?"

Lifting my hand, Ocean kissed my knuckles. "Of course. I think it's dope how you look out for your *friend*." Frowning at the way he said friend, I watched him carefully for a clue at what he meant, but he was too preoccupied staring at my lips to notice my confusion (or maybe he just didn't care), and when he spoke again, his voice was deeper and thickened with lust. "Now say thank you," he commanded.

"Th-thank you."

"No," he said firmly. "Not like that, Coby.."

Oh. Catching on to his meaning, I held his gaze as I slid off his lap and onto my knees between his legs. Ocean's dick was already a hard ridge trapped under his sweatpants when I ran my palm over it reverently. He bucked his hips in response, and I tugged on the waistline of his sweats. Ocean lifted his hips to help me, and I lowered them just enough to free him.

"Take off your shirt," he ordered as he stroked his dick. "Let me see you." I wasn't wearing a bra underneath my camisole, so when I pulled it over my head, my breasts were bared to him. "Beautiful."

He let go of his dick, giving me permission to take over. I was salivating for it.

I expected Ocean to go back to watching the game, but he was laser-focused on me as I wrapped my hand around him. Ocean was so hot and hard in my hand that I couldn't resist giving his dick a soothing stroke as I held his gaze. I continued holding it as I lowered my head and licked the tip, loving the way his nostrils flared slightly, so I repeated the action a second time. Ocean pushed my hand away from him with one hand and roughly fisted my short curls in the other before tipping my head back.

Replacing his own hand with mine, he tapped my lips twice with the head of dick and said, "Open your mouth for me, *mo aingeal*." I wanted to ask him what it meant, but he quickly silenced me with his thick length pushing between my lips. I felt his groan vibrate in my belly once he was seated on my tongue with the tip pushing the back of my throat. "There," he said with a satisfied sigh. "Now suck."

Doing as he ordered, I pulled back just enough to suckle the tip before sliding him back along my tongue. Ocean tried to watch me, but before long, his head fell back on the couch as I started servicing him.

I had never been so turned on sucking dick before, but watching the way his abs contracted, his Adam's apple bob, and his hand twitch on his lap had me eager to see what other reactions I could get out of him.

I wasn't aware of my hand disappearing inside my sleep shorts until I touched my swollen clit and spasmed with a whimper. Ocean's eyes flew open, and he lifted his head to regard me through dark eyes.

"What's the matter? That pussy needs me?"

With a mouth full of dick, I nodded.

Ocean stood up suddenly and pulled me from the floor before tossing me down on the couch. I landed on my stomach, and before I could even grasp what was happening, he shoved down his sweats and ripped my sleep shorts away. I barely made it onto my knees before he was lining his fat dick with my sopping wet hole. Because of his girth, he was careful when he pushed inside, but it didn't matter. My cry once he was fully seated would have been loud enough to wake the neighbors (if we had any).

And it didn't deter Ocean in the least.

He held nothing back as he gripped the arm of the couch with both hands and immediately began to fuck the shit out of me. I was in heaven, in utter fucking ecstasy as I fisted the cushions beneath me and sniveled like a baby as I let him have his way with me.

"Ooo—ceee-aaan," I cried out when he started hitting it a little too deep.

"Mmmh," he moaned like he was having the time of his life. "Don't weep, pretty girl. You're taking it so well for me. The praise did something to me, so I threw it back at him, making him growl as he started going harder. "Shit, fuck, Coby. Goddamn. You doing it like that, baby?"

All I could do was scream in answer. It felt like I started losing my mind the moment Ocean entered me because I had no idea how I could go on living even a second without this. As if my pussy agreed, I tightened around him.

"Fuck." He grunted. "I'm gon' come." It was the only warning before he stopped fucking me. "Give me a kiss." I twisted my head and tilted it so I could kiss him. Ocean gripped my neck possessively and tongue fucked my mouth, offering me a brief reprieve. "Sexy ass," he grumbled once it was over. "Now arch your fucking back. I'm far from done."

I did as I was told, and Ocean wasted no time pummeling my shit until I came.

Sensitive now, I started running from him after that, so he moved to stand from the couch, and I made a sound of protest, but Ocean simply dragged me along until my lower half was tilted upward and I had to hook my ankles around his back for leverage while my hands came to rest on the cushions—like a partial handstand. I was silently grateful for all the hours I spent in pilates because the strength it took just to hold myself up while he fucked me as if my pussy owed him money.

Well... technically, I guess it did.

Three million dollars worth.

In this position, I was completely at his mercy. He grunted and shoved and cursed above me as he used me like a rag doll. "Oh, yes. Oh, yes. Ocean!"

Delirium had my eyes lowering and mouth falling open. My pussy was so wet for this man that, together with our moans, combined juices, and sweaty skin, we created an erotic symphony that filled the penthouse. Every time my ass smashed violently into his pelvis, my lashes fluttered, and I squealed with delight until I came again.

I didn't know how much longer I would last.

Ocean didn't seem as if he was going to be done fucking me anytime soon.

His stamina was truly terrifying.

Just when I was about to come for a third time, he twisted us around and fell onto the couch.

"Nooo," I wailed as he re-sat me on his dick, facing him. "I was so close! Why'd you stop?"

"Shut up and ride this dick," he ordered gruffly with a slap to my ass that stung so hard it froze me in place for a second before all the pleasure that built up released itself in a violent shiver, and I slowly started moving again.

Loving this rare, harsher side of him, I was once again powerless to his will as I abused myself on his pole. "It feels so good," I whimpered more than whispered.

"I know, baby." He rubbed my ass soothingly right over the spot he abused. "I'll make it last. I promise."

With that assurance, I gave myself permission to show out, riding his dick like I was specifically made for this. I alternated between bouncing and rocking my hips until I finally came so hard my toes curled painfully.

"I want you to come," I panted while my skin was soaked in sweat and I could barely hold myself up. Only Ocean's hands were keeping me from collapsing. "I want to feel your cum dripping out of me."

"You know what that means, don't you?" he said as he kissed the top of my breasts. "Tell me you know what it means."

"You're going to breed me."

"Are you ready for that?" A moment later, Ocean wrapped his lips around my nipple and started suckling. "You gonna have my baby, *mo aingeal*?" He thrust his hips up, and my eyes rolled back.

"What does that mean?" I asked rather than answer. "*Mo aingeal*?"

"It means my angel, Coby. Because that's what you are," he said as he kissed my chest. "The only halo I'll ever own."

I was stunned into silence for a few moments before I finally answered, "Yes," with a soft sob. "I want to have your baby."

Ocean—as if he were able to simply command his body—kissed my sternum one last time and locked gazes with me as he started coming inside of me.

"Coby, I have something to tell you, too," he said much later as we lay spent on the couch together, with me sprawled on top of him.

We'd already gone two more rounds, so it took all of my remaining energy to lift my head and peer down at him in the semi-dark. "Okay...what?"

"We have to get married soon. Much sooner than I promised you."

"What? But I thought you said we could wait until June?"

"I know," he said solemnly as he stared at the ceiling. "It's not going to happen. I'm sorry."

Truthfully, he didn't sound sorry at all. I wasn't stupid. There was *some* regret at disappointing me, but moving up the wedding just meant I was his that much sooner. Whatever had forced his hand was just an excuse to force mine.

It wasn't just that I wanted a summer wedding. I needed time— time to reunite with Hunter, time to make sure Roshaun pulled through, and time to know that I wasn't making an irreversible mistake. I know Ocean said I could divorce him in five years, but time changed people. How could I really be sure it wouldn't change him? I was already falling for Ocean, and that's what scared me the most— how deep I'd gotten so quickly.

It terrified me.

And then there were these other feelings I still haven't been able to shake. They haunted me, and keeping them a secret from Ocean was getting trickier by the day.

Shifting onto the wide cushion next to him, I huddled close to him for comfort, even though he was the one knocking me off my axis once more. I tilted my head back to meet his gaze and found him already watching me. "So when are we getting married?"

"The day before Christmas," he answered.

My stomach sank, but I didn't have time to question the reaction because Ocean yanked me under him again and shoved himself deep inside of me with a conquering groan that set a deep chill in my bones.

"You want it again?" Ocean murmured just before sunrise after I woke him with my hand down his boxers. Addicted now, we'd spent the night fucking on every surface of the apartment before we finally fell into bed a few hours before sunrise.

"Fuck me," I demanded as I stroked him. "I want it so much."

"Yeah?" Ocean smiled as he rolled and shifted his weight on top of me and shoved my thighs apart. "Beg for it, wife."

"Please fuck me again," I whimpered as my head rolled back and forth on the pillow. "Never. Stop. *Fucking me.*"

"If you insist, greedy girl. Are you wet for me already? Good girl. Look at that fat ma swallowing my dick," he praised as he slid inside of me. "*Fuuuck,* Coby."

CHAPTER THIRTEEN

OCEAN

"Again," Coby pleaded as she writhed underneath me. "Fuck me again."

Chuckling, I lowered my head to her shoulder and tried to catch my breath. I had just fucked and licked her into three orgasms. My balls were fucking empty, and I was out of time. "I got to go, sweetheart," I said as I pulled out of her perfect pussy and kissed her soft lips. "The streets are calling, and you're meeting with my cousins today to finalize the wedding plans." Coby pouted as if she'd rather do anything else. I couldn't help myself when it came to her, so I kissed her one last time. "Be good."

I left the bed to shower and dress for the day, and then stepped back into my room to find Coby gone. Needing to set eyes on her one last time before I left, I tracked her down to her library and peeked inside to find her also dressed and perusing one of the shelves on the second floor.

Day by day, they were getting fuller and fuller as Coby put my credit card to good use after getting over her initial hesitation and realizing I wasn't one measly shopping spree away from being broke. It would take a lot more than that—generations of bad financial decisions—before that happened.

It's been a couple of weeks since my father threw down his ultimatum.

Two weeks and no sign or word from Hunter.

Unbeknownst to Coby, I've been spending every waking moment that I wasn't with her looking for her roommate.

It was as if Hunter vanished into thin air after her confrontation at the hospital with Kellan. We eventually caught up with him, but Hunter's been hard to find ever since. I've been writing some pretty fat checks to keep the police off her ass.

I didn't want anyone else getting near it before me.

I'd tried calling the burner a few times since she stole it from Kellan, but Hunter must have ditched it by now because my calls always went unanswered. *Smart girl.*

The phone wasn't traceable, but she obviously knew better than to leave herself open to temptation.

Because that's exactly what she was.

A temptress.

Don't you dare. Don't you dare. Don't you dare *think about it....*

With some effort, the pawns on my mental chessboard scraped back into place, and I left the penthouse with Abel. We rode the elevator down in silence.

"We might need to refocus our efforts outside the city," I said as we drove away from Glainne. "Have we looked far enough into Hunter's past to figure out where she might be holed up?" *Or who she might be hiding with.* I let that dangerous thought pass as swiftly as it arrived. I wasn't foolish or arrogant enough to believe that I could somehow accomplish what no man has been able to successfully pull off in the history of time.

One was enough.

One was *more* than enough.

"Everything before she turned eighteen is sealed," Abel told me. "We can get the information, but it will take time and money. A lot of it."

"Do what you need to," I responded with a sigh. Kellan was the one who handled this shit for me, but he was currently busy tracking down Hunter. The same as me.

Abel never complained, though, because he knew there were so few people I could trust, especially now with a regime change on the horizon—even my allies within and outside of the *Fola* could turn for not much more than the promise of a minor promotion.

Before Abel could get to work on it, he got a call on his phone.

"Whoa, say that shit again?" Abel screamed moments later. It startled Paul, who swerved a little but quickly regained control of the Denali with a mumbled apology. "Well, handle it! Nobody moves until we get there. Whoever isn't accounted for fucking dies." Hanging up, he punched the ceiling before turning in his seat to meet my gaze.

"What is it?"

"Someone just raided one of our caches."

I was already pulling out my phone to start ordering executions. "ATF?"

"No. They said whoever did it was alone. This person took out *fifteen* of our men, made off with some weapons, and left a message."

"Let me guess," I stated coldly. "For Michael Black." That trail was also getting colder by the day, but mysteriously, the raids on our flesh dens had also stopped. Maybe they'd chosen to refocus their attention.

"No." Abel winced. "The message was for you."

Fury wrestled with obsession now that I was forced to choose between finding out who raided my warehouse and chasing down Hunter.

I knew what I wanted to do, but I was heir to the *Fola*. It was never about what I wanted.

Coby was the first slice of heaven I'd ever taken for myself, and I was determined to keep her no matter how many people I had to kill.

"Boss?" Paul questioned as he waited at the light that had already turned green. My driver's hand hovered uncertainly above the turn signal that would take us to the apartment of a gifted hacker whom Hunter apparently met in juvie a long time ago. Horns behind us honked furiously as Paul waited for me to make a decision. Abel was noticeably quiet since he likely already knew my dilemma.

There was no reason to believe that Hunter still had contact with Destiny Arehart, but I wasn't about to leave any stones unturned. I could say my dedication to finding her was solely for Coby's sake, but why lie to myself? For now, my curiosity about Hunter Parrish was just that. A curiosity. She was a puzzle I couldn't resist solving, and the hold she had on Coby would need to be severed sooner or later. Coby's little speech about Hunter made that *very* clear to me.

I wasn't about to share my wife's heart with anyone.

"It's probably just another dead end," I whispered to myself.

"What's that, boss?" Paul asked.

"The warehouse," I answered tightly. "Take me to the warehouse." It was where my gut was steering me, and it had never led me wrong before.

Twenty minutes later, I was standing in front of a message written in blood with bodies strewn all around me. Abel was busy cross-checking the inventory to see exactly what was taken. There weren't any cameras because the risk outweighed the reward. Whoever did this was quick and efficient. They'd use the *Fola's* own hubris against us. In truth, the culprit did me a favor by taking out most of the crew because letting this happen in the first place had earned them a bullet.

One.

One person was all it took.

One reckless girl hellbent on reclaiming something that was never hers.

I studied the three words written on the wall and grinned.

GIVE HER BACK.

The threat behind it was just as clear as the angry letters on the wall: Give my wife back, or the next person's blood on the wall would be mine. Swiping my finger through the pool of blood under my feet, I wrote my response on the wall.

NEVER.

She'd never see it, but that was okay. I planned to deliver my answer in person. Done with this shit and ready to hunt, I turned away and gave the dead men no more than a cursory glance. I'd make sure their families were taken care of before erasing them from my mind completely.

"*Fuil a-steach, fuil a-mach*[6]," I uttered like a prayer on my way out.

And whether Hunter liked it or not, after this stunt, she was *in*. You don't destroy potential like that for something as petty as dick measuring. You nurture it.

Hunter Parrish was mine.

The first stop I made after leaving the warehouse was Glamis to inform my father of what happened. Of course, he wanted to know who was responsible, and I told him, with great pleasure, that it must have been the same person hunting Michael Black, and stressed what a shame it was that we couldn't interrogate him.

I wasn't stupid.

I knew that my father knew exactly where Black was. What I didn't know was why he was going to great lengths to keep the man hidden.

After leaving Glamis, I popped up on my baby at the restaurant where she was having lunch with Chiara and Priscilla. They were going over the very exclusive guest list since our wedding was a forbidden secret that could end like the Red Wedding in *Game of Thrones* if we weren't careful.

"Oceeeean!" Coby's eyes widened when she saw me, and then she greeted me with a drunken smile. "Whassup, my brotha?" She and Chiara started snickering at the former's imagined joke while Priscilla rolled her eyes in exasperation.

"Too many Bloody Marys," she explained. "They've been like this for an hour."

I nodded at my cousin before regarding my wife. "Having fun?"

"Sooo much fun." Leaning over, Coby wrapped her arms around

---

6   Blood in, blood out.

my neck and kissed me. I could taste the tomato juice and vodka on her lips. "I missed you."

"Missed you too." I pecked her cold lips a second time while she rubbed the side of my face.

"You're so handsome."

"And you're so drunk."

"I am not." She hiccuped. "You were supposed to say I'm handsome too." Pinching my bottom lip, she started moving it up and down before I could say a word. "Coby...*mo aingeal*," she mocked in a deep voice. "You're so handsome. Marry me, woman. Give me lots of babies."

Across the table, Chiara clapped and cackled. "Oh my God, cuz! She sounds just like youuuu!" She squealed that last part.

"All right." I batted Coby's hand away from my face. "Time to go home."

"Can Chiara and Pri come?"

"Uh, no. Chiara has to go home too, and so do I," Priscilla said. "If I wanted my nerves worked, I would have stayed at home with my kids, hell."

Coby blew kisses at Priscilla.

"Y'all gon' head and go. I got her," I told my cousins.

Priscilla sighed with relief before standing and helping Chiara's drunk ass up. Priscilla kissed Coby on her forehead and then waved her fingers at me as they left the restaurant.

"Are you mad at me?" Coby asked the moment we were alone.

"No. Why would you think that?"

"I don't know." She shrugged. "You feel mad."

"I *feel* mad?"

"Yes. It's a feeling," she explained needlessly.

"Come on, pretty girl. Let's get you home." I threw down some cash to cover the bill and tip, and then picked Coby up with my arms under her back and legs. I ignored the curious gazes that followed us as I carried her out of the restaurant with her head on my shoulder.

She was asleep by the time we reached the car.

Unknown: Hey thief... u there?

It was just a little after two in the morning, and I was standing in an apartment building just seconds away from knocking on the front door of one Destiny Arehart when I received the text message.

A message that came from Kellan's stolen phone.

I held up my hand to signal my men to wait as I typed a response.

Yes. What can I do for you, Hunter?

Her reply came instantly and didn't disappoint.

Unknown: You're lurking outside my friend's apartment like the boogeyman.

Unknown: It's making her very nervous

I didn't give a damn, but I typed anyway...

That's unfortunate. Where r u?

I didn't believe in mincing words. To my surprise, neither did Hunter because a minute later she texted an address where to meet her.

Unknown: But you should know that I'm not interested in talking

Good. Neither was I.

I didn't bother to text back as I pocketed my phone and gave the order for my men to retreat. It was likely a trap that Hunter was leading me into, but I didn't give a single fuck.

I had to see her.

I had to know because I was starting to understand why Coby

was so attached to her roommate. That shit spelled nothing but trouble and would probably get me killed.

Coby was soft and sweet but savage when she wanted to be.

Hunter was…something else. I didn't know yet, and it bothered me how much I wanted to find out.

"What's up?" Abel asked me as we left the complex.

"That was Hunter," I said while waving my phone. "She gave us her location."

"And you believe her?"

It only took me a second or two to think about it before I nodded. "I do so look alive. She's got something up her sleeve."

"Yeah, no shit," Abel grumbled as he fell back to start disseminating orders. I was going to have to give him a raise soon. He's more than earned it.

On the way to the location, I texted Kellan on his actual phone. *Any news?*

> Kellan: I tracked her to the north side. She disappeared inside a building on Senna Ave and hasn't come out yet. I'll let you know if anything changes.

Kellan's confirmation of Hunter's location aligned with the address she'd given me, so I backed out of the thread and reopened the one with Hunter.

> Whatever you're planning, I'd advise against it.

> Unknown: What am I planning?

> Don't fucking play with me, Hunter.

> Unknown: And don't you fucking think you can order me

"What the fuck?" The incredulous tone in Abel's voice drew my attention from my phone as Paul cursed and slammed on the brakes.

We were still a few blocks away from Hunter's location, and the streets were empty due to the late hour, so it didn't explain the lone figure standing in the middle of the one-way street just a couple of hundred feet ahead.

I couldn't see their face this far away, but there was something familiar about the shape of the shadow that felt like a warm vise around my dick. It must have been windy outside because the person's hair suddenly shifted, showing the tail end of a long braid. Goosebumps spread over my skin when I began to suspect who it was.

"Boss, how do you want us to handle this?" Abel questioned when the person started walking toward the truck.

Only then did I notice they were carrying something. It was long and slender with a cone-shaped end that made me squint.

"Abel," I said calmly once the dark figure slowly taking form stopped a hundred feet away. A moment later, they hoisted the mysterious cargo on their shoulder. "What were the weapons that were missing from the cache?"

"Not much. A couple of pistols, an automatic rifle, some smoke grenades, and a—"

"Shit!" Craig, the guard sitting next to me, shouted, cutting Abel off as he pointed straight ahead. "RPG!"

While everyone else in the SUV watched helplessly as a rocket-shaped grenade was launched at us, time slowed as "Suddenly" by Billy Ocean played in my head. There was no time to react as we watched the missile cut through the air.

A moment later, there was an explosion, flames, glass shattering, the feeling of being lifted in the air, and then my world turning upside down as screams and shouts surrounded me. The last thing I remembered was the screech of metal against the pavement. My brain felt like a ping-pong ball inside my skull once the Denali came back down. I think I even blacked out for a second.

When I came to, there was gunfire all around me. I was upside down, still strapped in my seat, as I looked to my left and then my right.

Craig was definitely dead.

The door he had been sitting next to was gone, and so was he.

Gritting my teeth that tasted like blood, I unlatched my belt buckle and fell the short distance onto the crushed roof of the Denali as the gunfire around me went on. I shuffled over broken glass to squeeze between the crushed seats in front of me to check Paul and then Abel's pulse.

"Shit," I said with a grateful exhale at discovering they were both unconscious but alive. "You're all right, man. You're all right." I patted Abel's slashed cheek that would need stitches, and then grunted as I pulled my gun free before checking and reloading the clip.

I didn't want to have to kill Hunter, but her stubbornness might not leave me much choice. Outside the truck, there was a sudden flash of light, followed by a long bang. More screams followed, and then almost all at once, the gunfire stopped.

Panic began to slice at my chest and temple, but before I could come up with a game plan, my door was ripped open.

I raised my gun automatically, only to be arrested by the sudden appearance of a gorgeous face wearing a scowl. Hunter's upturned eyes that were sharp at the corners were narrowed with displeasure at finding me still alive. Her deep, dark skin was so supple and soft-looking, even while the rest of her was covered in dust, cuts, and blood. Some of her naturally curly hair had come loose around the perimeter of her hairline, softening her blood-splattered features despite being dressed and strapped for battle.

"Ah, Hunter," I cooed through my pain. "You really are a bloodthirsty beauty, aren't you?"

Hunter's lips parted, but no words came as we continued to stare at one another, guns drawn and aimed, but neither of us seemingly able to pull the trigger. Reluctantly, she dragged her gaze away from me and frantically searched the destroyed SUV with her eyes before exhaling her relief at discovering that her friend wasn't here. I was still staring when Hunter's angry gaze snapped back to mine.

Temptress.

I'd heard her call from the moment I first saw her in the

surveillance photos of Coby. I knew she was attractive, but lots of women were. Needing more—a beautiful mind and heart—I'd grown bored with surface beauty years ago. Still, none of those photos had done Hunter Parrish justice.

She was exquisite.

"Oh, fuck!" Abel shouted. I was so captivated by Hunter, I hadn't realized he'd woken up. His shout was Hunter's only warning before my head of security pulled his gun and started busting.

"No!" I roared.

Gunshots rang out, making my ears ring. I shook off the sensation just in time to hear rapid footsteps retreating as Hunter safely got away.

"Crazy ass bitch," Abel grumbled once she was gone. He looked at me weirdly when he noticed my gun was already drawn. "Why the fuck didn't you shoot her ass?"

Ignoring him, I pushed past the aches and pains in my muscles and limbs as I climbed out of the SUV with Abel right behind me. The lead SUV that had taken the direct hit from the RPG was a ball of flame next to us. There was also smoke everywhere from the explosion and the grenades Hunter must have set off to maintain the advantage of her ambush. Abel and I helped drag Paul out and then left him lying on the ground since he was still unconscious.

"What the fuck!" Abel screamed as he looked around at the carnage left behind. It definitely told a story. Doors from the trailing SUVs were thrown open. Bodies were slumped over the open windows, some bleeding out from a slashed throat or a knife stuck in their backs. "She fucking…she fucking killed everybody!"

Laughing maniacally while holding my bruised side, I fell back against the upturned Denali. "Goddamn," I said as I fought to catch my breath. I think I'm IN LOVE!" I shouted my confession to the storm-darkened sky. Overhearing, Abel shot me the dirtiest look, but I didn't care. It was the truth. Fires burned all around us, but none compared to the one Hunter and Coby had lit inside me. Lightning flashed, and thunder rolled as if it had heard my thoughts. A moment later, rain poured in sheets, washing away the evidence of what Hunter had done and turning all the blood into pools of dark pink. My wife's favorite color. "Shit," I croaked at the reminder that I was spoken for. This cat-and-mouse game with Hunter was making my dick hard and blocking access to my brain. "I think I hit my head too hard," I mumbled.

"You think?" Abel shouted over the rain. Once again, I ignored him.

Hunter had stolen my weapons and then used them all against me to reclaim my wife. *My* wife. Mine.

I think it's finally time I had a real-ass discussion with *my wife*.

Abel called in reinforcements, and we made it back to Glainne without anymore run-ins with Hunter. *Shame*. Niamh was already there waiting for us, but I waved her off when my cousin tried to make a fuss over me, and then I made Abel sit so she could attend to him instead.

The commotion had drawn Coby out of bed, who took one look at me bleeding all over the marble floor and ran to my side. It took almost an hour to console her and then another ten minutes to peel her off me once she was convinced I wasn't dying. Niamh had finished patching up Abel and moved to help me, but Coby wouldn't let my cousin touch me, so Niamh patiently showed her how to stitch my side where the glass had cut me.

"Who did this to you?" Her horrified whisper drew Abel's attention, but one look from me silenced him before he could pop off.

After sending Niamh home, the three of us retreated to the office that I rarely used since I was never home. I took a seat behind my desk and pulled Coby to stand between my spread legs. She'd been asleep, so she was only wearing a dark pink nightgown that was now stained with my blood and a matching robe that was left open.

"Why are we in here?" She sniffled and tossed a concerned glance at Abel, who was across the room, angrily pacing a hole in my imported rug. "A-are you going to tell me what happened now?"

Leaning back in my chair, I rubbed my temples. "Coby...I need you to be honest with me, baby, and it needs to happen now. Do you understand?"

"Y-yes, I think so, but you're scaring me."

I swallowed the apology on my lips and held her gaze. "What the fuck is going on between you and Hunter?"

"What?" She visibly paled, and I felt my eyes narrowing at the nearly imperceptible step she took away from me. "What are you talking about? I already told you. She's my best friend."

"Cut the bullshit!" Abel roared. The stitches in his cheek that Niamh had just sewn together stretched tautly with his anger. "That bitch just tried to blow us up! Ain't no *friend* doing all of that!"

"Aye!" I shouted at my head of security. "Unless you want me to finish what Hunter started, check your goddamn tone when you're speaking to my wife."

I heard a gasp and swung my attention back to Coby. "What is he talking about? Are you saying *Hunter* did this?" Coby's gaze swung back and forth between Abel and me. I honestly didn't know if her confusion was genuine or a ploy to throw me off the scent, and that's what worried me, especially when her next question made it even more clear where her allegiance stood, even now. "Is she okay?"

Abel tossed back his head and laughed hoarsely at the ceiling before staring at me like I was the dumbest man in the world. "What more proof do you need, Ocean? Open your goddamn eyes. You almost get blown to pieces, but your *wife* is only worried if *Hunter* is okay."

"First of all, I can clearly see that my man is fine, so how about you kiss my ass? You don't know me!"

Abel's only response was to suck his teeth and then kick a chair across the room, which made Coby jump. And that I couldn't have.

"Abel…" I inhaled a calming breath. "Go take a walk, man. I got this." It was an order that he knew to follow because I was one more dirty look thrown at my girl from fucking him up.

Abel left without another word but made sure to slam the door so hard that a framed picture of my great-grandfather fell from the wall and crashed to the floor.

I didn't react. Quiet as it was kept, I understood his anger. Would I go to war for Abel? The closest person I had to a friend?

Yes.

But I would be smart about it. I wouldn't recklessly throw myself into the line of fire when there was a smarter way. Hunter had won a few battles, but the war was far from over when it had barely even begun. Most importantly, she couldn't win. Eventually, when her rage subsided and reality set in, she would be forced to see that.

The question is, would it matter? Or would she throw her life away to rescue a friend who didn't care to be saved? If Hunter kept going like this, by the time she realized it was all for nothing, that Coby was here of her own free will, and that she was marrying me because she wanted to (something I don't think even Coby has realized yet), it would be too late. My mercy and that of the *Fola* would be long spent.

The crushing weight of that impending eventuality had me replaying my argument with Abel on the way home.

"Ocean, this bitch is drawing too much attention," he argued. *"She's more than just some loose end. She's clearly a threat. We need to neutralize her right fucking now."*

"I'm not killing my wife's best friend."

"You think it will be any different once your father finds out who's doing this and puts a price on her head?"

No.

It won't.

Coby would still blame me, and rightfully so.

I've been dealing with Hunter with one hand tied behind my back and wrapped in kid gloves because of what she meant to my wife, but as the death toll rose, it was becoming clear that it wouldn't be enough.

Coby was soft and ripe for the picking like a grazing doe in the woods, but Hunter was clearly a different kind of animal. She was an apex predator stalking from the shadows and just waiting for the right moment to pounce. Like me.

It was past time I started acting accordingly.

Resting my head back against the seat, I closed my eyes and prayed to God I'd have the strength to resist temptation. I waited for an answer, but God was woefully silent, making it clear I was on my own.

All too quickly, the SUV turned into the underground garage at Glainne. I'd run out of time, so I opened my eyes and met Abel's bloodthirsty gaze. Anticipation was already injecting itself into my veins, setting my blood on fire at the promise of possessing Hunter soon.

The chess pieces were already moving, except this time from the opposing side of the board. Pawns, knights, and rooks were knocked over as the second-tallest piece—and easily the most important—did the unthinkable. The impossible. It slid across the center of the board until it stood tall by my side.

Two queens, one king.

With that eager burn stirring in my gut, I gave the order that I've been resisting for far too long because I knew... I fucking knew that it could shatter everything. "Find Hunter. Bring her to me. Spread the word that I want her captured alive and make it known to everyone that anyone caught helping Hunter Parrish will be dealt with."

Coby's best friend now had the highest bounty on her head in all of Black Veil.

She was officially duine gun fàilte[7]. *Persona non grata.*

Hunter was all alone and had nowhere to run except straight into me.

"Coby, is Hunter your girlfriend?" I questioned softly. It was an unusual thing to ask about platonic friends when there was no real evidence to suggest otherwise—only my gut feeling. Coby's brows dipped a little as she subtly shook her head, only to wince as if the denial—or the acknowledgement of the truth—pained her. None of it escaped my notice. Not even the sharp little inhale or the way she slightly turned her head to discreetly blink away her tears. Tamping

---

7   An unwelcome person.

my need to turn this room inside out, I kept my tone gentle and patient because it was what *she* needed. "Was she ever?"

My bride, who was already my wife in my heart, was slower to answer this time. "No." Looking up from the floor where her attention had been, she finally met my gaze. "Hunter was never my girlfriend. She's my sister. If she did this, it's because she's angry and scared. Wouldn't *you* be if someone took me from you and you didn't know if I was alive or dead?" *Yes.* But I remained silent as I listened. "I told you, Ocean. We've never been apart. You need to let me see her."

Inhaling deeply, I could feel the ice forming around my heart and bleeding into my tone as I spoke. "Hunter is backing herself into a very dark corner," I explained while ignoring her request. "Her actions tonight cemented that. I'm sorry, *mo aingeal*, but it's war."

"What?" Coby blinked and took an astonished step back. "W-what does that mean?"

"It means," I said slowly, "that I don't have to imagine how scared and angry your friend is feeling because I would never and *will never* allow anyone to take you from me. Hunter included."

In my peripheral vision, I spotted the door to the office slowly creeping open and someone quietly slipping through. I kept my gaze straight ahead at Coby, who was currently eyeing the paperweight on my desk.

"What are you going to do?" she asked nervously.

"What I have to."

Coby lunged for the small, round glass with an ocean wave trapped inside its prison, but still rising high to swallow and drown everything within its orbit. Ironically, it was a cherished and recent engagement gift to me. From my wife.

"NOOO!" She screamed when Abel grabbed her before she could bash my head in with it. Fuck, I loved this rare side of Coby just as much as her sweet and softer side. Abel lifted her up and carried her away from me as she kicked and screamed. It was all I could do not to kill my loyal friend for touching her. He was just following my orders after all. "Ocean! Don't you touch her! Leave her alone! I'll fucking kill you! Do you hear me? Ocean!"

Abel carried her out, and the door to my office slammed closed behind them, leaving me to sit in the dark alone. I didn't move long after my baby's enraged screams had faded.

She'd probably never forgive me, but it was a risk I was willing to take since I was more than committed to making sure my wife had *all* her heart's desires, even the ones she was determined to keep from me.

But this new game of ours was a delicate, treacherous one, and I had no moves to spare, so it must be played *carefully*.

CHAPTER FOURTEEN

COBY

I'VE BEEN TRAPPED IN THIS ROOM THAT I ONCE THOUGHT beautiful for a week. The first three days were spent banging and screaming at the door. The only people I saw during that time were the staff who brought me food and books, restored the room after I tore it apart, changed my sheets that are thankfully no longer silk, and ignored my pleas for help.

Ocean hadn't come to see me once.

He was too busy hunting down my best friend so he could... what? Kill her?

It was certainly the impression he'd given me right before he locked me in here again. *So much for not being a prisoner.* I spent my days reading but not hearing the story, eating but not tasting the food, and sleeping but not allowing my mind to rest.

That last part was the reason why it was early morning when I crawled back into bed from exhaustion after contemplating if I could survive jumping from the fortieth(?) floor.

Probably not.

I don't remember falling asleep, so I had no idea how much time passed before I was woken up by a finger trailing softly down my cheek. A lone man stood over me, but I knew from the scent of the rich cologne who that man was.

My future husband.

"Ocean?" I slowly sat up and blinked until I was sure I wasn't hallucinating. It was definitely him. The moment sleep faded, the blurred edges of him sharpened into focus. He was dressed in a dark blue hoodie and jeans, with an overgrown beard and tired eyes. I subtly inched away from him. "You're here."

"I missed you." I stared back at him, dumbfounded. After threatening to hurt my friend and locking me in here for a week, all he had to say was that *he missed me.*

Rage filled me too fast to regulate before I lunged at him and started punching him in the head.

"Coby, stop this shit," he ordered as he wrestled me under control.

"I haaaate youuuu!" I sobbed while lying on my back with my hands pinned to the bed. Ocean lay beside me, kissing my face.

"Shhh," he quietly soothed. "It's going to be okay, Coby."

"No, it won't," I cried. "You're taking her away from me."

"So there ain't no way forward?" he questioned as he searched my gaze. "We can't get past this?"

I quieted my sorrow enough to ask, "Are you still looking for Hunter?" Dead silence stretched between us. "Then no, Ocean. We can't get past this." With a lump in my throat and a tearing in my chest, I said, "It's o-over."

His grip on my wrists loosened when he stiffened. "Over?"

"Yes." I snatched my hands away. "I won't marry you. I can't even stand to look at your ass." Gritting my teeth, I mushed his face. "This is all your fault. Why does Hunter have to die?"

"Coby—"

"No!"

Ocean stared at me in shock that swiftly turned to anger. "That's it then? You don't love me anymore?" He sounded genuinely curious and hurt while I stared at him in shock.

"I never told you that I loved you," I denied hoarsely.

"You didn't have to. It's a feeling," he explained arrogantly, throwing words spoken by a happier, stupider me back at me. "And by the way, this isn't *all* my fault," he said as he stood from the bed. I followed him until we were facing one another. "Believe me, your bitch-ass brother carries a lot of the blame."

"Don't talk about Roshaun!"

"Fuck Roshaun!" Ocean roared. "He didn't even hesitate to sell you out. Don't you dare defend him to me unless you want me to find him and break his neck."

Unwilling to face the truth, I did the only thing I could to hide from it. I slapped the shit out of Ocean. He yanked me into him before pressing a hard kiss to my lips that made me whimper and wish things were different so I could beg him to never stop. "Make that the last time you put your hands on me," he warned before shoving me onto the bed.

Fuck that. He'd already pissed me off too much. I choose violence.

I kicked out at him as he went to leave, but Ocean's reflexes were lethally quick. He grabbed my ankle and dragged me to the edge of the bed. I quickly flipped onto my stomach and tried to crawl away, but Ocean just flipped my ass right back over before ripping my nightgown clean off.

My skin burned where the straps broke, and my breasts jiggled from the force of the movement. I was so shocked I couldn't move for several moments. Ocean didn't miss a beat, though. He pushed his jeans and boxers down his thighs and then shoved my panties to the side.

"Goddamn," Ocean growled appreciatively when I spread my thighs to show him my glistening pussy. He ducked his head and spat on it nastily before lining up his thick, long dick with my opening. There was no need to get me ready for him because I was already sopping wet, which he soon discovered the moment he pushed inside. "Ah, fuck, Coby." He laughed, but the sound became strangled when I tightened around his invading length. "Why are you so wet, baby? Huh? You missed me?"

Keeping my attitude, I refused to respond, so he started going ham on my pussy right there at the edge of the bed. I clutched at his arms and tried to stifle my cries, but it was impossible with how hard he was fucking me.

"Ocean, ocean," I eventually whimpered when the pleasure building inside became too intense to keep quiet.

"Ocean, ocean," he mocked in a high falsetto. "Nah, you gon' take this fucking dick however I give it to you," he said as he lifted me up until he was standing with me wrapped around him. "You wanted it, remember?"

Nodding, I stared at him, but he wasn't moved by my pleas or my tears.

Why was I crying when it felt so good? Because it also felt like betrayal. Hunter would never understand why I gave in because she didn't know what it was like to be caught in Ocean's vortex. The storm might calm or retreat for a while, but there was no true way to be free once caught.

And Ocean knew everything I was feeling inside and was forcing me to face it, so I did.

At least for a while.

Moaning deep in my throat, all I could do was hold on as he made me fuck him back. I wrapped my arms around his neck as I impaled myself on his dick until I came with a cry while Ocean watched me with a dark possession in his eyes that both terrified and elated me.

He didn't even come. He just set me down once I was done acting a fool on the dick and then made me clean my juices off him with a warm, soapy rag that I got from the ensuite. Once his dick was come-free, Ocean carefully stuffed his erection back inside his jeans with a pinch in his brows that confused me.

He'd rather be in pain than come for me? The rejection stung enough to revive my anger.

"Don't get it twisted," I said as I pulled my robe on. "This changes nothing. I'm done with you."

Ocean stared at me for a long, long while. "So you want to leave me and go back to Hunter?" he asked calmly.

I shrugged and lied through my teeth. "Of course I do."

Ocean inhaled sharply, and then his expression crumpled before he quickly looked away. Feeling his devastation crash into mine, I wanted to take the words back, but it was already too late. All trace of emotion had been wiped from Ocean's face when he gathered himself enough to look at me again. And even though he was standing close enough to touch, he never felt more unreachable.

"All right then."

Convinced I was hearing things (or maybe hoping I was), I asked, "W-what?"

"I'll take you back to Hunter," he repeated.

"Ocean, please try to understand—"

"Do you want to marry me or not?" he snapped.

The chill in his eyes had me afraid to answer, but I knew he'd never hurt me, so I forced myself to shake my head while feeling my heart tear in two at the lie. Of course, I wanted to marry him, but how could I, knowing it meant Hunter had to die? How could he love me, knowing I was fine with giving up my soulmate? I wouldn't be the woman he was so determined to possess because if Hunter died, so would I.

"So let's go. There's no need to drag this out." Ocean walked away, and I was left gaping at his back until the door slammed behind him.

I was going home.

He was letting me go home.

Why didn't it make me feel better?

Still unable to believe Ocean was willing to let me go so easily after all his talk and thinly veiled threats, I stepped out of my bedroom empty-handed and wearing only the clothes I wore the night Ocean took me on my back.

I went downstairs and found him waiting by the elevator with Abel, who watched me with his brows raised like he was surprised I'd actually shown up. I rolled my eyes at his ass since I still hadn't forgiven him for how he was coming at me that night. Abel had been surprisingly gentle when he left me in my room, but I didn't give a damn. Neither he nor Ocean had apologized for declaring war on my bestie.

"Okay," I said sadly. "I'm ready to go."

Bold words for someone whose sore pussy was a constant reminder of what we just did.

There was an emotional dissonance in Ocean's dark brown eyes as he stared at me before tearing his gaze away and nodding curtly at Abel. The bodyguard swore something under his breath and then pressed the button for the elevator. The three of us stepped inside when it opened immediately, and the elevator quickly became stifling as we rode down in silence.

The lobby was mostly empty when we passed through.

It was so goddamn cold outside, I gasped the moment we stepped through the glass door because I was far from dressed for the weather in my tiny black shorts and green sequin corset. Warmth surrounded me a moment later, and I looked up in surprise to see that Ocean had given me his coat.

"Th-thank you."

Ocean dipped his head, and then we shared a long look before he broke the connection and stepped away to hold open the back door for me. There was a thick pile of snow on the ground while more white flurries continued to fall from the sky. The roads were already cleared at least, so once we climbed inside the bulletproof Denali, Paul, who still looked a little banged up, drove off immediately.

The drive was over too quickly.

I still hadn't been able to sort all the things I wanted to say to Ocean before the SUV stopped in front of a familiar brown building.

Yes, I love you.

No, I don't want you to kill Hunter.

Yes, I wish it could be different and that I could marry you, have your children, and live happily ever after.

Now that some of my anger had faded, I was thinking so much

more clearly, but I feared it was too late to turn back. I also didn't want to. I needed to see Hunter. I needed to talk to her and tell her everything that happened. If this was the only way to do it and keep her safe, so be it.

Ocean would just have to understand.

And hopefully, one day, forgive me for leaving him.

After staring out the window at my building, I turned to Ocean to find him watching me. "I—" He held something out to me, and I looked down to see him holding my phone. I managed to steady my hand as I accepted it from him, but I couldn't stop a lone tear from falling. "Thank you."

"Have a nice life, Coby."

I flinched at the coldness of his dismissal, but he thankfully had already turned his head to stare out the window, so I slowly climbed out of the Denali with my heart in my throat. I was too busy fighting back tears to hear the car door open and slam shut, or the footsteps quickly approaching from behind, until my arm was caught in a tight hold and I was turned around.

I barely got a chance to glimpse his face before Ocean was coaxing me into a drugging kiss with my face caged between his hands. I would remember it for as long as I lived. My tears fell freely now, pouring into my mouth and his, but he just kept kissing me long past us both needing air.

Ocean kissed me until we were forced to stop or die.

I think I would rather die.

"Go," he begged me. "Go now before I change my mind."

Change it! I wanted to scream at him. I may have been his weakness, but mine was Hunter. It always has been. I couldn't turn back now, even if it meant I would never be happy or fall in love again.

Ocean had my heart, but Hunter was my soulmate. Right now, my soul was dying. I couldn't even be whole for Ocean without her, so I pulled away from him and turned to walk down the path to the walk-up apartment building. It was nothing special, but it was the home I shared with Hunter. That made it everything.

Every step felt as if I was being torn in two. I wanted to turn back, and I wanted to keep moving forward.

"Coby," Ocean called out to me. I spun around to see a plea in his eyes that made my stomach ache so bad that I unconsciously pressed my hand to it. His gaze dropped to follow my movement, and then he seemed to collect himself before shaking off whatever it was he was about to say. "If you're pregnant..." He paused to swallow, the knot in his throat bobbing. "I want you to come straight to me, do you understand? It doesn't matter what we are or aren't to each other. I'll take care of you and my baby." My eyes widened because I hadn't even thought of the possibility that I could be pregnant right at this moment. And still, he was letting me walk away with his child because he thought it was what I wanted. "Coby," he urged when too long passed without a response.

"I understand."

Ocean didn't leave right away. His eyes roved all over me like he knew this would probably be the last time we saw each other. And then he slowly backed away so that he could drink me in a little longer. I still didn't move when he reached the Denali and climbed inside. Not even when it drove off slowly, and I was stuck staring at the red taillights until it disappeared around a corner.

It wasn't a ploy.

Ocean had let me go.

I glanced up at the sky to see if pigs were flying because it seemed more believable.

A part of me that I should have probably listened to still didn't want to believe it. The other half of me that still belonged to Hunter brushed aside my paranoia and raced up the stairs to our apartment while my heart pounded excitedly.

I could barely breathe by the time I reached my door, but that didn't stop the grin from tugging at my lips at the sight of our door with our names decorating the front. Pale pink letters and the sun for Hunter, dark pink letters and the moon for me. Yin and Yang.

Luckily, I still had my key tucked inside my clutch, so I unlocked the door and stepped inside.

"Hunter?" I called out.

The apartment was quiet and yet unrecognizable as I looked around in horror. There were weapons, pictures, and liquor bottles taking up almost every available space, including the floor—more than what she had before—and blood-soaked rags covering the counter and coffee table that made me gasp and cover my mouth.

Was Hunter hurt?

I ran to the back of the apartment, checking her room first, which looked like it hadn't been slept in a while, and then mine. I always made my bed every morning, and the day Ocean kidnapped me had been no exception.

My bed was in shambles.

It looked like it had been slept in and more than once, and I knew Hunter must have been sleeping in my room to feel close to me. I knew she would take my being gone hard, but I never imagined it would be this bad.

It was decided.

I was the shittiest friend in the world. While Hunter was going through all of this, I was busy falling in love. I should have fought harder to get back to her, but I had given in to my own selfish whims.

With no choice but to wait for her return, I started cleaning up. It took me hours to get the apartment back right. By the time I was done, it was nighttime, and I was exhausted. I dragged myself into my room just to stare at the unmade bed.

My lips started to tremble as I wondered where Hunter could be, and then I remembered I had my phone now. I left my phone in the kitchen, so I turned to get it and screamed when I saw someone standing in the doorway.

"It's really you," the shadow croaked. "You're really here. What happened?" Light suddenly flooded the room, and I cried out when I saw Hunter leaning against the door jamb with a bandage around her thigh. "Did you escape?"

"Hunter? Oh, my god! You're hurt! What happened? Who did this to you?"

Hunter gave no indication that she heard me. She just stared at me as if I were an apparition, so I closed the distance between us and pulled her into my arms, but she didn't hug me back. I wanted to cry. "It's me, Hunter. I'm here. I'm back, and I won't leave you again, okay?"

Finally, I felt her arms close around me, and then she nodded against my shoulder. "Okay," she said hoarsely.

I pulled away so I could get a good look at her, and it became horrifyingly clear why I hadn't recognized her immediately. Hunter's long, beautiful hair was tangled, her lips were horribly dry and cracked like she hadn't had a drop of water in weeks, her skin was smudged with dirt and blood, her clothes were filthy, and she smelled like she hadn't bathed in days.

She'd even lost weight and a lot of it.

Her tantalizing curves had been diminished so much that I wondered about the last time she'd eaten.

"I don't understand," I said. "Where were you? *Where have you been?*"

Hunter smiled sadly. She looked so exhausted. "Shouldn't that be my line?"

Swallowing past the thick knot suddenly lodged in my throat, I guiltily skated past that disaster and ushered her into my room. "Come on, bestie. Let's get you cleaned up."

I sat Hunter on the toilet inside my bathroom while I filled the tub with warm water and prepared a bubble bath for her. Hunter was quiet, and every time I looked back to check on her, she was just staring at me like she didn't think I was real.

While the water continued to run, I helped Hunter stand and undress and swallowed my cry of anguish at all the cuts and bruises marring her beautiful body. None of them looked too serious, but it still made my heart hurt.

"Hunter...I...I'm so sorry." My vision blurred suddenly, and I blinked furiously to clear it. "I never meant for anything of this to happen."

"I know that, Coby. No one asks to be kidnapped. It's not your fault. I'm just sorry I couldn't find you sooner."

"Don't be sorry," I pleaded. "Please don't be sorry."

"All right," she said, sounding more like herself. "Let's agree that neither of us should be sorry. We both know who's to blame anyway." It was silent for a few moments, and then she inhaled and finally asked the question plaguing her. "Did he hurt you?"

"No," I answered quickly. "Not once." But that was a lie. Because he hurt me when he let me go. I obviously couldn't tell Hunter, so I changed the subject. "Come on. Let's get you cleaned up. No offense, bestie, but your armpits smell like chopped onions. My eyes keep watering. I thought a bitch was just happy to see you, but now I know what it really is."

"Girl, fuck you," Hunter retorted with a smile and a laugh.

I helped her into the tub, then grabbed a fresh sponge from under the cabinet and returned to Hunter's side. The bubbles covered most of her body from the shoulders down, but I've seen Hunter naked a thousand times. She wasn't shy about her body. Content to just be together again, we didn't speak for several minutes as she allowed me to bathe her. The bathroom was silent except for the trickling of the water and our neighbors arguing on the other side of the wall.

"He said you were here. I thought it was a trap," Hunter whispered, sounding exhausted again as she rested her cheek on the lip of the tub. "But I had to come. I had to be sure."

I frowned in confusion as I took my time scrubbing the dirt from her inner thigh beneath the water. "Who said I was here?"

Hunter's eyes found mine briefly before she looked away and then closed them with a sigh. "Ocean."

Exhaling past my longing and guilt, I once again avoided the subject of him and became hyper-focused on my task: taking care of Hunter.

Nothing I did could undo the last five and a half weeks for her, but I could try.

A couple of hours later, Hunter and I were huddled together on my bed watching TV and eating pizza—vegan for me, carnivore for her—like nothing had ever happened. We were both wearing robes after bathing. Hunter's hair was still damp from my washing it. She now wore two long braids with her hair parted down the middle.

"Are you ever going to tell me what happened to you?" Hunter asked out of the blue with her gaze still on the TV. "What did Ocean want with you?"

Knowing that I couldn't avoid it any longer, "He wanted me to marry him."

"What?" Her eyes flared wide with shock, and then she not-so-subtly looked down at my hand. Her relief was palpable at the sight of my empty ring finger. My guilt quadrupled.

"He asked me…and I said yes." Hunter flinched and then re-coiled once my confession sank in. Her beautiful mouth opened and closed several times, and then her breathing deepened.

"Apparently, Roshaun stole a lot of money from Ocean, and he had no way to repay him except for… me."

"What does that mean?"

I sighed. "Ocean has to marry so that he can take his father's place in the Fola."

"Okaaaay," Hunter said slowly. "But what does that have to do with you?"

"Ocean needed a wife, and I needed to keep my brother alive, so I…I said yes," I confessed.

Hunter pinched her nose, and the move weirdly reminded me of Ocean whenever he got frustrated. I never realized before how alike they were. "So wait, he asked you to marry him or told you that you had to?"

I thought about it for a moment before I shrugged. "Both."

After hearing that, Hunter had finally reached her tipping point and exploded. "Coby Perry, have you lost your mind?" she shouted.

"I had to say yes, Hunter! He was going to kill Roshaun!"

"So? Coby, I know you love your brother, but I told you he was a snake. He damn sure isn't worth you sacrificing yourself to the mafia!"

"That's not for you to decide, Hunter. He's my brother."

"Yeah, well, he doesn't fucking act like it."

"You're right." I nodded. "He doesn't. Roshaun stopped being my brother a long time ago when our parents died, and he was forced to become my guardian. Roshaun gave up everything for me. The least I could do was save his life."

"By getting married to a stranger? A dangerous one at that?"

Exhaling slowly, I prepared myself to make Hunter possibly hate me forever. "Ocean isn't a stranger, Hunter. I've sort of been seeing him for years. Nothing serious," I quickly added at her look of alarm. "We never even spoke to each other until the night he took me, but we *weren't* strangers either."

"How?" Her voice cracked as she stared at me through wide eyes glistening with tears.

"I would sneak away on the nights I told you I was doing Pilates to see him at the Diamond Lounge. Ocean was the silent investor in Roshaun's club."

"You lied to me?"

"I knew if I told you about him, he would end up being like all the others, and I wanted to keep him for a little while longer."

"What the fuck does that mean, Coby?"

"Hunter, don't play dumb." I sighed. "You know how it goes. It would have been fine for a while, but then either you would have gotten jealous, or he would have. None of the men we date has ever been able to understand that you're my soulmate and what it means. It's always been easier for you to accept because you don't let yourself form attachments, but I'm not you, Hunter. I want to fall in love. I want marriage and babies. I want something that lasts forever."

"And you think *Ocean Kilpatrick* can give you that? Do you know what they call him in the streets? Somehow, I doubt he'd win any husband or father of the year awards."

I smiled a little as I thought of him. "You'd be surprised. Ocean's actually kind of...sweet."

"Sweet," she echoed incredulously.

I shrugged. "Well, he is to me. I think I lo—" Suddenly, Hunter started touching my head. Her hand moved to several different spots before she leaned into my space to peer into my eyes. "Whaat are you doing?" I asked nervously.

"Checking for a bump. I suspect you must have hit your head during your escape. It's either a concussion or Stockholm syndrome."

I tugged her hand away from my head. "I'm fine, Hunter. I know how it sounds, but I don't care. I know what everyone says about him, but he's different with me. Softer."

Ignoring that she said, "By the way, how did you escape?"

"I didn't. He brought me back."

Hunter's expression soured even more. "He what?"

Unsure of how much detail I should share, I downplayed it a lot when I said, "I told him I couldn't marry him and that I wanted to go home. He brought me back."

"And you...believed him?" She frowned at me like I was the dumbest bitch alive.

"Why wouldn't I?"

"Because a man like Ocean Kilpatrick *doesn't lose*, Coby. There's no way he just accepted you not wanting to marry him." She was full-on hyperventilating now as she stood from the bed and started pacing.

Feeling the need to defend him, I argued, "You don't know him. He's a better man than you think, Hunter. You just have to—"

"*Coby!*" Her shout shut me up. "Do you know *why* I looked like I've been through hell when I found you tonight?" All I could do was shake my head. "It's because I have. And not just today. I've been running from your fucking fiancé for a goddamn week! He put the word out, and now *everybody* is gunning for me. Coby…there's a bounty on me for half a million dollars," she said with tears streaming down her cheeks. "I couldn't even turn to friends because with that much money on the table, I didn't know who to trust. As for the ones I could, it would only mean putting them in danger, so I've been sleeping in Deborah," she said, referring to her '93 Ford Thunderbird. "At least, I was. She's… she's gone."

It wasn't the first time Hunter had been forced to sleep in the cranky old bitch. The last time had been shortly after we met. I remembered thinking how cool Hunter was for already having her own car at fifteen until I learned she'd been living in it and had no one else. It hadn't been easy convincing Shaun to let Hunter move in with us. It wasn't until my brother met her for the first time that he finally gave in, elevating him from my bossy older brother to a hero in my eyes. Hunter lived with us until we both turned eighteen and moved on campus at the university. Not long after that, Hunter and Roshaun fell out for good, but I still remembered when they got along.

"Wait, what do you mean gone? What happened to her?"

"Prince Charming happened," she answered acerbically. "He sent one of his goons after me, and I got caught slipping. Sacrificing Deborah was the only way I could get away."

"Hunter, I'm so sorry. I know how much she meant to you."

I nodded. It hurt too much to think about Deb, so I quickly moved on. "I only came back here because I was getting ready to leave the city," Hunter went on to explain, "but then I found you here, and it was like you never left. I just…forgot about it all." It was silent for a moment while Hunter gathered herself. A week of running from a man with more power than God had obviously taken its toll. "So no," she said once her voice was steady once more. "I may not know Ocean, but I've known men like him all my life. He didn't go through all of that trouble backing me into a corner just to give up because his *fiancée* was homesick. If he let you go, it's for a reason."

I started to wonder if she was right until I remembered something she said earlier. "But he told you I was here, right? Ocean could have easily grabbed us both the moment you showed up, but he didn't. Why?"

"I don't know, Coby. Maybe you're right," she admitted while still looking ready to bolt. "But my gut is telling me that I am. I can't explain why. I just feel it."

"So what do you want to do because I'm with you no matter what," I assured her. "Where you go, I go." And then I smiled. "Ride or die, bestie."

Hunter shakily returned my smile, but all it did was highlight the dark circles under her eyes. "Ride or die," she whispered.

CHAPTER FIFTEEN

COBY

I WOKE UP THE NEXT MORNING, CUDDLED WITH HUNTER IN MY bed, and my first thought was how glad I was that the heat was working. She was still sleeping when I slipped out of bed to get started on breakfast.

I padded barefoot into the now spotless kitchen, only to end up staring at an empty fridge and emptier cabinets. Right…no food.

I picked up my phone to check my bank account to see if I even had enough money for groceries, but I somehow ended up staring at my phone as I went back and forth over texting Ocean to confront him about all the things Hunter told me last night. And then I remembered that I didn't have his number, so I put my phone down and forced him out of my mind.

With any luck, I'd never see him again.

I told myself it was better this way.

Almost immediately after, I remembered my brother, and my heart twisted painfully with guilt.

I had no idea if he was alive or dead, if he was still recovering in the hospital, or if he'd been discharged. I picked up my phone again to call him. The line rang until the voicemail picked up, so I steeled my nerves and forced myself to leave a message.

"Hey, Shaun. It's me. I just wanted you to know that I'm okay. I'm back home with Hunter, and I'm safe. And I want you to know that I don't blame you for anything that happened. You've always done the best you could for me, and you'll always be my big brother. I'll never forget that. Call me back, please. I love you. Okay. Bye…"

Hanging up, I took a deep breath and shook off the feeling that my brother hated me. *He'll call me back.*

I went back to my room and dressed myself in layers for the short trek to the grocery store. Once I was dressed and had left the apartment, I logged into my banking app to check my balance and stopped in the middle of the sidewalk when I saw it.

Checking Balance: $3,147,613.89

Confused, I checked the history and saw that $3,147,603.66 had been deposited into my account a week ago. The specific figure scratched at my memory, so I searched until I arrived on the night Ocean took me. Every penny that Roshaun had stolen from him had been paid to me, but why?

It also meant that, up until a few days ago, I had only a little over ten dollars in my account.

The wind was blowing so hard I could barely trudge through the two blocks of snow and ice until I reached the store.

Always the one stuck doing the grocery shopping for both of us, I quickly selected all of Hunter's and my favorite foods before checking out and leaving with my arms loaded with two paper bags. As soon as I left the store, my phone started ringing, so I shifted the bags in my arms to free it from my coat pocket. Heart galloping, I answered quickly when I saw the caller ID.

"Hello? Shaun?"

"What the fuck do you mean you're back?"

Taken aback by his furious tone, I didn't respond right away as I stopped walking. "I'm home. O-Ocean let me go."

"Why the fuck would he do that, Coby? What did you do? Did you piss him off?"

"*No.* I didn't do anything. He let me go. And what the hell is your problem? I thought you'd be happy to see your sister home safe and sound."

"Of course I'm fucking not, Coby. Are you fucking stupid? If Ocean can't get his payment from you, that means he's coming after *me*. I asked you to do one fucking thing, and you couldn't do it."

Um...*what*?

All I felt was this gaping hole at the end of my brother's tirade that was quickly filled with everything Ocean and Hunter had tried to warn me about him. "Roshaun..."

"What?" he snapped.

"Did you give me up?"

"What?"

"You heard me! Did you sell me to Ocean?" I shouted in the middle of the sidewalk while people skirted around to avoid me.

"Of course I did," he admitted with zero emotion. "He was going to kill me. I had to offer him something, and you owed me."

Roshaun ended the call, and I swallowed the urge to scream. The worst part of all was that I wasn't even surprised. I'd only been living in denial because I didn't want to believe that my own brother hated me for something that wasn't even my fault.

My phone rang again, and the little girl inside me, who once looked up to Shaun, hoped it was him until I read the name on the screen.

"Hey, Hunter."

"Coby! Thank God. Where are you? Are you okay? I woke up, and you were gone. I didn't know what to think. I—"

"I'm fine, Hunter. Breathe. We didn't have any food, so I went to the store."

"Oh." I heard her relieved exhale. "Well, I'll come help you then."

"No need. I'm on my way back now."

"Sorry, bestie, but I was already heading that way. See you soon." She hung up.

Shaking my head, I smiled as I started walking toward home again.

Hunter turned the corner less than a minute later.

Her thick thighs and wide hips were encased in skin-tight

medium-wash jeans, and she was wearing a cropped knit sweater like it wasn't twenty degrees outside, a long brown faux fur, and a blue NY Yankees ball cap. There was a hunting knife sheathed inside the holster on the side of her small waist, but it was mostly hidden, peeking out from under her heavy coat with her movement.

When I saw her appear at the end of the block, my smile stretched even wider as a thousand tiny wings fluttered in my stomach.

She was so beautiful.

The YNs already hugging the block certainly thought so. They called out to her as she passed, and true to form, Hunter looked over her shoulder to talk shit to them as she kept walking. She was so preoccupied roasting those little boys that she didn't notice the white van trailing slowly behind her. It hugged the curb as it steadily gained on her.

My lips parted to call out a warning, but it was already too late. The van slammed on the brakes, and the back door slid open. A man dressed from head to toe in black jumped out and snatched her right off the sidewalk.

"Hunter! Noooo!" Dropping the bags, I was already running for them.

The boys who had distracted Hunter quickly made themselves scarce while the man wrestled Hunter into the back of the van. She fought like hell, but her assailant was stronger and had the element of surprise. I screamed for my best friend again when the door closed behind them, and then the van peeled away from the curb before I could reach it.

Falling to my knees, I screamed until my throat was raw as I helplessly watched the white van disappear around a corner with Hunter trapped inside. Losing my best friend when I just got her back felt like deja vu, except this time, I was the one left behind.

A trap.

Hunter had been right after all.

Ocean didn't lose.

I did.

ACT II

THE TEMPTRESS

CHAPTER SIXTEEN

HUNTER

Five and a half weeks ago…

T HE PINK SUBCOMPACT RUGER RESTED AT MY SIDE AS I watched the taillights of the Denali disappear with my best friend trapped inside.

I know damn well that did not just happen.

And yet…I was painfully and terrifyingly aware that it *did*.

I'd barely gotten a glimpse of the man who'd taken her, and the only other witness was fighting for his worthless life in the back of an ambulance. I didn't know what drama had transpired between Coby and her brother, but I knew Roshaun was behind it.

Swallowing my enraged scream, I tucked my gun back into my clutch and jogged toward Deborah. She was my off-white 1993 Ford Thunderbird and the bane of my existence. However, the tragic history we shared meant we were stuck together.

"All right, you cranky bitch," I warned the rust bucket once I was inside. "I don't want any problems out of you. I'm not in the mood." Deb's engine was well past its last legs and would often stall in the cold. Since it was winter, and I lived in a city that spent a third of the year buried under snow, that was all the fucking time.

Thankfully, when I turned the key, Deborah sputtered and coughed her ancient ass to life. Patting the dashboard affection- ately, I exhaled. "Thanks, Deb."

I didn't bother with the heat since it stopped working ages ago. However, I paused long enough to try tracking Coby's phone.

When it said a location couldn't be found, I knew her phone had been shut off, so I texted Destiny. She was a skilled hacker and fellow delinquent who owed me a shit ton of favors simply for the fact that she was still breathing thanks to yours truly. Once she sent me a thumbs up that meant she was on it, I sped away down the street away from The Diamond Lounge.

Ten minutes later, I was parking Deborah in front of the nearest police station.

I wasted no time climbing out and hurrying for the icy steps. I was so busy fighting not to bust my ass or break my neck (because who would help Coby then) that I didn't notice the man leaning against the wall where he watched me with his foot propped against the brick. I paid him no mind since he wasn't doing anything but standing there. That lasted until he spoke.

"Are you sure this is wise?"

I huffed my irritation because I just knew he was talking to me. Every second counted, and I didn't want to waste a single one on some stranger. I couldn't be sure how much time Coby had since I didn't even know why she was taken in the first place.

"Look, man, I don't have time for your bullshit today. I ain't signing up for shit, and I ain't got no money, so go on somewhere. I'm busy."

"Busy snitching?"

His question caught me off guard enough that I paused to get a good look at him.

Lord, help me, it was a White man.

His blond hair had fallen over his forehead and past his brow, while the dark leather of his jacket made his fair skin and green eyes look even paler in the moonlight. He looked young, but his eyes told a different story. He had this fatally gorgeous, tragic bad boy thing going on that I was sure wet many cats.

Unfortunately, mine was as dry as Popeye's biscuits.

I've taken down a few White boys before. Another day, another time, maybe I would have given the cutie some play, but not now. All I could think about was my best friend being tortured and hacked into little pieces or trafficked to god knows where to do god knows what.

Sighing, I stared straight ahead at the door, but something wouldn't let me walk through it.

As if reading my mind and knowing exactly why I hesitated, he said, "You never know when a chance encounter is really by design, or when a stranger isn't a stranger after all, Hunter."

Pivoting on my heel, I slipped my hand inside my clutch where my Ruger rested. "Who the hell are you?"

"No one important," he evaded. "But you can call me Kellan."

"Hmm…sounds made up. What do you want?"

Kellan lowered his foot and shifted until his shoulder was propped against the wall. "I want to know why you think talking to the cops will help your friend."

Unmindful that we were in spitting distance from a building full of cops, I rushed him and pulled my gun before shoving it under his chin. "Where is she?"

Kellan didn't care that I held him at gunpoint, and it told me one of two things—he either didn't believe I'd shoot him, or he wasn't afraid of dying. The first made him stupid, and the second made him dangerous. "Coby's safer than you are right now."

Hearing him say her name, I pressed the muzzle deeper into his skin. "Do I look convinced, Kellan? Take me to her."

"Can't do that."

"That wasn't a goddamn request!"

"My boss, who has some very powerful friends, would like me to inform you that going to the police is a mistake he will not forgive."

"Good. Then you can tell him that taking my friend was one I won't forgive either."

Kellan's green eyes twinkled. "He thought you might say that."

"Am I supposed to care?"

"He also wants me to tell you that he'll pay you well to forget what you think you saw."

I lowered the gun until it was pointed at his crotch. "Say that shit again, and I'll blow your dick off."

Kellan's green eyes twinkled with a grin. "I think I'm in love."

"That's what they all say."

The door next to us opened before Kellan could respond. Five uniformed cops filed through, talking amongst themselves. Kellan yanked me into him until I was pressed against the full length of his body—so close I was sharing his heat. Our closeness also hid the very illegal gun I still had pressed to his crotch just as they gave us curious glances.

"Okay, love birds," the last officer, who had a thick mustache, said with a wave of his hand. "This is a police precinct, not the backseat of a car. Move it along."

I discreetly slipped my gun back inside my clutch and then slowly backed away from Kellan, braving the treacherous steps blindly this time because daring to take my eyes off him seemed twice as risky even with a boatload of cops around.

Reading my mind once again, Kellan smiled. "Be seeing you, Hunter."

Rolling my eyes, I darted off and dove inside the safety of Deborah, but I couldn't bring myself to drive away. My emotions overcame me the moment I was alone, and I ended up sobbing with my forehead pressed to the steering wheel as I imagined all of the horrors Coby would likely face.

Getting her back was never going to be easy, but Kellan boldly showing up to stop me from filing a report mere feet away from the precinct told me I wasn't dealing with the average street thug. No, there was something much larger at play here.

Whoever took her was clearly watching me, so I would have to find another way to get my best friend back, and I would. There were so many things I never got to say—so many things I was sorry for. But I couldn't turn back time, so I would do everything in my power to make sure Coby had a future. I would defy the devil himself to reclaim what was mine.

Even if it killed me.

CHAPTER SEVENTEEN

HUNTER

Two weeks missing…

FOR TWO WEEKS, I'VE BEEN PLAGUED BY THE SAME DREAM OF the night Coby disappeared without a trace. A nightmare, really. And no matter how it goes, it always ends the same—with the taillights of a black Denali speeding away with my best friend trapped inside. And when I wake up, I'm haunted by the shadowed outline of the man who'd taken her.

The only cure was to hold off sleep for as long as I could, so I've spent every waking moment since she was taken combing the streets for my other half. And whenever I eventually collapsed from exhaustion, I made sure I was too intoxicated to dream.

Like now.

Tipping back my head, I poured the last of the vodka down my throat while a river of fresh tears soaked my face. All around me were pictures of Coby and me scattered all over the floor. They were all hers since she was more sentimental than I, and now I was the one drawing comfort from them, wondering if I'd ever see her smile again.

I've been putting feelers out to find out who the hell had taken Coby. I'd only gotten a glimpse of the dark-eyed stranger, but his description and the circumstances were enough to spook anyone who knew anything from talking.

And now there was this anxious twisting in my gut telling me that I'd never see Coby again. None of it made any sense. All the evidence pointed to a targeted attack, but there was only one problem.

Coby didn't have an enemy in the world.

Coby didn't, but that didn't mean the people in her were without them.

My gaze fell over the pile of glossy four-by-sixes until it zeroed in on one of Coby posing with her brother in front of his club before it opened. The picture was taken the day Roshaun got the keys to the building, and Coby insisted on being there to celebrate with him, dragging me along.

"Bitch ass," I growled at that grinning piece of shit before crumbling the photo in my fist and tossing it away. Picking up my gun that had been resting by my side and stumbling to my bare feet, I spent the next half hour trying to sober up fast. Once I was steady on my feet, I left the apartment I shared with Coby.

"Aye, what's up with you, Hunter?" Gary greeted me with a smile as I passed him on the stairs. He lived a couple of floors above me and had been trying to fuck for years.

"Not now," I snapped as I stormed past him.

"Damn, my bad," he grumbled.

Ignoring him, I jogged across the parking lot toward Deborah, who was parked by the pond overlooking our apartment building. It was the wee hours, so the streets were empty, charging me only ten minutes before I reached the hospital. I'd come the night Coby was taken to question Roshaun about what the hell happened, but the bitch had suffered a pneumothorax and had been surrounded by doctors and nurses in the ICU.

I prayed all night that his ass would die, but he just kept right on living.

I hadn't returned since that night, but there was no time to kick myself for it. I didn't even know if he was still here, but I wasted no time parking and rushing inside the hospital.

It took another ten minutes of navigating the hospital maze and a little white lie with the nurse at the desk to find out what room he was in, but then I was walking into his private suite without warning, paying no mind to the startled nurse on the other side of his bed, who was swapping his IV bag.

"Oh!" she gasped when she noticed what I was clutching. "Absolutely not. No, ma'am. You can't bring that in here!"

"Shut up and stand over there," I ordered with my gaze fixed on a sleeping Roshaun and my gun pointed at the corner where I wanted the nurse to stand. After a brief hesitation and realizing she'd never get between me and the door in time, she stumbled into the spot I'd pointed out.

The pain meds they had Roshaun on must have been heavy because he was still out of it when I stepped up to his bedside.

"Wake up," I ordered with zero emotion as I slapped his cheek with my gun a few times.

It took a few minutes for Roshaun to fight off his meds and the initial confusion after a long and deep sleep, but then his gaze widened when he noticed me standing there and felt the muzzle of my Ruger on his cheek. "What the—Hunter?" He blinked at me. "Fuck are you doing here?" His gaze darted around the room, unfocused and hazy. "Where's Coby?"

Roshaun was one of those types who assumed having a dick between his legs put him in charge. Being ordered around or bested by a woman would strike a huge blow to his pride and damage him more than any physical blow.

Still...

The nurse cried out when I adjusted my grip and began smashing the butt of my Ruger into his face without a word. "Arrgh! Shit! Arrrgh!" Roshaun shrieked in pain while curling into a ball and trying to duck out of the way. "Fuck are you doing?" he shouted.

I didn't stop until I heard a satisfying, sickening crack, followed by blood gushing from his shattered nose. Some of it splattered onto the machines reading his vitals and the whiteboard on the wall next to his bed.

"Oh, God! Oh, God! Oh, God!" The nurse muttered hysterically before opening her mouth wide to scream. "Help! Somebody help!"

Swinging the gun the nurse's way, I met her terrified gaze and felt no mercy in my heart—not even for an innocent woman just trying to do her job. The only good thing about me was gone, and without Coby, I had nothing to fucking lose. "Last warning to shut the fuck up. I'm not here for you. I'm here for him. He's not worth getting shot over, sis. *Believe me.*"

That seemed to calm her down. "Okay," she said with a quick and jerky nod, making the large bun of her box braids loosen. She threw her hands up in surrender. "Okay."

Returning my attention to Roshaun, who was groaning in pain and clutching his side, I felt nothing but hate for Coby's brother—a man I once trusted and looked at like a brother. "Don't play games with me, Roshaun. Tell me who they took her, where, and why."

"Who?"

Snatching the pillow from behind his head, I placed it over his thigh, pressed the Ruger into the pillow, and pulled the trigger. The muffled shot was punctuated by Roshaun's scream of pain and the sound of a body hitting the floor across the room.

The fucking nurse had fainted.

"Arrrgh! My leg! My leg! Aww, fuck! You shot me, you crazy bitch!" The pussy motherfucker was crying now as he reached for his leg, only to be stopped by the pain of his broken ribs.

"You're in a hospital," I reminded him. "The sooner you tell me where she is, the sooner the doctors can save you."

"Save my—what are you talking about? You only shot my leg."

I retrained the gun, aiming for his liver this time. "So far."

Roshaun collapsed against the bed with a groan and spent a few precious seconds trying to catch his breath. "It's no use…Hunter. You'll never…g-get…to her. She's gone."

"Where?" I urged through gritted teeth.

"He has her now. Kilpatrick." The name made my stomach sink because I knew what it meant. Coby hadn't been kidnapped by traffickers or garden-variety creeps. She'd been taken by the *Fola.* People with the power to make her disappear forever and get away with it. Roshaun chuckled, baring his blood-stained teeth as he stared at me knowingly. "I doubt Ocean will want to share."

"What does he want with her?"

Roshaun coughed before shaking his head weakly. "Don't know. Didn't matter."

"It didn't matter, or you didn't care?"

"Just kill me," he muttered as he looked away, a stubborn look that reminded me of Coby entering his eyes. I hated how much they looked alike. Coby was fucking beautiful. Looking at Roshaun's ugly mug just made me want to vomit. "I'm dead anyway."

"No." I shoved my gun inside my thigh holster to keep from using it again.

It's not that I didn't want to kill him. I *really* did. But I knew Coby would never forgive me. She loved her brother, and that love kept her from seeing just how much he resented her.

Having what I needed, I grabbed the remote-looking device, pressed the button to call another nurse in, then turned to leave without another word.

"Hey…"

Roshaun's voice stopped me in my tracks just as I reached the door. Reluctantly, I turned to face him and found him glaring daggers while his breathing grew increasingly unsteady. "Judge me all you want, but Ocean gave me no choice, and Coby owed me. You should know better than anyone that I always collect my debts."

Chuckling without any humor in the sound, I leaned my weight on one leg and crossed my arms. "You know what, Roshaun? I do know. I know you still ain't shit and you don't deserve Coby. She didn't kill your parents. A drunk driver did. And it's not her fault she was born second, and that responsibility of guardian fell on you, but even if it had…" My heart felt a thousand times lighter thinking about how much larger Coby's was. "She would have done the same for you, and she wouldn't have blamed you for any of it. Not for a second."

He shrugged while looking away. "Guess we'll never know."

Hearing multiple footsteps outside the door, I quickly pulled it open and left the room. Down the opposite end of the hall, where the elevators were, two security guards jogged this way with their hands clutching their holsters. The nurse posted at the reception desk was nowhere to be found. She must have heard the screams and alerted them.

"Hey!" one of the guards shouted when they spotted me. "Stop right there!"

Nope. I immediately ran in the opposite direction toward the stairs. There was no reason for me to linger now that I had a name.

Ocean Kilpatrick.

I wish I could say I'd never heard of him, but as I flew down the stairwell in an attempt to avoid capture, my bravado slipped until I was having a full-blown panic attack.

What would the *mafia* want with Coby?

I made it to the parking garage and through an unguarded exit, but as soon as I stepped through the door, a heavy weight slammed into me, and I hit the nearest parked car with a yelp, setting off the car alarm.

I only had time to pull my gun before my assailant—with a speed I begrudgingly envied—grabbed my wrist and slammed my gun hand repeatedly into the car behind me to get me to release my only protection. *Fuck. That.* I drove my head into his face and immediately saw a thousand bright lights while my attacker stumbled back.

Some days, it paid to have a hard head.

Taking advantage of his disorientation, I pressed my gun into his stomach before he could recover, and he dropped his hand to scowl at me.

Kellan.

"Why the fuck are you following me?" His lips parted. "Never mind. Dumb question," I said before he could speak. "Get your hands up."

Kellan attempted to eviscerate me with a look, but he didn't know I was empty inside. Coby had taken it all with her, so I waved my gun at Kellan to signal him to hurry the hell up. His jaw twitched as he slowly raised his arms.

I wasted no time quickly searching his pockets. His jeans were empty, but I struck gold when I searched his jacket.

"I promise you don't want to do that," Kellan warned when I relieved him of his burner phone. He no longer sounded amused, which meant he was finally waking up to the fact that I wasn't easy to scare.

"Shut up."

I brought the gun down hard on his head, and Kellan crumpled to the ground. With great effort (he was heavier than he looked), I dragged his unconscious body into the stairwell and then jogged to Deborah before speeding all the way back to the apartment I shared with Coby.

I'd already forgotten about the phone by the time I was turning into the complex when I startled at hearing it ring. Truth be told, I didn't know why I'd taken it. Maybe I hoped it would lead me to his boss, or maybe I just wanted to be a bitch and piss off my annoying stalker.

Whatever the reason, I wrestled with whether to answer or ignore it before remembering I had nothing left other than lose. I blindly grabbed it from the passenger seat where I'd tossed it, and glanced at the screen. The number calling hadn't been saved, but it didn't matter.

I answered.

"Hi," I greeted cheerily. "Kellan can't come to the phone right now. He's currently nursing his head and his ego, but I can take a message." Nothing but silence greeted me as I let paranoia steer my car around back instead of my usual space. "Look, pervert," I said as I hopped out, "if you're not going to talk, I'm hanging up. I got shit to do."

"Who is this?" the caller demanded in a voice so deep I actually stumbled a step.

He'd only spoken three words so far, but each was measured as if he spent too much time wondering how they might be used against him later. Another puzzle piece slid into place, but I was still far from seeing the whole picture.

"Me?" I teased as I entered my apartment. My heart twisted painfully when I didn't find Coby waiting for me like usual. She preferred staying home and reading her porn, while I liked to run the streets. The only problem was Coby couldn't stay away from me any more than I could from her, so we often wandered them together or stayed in and pigged out in front of the TV. "I'm the new owner of this phone. Who are you?"

"The former owner of this phone," he barked back.

I entered my bedroom and put the burner on speaker before setting it down on the small desk I had wedged in the corner. "Well, that's impossible since you sound nothing like the handsy bastard I lifted it from."

The other end of the line grew quiet again. "Kellan touched you?"

Was it me, or had the temperature dropped a thousand degrees?

"Yup," I said, not caring what that meant for Kellan as I toed off my sneakers. "You should really try teaching your goons some manners. I had to squeeze his balls, literally and then figuratively, but I think he's getting the message. *You're welcome.*"

The rest of my clothes followed my shoes into a pile on the floor. Wearing only my glitter thong (Don't judge me. It's laundry day), I grabbed the stolen phone and my purse, walked over to my unmade bed where I deposited both items, and pulled out the heavy but flat safe hidden underneath.

He chuckled, and the sound was like liquid silk being poured over gravel. Worse, my heart quickened at the sound of it. I was already beginning to crave more of it. "I underestimated you, Hunter."

I forced myself not to react to my name being uttered in such a deep tone or to the fact that the man who took Coby indeed knew who I was.

"People tend to do that," I said as I keyed in the safe's code.

One-two-one-six. Coby's birthday. Hearing the safe beep, I pulled out the long drawer, replaced my compact Ruger with two larger Sigs, and checked both loaded clips before slamming them back into place.

After, I carefully braided my long hair into a single plait. It took a while since my hair was thick as fuck, and my nails kept snagging on the 4C texture. The man on the other end didn't speak the entire time, so I flicked my gaze toward the phone to check if he'd hung up.

He hadn't.

Either he had the patience of a saint, or he must really like listening to me breathe. Exhaling slowly, I steadied my nerves, let go of my finished braid, and began redressing for war.

"So here's the deal," I said once I was donned in all black, complete with a bulletproof vest. "I know you're the one who took my Yin. I don't know why, and I don't really give a fuck. You're going to give her back in one piece, and it's going to be now."

A bitch was starting to feel like the dad in *Taken*. *I will find you, and I will kill you.* Nothing less than painting this city red in order to get her back would be enough.

"Don't leave me in suspense when you've worked so hard to intrigue me, Hunter. What will you do if I don't?"

Excuse me? I hadn't worked hard for shit! Everything I've done was to get Coby back. Nothing more. *Arrogant prick,* I thought. "I'm sure you can fill in the blanks." I grabbed a box of ammo and an extra mag and began loading the clip.

"Do you even know who you're threatening?" There was no anger or arrogance in his tone—only amused curiosity.

"Should it matter?"

My mysterious caller fell quiet again, but when his answer finally came, I could hear a hint of respect in his tone. "No." And then his voice deepened until there was a slight growl in every syllable. "It sure as fuck wouldn't matter to me."

It could have been my imagination, but I was pretty certain my thong just became a little damp. "I'm glad we understand each other."

"Hunter, I think we're far from understanding each other. Stand down. This is your last warning."

Standing, I strapped one holster around my thigh and another around my waist. I was previously prepared to get Coby back the legal way until Kellan showed me that whoever took her wouldn't be swayed by the boys in blue. Yeah, he'd been there to stop me from filing the report, but that was only to flex his muscles and show me that it wouldn't have done me any good.

"And this is my warning. You have less than an hour to return my friend. By the end of that hour, I'll be on your doorstep shooting anything that moves."

Destiny was working overtime to find out where Coby was being held and to make sure I had what I needed to get her out alive.

"Show me yours, and I'll show you mine," the man on the phone promised. "And Hunter?"

"What?" I didn't bother to veil my aggression. My trigger finger was already itching.

"I promise mine are bigger."

I snorted. *Sure, buddy.* "Okay, I hear you. I guess we'll just have to pull them out and see."

"I'm looking forward to it."

Ocean hung up, and I quickly gathered everything before hurrying across the hall to Coby's once pristine room, where her green apple scent was the strongest. I'd already torn it apart looking for answers. Looking for secrets.

Had she been keeping them while I'd been bearing my soul?

I didn't want to believe so. I wanted to keep believing that we told each other *everything,* but with each day that passed, I became less sure.

Inhaling the lingering remnants of her perfume one last time, I left the apartment in a hurry. For now, I'd lost my tail at the hospital, and if I wanted to keep it that way, I had to make sure I never came back where he could find me.

Destiny's place it was.

CHAPTER EIGHTEEN

HUNTER

Another two weeks…

I WAS NOTHING BUT ASH BEFORE COBY FOUND ME. IN TROUBLE with the law again, I was forced into counseling for the profound grief over the loss of my mother. My public defense attorney had cleverly attributed it to my bad behavior in order to keep me from doing hard time after I was caught burning down my father's house with him inside of it.

Unfortunately for the world, my sperm donor survived.

Coby's relentless optimism had pushed back the hopeless obscurity, laying siege to my mind until there was only her. I'd become so dependent on her light that I could barely last a few hours without seeing or hearing from her before I began to slip back into darkness.

She had been the only person I could count on in a long time and the one time she'd needed me…

My chest cracked when a sob was trapped inside.

I'd failed her.

I wouldn't fail her now.

And that, ladies and gentlemen, was the reason I was standing alone in the middle of the street with a rocket launcher hoisted on my shoulder. Was it slightly over the top? Maybe. But for Coby, I would travel to the depths of hell to get her back.

"Okay," Destiny spoke into my ear. She was safely hidden on

top of one of the buildings with the handgun I taught her how to shoot, just in case. I'd taught Coby, too, but she was determined not to ever use one. "According to the security feed, he's in the second vehicle. A direct hit will almost definitely kill him, so unless you want to never find Coby…"

"Got it."

In addition to offering me temporary shelter from the Fola's reach, Destiny was the one who located one of their weapon caches, and with her help, I was able to escape with enough hardware to make sure Ocean got the message of just how serious I am.

I knew he could see, but I would give almost anything to know if he was scared yet.

Smiling a little at the thought of him pissing his pants, I pressed the trigger and fired the rocket.

The lead vehicle exploded, but the blast's force launched the second vehicle into the air, flipping it and landing it on its roof.

I only had time to toss the rocket launcher away and grab a couple of smoke grenades before the doors of the trailing SUVs flew open. Snatching the rings free of the canisters, I ran forward and tossed them on the ground toward the SUVS. While they rolled to a stop, I quickly removed the automatic rifle from my shoulder. Heavy smoke started filling the street as I ducked behind one of the parked cars.

"Where did she go?" one of the goons asked.

"I can't see shit!"

"Someone check on the boss."

"You've got two heading toward Kilpatrick," Destiny whispered in my ear. "Ten o'clock. Good luck."

Breathing heavily, I closed my eyes and said a prayer before shooting to my feet, aiming in the direction Destiny indicated, and unleashing on the men. With their backs turned to me, they stood no chance as my bullets dropped them like flies.

"Oh shit!"

"There she go! There she go!"

Ducking just in time to avoid their bullets, I belly crawled to another car and returned fire.

"Fuck! There!"

None of their bullets could touch me since it was so hard to see past the smoke. I was shooting just as blindly until I remembered the thermal imaging camera I'd also pilfered from Ocean. Heart pounding in my ears, I ducked behind the car once again and freed it from the pouch on my waist as the shooting continued around me.

Moments later, I had their heat signatures showing on the small screen, so I swapped out my rifle for the handgun in my holster and weaved between the cars as I hunted down Ocean's men within the smoke and shadows.

Time stretched endlessly, but in reality, it was only a couple of minutes before the white opaque smoke thinned out and the hunter became the hunted.

I was ducking behind a red car riddled with bullets and broken windows when I peered around and saw them. There were only three left now, but they had regrouped and were slowly stalking the street in a triangulated formation.

And I was out of bullets.

"Well, fuck..." I shook my head and swallowed my whimper. "The things I do for you, bestie," I whispered as if she were here. I would need a massage, a pedicure, and a good ass nut after this. The likelihood of any of those happening was a firm zero. Pulling the stun grenade free, I tossed it over the trunk of the car without looking.

There was a flash, and then a chorus of shouts rang out before the bang.

Rushing from my hiding spot, I unsheathed my hunting knife as I sprinted for the one in the middle. As soon as I reached him, I didn't hesitate before burying the blade deep in his gut and driving it up toward his sternum. Blood spilled from his mouth through clenched teeth and splattered my face (yuck), so I turned my head to the man gaping next to him and smiled.

"Ah, hell nah! Fuck this!"

Realizing that they were on the losing side, the remaining two retreated in desperation to the safety of the armored SUVs, but my bloodlust could not be sated.

One slit throat and a stab in the back later, *I* was the last man standing.

Well…almost.

Remembering the spare bullet I always kept in a special place, I wedged my fingers underneath my vest and dug into the space between my breasts until I was able to pinch the warm metal between my fingers.

I strutted toward the overturned Denali as I loaded the single bullet into the magazine and slid back the slide. It took some effort to wrench open the door, but when I did, I was immediately facing down the barrel of a gun.

"Ah, Hunter," the underboss of the mafia casually greeted, as if I didn't also have a gun pointed at him. "You really are a bloodthirsty beauty, aren't you?"

A multitude of responses entered my mind as I looked around the SUV. I knew Coby wasn't with him, but I still had to see for myself before I finished this.

Where's Coby?

I should have barbecued you.

Where's Coby?

Villains should not be allowed to look this good.

Where. Is. Coby?

In the end, it wasn't meant to be because I didn't get a chance to say a damn word before I caught movement in my peripheral vision.

"Oh fuck!" the man in the front seat shouted.

"No!" Ocean roared.

I threw myself out of the way in time to avoid the bullet his head of security had for me, and I weaved through the enflamed and bullet-riddled cars until I was standing out of sight but still within earshot.

Panting, I rested my head against the brick building and fought to catch my breath as I listened to Ocean and his bodyguard climb out of the Denali and then drag the driver out.

"What the fuck!" the bodyguard screamed moments later. "She fucking killed everybody!"

The last thing I expected to hear in response was Ocean laughing, as if the carnage delighted him. I guess his moniker as the Bloodthirsty Prince was well earned. Those were his men, and he didn't even care. Peering around the corner, I saw him tipping his head back to the sky while lightning flashed.

"I think I'm in love!" he shouted.

Gasping, I ducked back into hiding and closed my eyes while my heart raced all over again and butterflies erupted in my stomach.

I couldn't have heard him right. There was no way.

Confusion, mixed with shock, held me in place until it started raining, and then I did the only logical thing when I heard them start calling in reinforcements. I peeked around the corner of the building again to see Ocean looking around, swiveling his head back and forth as if he was searching for me. When his gaze reached my hiding spot and peered a little too long in my direction, I gasped again and ran like hell in the opposite direction.

I told myself that was the only reason I ran and not because of what I thought I'd heard.

I sprinted all the way to the meeting point with Destiny, and then I saw her home safely before choosing to sleep in my car. Fortunately, Destiny hadn't actually been home as I led him to believe when Ocean had shown up, but if he was looking for me there, it meant staying at her place wasn't an option.

Destiny insisted that it was fine. Her over-the-top security measures meant we would see Ocean coming long before he arrived, but I wasn't willing to take that chance, so Deborah it was.

I didn't mind.

The Thunderbird and I go way back. She was the first real home I ever had.

Coby was my second.

I think I'm in love. Ocean's words replayed in my mind as I got comfortable in the backseat of Deb. Eventually, they lulled me to sleep, but not before I had the disturbing thought that in another life, I could have been too.

The next morning, I woke up to three messages from Ocean that chilled my blood and ignited my fury.

> **Unknown: I hope you're as good at running as you are at killing, Vengeance.**

> **Unknown: You can run, but there is nowhere you can hide where I won't catch you**

The third message was an attached photo of Coby standing on the balcony of some library that looked straight out of a fairytale. She was smiling widely down at the cameraman like she didn't have a care in the world.

Like she didn't miss me at all.

CHAPTER NINETEEN

HUNTER

I T WAS RISKY GOING BACK TO THE APARTMENT, BUT I HAD NO
choice after Ocean had declared war on me. The only thing I had
to defend myself with was a single bullet. I staked out the complex
for a few hours, watching everyone who came and went before I even
dared approach the building.

Two minutes.

It was all the time I would allow myself to gather everything I
needed.

When I entered the apartment, I looked around expecting to
see it ransacked or someone inside waiting for me, but it was just as
I left it. Still, I took my time clearing every room, door, and corner
before I allowed myself to breathe.

And then I went into my room and started loading all the guns,
clothes, and bullets as I could into a pink duffel bag. I left the apartment as quickly and quietly as I'd arrived and jogged down the stairs.

I slinked through the breezeway until I reached the back of the
building, where Deborah was parked in her usual spot by the pond.
That was my first mistake, but a night spent shivering in my sleep inside my cold car left me anything but on top of my game.

Reaching Deb unscathed, I threw my duffel bag across the console and into the passenger seat and quickly dropped into the driver's

seat. It was only after I jammed my key in the ignition, turned it, and listened to Deborah struggle to wake up that I realized my mistake.

I didn't check the backseat.

A cloud of Axe body spray and cigarette smoke drifted over my shoulder as I stared straight ahead in horror. Snapping out of it, I dove for my gun, but the intruder was faster.

A long arm encased in leather whipped out from the backseat where he had hidden and wrapped around my neck in a brutal hold that had me gasping for air in seconds. The second arm joined the first when I struggled, putting pressure on my carotid and pinning me to the seat.

"You should have known better than to think you were getting away from me that easily," a familiar voice whispered.

Fucking Kellan.

I gurgled obscenities as I struggled, but his hold was too secure, and none of the rigorous defense training I'd put myself through over the years could slow the fog creeping in from the edges of my vision.

I'd be conscious again in less than a minute, but it didn't matter. It was time enough for Kellan to incapacitate me permanently if he wanted.

Stop panicking, I scolded. *Think.*

My door was suddenly snatched open before I could form a plan, and a man I didn't recognize in a simple black suit and chauffeur's cap crouched next to me. My eyes met his apologetic ones briefly before widening at the sight of the long needle the older man used his teeth to uncap.

Kellan's arms loosened only enough to keep me conscious while ensuring my flailing body remained secured. "Do it," he snapped at the older man.

It didn't matter how sorry he was. The driver made a decision and leaned forward to follow orders, so I hawked and spit in his face before he could stick me in the arm.

Using their mutual horror to my advantage, I surged forward

before Kellan had a chance to tighten his hold again, and then, shifting the gear into reverse, I slammed my foot on the gas.

The chauffeur's shout of surprise was cut short when he was knocked over, Deborah's front left tire narrowly missing his head.

Pity.

I kept my foot on the pedal as the car shot across the small parking lot, and then I felt Kellan shift as he turned to peer over his shoulder.

"Oh, fuck," he whispered. Fright had his arms slackening a little more when he saw where we were headed. A large and seemingly bottomless pond was nestled between the parking lot and the small grouping of trees. "Stop the car!" he screamed. I kept going. "Hunter, for fuck's sake, stop!"

Ignoring him, I turned my head and sank my teeth into his bicep, digging into the skin until I tasted blood.

Cursing, Kellan was forced to let me go, and I risked precious seconds waiting for the right moment. I'm sure Kellan had the same idea, but he'd made one mistake.

Deborah was a two-door.

Kellan had allowed himself to be trapped in the backseat with nowhere to go.

Finally, concrete gave way to grass and dirt as I twisted in my seat. With the only second that I had to spare, my determined gaze collided with Kellan's shocked one, and I smiled.

Adios, asshole.

I threw myself from the car just as Deborah sped over the grassy knoll.

My back, thankfully, absorbed most of the impact with the ground as I allowed my body to roll across the grass. When I finally lost momentum enough to stop, I looked up just as Deborah cleared the small hill and plunged into the pond.

I was frozen momentarily as I watched thousands of pounds of water rush inside the open door and Deborah quickly sink beneath the surface. My mouth parted in a silent scream, and tears I hadn't shed in a long time spilled from my eyes when I realized what I'd done.

After I was released from juvie for putting my father in the hospital, I'd found Deborah all alone with a sign stuck in her window that said one word…

Worthless.

Someone too stupid to see her value had abandoned her—just as I'd been.

Homeless and penniless, I tracked down the shady owner and bartered my body and a small piece of my soul in exchange for her.

Why?

Because like recognizes like. Deborah had called to me.

I couldn't explain why or how, but if I believed in fate, I might think it had been for this moment.

Saving my life.

Saving *Coby's* life.

Thunderbirds represented protection, and she had been exactly that for me. My home, my shelter, and salvation.

That car was all I'd had before Coby came along, and in one desperate move, I'd sacrificed her without a thought.

Deb…I'm so sorry.

Gritting my teeth at the pain in my leg, I forced myself to my feet. Instinct told me that Kellan was just the first of the onslaught headed my way, and once again, I had nothing but a single bullet I'd carve Ocean's name into.

Assuming he could swim, I knew Kellan wouldn't be trapped for long, so I charged across the parking lot like vengeance itself.

When my shadow fell over the nameless driver crawling onto the sidewalk, he looked over his shoulder, eyes widening with fear when he saw the barrel of my gun pointed at his head.

"Take me to your boss," I ordered. When he hesitated, I flipped off the safety. "Now."

I wasn't going to waste the only bullet I had on him, but he didn't need to know that.

With a grim expression, the driver nodded and slowly stood while watching me warily.

Together, we traveled back through the breezeway to the front of the building. We climbed in the Denali—he in the driver's seat and me directly behind him with the gun pressed against his side.

He cranked the SUV, but he paused to look in the rearview mirror instead of driving away. "Are you sure you want to do this, darling?"

"Drive, *darling*."

The Denali rolled forward, and I allowed myself to have a moment by resting my forehead against the back of the seat. The journey was silent, and I was perfectly content to keep quiet until I realized we were leaving the city limits.

I frowned.

"Where are you going?" I questioned, even though it was a little too late for that now.

"I'm taking you to the Boss as you requested."

The Boss. Not *his* boss.

Oh, shit.

He wasn't driving me to see Ocean. He was taking me to the very top of the food chain, where I was sure to be devoured.

Suddenly, my skin became clammy, and I wanted out. "Stop the car," I ordered anxiously.

"I can't do that, darling. You've caused enough trouble."

"You realize I have a gun aimed at your kidney, right?"

He glanced in the rearview again. "They won't do me much good if I lose my head."

"Touché, dude."

"Paul," he corrected good-naturedly. "I'm too old to be a dude."

I guess that meant there were no hard feelings about me holding him at gunpoint…and almost running him over with my car. I wouldn't apologize since he tried to drug me, so for that offense, I'd say we were *almost* even.

Seeing that we were entering a heavily wooded area with no

other traffic, I raised the gun and brought the butt down on his head. Paul slumped in his seat as I dove for the steering wheel to keep the SUV from leaving the road.

Now we were even.

All I could do was steer through as we swerved the empty road at high speed. His leg was deadweight on the gas pedal, so I had to crawl over the unconscious man to engage the emergency brake.

I felt triumphant when we started to slow until I realized it wouldn't be in time to avoid the deer that just leaped out of nowhere.

Today was truly not my day, but little did I know, the next few days would be even harder.

CHAPTER TWENTY

HUNTER

One week later...

A STORM HAD BLOWN IN.

With no other options after days on the run, I was forced to take shelter in the second-to-last place I hoped to never see again. I stood on the sidewalk staring up at the brick two-story home with an overgrown tree in the front yard and an empty driveway.

Roshaun had inherited it from his parents after they died, and according to his social media, he was currently out celebrating his second chance at life. Knowing him, he wouldn't be back until morning, so here I was trudging up his driveway through two feet of snow.

At least he still kept the spare key where his parents had kept it.

Injured and hopeless after countless near escapes, I didn't make it further than a few limping steps from the front door before I collapsed in the entryway with the wind, snow, and cold blowing in.

I didn't have the strength to get up and close the door, so I used the last of it to pull the stolen burner phone from my pocket, which I was still clinging to like a lifeline. I knew the reason. It was my only connection to Coby because it was the only connection I had to *him*.

And that's why, when I passed out, I did so with it cradled in my palm.

When I woke up hours later, it was with the startling knowledge that I wasn't alone. I was lying on the couch with a blanket tossed over me, and the house was quiet and warm. My eyes drifted around the room until they landed on the armchair near the couch with the last person I wanted to see sitting in it. Through the window behind him, the sun was setting.

God, I'd slept all day.

"You're up. Good," he said, sounding relieved when he noticed me. "I thought yo' ass was dying."

"What the fuck?" I croaked as I fought off my grogginess and sat up. "What are you doing here?"

Roshaun gave me a blank look. "It's my crib, Hunter. I should be asking you that." He stood before I could come up with an answer and left the room. When he returned, he was carrying a bottle of water and tried to hand it to me. I hadn't had a drop of water in two days, but his offering—like all the others—more than likely came with a hidden price.

"Thanks, but I need to go." Panic suddenly speared my chest when I realized I didn't have the burner phone anymore. I started frantically searching the couch until I found it wedged between two cushions and sighed. Roshaun was staring at me like I'd lost my mind. "I need it to find Coby," I explained.

Roshaun took a seat on the coffee table in front of me, and it was all I could do not to move away and give him the satisfaction. "Why?" He sounded genuinely curious, as if it wasn't his sister in bed with the mob.

"Why?" I echoed incredulously. "Because she's in trouble, Roshaun. Why else?"

"My sister is gone, and she ain't coming back," he snapped like I was dumb for thinking otherwise. And then he reached his arm across the small space between us to run his hand up my thigh. "But that doesn't mean you and I can't get our shit started again."

Jerking my leg away, I snarled, "Don't fucking touch me, Roshaun."

All pretense of amity dropped from his face. "Oh, you too good for it now?"

"I was always too good for it. You were just better at taking advantage."

"Ain't nobody take advantage of you!" he roared, losing his composure.

"I was sixteen, Shaun, and you were a grown ass man, so what would you call it?"

He waved me off with a scowl, and I truly hated how much he looked like Coby, sans the copper-colored curls. His hair was a dark brown with the sides shaved into a fade. "Don't act like you were some innocent virgin. You were already fucking so what's the difference? And don't pretend you didn't enjoy it."

"The difference is you knew I'd do anything to stay with Coby, including lying down with a dirty dog."

Roshaun's features contorted with rage. "Get the fuck out!"

"*Gladly.*" Happy to have gotten under his skin, I smirked and pushed the blanket off me before rising unsteadily from the couch where he'd carried me while I was passed out—probably thinking it would earn him enough goodwill that I'd actually fuck his ass. "One of these days," I said, turning to see him glaring at my back, "Coby will see you for what you really are, and when that day comes, I'm *going* to kill you. Just thought you should know. For old times' sake."

"And what am I, Hunter? Tell me."

Scoffing, I shook my head. "It doesn't matter what I think. What matters is how Coby sees you, and right now, she still thinks you're a hero for what you did for her, but she doesn't need you anymore. She needs…" An image of a dark-eyed villain with a panty-melting smile entered my mind, and a wave of comfort unexpectedly washed over me, knowing that Coby was safe from Roshaun at least. "She needs something much darker and less forgiving than you or me." Opening the front door, I stepped out onto the porch while keeping my eyes on him. "You fucked up when you sold her to Ocean."

I closed the door behind me and, out of habit, checked the burner phone to see an unread message waiting for me.

> **Unknown: Go home, Hunter. Something precious to us both waits for you there.**

Back in the cold once more and with nothing left to lose, I started my trek back toward the center of the city—toward home and the one trap that Ocean knew I wouldn't be able to resist.

It was dark by the time I reached our building, so I used the cover to sneak inside undetected. I didn't have my key, but the door wasn't locked. It was the first spark of hope I felt in days, not because of the easy entry but because Coby always forgot to lock it.

Opening the door, I stepped inside, and the first thing I noticed was that the apartment had been cleaned. The bottles were gone, the countertops and floors glistened, and the pictures of Coby that I'd been living off of were put away.

"Coby?" I whispered with a clatter of my teeth. No answer. The walk back through the snow and ice had been brutal. In my hurry, I even slipped and hurt my knee coming up the stairs, so I was hobbling once more as I ventured deeper into the apartment.

The only light came from the living room behind me, casting the short hall in shadow as I came to stand in Coby's open bedroom door. Someone was standing in the dark in the middle of her room, but I'd recognize that petite frame and short crop of copper curls anywhere.

"It's really you," I said hoarsely, feeling my cracked lips and parched throat protest. I watched Coby spin around and startle with a yelp at my presence. I could barely hold myself up, so it was good that she didn't subscribe to the *shoot first* motto like me. "You're really here."

It was a few more seconds before Coby finally spoke, and I nearly wept at the sound of her sweet voice. "Hunter?"

CHAPTER TWENTY-ONE

HUNTER

One short day later...

THE VAN DOOR ROLLED SHUT WITH A SLAM, THEN PEELED off with a squeal of tires as it sped away from the curb. There were grunts and curses all around as what felt like a gang of dudes held me down and tied my hands around my back.

No defensive measure I attempted could ward them off in such a tight space, so before long, I was subdued and blindfolded. One of them lifted me up to sit against the wall of the van, and I didn't like the way his hands lingered before he finally released me. Everyone's face had been covered even before I was blindfolded, so I had no idea who was behind this latest attempt of many to deliver me to Ocean.

Apparently, the underboss had made it clear that he wanted me captured alive and without a scratch, which had put everyone dumb enough to come after me at a disadvantage as I escaped time and again.

But there was one trap I couldn't escape.

I knew Coby was bait, but I hadn't cared because for one short day she was mine again, and it was just as it had been before. But now she was alone, probably feeling the same crushing terror that I had when she was taken, and there was nothing I could do about it.

"So what's the plan?" I heard someone ask.

"I made contact," a muffled voice responded. "He said to sit tight. It will be a while."

"What the fuck?"

"Bro, I don't fucking know. He said something came up."

The men who snatched me talked amongst themselves. Before long, they forgot I was even here, thank God. I wasn't sure how much time passed sitting in the cold van. It felt like hours before the leader got the call and we started moving again.

The ropes tying my hands and ankles together dug painfully into my skin as I wriggled around, searching for the tiniest bit of slack. There was none. Suddenly, the blindfold was ripped off, and the man directly across from me yanked off his black ski mask. The familiar face staring back at me made my blood boil.

"Really, Gary?"

My neighbor had the nerve to look offended. "Aye, don't judge me. Half a million is a lot of money, girl." And then he smiled lewdly. "I guess your pretty ass should have fucked me when you had the chance."

"Gary, I wouldn't fuck your sorry ass if you were the last man on Earth and God promised me a spot in heaven for sleeping with the unfortunate."

"You got a lot of mouth for someone who's going to be dead by the end of the day."

"Funny. I was just about to say the same thing to you."

Ignoring my very real threat, he looked me up and down. "So what did you do anyway?"

With a straight face, I answered with a smile. "I stole a rocket launcher from his warehouse, blew up his men, killed the rest, and stole his girl." That last part hurt to admit, but after what Coby told me, I'd be a fool to deny it. Coby was Ocean's, and it was all my fault. I should never have lied to her two years ago, telling her we had no chance. Finding comfort in my rage, I smiled sharply at Gary. "But that's nothing compared to what I'll do to you."

Gary's eyes widened while his boys shifted nervously.

"Whoa, wait a minute, wait a minute," Gary said after a short silence. He leaned forward and stared at me like I had grown two heads and he'd never seen me before. "You're *gay?*"

It's like he hadn't heard a single thing else I said.

Rolling my eyes, I turned my head and refused to answer. No, I wasn't gay. It wasn't nearly that simple. Sure, I liked dick, but I loved Coby even more. My heart didn't care that she was without my favorite appendage. It craved her anyway. End of story.

Unperturbed by my silence, Gary suddenly grinned and relaxed against the side of the van. "I guess that explains why you wouldn't fuck me, huh?"

"No, Gary. Evolution explains why I wouldn't fuck you."

His smile fell while snickering erupted around the back of the van. A moment later, he slapped fire out of my ass, and the van suddenly became quiet.

"Gary, you better hope that shit doesn't leave a mark, man!" one of his partners scolded once the initial shock wore off. Cryptically, he added, "You know what happened to Terrance and 'nem."

The masked goon was referring to the last crew that tried to snatch me. Terrance had lost his composure like Gary and kicked me in the ribs. I guess word had gotten back to Ocean somehow.

Huh…

Another one of Gary's masked friends spoke next. "Man, I heard they're still finding Terrance's body parts all over the city." And then he stared at me with something like pity in his eyes. "No one touches her again. The crazy motherfucker who wants her ain't fucking around."

We rode in silence for over an hour before the driver called out from the front. "Look alive! We're almost there."

There was shuffling as everyone got ready, their eyes eager to collect their reward.

"Aye," Gary whispered after sliding across the van to sit next to me. "This is your last chance. Say you'll fuck with me, and I'll turn this van around right now. I'll just tell Kilpatrick that you got away."

Inhaling deeply, I pretended to think about it for a while before nod-ding faintly. Gary's eyes flared with surprise, as if he didn't believe me, so I smiled coquettishly. All doubt was erased when he slowly smiled back. "Yeah?"

"What do I have to do?" I whispered with a touch of fear to gar-nish the ruse.

"Let me kiss you."

Batting my lashes, I smiled harder and said, "Come closer."

Gary glanced around to make sure no one was looking at us be-fore he inched closer to me until our thighs were touching. I waited until his face was hovering above mine and I was breathing in his foul breath before I made my move.

Rearing my head back, I sent it crashing into Gary's nose when I brought it forward again.

"Aargh!" he yelled in pain as he fell back and clutched his ugly mug.

Without missing a beat, I scooted forward and then threw my-self on top of him to deliver another blow that made his friends freak the fuck out.

"Hey, Stop! Stop!" they screamed at me as I used Gary to bash my own face in repeatedly.

Unfortunately, Gary's weak ass couldn't even slap a bitch prop-erly. It barely stung, so I knew there was no mark for Ocean to see. Guess I'd have to make my own.

Never send a man to do a woman's job.

Hands closed around my arms and yanked me back just as the van slammed to a stop. I felt warm blood leaking from my nose when I peered through the windshield and saw nothing.

It was pitch black outside and utterly silent.

A terrified chill snaked down my spine as goosebumps prick-led my skin.

For a few haunting moments, no one moved or spoke. Suddenly, there was this blinding bright light. It flooded the cab and cargo of the van, and I tried to look away, but it didn't matter which way I turned, so I lowered my gaze to the floor when I felt the strain in my corneas.

Everyone in the van jumped when a phone started ringing.

Gary, who was still regrettably conscious, fished his phone out of his pocket and answered with the phone on speaker. "This is— this is Gary."

A familiar voice so deep and commanding that it made my pussy clench answered with a command. "Bring her to me." The call immediately ended.

Oh shit, oh shit, oh shit.

"Come on," Gary said forlornly as he cut the ties on my ankles but left the ones on my wrists before he took my arm.

None of the men who kidnapped me looked excited anymore. They were all scared shitless of facing Ocean now and for good reason. The man was unpredictable as shit.

The door slid open, and I couldn't see shit as I climbed out of the van. The moment I was out in the open and completely exposed, all the headlights surrounding us shut off simultaneously.

I blinked to clear my vision until I could make out the outline of fifteen vehicles surrounding the van. There were even larger off-road pickups parked in the trees, too.

I had never seen anything like it except in movies. Ocean had obviously been prepared to give chase in case I had somehow escaped him again.

Now I was the one pissing my panties.

I was too consumed by vengeance before to believe it, but it was clear to me now that I was dealing with a man used to thinking two steps ahead of his opponents.

Suddenly, a freakishly tall figure broke rank from the others waiting by their vehicles and swaggered forward. The closer he got, the bigger he seemed. He wasn't overly bulky, but he clearly spent a lot of time in the gym. If the situation weren't dire, I'd roll my eyes at the idea of suffering the company of another gym rat. Coby's obsession with fitness was enough, thank you.

With no choice but to wait, I forced myself not to fidget as my heart sped up with every step that brought him closer.

It wasn't fear. It was anticipation.

I was once again coming face to face with Coby's kidnapper, but this time our roles had reversed.

I held my breath until it felt like it would burst, and I exhaled. Only then did the shadows clinging to the underboss's features finally part, revealing his handsome face.

I probably wouldn't be alive to remember this moment later, so there was no shame awaiting me later for the tiny step I took backward. It had been a while since I last felt it, but I still remembered what fear tasted like.

Finally, he stopped walking just a few feet away.

"Hello, Hunter." Ocean's gaze roved my face before he rolled his shoulders to shake off the promise of violence that flashed across his features. "Who did this to you?" I said nothing. I just held his dark gaze and let him come to a conclusion on his own. "Well, that's unfortunate because I made a promise." A moment later, Ocean once again lived up to his reputation when he coldly ordered, "Kill them."

"Whoa, whoa, wait!" Gary pleaded as Ocean's men raised their guns. "I swear this wasn't us! She did that to herself! Hunter!" He then shifted to stare down at me pleadingly. "*Tell* him."

"Bye, Gary."

"No, wait! It was her!" One of my kidnappers threw an accusing finger at me while another tried to run.

Ocean's men started firing.

Also in the line of fire, which I suspected was by design, I closed my eyes and waited for my turn. For the bullet with my name on it to come. On either side of me, I listened to Gary and his boys scream as the bullets tore through them—some even hitting the van behind us. They never even had a chance to pull their guns.

Numbness eventually washed over me as I waited and waited and waited. I waited so long I didn't even notice when the firing ended, and it was dead silent again. My eyes flew open, and there was Ocean, staring at me like he found me amusing.

I narrowed my gaze, and he stepped forward.

I didn't notice the black duffel bag he was carrying in one hand until he dropped it in the pool of blood quickly gathering near the bodies. My brows dipped in question when I spotted multiple bands of cash inside and realized belatedly what it was—the promised reward.

Five hundred thousand dollars in cash.

To deliver me unharmed.

Gary's unseeing eyes stared at me from the ground.

"I believe his mother lives in Renwood," Ocean announced as he turned to me with his stern gaze locked on my face. "Someone make sure the money gets to her."

I swallowed.

Yeah, I lied, so what? *Fuck* Gary.

Ocean had obviously known it and decided to kill them anyway. Neither of us had the moral high ground as far as I was concerned. Not even dead-as-hell Gary.

Ocean shifted and moved over to stand in front of me, the tips of his boots meeting mine. All too soon, I was drowning in him. I could smell the mint on his breath, the spice in his cologne, and a familiar hint of sugar and tartness clinging to his clothes. It didn't take me long to identify the familiar and yet out-of-place scent.

Green apples.

I was smelling Coby's perfume.

The scent was strong as if he'd been exposed...recently.

Before I could remind myself why attacking the underboss of the Fola wasn't wise, my rage swiftly returned, rising high and crashing into me like a tsunami wave until all I knew was the name he'd called me earlier. What was it again?

Oh, yeah...

Vengeance.

Snatching my knife from the hidden sheath by my hip, I lunged.

ACT III

THE GROOM

CHAPTER TWENTY-TWO

COBY

A few hours before…

WITH NO IDEA WHO TOOK HER, I WENT TO THE ONLY person who could get her back.

Wayne, the doorman at Glainne, tried to stop me at the door, but I managed to convince him with a knife to his throat. Hunter's idea of a Christmas present had finally come in handy. The receptionist had taken one look at me and reached for the phone. Somehow, I knew he wasn't calling the police, so I kicked the back of Wayne's leg to make him kneel and waited.

I'm sure the scene I'd caused in the lobby was a sight to behold when Ocean finally stepped off the private elevator to see me with his doorman on his knees and me crying uncontrollably like a lunatic. That knife at Wayne's throat shook in my grip, cutting him a little in the process.

Ocean observed it all with the casualness of someone watching a bird drop a deuce. "This is a surprise. How can I help you, Coby?"

"What did you do?" I demanded. All the betrayal I felt curdling in my gut was reflected in my voice.

"Coby, drop the knife."

"Someone took Hunter," I told him desperately.

Ocean repeated his command as if I hadn't spoken. The attentive man I'd grown used to was nowhere to be found. "*Drop…*" He stepped forward, and I inhaled sharply. "The knife. I won't ask you again."

Forcing my fingers to relax, the knife fell from my hand and clattered on the marble floor. A moment later, I was engulfed in Ocean's strong arms as he wrapped them around me and attempted to console me.

For a moment, I forgot why I came.

"Ocean," I sobbed his name as I came to my senses and pulled away. I tugged on his shirt, attempting to pull him to the door. "Please, you h-have to h-help h-her."

"Coby, calm down, *mo aingeal*."

"No! Don't tell me to calm down!" Unable to force him out the door, I turned and started shoving at his chest. "This is your fault! You did this!"

"And I'll fix it, but first, I have to take care of you. Come here." Before I could say no, Ocean lifted me into his arms and then carried me into the elevator. Already, I could feel my muscles relaxing and exhaustion creeping in. "Hush," he soothed when I fought off sleep to beg him some more. "I'll get her back. No harm will come to Hunter. Not even a scratch. You have my word."

Believing him because I had no other choice if I wanted to see Hunter again, I closed my eyes and allowed my mind to settle as the elevator descended into the underground garage.

CHAPTER TWENTY-THREE

OCEAN

TEMPTRESS.

She was a restless soul.

Hunter stayed in the streets like it was a second home. I knew she kept company with thieves, hitters, and corner boys— some of the worst in Black Veil. And she did it without any regard for the danger she courted. No longer just pixels in a photo but flesh and blood, Hunter stood before me now with murder in her eyes.

I should have seen the blade coming before it was inches from my heart, but her aura was a distraction that nearly cost me. At the last moment, I grabbed Hunter's wrist before she could plunge the hunting knife between my rib cage and quickly disarmed her.

She cried out her frustration and anger when the knife clattered to the asphalt. I gripped her fingers, pushing her hand into her face and transferring my hold to her thumb, and then I grabbed her elbow before shoving it down until it forced her back to bend into a ninety-degree angle with her face toward the ground.

"Let me—"

I locked my elbow to apply pressure to her wrist until it cinched, and she screamed. "Go?" I finished for her. Hunter focused on controlling her breathing rather than responding. "You're Coby's friend. I'm sure you mean a lot to her, which means I'd prefer it if I didn't hurt you and upset her."

Hunter renewed her struggle at hearing Coby's name, which only made her cry out in pain when she realized my hold was unbreakable. Moving my grip from her wrist to her arm, I grabbed her nape before she hurt herself.

Forcing the front of her body over the hood of the van, I locked her arm behind her back before planting the hand that held her neck next to her head. Once my hold was secure again, I leaned forward until my lips brushed her ear, and that delectably round ass was nestled right against my dick. "Are you going to make me hurt you, Hunter?""

"You'll never get the chance," she threatened while trying to wrestle free. "I'm going to make you bleed."

All she managed to achieve was making me hard.

"Cut it the fuck out," I commanded as I drove her arm upward. She whimpered. Liking the sound, my dick jumped in my jeans, so I took a deep breath to keep my mind off getting into hers. *Down, boy.* "As thrilling as chasing you has been, I've had enough. I'm tired and have something warm waiting for me in my bed."

Knowing exactly who I meant, Hunter growled. "She said you let her go—"

"I did no such thing. That would only ruin my plans."

Hunter huffed and shook her head. "Then you lied to her," she accused.

I studied Hunter before I coldly replied, "And now she knows how it feels."

She laughed right in my face, and all I could think was that if all I had was that sound and Coby's smile for the rest of my life, I would never want for another fucking thing. "If that's true, then I can promise you're not getting any sleep tonight unless you can do it with one eye open."

I'd feared as much.

These women were going to ruin me.

I couldn't remember the last time I had to work this hard to win. The game had started long before Coby or Hunter even knew, the board meticulously set, but within a few weeks, I was already questioning if I'd made a grave miscalculation.

My plan for choosing a bride had been simple: take one with everything to lose or one with nothing.

In a bizarre twist of fate, Coby Perry had been both.

Extorting her hand in marriage wasn't my first choice. It was insurance. I couldn't have her backing out later once I won her over. In the meantime, I'd make her fall so hard for me—make it feel so real—that she forgot about how we came to be. Until nothing else mattered.

But I hadn't counted on Hunter.

Their bond.

Their…affection…for one another.

But I could offer Coby more than just my heat. I could give her status, wealth, and protection. All things she was sorely lacking.

My thoughts were interrupted by an explosion of pain when the girl trapped in my hold drove her foot into my shin.

Almost as if Hunter had read my mind and sought to prove me wrong.

Her message was clear.

Coby had a champion. Someone willing to wage war against the *Fola*—against *me*—for her.

It was admirable but foolish. Hunter would eventually lose, and Coby would still belong to me.

As amused and impressed as I was by Hunter Parrish, I didn't like loose ends. I'd been prepared to leave her be—if only to keep my new bride happily chained to me—but she'd forced my hand by coming after me.

"Why didn't you take the money?" I asked. The answer to that question had been plaguing me ever since Kellan told me she turned it down.

Hunter stopped fighting me as if I'd surprised her. "What?"

"The money Kellan offered you. Why didn't you take it?"

"Because there's no amount you could offer to make me give up my best friend."

"It was two million," I stated flatly.

Hunter let out a laugh that sounded both condescending and hysterical. "Then you clearly don't know Coby."

I didn't respond as I quickly checked her for more weapons before releasing her. Abel had already moved closer after Hunter's misguided attack, and I knew I'd have to listen to him bitch about the close call later.

"Explain," I ordered once she was facing me.

If looks could kill…

Her pretty ass wanted to finish me off so bad. I don't think she ever wanted anything more.

Hunter was smart enough to know she'd reach the end of my forgiving nature.

I mean…it's not like I needed a second wife.

Hunter sighed and said, "She's my best friend."

I guess that was all the explanation she felt compelled to give.

"You can buy new friends."

Hunter shook her head. "Not like her."

I just stared at her. I might have given Hunter too much credit. She was more naive than I thought.

"I disagree," I told her. "Anyone can be bought when you have the world to offer."

"Speak for yourself, asshole. I'm priceless."

I smiled widely. "I'm starting to understand that." I began circling her and laughed to myself when she turned with me, keeping me within her sight always. "But money isn't the only currency, so tell me your price."

Hunter blinked. "What?"

"Tell me how much it will take to make you go away and forget Coby Perry ever existed."

There was nothing but silence between us for several moments.

"All right," she said eventually and then folded her arms. "Eat a dick."

Stopping in front of her again, I turned my head to the side and cupped my ear. "Run that back?"

Hunter batted her false lashes innocently. "Eat a dick," she repeated, "and I'll let you have my friend."

I said nothing as I let my gaze roam her face and those arresting eyes one last time.

So tempting.

And an utter waste.

"Have it your way, Vengeance." I held her gaze as I backed away and lifted my hand.

My men immediately took aim.

She'd never even noticed them closing in and forming a kill circle while we spoke. As one, they tightened their ranks until Hunter had nowhere to run. Their grim faces would be the last thing Hunter Parrish would ever see.

Suddenly, I felt a wave of anxiety as I forced myself to walk away from her. *Come on*, I silently begged her. *You're smarter than that.*

Two of my men had just parted to let me through when I heard, "Wait."

My chest felt like it had caved from all the relief rushing in. I let none of it show as I paused at the circle's edge and turned to face her. "Yes, Hunter?"

"I-I can work for you."

Now, why did this sound familiar? "I'm sorry, Vengeance. All positions have been filled."

"You wouldn't have to pay me," she rushed to add. "Just let me be with Coby." Remembering at the last moment to play the part, I turned to go without a word, adding to Hunter's desperation. "She'll never forgive you!"

"She'll never know," I returned. *But she could*, my paranoia warned.

"Coby is smarter than you think," Hunter argued. "She's smarter than you and me. She'll figure it out."

I barked a laugh so loud it startled the birds in the trees. They flew from their perch, where they had no doubt been watching the drama unfold. I was still laughing when I turned to face Hunter. "You mean the same way she figured out that her brother sold her to me?"

Hunter balked. "What?" I just held her gaze. Hunter eventually saw the truth in my eyes and swore. "That grimy piece of shit!" Her eyes were wild as she started to pace, seemingly forgetting about the guns pointed at her. "I should have killed him a long time ago," she mumbled. *I couldn't agree more.* I didn't realize I'd fallen into a trance watching her prowl like a caged lioness until she suddenly whirled on me. "Well?"

I blinked. "Well, what?"

Hunter's gaze narrowed as she shifted her weight to one leg. "What are you planning to do about it?"

"I'm going to kill him, of course. When I'm ready."

Her eyes widened—with surprise or glee, I didn't know. Maybe both. "I can help you."

"I don't need your help."

"You will if you want Coby to forgive you after."

I paused to consider that and felt Abel's agitation the moment I did. I already knew he thought killing Hunter was the safest move, and this was coming from a man who despised offing women. That was how far Hunter had pushed us. "I don't need to convince her," I decided after a while. "She'll do what I say and think what I tell her."

It was Hunter's turn to howl obnoxiously.

"Oh, my God." She cackled as she bent and braced one hand on her knee while wiping a tear from her eye with the other. It took everything in me not to smile along with her. "Forget not being ready to die. I just want to live so I can be there when you tell her that."

Losing the battle, my lips turned up at the corner as I watched her.

The shadows in her eyes had cleared a little, and in that moment, Hunter looked younger. Supple. Pliable.

Mine.

Fuck.

Done with this game, I reached for my coat pocket. There was no going back now. A decision had been made. I pulled free the rope I'd hidden inside and started toward Hunter.

Abel swore.

Noticing, Hunter rose to her full height and eyed me warily as she backed away.

"Turn around and put your arms behind your back." I paused when she shook her head. "Or die, Hunter. Those are your choices."

She stopped backing away, but her stubborn ass still felt the need to make me wait as she considered whether or not to obey after bargaining beautifully for her life just moments ago.

The tension coiling around my muscles and my patience eased when Hunter slowly turned and stayed still for me while I used the rope to tie her wrists. I didn't miss the raw skin that was already there, and if I could, I'd kill the men who brought her to me a second time.

Once she was bound, Abel gave the signal, and my men all lowered their guns. I pulled the knot to check that it was secure and then used the rope to yank her into me until her back was flush with my chest.

"Don't make me regret this," I quietly warned in her ear. Her jasmine scent was earthy, whereas Coby's was sweet. I wanted to bathe in them both, but I knew better than to say so.

Hunter turned her head and flashed a smile filled with the promise of violence. "Not even a little?"

I didn't respond as I pulled free the other item I was hiding in my pocket. "Open your mouth." She didn't hesitate this time, probably to tell me to fuck off, so I quickly shoved the red ball between her lips and then quickly buckled the black leather straps behind her head before she could get over her shock of being gagged. "Keep testing me, and I'll spank that ass black and blue," I warned.

Hunter's eyes widened.

Smirking, I gently turned her around. And then, to her surprise and mine, I bent and lifted her over my shoulder.

I left Abel to issue orders to the men as I carried her to the Denali.

Paul was at home recovering from his run-in with Hunter. Apparently, she knocked him out while he was driving. When he woke up, he found himself alone inside the totaled Denali with nothing to explain what had happened except the dead deer in the road.

Hunter was chaos.

She was violence and vengeance.

And now...she was mine.

Kellan, who was filling in for Paul, held the back door open for us while grinning at Hunter, who merely rolled her eyes at discovering he was still alive after trying to drown him.

I shifted my hold on Hunter before climbing in. Once settled, I pushed her to sit between my legs on the floor. Trapped between the back of the front passenger seat and me, there was nowhere for her to go unless she wanted to sit in my lap. Kellan hopped into the driver's seat, and then we were off.

I didn't realize I was keeping track of how much time had passed until ten minutes into the drive when Hunter finally capitulated and rested her cheek on my inner thigh to ease the strain in her neck.

I couldn't remember exactly when I reached out for her, but before long, I was playing with the end of her long braid as I stared out the window, trying to figure out what I'd done.... My gaze shifted away from the window and down to Hunter.

And what I was going do now.

We didn't go back to the city—back to Glainne. Instead, we headed north, where none of us would be safe. I took Hunter with me to Glamis.

Hunter perked from her doze on my lap when she felt the shift from paved road to dirt and the Denali slowing. Forgetting she was bound, she shifted to rise onto her knees and see where we were, but I wrapped her braid around one hand, yanking her head back and keeping her eyes on me while I pulled a scrap of silk from my pocket with the other.

Her eyes flashed with hatred, but her nipples...the way they pushed against her sweater told a different story. The other half of the truth. Hunter wanted to kill me, but she craved what I could do to her just as much.

"You must be wondering why this is happening," I said as I let her hair go and tied the blindfold around her eyes. Hunter didn't make a sound, but I knew she was listening. "You're wondering what Coby could have done to earn my attention. If she'd been keeping secrets from you." I finished tying the blindfold as Kellan drove us around the main house overlooking the lake. "The answer is simple, if not at all conventional. Your friend intrigued me, Hunter, and that doesn't happen often. I never intended to act on it, but when I encountered an obstacle, I could think of no one else to help me get around it. Maybe it's love," I mused, just to fuck with her. Hunter's eyes flared with alarm when my comment hit its mark. "Whatever it is, I can't shake it." I grew quiet as Kellan carefully steered us through the thicker part of the foliage, driving us deeper into the property and away from the main house. "And now, here you are—stubborn and steadfast like a rock forcing the river to go around it. You're in my way, Hunter Parrish."

The small cabin, the first home my great-grandfather had built after he immigrated to America, finally appeared.

"Fortunately for you, you intrigue me, too. It's... distracting. But you and I need to get some shit understood, Hunter. Coby is mine. Her heart is mine. Her loyalty is mine." Leaning down, I brushed my lips against her forehead, cheeks, and chin. The only part of Hunter's lovely face that was still bared to me. "Her pussy is mine too," I whispered in her ear. "And I don't share. If you'd like to keep breathing, make sure you remember that."

Hunter made a sound then, but her muffled screams went ignored as the Denali stopped in front of the cabin. It was treated like sacred ground, so we hadn't used it in years—not even as a guest house.

That was all about to change.

"Welcome home, Hunter."

"Are you fucking kidding me!" Abel shouted as he followed me through the main house an hour later.

I rubbed my throbbing temples and sighed. "What?"

"Quit playing with me, Ocean. You'd already brought that rope and gag, so tell me the truth. When did you decide to take her?"

"Does it matter?"

"Was it worth it?" he shot back.

I didn't answer since that remained to be seen, but God, I hoped so. I wasn't sure what I wanted from Hunter, but she wasn't going anywhere until I figured it out.

I turned down the hallway that led to my suite of rooms with Abel still on my heels, so I stopped in my tracks before I reached the door and kept my voice low just in case Coby had awakened.

"Put men on Hunter's guard detail, but only ones you trust, and keep their shift rotation sporadic so she doesn't learn their routine."

"This shit is crazy." Abel huffed with his hands on his head as he eyed me like he didn't know who I was anymore. He was probably onto something because I wasn't so sure either. "You don't think you're being a little greedy?"

"Last I checked, I was the one paying you, not the other way around. I give the orders, and you follow them. If you can't understand that, maybe I should find someone who will."

"Well, don't come crying to me when your fiancée finds out, or one of them kills yo' ass." Dropping his arms and shaking his head, Abel spun around without another word and stormed off.

He was probably right, but I couldn't see myself letting either of them go or worse—choosing between them. I wasn't dumb enough to think the choice would be up to me anyway.

Reaching the double doors of my suite, I pulled a black key card from my pocket—similar to the ones I used at Glainne—and scanned it before pushing inside the dark room.

My eyes immediately went to the Alaskan king, expecting to find the bed occupied, but it was empty, so I followed the sound of running water.

There was light pouring in from under the closed bathroom door.

I was still torn between giving Coby privacy and interrupting to settle my own peace of mind when I heard a faint sound behind me.

Exhaustion had slowed my reflexes.

Something heavy crashed over my head. Pain erupted through my skull as I went down. My knees hit the carpet, and the base of the lamp landed next to me with a thud.

I reached back and touched the spot on my head where I'd been hit and felt blood.

A soft gasp came from behind me when Coby realized she hadn't succeeded in knocking me out, and then I heard hurried footsteps retreating from the bedroom.

Coby was halfway down the hall when I finally shook off my disorientation and rose to my feet. I staggered out of the bedroom just as she reached the end of the corridor. I started to call out to her when Coby ran into the open to turn down another hall, but then Abel appeared out of nowhere, catching her around the waist and lifting my fleeing fiancée off her feet.

"You bitch ass dick-sucking cunt! Let me go!" Her short legs were flailing wildly, and she even managed to knee Abel in the stomach, making him grunt before he threw her over his shoulder.

"Is this a good time to remind you why you keep me around?" Abel shouted as I approached. "We both know you left her alone too long to chase the other one. I figured her ass was plotting, so I stuck around." A smug grin took over Abel's scarred face. "I guess that means you should listen to me more."

"I thought you were going to let them kill me?" I took Coby from him, and as soon as her back was to my chest, she kicked out at Abel, which he narrowly dodged. I tightened my arm around her waist until all the breath left her and she piped the fuck down.

"Yeah, well, I can't get paid if you're dead, and I'd rather not work for your damn daddy." Abel left without another word.

I peered around the corner to ensure we were alone this time before wrapping my free hand around Coby's throat and shifting her until she faced me. I drove her back into the wall hard enough to rattle the framed art above us.

"My patience is running thin, Coby." She pursed her lips to spit in my face, but I clapped my other hand over her mouth just in time. "If you won't at least behave for your brother's sake, I'll have to assume he's no good to me and pay him a visit. Is that what you want?"

Coby's eyes flared wide and then filled with unshed tears before she shook her head no.

"Good girl."

Coby sniffled and then stared up at me. "Did you find Hunter?" Slowly, I nodded but didn't offer more information than that. I should have known it wouldn't be enough for Coby. "And? Where is she?"

"Home," I answered carefully because I didn't want to lie to my wife. "Safe and sound. All tucked in."

Coby visibly relaxed against the wall. We stood like that for a full minute before she began looking at me warily. "Why am I here, Ocean?"

"My father is in Ireland dealing with a family dispute. He'll be gone for a few weeks."

"No," she said with a shake of her head. "Why am I *here*... with you?" She bit her bottom lip.

"Because you are my wife," I stated simply. "Or at least you will be soon."

"Are you still going to kill Hunter?"

"Not unless she gives me a reason, Coby."

It was incredibly telling that my answer wasn't very assuring to Coby. Hunter was never going to give up fighting to be reunited with Coby, and my bride-to-be didn't seem any closer to letting go of Hunter either. These two were making it harder and harder for me to do the honorable thing and keep my hands to my fucking self.

I didn't know if they were just committed to the lie that they were only friends or in denial, but I wondered how much longer I could resist calling them both out on it.

"Come on," I said when it began to look like Coby would pass out from exhaustion right here. "Let's get you to bed. You need the rest. You have a big day tomorrow."

"What's happening tomorrow?" she asked with a confused frown aimed up at me.

Staring straight ahead, I ushered into my room. "You're meeting my mother."

CHAPTER TWENTY-FOUR

COBY

OCEAN HADN'T PUT ME TO BED. HE SAID I WAS WELCOME to sleep, but how could I?

The muscles in my arms gave another spasm when I shifted to ease the crick in my neck. I caught my sob before it could escape, refusing to give that sadistic fuck the satisfaction. I noticed the rings in the ceiling and thought they were strange, but I hadn't given them much thought. And then last night, Ocean made me regret it when he showed me what they were for.

After announcing that I would be meeting his mother today, he stripped me naked and bound my wrists together, leaving little slack in the ropes. If I sat back with my butt on my heels, they stretched my arms so tightly I thought they'd snap. My only relief was if I rose onto my knees, a pose I could never hold for long.

It had been a long day and an even longer night.

And now my inner thighs were soaked. My pussy wept from going so long with no relief. All the while, Ocean had slept soundly in his big comfy bed. He'd woken ten minutes ago and disappeared inside the bathroom to shower.

Not for the first time, I wondered what Hunter was doing.

She was safe now.

It was all that mattered.

And now she knew I was safe too. In good—if not slightly

tormenting—hands. I just prayed it would be enough for Hunter. That she wouldn't try to find me again. Hunter was fearless and could take care of herself, but she couldn't take on the Blood mafia alone.

I could do this.

I could marry Ocean and try to be happy, and then in five years, divorce him and try to move on with my life—with Hunter.

I didn't realize the water had shut off until the bathroom door opened and steam poured out. Ocean waltzed into the bedroom with only a towel wrapped around his narrow waist. He was built like he'd been carved from marble. Water glistened on his dark-brown pecs and dripped between the ridges in his stomach as he moved into the walk-in closet. A few minutes later, he emerged dressed in black joggers with white stripes down the side that accentuated his muscular ass and legs, and a hooded pullover. Only his large feet remained bare.

I held his gaze as he crossed the room to tower over me. My stomach dipped with anticipation when he reached out and seized my chin and jaw between the V of his pointer and thumb.

"Are you sorry?"

No. I would do it all again for Hunter. My arms spasmed again—a reminder of the hours I'd spent with them trussed up like an ornament. "Yes."

Ocean gave me a small smile at my blatant lie. His thumb swept my bottom lip affectionately before letting my face go. He then started on the knot binding me and worked it free. The rope fell away, and my weakened arms collapsed to my lap. I winced when my shoulders protested the movement.

"What do you say?" he prompted.

"Thank you for helping me see that I was bad," I recited. We'd rehearsed it last night before he went to bed and left me here. *Fucker.*

"You're welcome, sweetheart."

Ocean helped me stand, just as there was a knock on the door. He grabbed the blue throw from the foot of the bed and used it to cover my naked body. His room at Glamis was a lot like the one at

Glainne—dark, masculine, cavernous, and opulent. The only real difference was the high ceiling with its exposed wooden beams.

Ocean went to open the door. It was Abel, but he spoke too low for me to catch more than bits and pieces.

"…got out."

"Injured two of the men…"

"…back in the cabin."

"Wants to talk to you…"

I could see the muscles in Ocean's jaw tick as he listened. When Abel was done with his report, Ocean rolled those powerful shoulders like he had last night when I pushed him too far.

"She'll have to wait," Ocean replied, making my heart stop. She? "I'm taking my fiancée on a date."

Abel looked at me then, so I flipped him off with a smile. Ever the grump, he shook his head as he turned and left. Ocean had already closed the door and was walking toward it when the plans he shared with Abel finally registered.

"We're going on a date? I thought I was meeting your mom today."

"You're having lunch with her on the terrace after."

"Oh…okay." Nervous butterflies flitted around my stomach as I gripped the blanket tighter and followed him into the bathroom. My eyes went straight to the enormous sunken tub I'd internally squealed over last night. Knowing I preferred soaking to showers, Ocean had already filled it with water and bubble bath that smelled divine. "You know, for a psycho, you're incredibly sweet and generous."

"Whatever I am, I'm yours," Ocean said as he turned and forced my fingers to let go of the blanket. I don't know why I was shy around him all of a sudden. I guess it was because we sort of broke up, even though it only lasted a day, and now we were back together. "Till death do us part, Coby Perry."

The blanket fell to the floor, and I was naked once again.

"We haven't said our vows yet."

"We will," Ocean promised.

It sort of sounded like a threat. A gentle reminder that he wasn't letting me go without murdering a few dozen people. Ocean kissed my knuckles before helping me inside the stone tub. Once I was sitting in the water, he did too—except he sat on the flat, wide ledge and pushed up his thick sleeves. He then grabbed one of the sponges stored in the glass container next to him.

"I know it's a bit late," I said as he dipped his hand in the warm water. "But I have one more condition for marrying you." Immediately, I sank my teeth into my bottom lip. While Ocean was incredibly patient, gentle, and generous with me, I didn't know if this latest request would send him over the edge. I didn't want him to think I was taking advantage of him, especially when our relationship only existed because my brother stole from him.

"And what's that?" Ocean didn't miss a beat as he brought the sponge to my neck and began washing my skin. Slowly and thoroughly, he made his way down. "I-I want Hunter taken care of. Everything you're offering me, I want her to have it too. For every year we're apart, I want her compensated and protected. She doesn't want for anything. Ever."

Something shifted in Ocean's gaze, his eyes becoming so molten, dark, and predatory that I stopped breathing. And then in a blink, the look was gone as if it had never been. "If that's what you want, then I promise you, *mo aingeal*, your friend will receive my full and undivided attention."

After my bubble bath, I dressed in the red athletic leggings, white cropped pullover, sports bra, panties, windbreaker, headband, gloves, and hiking boots that Ocean provided. I was starting to think of him as my own personal genie—granting all of my desires before I even knew I needed them.

I was curious and excited about our date as I followed him down one hallway after another and then out of the enormous house and into the early morning.

The cold smacked me in the face as soon as I stepped out.

Winter was weeks away, but this far north, it felt like it had come early.

I held Ocean's hand as we approached a sleek, matte-gray sports car with red calipers waiting further down the path. He opened the passenger door for me, and I went to climb in when he stopped me. Ocean stared into my eyes, and I didn't know what he was waiting for until I smiled. Satisfied, he leaned down to kiss me, and I rose onto the tips of my toes to meet him.

I guess we'd forgiven each other.

We drove for hours to reach the hiking trails.

The air was brisker, and the winds were harsher this close to the enormous lake and Canada's border.

I cut my gaze at Ocean as I followed him up the cliffside, wondering if this was more punishment for attacking him. I loved to hike (as I'd previously shared with him), but I wasn't fond of the cold—something I forgot to mention. Fortunately, the views made it a teeny tiny bit worth it.

An hour into the hike, I barely noticed the temperature.

After a few more miles of silence, Ocean led us through a break in the trees. The trail had reached a plateau bordered by trees on three sides, some of whose gold and red leaves were already decorating the ground.

My steps faltered when I saw the multicolored sandstone of the cliffs beyond. They surrounded the sparkling beaches below, and I could see more than one rushing waterfall peeking out from the gilt and ruby foliage. I'd never seen anything like it, only pictures of places like this online, but never through my own eyes.

It was breathtaking.

"I guess that look on your face means I chose correctly for our first date?"

I couldn't take my eyes away from the view to see where Ocean was, but I could feel him, and that was all that mattered. This minuscule wonder so close to home looked untouched by human corruption. Somehow, it had escaped the plague we humans wrought.

I stumbled toward the edge, and I could feel Ocean keeping close, ready to catch me if I fell from the cliff or save me from an errant rock.

"It's beautiful." Like something straight out of a painting.

"Yes. It is."

Something in his voice lured my focus away from the miraculous scenery to peer over my shoulder. While I'd been admiring the view, Ocean had been staring at me like he'd found heaven. My cheeks warmed, and I suddenly wished Hunter were here to tell me what to do. I'd never been good with boys.

But then, Ocean was all man, which was even more worrisome because I had no idea how old he was. He looked young, with no sign of aging, but his maturity gave him away.

"How old are you?" I blurted.

Ocean had fallen into a trance while staring at my lips, so it took him a second to realize I'd spoken. His gaze flew up to meet mine. "Huh?"

I giggled as the wind kicked up. "How old are you?"

"Thirty-five."

"Oh."

The corner of his lips tilted up as he raised a brow. "Is that a problem?"

"No," I told him honestly, my gaze drifting to the ground. Ocean was ten years older than me. A little more shyly, I added with a shrug, "I like it."

"You do?"

I nodded eagerly, feeling my nipples harden to painful points under my sweater. "Mhmm." I met his gaze. "You're like my dirty old man."

Ocean barked out a harsh laugh, his dimples appearing and his eyes sparkling. "Hilarious."

"Sugar daddy?"

His smile faded, the look in his eyes becoming less playful and more predatory as he cocked his head to the side. "Would you like that, sweet thing? You like the way I spoil you?"

I nodded and then rushed to clarify. "It's not the gifts and material things." I didn't want him to think I was after his money. "I just love that you make me feel..."

"Yes?" he urged when I fell silent.

"Precious."

The wind blew through the trees again before I could have the chance to feel embarrassed. The gust was strong enough to push me forward and right into Ocean's arms. My teeth started to chatter from the onslaught, so he turned us around so that his back took the brunt of it, and he became my human shield.

"Ready to go?" he asked when my entire body began to quiver.

"Not yet, please. I l-l-like it h-h-here." And I didn't know when I'd get another chance like this.

Ocean didn't seem to mind, but I still wanted to explain why I wasn't ready to leave this place that most would take for granted. "A few years ago, Hunter and I started a list of places we hoped to visit one day. It's pretty ordinary stuff, I know. Who doesn't have a bucket list? But we've been adding to ours for years, and the thing is...it never got any shorter. It just kept getting longer and longer until it felt more like a running joke than an actual plan. Maybe we were just quietly telling each other that it was okay to keep dreaming," I said after a while.

Hopeless optimism - 1

Reality - 0

The last strong gust blew by, so I reluctantly pulled away from Ocean with a grateful smile. Like a magnet, I was drawn to the landscape beyond, so I stepped around him to enjoy the view.

"Being here," I said while staring at the waterfall peeking through the trees, "it makes me think we were right to keep dreaming." I looked up at Ocean, who was still staring at me instead of the view. He looked at me like I was the escape he'd been dreaming about for years. "Thank you for bringing me here. I'll never forget it."

"Honestly, I don't know if I'm happy or hating the fact that you love the view so much because now I don't know if this can top it."

I didn't see the small box in his hand until he flipped it open, and I saw the diamond ring inside. It had a simple platinum band with two trillion-cut pink diamonds, their pointed ends facing each other and held together by a smaller band of pink diamonds in the middle, forming a bow.

I had never seen anything like it and doubted that another like it existed. God, it must have cost him a fortune.

"Ocean…"

"My mother is dying to meet you today. She'd kick my ass if she found out I've been letting her future daughter-in-law walk around without a ring on her finger for this long."

I shifted nervously even as I blushed. "You really told your mother about me?"

His soft lips twitched with amusement. "Of course I did."

"And what did she say?"

"I told her…" Ocean reached for my left hand and pulled off my glove. He then plucked the ring from the velvet bed and tucked the box back into his coat pocket. "That she would love you almost as much as I do."

My heart started galloping in my chest, and it felt as if the world around us ceased to exist. There was only us. "You love me?"

"I do, *mo aingeal*. I love you so much that I'd do anything you asked of me. Do you hear me? *Anything*. As long as you're honest with yourself and with me, there's nothing I wouldn't do for you, do you understand me?" The intensity of Ocean's promise made me nervous for some reason. "And that's why," he said after a long and pointed pause, "it broke my heart to look at this beautiful hand and not see my ring on your finger."

Ocean gently slid the ring on, and I wasn't surprised at all that it was a perfect fit. He never seemed to miss anything. For some reason, my mind wandered to Hunter as Ocean drew me into a kiss. I forced her from my mind and focused on the man in front of me.

"I love you too," I whispered to him once the kiss ended.

Ocean stared down at me with adoration before pecking my lips one last time. "I know."

We stayed for another half hour, and I couldn't keep the smile off my face when Ocean lifted me onto his back and carried me the entire way down.

CHAPTER TWENTY-FIVE

OCEAN

AFTER DROPPING COBY OFF ON THE TERRACE WITH MY MOM and making sure they were hitting it off, I left the two of them to get to know each other better, since my mom started crying when she saw the ring I had custom-made for Coby.

Abel was waiting for me at the edge of the path that led to James's cabin. We took the ATVs since the cabin was on the other side of the lake, and I was eager to arrive. When we reached the house, I was relieved to see two guards posted outside the door and knew more were hidden within the tree line.

I dismissed the guards at the door and pulled the skeleton key from my pocket before entering the cottage. There was a fire crackling in the fireplace because the house didn't have central heating, but otherwise it was eerily quiet.

I discovered why when I entered one of the bedrooms and found Hunter blindfolded, bound, and gagged. Her hands and feet were tied to the bedposts with tape over her mouth. Abel's doing no doubt since Hunter had barely made it the night before attempting to escape and costing me two more men.

She stiffened the moment I entered the room, her head whipping toward the door and her breathing becoming fast and unsteady. I swallowed the urge to comfort her as I approached the bed. Hunter started pulling at her bindings once she felt me standing over her, but I still didn't speak because scaring her made my dick hard.

She still wore her clothes from the night before, but they were ruined now, telling me she put up a good fight when she was recaptured. My gaze swept over her, looking for injuries or signs that she'd been abused. I'd fucking kill every last person responsible if I saw so much as a broken nail.

I didn't speak until I was satisfied she hadn't been harmed.

"I'm disappointed in you, Vengeance. I thought we'd come to an understanding."

The knot in my chest eased a little when she relaxed at the sound of my voice. Sitting on the edge of the bed, I removed the blindfold and saw that her mascara was smudged and her eyes were red and exhausted.

"I'd like to talk to you about something important, and because you need to listen, I won't remove the tape until I'm done. Do you understand? Nod or blink once for yes. Shake or blink twice for no."

Hunter blinked once.

"Did they hurt you?"

Blink blink.

"You tried to escape last night—" Two more blinks were my answer before I could even pose the question, so I paused, wondering why she'd lie. And then it clicked. "You were looking for Coby?" I asked gently.

Blink.

"Have you reconsidered my offer of letting you live then?"

Blink blink.

"So you wish to stay?"

A pointed pause and then...

Blink.

"Then why did you run from me, Vengeance?" My voice was tight with restraint. It was only when Hunter just stared at me that I realized she couldn't answer with her mouth taped, so I forced myself to let it go. I hadn't planned to ask her that anyway. It just came out. "I know that Coby told you why I took her."

I sat and watched them on the security cameras the night they spent together and heard it all, but I left out the part about how I knew. Let Hunter think Coby confided in me on her own.

"We're getting married," I confirmed. Hunter's nostrils flared. Her only reaction. "And no matter how hard you fight to prevent that, Coby will be my wife." I left out the reasons why since they no longer mattered. I'm not sure they ever did.

I've wanted Coby since the moment I first saw her. The craving was fucking relentless. It grew stronger until I was past willing to do anything—cross any line—to have her. It started with having her surveilled. At first, I'd hoped to find something to cure my obsession once her guard was down, but there was only one thing hidden in Coby's life that had given me pause.

Hunter.

She never came around whenever Coby visited her brother's club, so I hadn't been prepared for the beauty when I started stalking her best friend. Instead of my interest in Coby shifting, it continued to embed itself into my psyche the more I learned about these women and how they had formed some kind of symbiosis.

Hunter and Coby had much in common.

They were strong, independent, and unafraid to fight for themselves and each other. They both loved hard and liked to be dominated—although one resisted that kink a little more than the other.

But there were differences impossible to ignore and easy to arouse.

Coby liked bows, and pretty ribbons, art, reading, nature, and saving cute little animals from the human race.

Hunter liked guns, knives, fighting, modeling on the side, and surviving. Clearly, something happened in her early life to make her so determined to never be helpless again. She was staring at me now, her upturned eyes already wide with alarm when I hadn't even delivered the most damaging blow.

"She told me today that she loved me."

Hunter shook her head in denial, blinking twice over and over and screaming behind the tape as she fought against the bindings again. The shredded skin around her wrists was starting to bruise, and I knew she would gladly hurt herself if I didn't take control, so I reached for her face and gripped the tape at the corner before ripping it off.

Hunter let out a wail that broke me in fucking two.

I let the inflection in my voice harden until there was no room for disobedience. "Stop."

Hunter's next cry died in her throat, and then she turned her face into the pillow to hide her tears. I used gentle fingers to turn her face back toward me and wiped them away.

"Vengeance, look at me. Please."

Hunter's eyes opened, and I almost wished she hadn't listened because I wouldn't have to face her sorrow. "How could she do this to me?"

"Coby doesn't know you're here, Hunter."

"That's not what I mean. I—" Feeling the urge to scream again, she squeezed her eyes closed and attempted to compose herself. When they opened again, her brown eyes were pools of pain. "How could she marry you?"

Not knowing what to say, I stalled for time by reaching out to untie her hands before moving down to her feet. Hunter sat up gingerly, rubbing her wrists and eyeing me warily when I climbed onto the bed to sit beside her with my back against the headboard.

"I made Coby an offer she couldn't refuse," I finally answered.

"What was that?"

"A fuck ton of money for five years of marriage." My decision to downplay Coby's reasons for marrying stemmed from my need to erase that look from Hunter's eyes. A look that said her heart had just been ripped out of her chest. I didn't know why I cared about Hunter's pain when I was getting what I wanted. I just did. Maybe

Coby was making me soft. Maybe I was the greedy asshole Abel said I was.

Hunter glared at the bedspread, angry at her own curiosity when she asked, "How much is a fuck ton of money?"

I smirked at her question since it once again showed how protective she was of Coby. I may have begrudged Hunter the very obvious fact that she wanted to fuck my wife, but I couldn't resent the idea of Coby having someone besides myself so dedicated to her.

"You know," I said slowly as I chuckled. "We never actually set an amount. I promised her whatever she wanted, but she still hasn't named a figure."

Hunter blew out a breath and shook her head. "That's Coby. Always so trusting. She doesn't really care about money anyway, so it may not have crossed her mind to care that much."

"So what do you think?" I asked when Hunter fell quiet. "What is Coby's hand in marriage worth?"

She narrowed her gaze at me. "There are some things you can't put a price on, Ocean."

"But if you could…" I urged.

"Three million," Hunter blurted. "Per year." When I raised a brow at the amount, Hunter shrugged, ready to go to bat for her friend. "I assume Coby will become accustomed to a different quality of life while you're married, so think of it as alimony."

Teasing her, I whistled. "Still, six million dollars a year for five years. That's a lot of cheddar."

Hunter frowned at me. "But I said three million."

"Coby may have convinced me to sweeten the deal this morning."

"How?"

"She wants me to pay you the same for every year you're apart, and I also promised to forgive her brother's debt and sign over my ownership of the club."

"Why would Coby do that for Roshaun after he—" Hunter's eyes widened, and she hopped up from the bed. "You haven't told her yet?" she shouted.

"Would she believe me after last night?"

"Probably not, but that's your problem, not mine," Hunter said as she paced.

"I disagree. I think it's our problem."

Hunter paused and then faced me, planting her hands on those wide hips that got me hard every time. "Excuse me?"

"I recall you asking to help me kill him and deal with the Coby aftermath."

"And I recall you saying you didn't need my help."

I folded my arms behind my head and grinned. "What if I promised you the honor of killing Roshaun yourself?"

"It sounds like a setup to make me take all the blame and have Coby hate me forever. I'm sure that would make your life much sweeter."

"It's definitely something I would do," I admitted, more than a little impressed that she'd read me so easily. "But that's not my intention, Hunter. And you have no idea of what I'm thinking will make my life sweeter." I stared at her hard and meaningfully, and then quickly pushed past the subject when I saw her getting ready to dig. "We both have the same goal—to keep Coby safe and happy." I paused, wondering if it was wise to admit this next part, but I decided I didn't care. "But I also want the same for you."

Hunter scoffed and began pacing again. "Roshaun doesn't scare me."

"He should," I warned, though I chose not to elaborate. Roshaun had committed much bigger atrocities than just stealing from me. Things that would break Coby's heart if she knew.

My mind wandered as I imagined all the ways I wanted to kill Roshaun slowly until I heard a sound, looked up, and saw that Hunter was hyperventilating.

I shot off the bed and across the room, but the moment my fingers grazed her arm, she whirled around and backed away with a clear warning in her eyes, so I forced myself to stay where I was and give her space.

"Tell me what just happened," I gently demanded. "What did Roshaun do?" It didn't take a whole lot of intuition to connect that Roshaun Perry was responsible for Hunter suddenly acting like cornered prey.

"It's nothing."

"That didn't look like nothing to me."

"Sorry. I meant it's *none of your business*, Ocean."

That wasn't good enough for me. Every time I mentioned Roshaun, Hunter's entire demeanor changed. She'd either shrink into herself or turn vicious and deflect.

"Coby wants you at the wedding," I blurted, choosing to drop the subject. For now.

Hunter's gaze flew to mine, and once again, she was vengeance. "There's not going to be a wedding."

I cocked my head. "You don't trust her judgment?"

Hunter barked a laugh and then made the most daring move of all. She stepped into my face until her bare toes touched my shoes. "Nice try, asshole. I don't trust you."

"She wants you there, you know." Just as I expected, Hunter had nothing clever to say to that. "Coby wants you to give her away."

"*Never*," Hunter hissed.

It was my turn to crowd her space. I forced her backward until her back was against the wall, and she had to tip her head back to hold my gaze. The moment she did, I got comfortable, bracing my forearms on the wall by her head.

Fuck it.

I heard the words before I even realized I was saying them.

"Coby is already mine, Hunter." I leaned down until our lips were just a breath away. "But I haven't won yet. My acquisition isn't complete. Can you guess what's missing?"

"No."

Feeling like I'd die without it, I let our lips touch. The faintest brush. When Hunter's breath hitched, I knew she'd felt it, too. "Try, Vengeance. Try to guess what else I want. What I need."

Chest rising and falling fast, lips parted in shock, she shook her head as my meaning slammed into her. "You can't."

"I will."

"How would that work?" She whimpered. "You're marrying my best friend."

"It'll work because I say it will," I assured her. "I'm marrying Coby because I want to. I'm marrying next month because I have to, but make no mistake, I want you both in my bed."

"You're crazy."

"Then why aren't you running, Vengeance? Why are you looking at me right now like you want me to fuck you?" I daringly dropped my hands to her hips, and when she didn't object, they slid around to her ass. I swallowed my groan. Hunter Parrish was more than a handful—in more ways than one. "We both know you could disarm me if you wanted to."

"So your goons can catch me as soon as I walk out the door?" I smiled down at her, and she rolled her eyes again. "Whatever."

My phone chimed then, cutting off my response. The only contacts I didn't have silenced were Abel and Kellan, so I reached into my pocket and pulled it free.

I swore after reading Abel's message, but I could feel Hunter watching me closely now, so I put a leash on my temper.

Pocketing my phone after texting orders to Abel, I lifted Hunter off her feet.

She immediately wrapped her thick legs around my waist to keep from falling while I carried her to the bed and sat on the edge with her in my lap. I couldn't help massaging the plump globes of her ass and watching her lashes flutter.

Fucking beautiful.

"Talk to me, Vengeance. Do you want out of this cabin, or don't you?"

Hunter's eyes snapped open, and she pushed my hands away. "Stockholm Syndrome hasn't set in yet, sir. I'm not fucking you."

Letting myself give in to what led me here in the first place, I said, "Then kiss me."

"What?"

"Kiss me like you mean it, and I'll let you see Coby." Hunter's lips opened and closed as she searched my gaze to see if I was telling the truth. "It's not a trick, Vengeance. I don't want to keep you apart any more than I want to choose."

Still unsure, Hunter swallowed hard. "One kiss?"

"One chance," I warned. "So make it good."

Hunter thought about it momentarily before closing her eyes and leaning forward. Her back was rigid as she tried to maintain space between us, so I stayed where I was, letting her come to me.

When her plush lips finally met mine, I didn't return her kiss.

I watched her brows dip with determination right before she tried again. Over and over, she pecked my lips while I feigned detachment. A frustrated moan tore from her throat as I drove her to desperation. She moved closer and wrapped her arms around my neck until her heavy breasts were pressed against my chest.

I didn't think my dick could get any fucking harder.

Hunter kissed me again, and then I felt her hot tongue lick my lips before she whimpered. "Please?"

The last of my will crumpled, and I finally gave in, parting my lips and meeting her tongue with mine.

Our kiss was slow and hesitant, but quickly turned desperate and uncontrolled. Hunter began grinding down on my lap, and I lifted my hips, trying to feel her hot pussy through her jeans. Pretty soon, we were dry-humping on the bed like two teenagers.

I was still kissing her when I felt Hunter's hands shift to my chest and push, so I gave in to her silent request and lowered my back to the mattress. Hunter followed me, and I savagely tore into the rip already at the back of her tattered jeans until I could feel her soft skin underneath. Her pussy was right there for taking, and all I had to do was lower my joggers and destroy what remained of her clothes. My hands roamed all over her bare ass, and I couldn't resist the urge to slap it, making Hunter moan and grind down on me harder.

I broke the kiss, knowing I had to slow us down before it went too far, but Hunter wasn't ready yet, so she chased my lips.

And I was too weak to resist.

We continued kissing a little longer until I felt her reach for my waistband at the exact moment I reached for her thong. And then I thought of my wife.

Stop, stop, stop. Do something.

"I ate her pussy before I came to see you. She let me," I said between kisses, making Hunter stiffen. It wasn't a lie. I really had eaten Coby out in the car the moment we finished our hike. "She was so sweet. Can you taste her, Vengeance? I wish you'd heard the way she screamed for me." I kissed Hunter's stiff lips one last time before pulling back to stare into her eyes. "Do you think it was Stockholm Syndrome that made her do it?"

Hunter cursed and tore away from me, scrambling to leave the bed, but I grabbed her throat before she could, slamming her back on the bed next to me. Her frustrated screams were ignored as I climbed on top of her and pinned her there.

"A deal's a deal, Vengeance, but let me clarify. Coby is mine, and so are you. That isn't changing now or ever. Tomorrow, you're going to join us in the main house, and you're going to pretend you came of your own free will until I say otherwise."

"And if I don't?" she challenged. I almost rolled my eyes.

"Then Coby's deal goes out the window, and I make her marry me anyway, except it won't be for five years, Hunter. It will be forever." Because I was an asshole and because I couldn't resist, I kissed Hunter's lips again.

"You bitch-ass—"

"I'm not done talking," I interrupted. "Right now, you're going to convince me that you'll play along, or else I'll keep you chained to this bed. And when Coby and I marry, she'll do it thinking you chose not to be there for her."

Hunter's jaw dropped, her wide eyes glistening with tears. "She'll never believe that."

"I'll make her."

"You're such a fucking bastard!"

"No, Hunter. I'm a man determined to win."

"Coby and I aren't prizes in a game, Ocean! I don't know if I deserve more, but I sure as hell know Coby does."

I felt my blood ice over. "I know that," I bit out.

"Do you?" She looked up at me like I'd grown two heads. "Think about what you're saying to me. Think about what you're doing."

I blew out a breath of frustration. I couldn't help the way I fucking felt. Neither could they apparently. I knew her and Coby were in love with each other, even if they weren't ready to admit it yet. Instead of holding up the mirror to Hunter and telling her what I knew, I asked, "What would you do if you were me?"

She gave me a perplexed look. "You can't ask me that, Ocean."

"I can, and I am. What would you do?"

"I'd let you choose. And I wouldn't scheme and cheat."

I stared at her for a long time before letting her go and climbing off her. I stood from the bed, and so did she, but on the opposite side.

"All right," I said after a while. "But Coby made this deal because she wants it, Hunter. I didn't force her. I gave her a choice, so I'll give you the same. My offer still stands. I'll let you be with Coby and help her through this marriage on one condition: you can't tell her about this until I'm ready to come clean."

Hunter was already shaking her head. "You can't ask me to lie to my best friend."

"Would you be telling Coby the truth for her sake or yours?"

"What kind of question is that?" Hunter spat.

"One that requires an answer," I shot back.

She lifted her chin. "For both of ours."

"Bullshit. You were just kissing your best friend's fiancé. Did you do that for Coby?"

"You know what, Ocean?" Hunter said with the driest chuckle.

"Go straight to hell, but until then, sleep with one eye open because not only am I going to get Coby away from you, I'm going to kill you in your sleep before I do!"

"That should be easy enough since you'll be sleeping next to me right along with Coby, and I guarantee when it happens, you'll both love it as much as I will."

"Kill yourself," she spat as she looked away from me to hide what my promise really did to her.

"Does this mean we have a deal, Hunter?"

Her gaze returned to mine to glare daggers. "For now."

"Come here."

Hunter hesitated just to piss me off, and then she slowly rounded the bed to stand in front of me. Once I was able to breathe her jasmine scent in again, she just stared at me like I was some great mystery she couldn't solve, but I knew what it really was.

Curiosity. Eagerness. Doubt.

She was thinking about what I'd said—about the three of us together in my bed just as I'd described. She was wondering if I'd really succeed. I'd gotten the same vibe from Coby when she demanded I give Hunter everything I offered her. I tried to tell myself she hadn't known what she was asking, but...what if?

I had the feeling Coby Perry was underestimated a lot.

My hand curved around Hunter's neck, and then my thumb gently swept her soft cheek. Even more surprising was that she let me.

"You may not know this, but I do. You deserve more than to be treated like a prize in a game, and I promise you, Hunter, it won't happen again. You're much too precious for that."

Her lips parted, but I kissed her forehead and stepped away before she could tell me to go to hell again. I'd already fucked this up because I couldn't let go of my upbringing. I couldn't stop approaching every fucking thing like a game or battle, and the people involved like opponents or chess pieces.

At this rate, it would take a miracle to win their hearts when Coby and Hunter had already stolen mine.

"I'll have someone bring you clean clothes, food, and whatever else you may need," I called at the bedroom door. And then I allowed myself one last look until tomorrow. "Good night, Hunter."

Walking toward the cabin door, I could have sworn I heard her soft voice parrot, "Good night, Ocean."

CHAPTER TWENTY-SIX

HUNTER

THREE DAYS AFTER OCEAN'S ULTIMATUM, I WAS LYING ON the bed, wearing only a towel. Ocean had delivered on his promise of clothes and food, but I hated him, so I was determined not to accept anything from him. None of the clothes were useful anyway. They wouldn't keep me much warmer than the towel if I tried to escape again.

Thankfully, the old cabin had running water and was stocked with the essentials, so after taking care of my hygiene, I decided to take a nap while I waited for him to fulfill his other promise—letting me see Coby.

Half the week had already gone.

Instinct told me that this was by design. That Ocean liked the idea of knowing I was waiting on him—anticipating his arrival. Why hadn't I killed him when I had the chance? I couldn't even say that if given the chance again, I wouldn't hesitate again.

The proof was in the kiss.

The one that set my body on fire and left me smoldering ever since.

As it turns out, Ocean had succeeded in torturing me after all.

I was just starting to nod off again when I heard a knock at the cabin door. My heart—which knew it could only be him—started pounding, chasing away my grogginess as I stood from the bed. I cautiously entered the main room that wasn't more than a kitchenette, couch, and fireplace, and looked around before slowly approaching the door.

I had no idea if it was even unlocked or if I was supposed to call out, but I wrapped my hand around the old knob. To my surprise, it wasn't locked. And then I realized why Abel or Ocean hadn't bothered.

At the bottom of the narrow porch, two armed guards stood sentry. Across the lake, I could see two more patrolling. There were probably more in the woods I couldn't see because I was beginning to understand Ocean Kilpatrick.

A tiny whimper drew my attention down, and I gasped at finding a little brown and black ball of fur standing on its hind legs with tiny front paws on the lip of the wicker picnic basket. The puppy was so tiny, its head didn't even reach the single arched handle. There was a red ribbon winding around the handle and another forming a bow at the front of the basket. It immediately made me think of Coby, who had worn one every day since her parents' death.

"Aww, hi. Hello, pretty baby," I greeted as I crouched to get a better look at the puppy. He looked like a tiny teddy bear with the sweetest face I'd ever seen. "Did the bad man leave you here all alone?"

The puppy whined and tried to rest his paw on my knee, but his little legs were too short.

"I guess we have that in common. Come on. Let's get you inside."

I let my gaze travel across the frozen lake one last time before lifting the basket and carrying both inside. The puppy was so small that he fit in the palm of my hand when I lifted him out of the basket. There was already a collar around his neck with a gold round name tag, but no name.

Hmm…

"What should I call you?" I asked rhetorically. He licked my palm and then started wriggling like he was restless, so I set him down before I could drop him. The puppy looked sort of fierce, like he was always frowning, and his fur was mostly black with pops of brown, but I knew from all my research that he'd change colors after a few months. It also occurred to me that I didn't even know if it was a boy or a girl. The red ribbon he was currently gnawing on didn't leave me any clues. "You must be hungry," I said as I watched him go to town.

I didn't have food he could eat, and there was only a single toy in the basket, so I fished out the chew toy and tossed it on the floor. The puppy immediately let go of the ruined ribbon and pounced.

After a couple of hours playing with him, I went into the bedroom and capitulated even further by dressing in the cute lounge set—thick heather gray fleece leggings, a matching bra top, and a long cardigan that reached my ankles. There were slippers too with a white fur trim.

Ten minutes later, I was grateful for the clothes when I caught the puppy lifting his leg in the corner and rushed him out of the cabin. Abel had taken my shoes so that I'd think twice about escaping, and the slippers offered little to no protection in the snow, so I ended up hopping around while pleading with the puppy to do its business already. I'm sure we looked a sight to the guards who watched my every move.

At some point, my focus shifted from the puppy, who was currently sniffing a blade of frost-bitten grass as if it held the secrets to the universe, to the grandiose rustic mansion on the other side of the closed lake, with gold light shining through the many windows. I'd never seen anything like it.

Coby was in there.

I was starting to question less and less whether she was safe, while gradually accepting that if she was with Ocean, it was almost certain.

Still...

I discreetly searched the grounds for weaknesses and blind spots—somewhere I could slip through and see for myself that Coby was unharmed, happy, and living her best soft girl life.

It's what she always wanted ever since she lost her parents and her brother began resenting her.

To be a part of a family again.

Once upon a time, I was dumb enough to believe that I could be family enough for her.

Maybe it was selfish of me to fight so hard to take this away from her if Ocean spoke the truth and it was what she wanted.

I stopped feeling my toes five minutes ago, so it took me too long to notice the puppy had stopped sniffing everything in sight and was now huddled on my slippered feet for warmth as its tiny body shivered violently.

"Time to go, cutie." Bending down, I lifted the puppy, who climbed up my arm and tried to hide inside the cradle between my neck and shoulder. He was so small that he actually fit. Turning, I came to a stop when I saw that I had an audience. Ocean was sitting on the steps and leaning back with his elbow resting on the porch as if he was watching his favorite show. Abel stood next to him, glaring at me like he was daring me to make a move. I smiled a little, glad to see that the bodyguard knew very well I could end him.

Slowly, I made my way over to the cabin, but neither of them spoke a word as my gaze darted back and forth, wondering why they were here.

Abel was keeping his boss safe. That much was obvious. It was Ocean whose intentions remained unknown. Especially when I didn't see Coby anywhere.

As soon as I was standing by Ocean's foot, he spoke. "Good evening, Hunter."

"Good evening," I returned amicably. I didn't want to piss him off and risk him taking my new friend away. I didn't think he was that kind of guy, but Ocean was unpredictable. Coby talked about him like he was Prince Charming or something, but I saw firsthand that he could be cruel, too.

"I see you found my gift."

"Yes, thank you." My gaze nervously flicked back to Abel again.

Not one to miss anything, Ocean stood and dismissed his head of security. Abel, of course, argued against leaving me alone with his precious charge. While the big, bad men bickered over the dangers of little ol' me, I slipped by them and returned to the warmth of the cabin.

My belly tightened and filled with heat when I heard the door open and close moments later.

I turned to see Ocean darkening the door, but he was thankfully alone.

Neither of us spoke for several moments, and yet somehow we both said far too much.

"How did you know?" I eventually allowed myself to ask, trying and failing to keep my awe and gratitude out of my tone.

Ocean moved deeper into the cabin while boldly eye-fucking me like I already belonged to him. "I may have heard it from a little birdie."

"Coby told you I wanted a puppy?" I asked as I sat on the couch and transferred the puppy to my lap. He immediately curled into a ball with a warning growl directed at Ocean. I didn't think it was possible to love the little cutie more. "She told you I wanted a Yorkie?"

"She let it slip," Ocean said while dropping down onto the couch next to me and stretching to get comfortable, when I scowled at him.

"Oh…well, thanks. You can go now."

Ocean grinned at my dismissal and stayed right where he was, so I ignored his ass while I petted the puppy's black fur. "What are you going to name him?"

"Coco," I answered immediately.

"It's a boy, Vengeance."

"Coco," I echoed. I turned my head to glare at him.

Ocean tucked his lips to keep from laughing, but his eyes were snitching on him. "Coco it is."

"Why are you here?"

Ocean sighed and mumbled, "I figured you could use some company."

"I thought that's what Coco was for?"

"And to bring you this." Ocean extended his leg and kicked over the reusable tote bag on the low coffee table that I hadn't even noticed he brought in with him. It was from the pet store.

Immediately, I stood and set the puppy down. He lifted his head to watch me, but stayed put while I searched the store bag.

My excitement grew with each new item I pulled out of the bag until I was full-blown grinning.

There were bowls, a small bag of food, treats, toys, puppy pads, shampoo, a bed…the list went on until the coffee table was filled with items. It wasn't everything, but it was more than enough to get started.

Grabbing one of the bowls, I tore open the bag of food and used the scooper to measure out some food before grabbing the second bowl and filling it with water. I arranged them both on the cute mat Ocean picked out, and Coco wasted no time barking and flying (more like tumbling) off the couch.

He raced over to the water first and started lapping at it before moving over to the food. Back and forth, he switched between bowls like he couldn't decide if he was hungry or thirsty.

I was so busy giggling at his antics as I set up his bed that I briefly forgot Ocean was even there until he called my name.

"Hunter." Spinning around like I'd been caught being bad, I stared at him wide-eyed. "What do you say?" I cocked my head at him, and he crooked a finger. Grumbling, I shuffled over to him until I was standing between his feet. His man spread meant there was plenty of room, and still I felt caged in by his long legs. "What do you say?" he repeated in a low tone.

Feeling indignant, I placed my hands on my hips. The movement made my breasts jiggle, which didn't go unnoticed by him. "Thanks, I guess."

Ocean laughed as my defiance delighted him, which stole my breath and turned my nipples into painful points. Only a man fully convinced of his dominance would brush off any half-hearted challenge to it. "You guess, Vengeance?"

I shrugged and looked away. I ain't gon' kiss his ass.

Suddenly, Coco came sniffing, paying special attention to Ocean's shoes and my ankles. Like his bowls, he couldn't decide which of our scents intrigued him more, and I thought of Coby again.

At least Coco would never leave me, I thought petulantly.

A moment later, Coco rose onto his hind legs and started pawing at Ocean's leg for attention. To my surprise, Ocean obliged him, lifting the puppy up with one hand and holding him suspended to stare him down. Coco growled, and Ocean kept staring until the puppy whined and licked Ocean's hand.

Feeling smug, Ocean looked up at me. "You see, Hunter? Even the dog knows when to submit."

"I'm not a dog."

"But you do know, don't you?" His deep voice had dropped even lower until it was nothing more than a sensual rumble. "When to submit?" Breathing heavier now, I couldn't move because I feared what I might do. "Here," he said indulgently. "I'll even make it easier for you."

Keeping his gaze on me, Ocean set the puppy on his lap, who turned to me and started begging for attention. I tried to pick him up, but Ocean lifted Coco out of reach and then set him back down once I dropped my hand.

I almost snapped at him to keep the damn dog, but Coco was just too cute and adorable not to be mine. The battle of wills between Ocean and me lasted a little longer until Coco began crying at the lack of attention. Ocean scratched between his ears, and even though it soothed the pup, who turned to lay his front paws on Ocean's chest, it made me seethingly jealous.

"Show me, Vengeance. Show me that you know how."

I inhaled a shuddering breath. There was an ache between my thighs that grew warmer and damper when I finally gave in, lowering to the floor until I was kneeling between Ocean's legs.

"So fucking gorgeous," he praised. "Such a good girl underneath all that violence."

Biting my tongue, my gaze pleaded as I tentatively reached out to pet Coco.

Ocean smiled and let me.

Not a minute later, Coco wandered off to chew on his toy. I didn't move from my spot. I didn't dare. Ocean rewarded me by threading his fingers through my bushy ponytail, paying me the same attention he'd shown Coco.

I should have been offended by it.

Instead, I ended up resting my cheek on his hard thigh while my heart pounded furiously and my stomach did back flips. I peered up at him, and he stared down at me. Neither of us said a word, content to just be in each other's presence.

I forgot I was supposed to hate him.

A knock on the door startled me awake, and I lifted my head from Ocean's thigh in time to see his head popping up too from the back of the couch.

I guess we'd both fallen asleep.

Stretching his powerful body, Ocean checked his watch and then leaned down to kiss my forehead affectionately, which succeeded in making me blush and want to kill him at the same time. He then lifted me under my arms and deposited me on the couch next to him like I weighed nothing before rising to his feet and going to the door. Smiling when Coco followed him, I curled up on the couch with my feet tucked under me.

Ocean opened the door, scooped Coco up, and then stood to the side.

A man in a chef's uniform rolled in a cart filled to the brim with silver dishes covered by plated domes. Abel walked in behind him, and then he and Ocean spoke in low tones before Abel turned right around and left again.

Good riddance.

Abel didn't like me because I'd bested so many of those weenies he called soldiers, and the feeling was mutual because he dared to get in my way.

The chef rolled the cart to the dining table, quickly and efficiently set the table with dinnerware that looked too fine for the old cabin, and lit a few candles to set the mood.

And then he just left.

Coco padded back over to his bed to sleep while I tried to figure out what the fuck was going on.

"What are you doing?" I questioned in a panic.

Ocean had removed his jacket and was already sitting down at the small kitchen table. He glanced up at me. "We're going to have dinner together."

No, no, no. It felt too intimate, even more than our kiss. It was bad enough that we fell asleep together. "What about Coby?"

Not quite sure what I was really asking, I let the question hang in the air, but Ocean wasn't having it. He held my gaze, and it felt like a challenge. "What about her?"

"I..." I wasn't brave enough to ask if Coby would appreciate knowing he was here having dinner with me like we were on a date, so I said, "I thought you were going to let me see her."

"And I will. When I'm ready."

Sighing, I sat down in front of the other empty place setting in front of him. "So what are you waiting for?"

"For one of you to tell me the truth."

While I gaped at him—a thousand responses flitted through my mind—Ocean stood up and started removing the silver-domed lids. My mouth watered at the sight of the jumbo shrimp cocktail, stuffed lobster tails, salmon, scallops, caviar, and oysters. Even the various side dishes looked amazing.

"I didn't know what you liked," Ocean admitted when he caught me salivating, "so I had the chef prepare a little of everything."

Coby must have also *let it slip* that I loved seafood. What exactly were the two of them talking about up in that big house?

I missed her.

I pointed out everything I wanted, and Ocean made my plate

before making his. I waited for him to sit down before I touched mine. Noticing, he threw me a wicked smile, and I rolled my eyes.

"I've never had caviar," I admitted a few minutes later as I used the tiny spoon to scoop some out of the chilled gold jar and onto the mini brioche toasts. I was nervous as hell to try what was essentially fish eggs.

"Try it with the champagne," Ocean suggested as he lifted the bottle from the bucket and poured some into a chute.

I made a face as I brought the tartine to my mouth and bit into it quickly like I was auditioning for Fear Factor. Ocean cackled as he watched me, and I realized I was still making a face as I chewed. I was so prepared for it to be gross that I didn't notice the butter and slightly nutty flavor until it slid down my throat. It was a little briny but not overly so.

I grabbed the flute of champagne and took a sip while Ocean returned to his food.

"So when is the wedding?" I asked.

He glanced at me before refocusing on his food. "Christmas Eve."

I raised my brows in surprise. "So soon? You really want your anniversary to land on a holiday?"

"Why? You think we should get married sooner?"

"No!" I shouted. Ocean nodded and kept eating. Damn, he was hungry. "When was the last time you ate?" I asked when he seemed to be devouring the meat and ignoring his sides.

"This morning. I had breakfast with Coby."

"Ah," I said, suddenly understanding. *Poor baby.* I set down my champagne and plucked a shrimp from the cocktail glass. "Did she tell you that you can keep eating meat if you want?"

Ocean nodded as he cut into his salmon. "Yes."

"She's lying."

"I know."

Coby had tried for weeks to get me to switch to plant-based foods before I had to curse her out to get her to back off. Prince

Charming wouldn't do that, though. Oh, no. He'd rather sneak away
to have dinner with me.

Ocean sat back and wiped his mouth after clearing his plate in
record time. We locked gazes, and amusement quickly filled his eyes
once he saw me laughing at him. He then stood up without warning and threw his napkin on the table before coming around the table and kissing me slowly. It felt so natural that I forgot that it was
wrong, especially when he pulled back with a possessive hand lightly
gripping my throat.

"Same time tomorrow?"

My heart plummeted at the thought of spending another night
alone, but I nodded, and he left after telling me goodnight.

Ocean visited every evening over the next week for dinner. Knowing
boredom and loneliness awaited me once he left, I attempted various tricks to prolong his visits after dinner, including showing him
the tricks I was teaching Coco. The pup still didn't fuck with Ocean
and growled every time he got too close.

Such a cutie.

After a while, I was forced to admit that it wasn't awful having
dinner with Ocean every night, but I couldn't help thinking about
Coby. Had she noticed his strange absences and the mysterious
holes in his schedule? Ocean was so magnetic that I knew the answer couldn't be anything other than yes. I certainly noticed every
second that he wasn't with me, and he wasn't even mine.

Then again, a man like Ocean wouldn't have a normal routine,
so perhaps not.

I went to bed still agonizing over it. I tossed and turned as what
Ocean and I were doing in secret plagued me with guilt in my sleep—
so much so that when I heard a thump late that night, it was easy for
me to shake off my drowsiness and go on high alert.

I didn't move from the bed as I listened for the sound again. When it didn't come, my killer instincts took over, and I slowly stood from the bed.

I was surrounded by enemies.

My gut wouldn't allow me to dismiss the disturbance as nothing.

There was a smaller bedroom at the back of the cabin, facing the tree line, while the room I was in faced the lake and the main house. Only one bathroom separated the two bedrooms, while the cabin's back door was padlocked from the outside. I also knew the window in the second bedroom couldn't close properly, which is how I escaped that first night.

Imagine my frustration after I'd wiggled all this ass I was carrying through that tiny window just to be caught before I could get more than a hundred feet. I hope the guard who reached me first and tried to manhandle me was happy with his new nose.

I quietly placed Coco in his crate to keep him safe, then tiptoed into the living room and small kitchen and looked around.

Empty.

I peeked inside the bathroom and found no knife-wielding psycho waiting behind the shower curtain either, so I crept to the second bedroom. As soon as I reached for the knob, the door flew open, and I came face to face with some crazy bitch wielding one of the chopped firewood.

I screamed.

She screamed louder.

Only when neither of us moved to attack the other did I get a good look at the intruder—petite, pixie cut with ginger-dyed curls, golden-brown skin, cute button nose, freckles, and round eyes. And she was barefoot, her periwinkle toenails on display while the T-shirt she wore—her only clothing—swallowed her small frame.

The crazy bitch was *my* crazy bitch.

"What the fuck, Coby? It's me!"

She lowered her arms when she realized whose head she was about to cave in, her confused gaze widening. "Hunter?"

"Yeah, bitch."

Coby dropped the log, and we ran into each other's arms. "How are you here? Why are you here?"

"Why else? I got kidnapped by a psycho just like you."

Coby released me, looking puzzled. "But... Ocean said you were home."

"What a surprise. The Strap lied," I returned dryly. "How did you find me?"

"It's a long story," Coby answered with a sniffle. "Ocean's been disappearing a lot. At first, I just assumed he was working, but then I'd see Abel and that pretty White guy wandering the halls, and that's when shit stopped adding up.

"Kellan," I said. Pity he was still alive.

"Yeah, him." Coby stared at me like she couldn't believe I was really standing here before shaking off her disbelief. "Anyway, I started following him to see where his ass was sneaking off to. I figured out it was the cabin, but I couldn't get closer without the guards seeing me."

I frowned. "So how did you get in?" As far as I knew, Abel and Ocean had every angle of this place covered. Or was I dreaming and Coby wasn't really here at all?

Deciding to test my theory, I reached out and pinched her arm.

"Ow! Bitch, what the fuck?" She looked at me like I'd lost my mind.

"Sorry." I winced. "I was just making sure I wasn't dreaming."

"You're supposed to pinch yourself, Hunter."

"Oh. Right." Coby reached out with fast hands and twisted my nipple. "Owwww!" I slapped her hand away.

"Well."

I laughed, suddenly feeling a million times lighter. "Seriously, though. How did you get in?"

"Ocean had some kind of emergency in the city. Whatever it was, it must have been bad enough to pull most of your guards. There's only a couple out front now, so I snuck around the back and found the open window." Coby shrugged like it was no big deal.

I'd be so proud of her if it weren't another of Ocean's obvious traps.

I gulped. "Oh."

"I've got to say I was not expecting to find you. Abel mentioned someone escaping. I should have known—" She shook her head in that self-deprecating way that told me she was beating herself up. "It all makes sense now."

I didn't respond this time.

Coby didn't seem to notice my trepidation as she turned and rushed back over to the window she'd snuck through. The same narrow window I'd used to escape, though she probably fit through a lot easier than I did.

"Okay, so let's go." She waved me over while checking to see if the coast was clear. I stayed put. "If we're quiet, we can run for the trees, find the road, and hitch a ride back to the city."

"Coby," I finally spoke. "You're only wearing a T-shirt, and I'd have to go barefoot. Even if we got away, we'll die from hypothermia before we get far."

"I know, I know," she said as she turned to face me. "But we gotta try."

"I agree, but this is not our moment."

"What are you talking about?" she whisper-shouted. "We have to get you out now! Ocean is going to come back soon, and then he'll know I'm gone."

"He already knows you're here, Coby."

Ocean probably never even really left. He was probably standing in the trees right now, patting himself on the back for manipulating us again like rats in a maze or pieces on a chessboard.

Coby gave me a perplexed look. "What?"

I licked my suddenly dry lips. "I already tried to escape, but I was caught before I got more than a few steps. Ocean has men hiding in the trees. If you got this far, it's because they let you. It's because *he* let you."

Even if Ocean was away, his men probably called him the moment they spotted her.

Coby's shoulders. "That...that doesn't make any sense."

"Doesn't it? Ocean's been one step ahead this entire time, Coby. Do you really think he just happened to mention his plans right in front of you?"

And even if Ocean had let his guard down, the fact that Coby made it this far said he'd already adapted, gaining one on us before we even realized the trap he'd laid.

After all, he promised to let me be with Coby.

Maybe he wanted us here together, locked in this cabin with no way out until he *let us out.*

I began to pace with one hand on my hip and the other palming my forehead.

"I'm so stupid," Coby said, sinking onto the edge of the bed and staring at the floor. I could tell her mind was racing and reliving every interaction—probably from when he first appeared in our lives. "How could I not see what he was doing? It was all right there."

Walking over to the bed, I sat next to her. "You're not stupid," I told her gently. "You're...in love." I immediately wanted to take one of my kunai and stab my own heart. My guess... it would hurt a lot less. I guess it's a good thing I didn't have them anymore. I kept reaching for it under my pillow and my thigh at night, only to remember that they were taken from me right along with my freedom. "You want to believe everything he tells you because he makes you feel safe and seen. And even when you know he's hiding the truth from you, you can't help but trust that he's doing it for your own good. You trust him, even though he doesn't always deserve it."

Coby groaned and then flopped onto her back and covered her eyes. Feeling exhausted from being caught in Ocean's vortex, I lay down next to her. At least, I wasn't trapped alone.

Coby turned onto her side to face me, and I turned my head toward her. "You've been here the whole time, haven't you?"

"Yup."

She picked at a loose thread in the bedspread. Something twinkled in the moonlight, and I got a glimpse of the huge pink diamond shaped like a bow now adorning her left hand. My stomach suddenly hurt. "And he's been visiting you...."

"Yeah." My voice sounded strangled to my own ears.

"Every night." I didn't respond, and my silence didn't go unnoticed by Coby. Her gaze was curious and trusting, making me feel even more like shit. "What were you guys doing?"

I sucked in a breath when I remembered my deal with Ocean. I get to see Coby if I keep my mouth shut, but that was never going to happen. I wasn't going to lie to Coby. That's not how we rocked.

I just hoped she wouldn't hate me too much.

Ocean made their marriage sound like a business arrangement, but the way he guarded her like a dragon hoarding treasure...

Yeah, no.

It was definitely more than that.

"I kissed him, Coby." The confession had been blurted out, and I wished I could say I felt better, but I only felt worse, especially when Coby sat up with a frown.

"What?" I'm going to be sick. "When?"

"Today," I confessed, my skin flushing while the room spun. "And yesterday. And the day before. And the day before that. It started with a deal. A kiss in exchange for...you."

"Why would you do that?"

My lips parted, but nothing came out. Every reason I wanted to give just sounded like an excuse. Because Ocean had been right. He'd given me a choice, and I made it on my own. I chose to kiss him, and I didn't care about the consequences... at the time.

"I don't know why," I said with a gulp. It was the truth. I had no fucking clue why I'd want to kiss a monster. And not just any fiend. The heir to the fucking mafia. My best friend's fiancé. "I'm sorry, Coby." She didn't speak for a long while, and I was too much of a coward to look her in the eye, so I kept staring at the ceiling. "There's something else you should know," I said after a few minutes. Coby still didn't respond, but I knew she was listening. "He said…" *Kill me now.* "He said he wants us both, Coby. Like on some sister-wives shit."

Turning my head finally, I watched as my best friend's lips parted and her eyes widened.

She was the picture of shock, except the thing is… Coby was a terrible fucking actor. When she remembered how well I knew her, she dropped her gaze and continued picking at the bedspread.

And then, finally, she spoke. "Isn't that illegal?"

I gave her a look. "Ocean's in the mafia, Coby. I don't think he cares."

She finally met my gaze. "Right. Well… what are we going to do?"

This time, I was the one to look away. I stared at the wall while I wrestled with my warring feelings. I couldn't recall Coby and me ever being afraid to tell each other what we were thinking. It just made me even more determined to get us away from Ocean Kilpatrick.

"I don't know."

We were quiet for a while, but even more surprising than Coby being the first to speak was the absolutely insane shit that came out of her mouth. "I think we should do it."

My stomach felt like Coby had just carved a hole into it, leaving desire to rush in and fill the emptiness. I used what last bit of my head not fogged by my lust to say, "Coby…bestie…sweetie…are you out of your mind?"

Sharing a man, much less our captor, was crazy. And out of the fucking question.

"What's the big deal? You and Ocean are the people I love most in this world, and he's offering to take care of us both and keep us together. *Clearly,* you like him, so I figured… why not?"

I shot from the bed and placed my hands on my hips. "Really? What the hell do you mean by *"clearly I like him"*? I do not like that psycho, Coby Perry!"

Coby groaned and tipped her head back. "Why are you yelling, Hunter?"

"Because you're talking crazy!"

She didn't respond until she was standing too. "Am I?"

"We don't even know Ocean, and you want us to become his little pets just like that?" I snapped my fingers for emphasis.

"It won't be like that, and you know it. Besides, it's only for five years. Did I forget to mention the millions of dollars?" she reminded me.

Who the hell was she kidding? Coby didn't care about money, and neither did I. It was just an excuse to be reckless with her heart. And now she was trying to drag me into this insanity with her.

"How do you know what he'll pay? You didn't even get the damn price first, Coby. I did!"

"If you think it's such a bad idea, why did you bother asking?"

"Because I was looking out for you!"

"Bullshit! You were curious, and you know it. If not about him, then about the money. Think of everything we could finally do together—"

"No."

Her cheeks bloomed with red, and I knew what it meant. We were in for one of our knock-down, drag-out fights. "You don't want to do it? Fine. But I will."

Panic speared my chest. *No, no, no. I can't lose you again.* "The hell you are, Coby. We're both getting away from that crazy motherfucker at the first opportunity."

"You can go." She crossed her arms. "I'll talk to Ocean and get him to free you."

"Coby—"

She barreled over me before I could finish. "I'm a grown woman, Hunter. I don't need you to baby, control, or decide what's right for me."

My gaze narrowed on her. "I thought we were best friends, and it was us against the world. Was one man all it took to change that?"

She fell back a step and then another until she was standing in front of the open window with her back to me. When her anger returned, it simmered this time, feeling like the ice gathering on the glass. "How is it," she spoke slowly, "that you always need me to choose you *except* for the one time when it truly could have meant something?" When she looked over her shoulder, tears pricked my eyes at seeing the crushing hopelessness in hers. The heartbreak I hoped to never see again. The first time I caused that look was two years ago. I swore I'd never do it again. "I know the real reason you don't want to share Ocean. It's because you don't want to share *me*."

"Of course I don't," I said softly, meaningfully. "You're my best friend."

"And is that all I am to you, Hunter?" Her voice was accusing when she turned her head to look out the window once more. "Is that all I've ever been? I distinctly remember a time when we could have had it all, but *you* said no. *You* broke my heart, and now someone else has picked up the shattered pieces and called it treasure. But you just can't let him have it, can you? You can't because you're a jealous coward. You say Ocean is wrong for me, and I say that he's perfect because he's the only man who wouldn't let you run him away. I bet that just kills you, doesn't it? I can't be happy with you, and I can't be happy with him. But I *am*. And I will be—with or without you." When Coby turned to face me this time, her beautiful face was soaked in tears and sorrow. "I just can't believe it took me falling in love again to finally see the real you. You are the most selfish person I've ever met, Hunter Parrish."

Coby turned away from me before I could do or say a word.

She fled, climbing out of the window and dashing off into the dark.

Running… back to him.

CHAPTER TWENTY-SEVEN

OCEAN

Three weeks until shit gets real…

EVER SINCE COBY SNUCK OUT TO THE CABIN ONLY TO COME back shortly after, she'd been giving me the cold shoulder. The space between us had grown so wide that today, I got my mom and cousins to take her out for brunch and a spa day. In the meantime, I would get to the bottom of her attitude. I knew Coby was angry at me for keeping Hunter my little secret, but something else must have happened because I'd overheard her grumbling shit about Hunter, too.

Once I reached the cabin, I let myself inside.

Hunter was sitting on the couch, a towel wrapped around her. Her dark-brown skin and the tight coils of her natural hair were still dripping water from her recent shower.

When she turned her head, I saw the tears streaming freely down her face as she stared back at me. As if it hurt to see me, Hunter inhaled a deep breath and then returned to staring at the flames flickering in the fireplace. I moved to the couch because I couldn't help myself. I had to be near her. But I forced myself to sit on the opposite end to give her space.

"Why didn't you go with them?"

Because nothing gets by my mother, she discovered that Hunter was staying in the cabin days ago and took it upon herself to check on her and bring her and Coco supplies. After meeting Hunter once, my mom fell in love with her instantly, which only got me an earful when she figured out alarmingly fast what I was up to. She'd given me a withering look and said, "Boy, you better be careful."

My mom had invited Hunter out with her and Coby, but apparently, the girl quietly sobbing on the couch alone had declined the invitation.

"I wasn't hungry," she whispered.

"Hunter," I said after we sat in silence for too long. "What happened with you and Coby?"

"I told her everything, and we fought. We fought because I couldn't." As if he could sense his mother's sadness, Coco whined from his spot between her feet, where he was curled up.

Unable to maintain so much space between us anymore, I pulled her into my side, and she came without a fight, curling into my side. Coco followed, and I scooped him up since he was too small to jump onto the couch himself and placed him in my lap. Once Hunter and Coco were settled, I tipped her chin back so that I could see her eyes. "What couldn't you do, Vengeance?"

"I couldn't be with her. I couldn't be with you."

"Why?"

"Because I was scared. I'm not meant to be happy, Ocean. I'll just ruin it for those who are."

"Who told you these things?" Hunter didn't come to this conclusion on her own, and I'll kill whoever put those thoughts in her head.

"It doesn't matter."

"It does."

"Ocean." She sighed, sounding more like herself already. "Let it go."

Never. But I will... for now. My murder list never ends.

"Well, since you don't want to hang out with my mom and Coby, you're spending the day with me. Go get dressed." I nodded toward the bedroom. "We're heading out soon, so wear something warm but comfortable."

The cabin fever must have been setting in because Hunter didn't argue. Ten minutes later, we were leaving the cabin.

"It's freezing," she remarked. Under her short, black winter coat with an oversized fur hood, she wore a black, fitted Dri-FIT jacket, matching leggings that highlighted her curves, and snow boots.

I touched my mouth, swearing I'd felt a little drool at the corner.

"We should be getting more snow soon," I replied, wondering about the last time I had to make small talk. I was used to having conversations about death, money, and power. And the people on the other side of it always preferred skipping over the niceties and getting right to it.

A fully recovered Paul was waiting for us as instructed. Hunter taunted him with a wave of her fingers, and I punished her with a hard slap to her delectable ass that made her yelp before she quickly climbed into the back of the Denali.

"I assume this means the wedding won't be taking place soon?" she asked once Paul drove off. Anyone else might think she was merely curious, but I knew better.

"The wedding will happen in a few weeks as planned," I confirmed.

The winters were particularly dreary and harsh this close to the Great Lakes, so a winter wedding wasn't ideal.

"You sure? I heard May weddings are all the rage," Hunter suggested a little too amicably.

I slid my tongue over my front teeth and stuffed my hands in my pockets to keep them to myself. Sometimes, I didn't know if I wanted to wring Hunter's neck or kiss her. "And it's time enough for Coby to get cold feet, huh?"

Hunter didn't reply, telling me I'd hit the nail on the head.

"It doesn't matter when Coby marries me," I said without hiding a damn thing I was feeling from her. "Only that she does. I know you want to stay, Hunter, even if you won't admit it. I suggest you stop trying to jeopardize what I have with Coby and start figuring out what it is that you want from her, or else Coby will never forgive you."

Hunter crossed her arms, and the movement had my gaze lowering against my will. The tops of her heavy breasts were now spilling from the unzipped portion of her jacket, and I briefly lost my train of thought. "You're one to talk."

"Yeah? How so?"

"Because you want to have your cake and eat me too." She smirked. "And when has that ever worked out for anyone?"

I grew hard at the thought of eating Hunter's pussy. "Probably never. But I'm not just anyone, Hunter, and once I get my dick deep inside you, you'll know it too."

"I hate you."

"No, Vengeance. You don't. You only wish you did."

I caught Hunter's nostrils flaring before she turned her head to stare out the window.

The rest of the drive passed in stilted silence.

When we reached our destination, I smirked to myself when I saw her perk up in my peripheral, but I pretended I didn't as I stepped from the Denali and held out my hand. Hunter ignored it and climbed out. As soon as her feet touched the ground, I placed my hand on the small of her back, and she stumbled a step.

Abel, who had beaten us here, strode forward to meet us as we approached.

"I did a sweep of the building. It's all clear," he said while glancing nervously between Hunter and me. I already knew what he would say before he spoke. "Are you sure this is a good idea?"

"It's fine," I told him as we entered the building.

It was unusually quiet since we had the entire place to ourselves today, but Hunter was already looking around suspiciously, as if she were seeking out another trap.

Or planning her escape.

I led her over to the heavy double doors with multiple safety signs hanging on them and a grim-looking man standing in front.

"Kilpatrick," the range safety officer greeted gruffly.

"Stoll." I shook the older man's hand.

He grunted grumpily and then turned to lead us inside the control booth—a long stretch of hallway between the bathroom, office,
and cleaning room on the left side and firing lanes behind a bulletproof wall on the right.

"Your man got everything set up for you," Stoll said after letting
us inside the firing lanes and over to one of the booths in the middle.
"Handguns, safety gear, mags, and ammunition."

"Thanks, Stoll."

"I'm told you have some experience. I assume you know the
safety and firing regulations, young lady? Same as any other range."

"Yes, sir." Hunter's smile was genuine now as she eagerly eyed
the array of weapons for her choosing.

"Okay, then. I'll leave you to it. Range is hot."

Stoll shuffled out, leaving us alone.

Well, mostly alone.

Abel had taken up guard by the door, and I knew more were
posted at every exit in the building to keep anyone from coming or
going without my express permission.

Hunter and I secured our eyes and ears with safety goggles and
earplugs, but when she reached for one of the handguns, she stopped,
and I tracked her nervous gaze toward the door where Abel was
openly watching her every move.

"No one will hurt you," I assured her.

Hunter forced her gaze away from Abel to regard me. "I think
he's more afraid I will hurt you."

"We're all afraid of that, Hunter. Even you."

Her expression was thoughtful now. "Then why did you bring
me here?"

I leaned against the divider separating this booth from the next
one. "Because I'm choosing to trust you anyway."

Hunter inhaled sharply and then turned away from me to snatch
up one of the magazines and a box of ammunition. "Well, don't expect me to return the favor."

I didn't respond as I pressed the button to call the backboard from the end of the firing range, and then I grabbed a paper target to hang. Once that was set up, I sent the target back while Hunter grabbed a handgun, locked the magazine in place, and chambered a round.

The target stopped ten yards away.

Hunter looked over her shoulder at me with her brow raised, and I grinned as I pressed the button again and sent it to fifteen yards.

She rolled her eyes but took aim as soon as the target stopped. I watched her shoot maybe five rounds before I was willing my dick to behave. I brought her here to see her shoot for myself, but I did not count on what it would do to me.

Remembering why I needed to see her shoot, I opened my eyes just as she emptied the clip. I pressed the button to retrieve the target, and even before it stopped in front of us, I could see the tight grouping at the center.

One look at Abel had him walking over to see for himself.

Hunter was silent but tense as she silently filled another clip.

Abel inspected the paper and tried not to look impressed. "Can you do that again?" he asked skeptically.

Hunter shrugged while avoiding our gazes. "Sure."

I hung another target and pressed the button. This time, I sent it to twenty-five yards. The maximum distance for the pistol range.

Hunter took aim and emptied the clip.

I called the target back and sent Abel a smug look when I saw the tight grouping. All fifteen rounds were dead center.

Abel's brows were damn-near touching his hairline as he studied the paper and Hunter with new eyes.

"Well?" I urged while bouncing on my toes. Vengeance was the fucking truth.

Abel rolled his eyes and sighed. "Are you any good with a rifle?" he asked her in a bored tone.

Hunter turned to face us, her wary gaze moving back and forth between us. I could see the curiosity in her eyes, but she didn't allow herself to ask what we were up to. "I'm okay." She gave a dainty shrug as if we hadn't just watched her shoot better than any merce-nary. "I prefer handguns."

Abel and I looked at each other.

Ten minutes later, we were outside at the rifle range located be-hind the building. Hunter was clutching a semi-automatic and listen-ing intently to Abel's instructions on how to operate it.

"You already know how to control your breathing and how to aim, so the key here is keeping the butt of the rifle firmly against your shoulder to brace against the recoil. It takes some getting used to, so don't feel bad if you need practice. Everyone does. We can adjust your sights once we see where your grouping is."

Hunter nodded, but I could tell under her excitement she was nervous—not just of the weapon, but of me. It was evident by now that I hadn't simply brought her here for a good time.

She glanced at me before quickly looking away and taking aim once Stoll confirmed the range was hot.

Hunter's grouping was all over the place this time, but that was to be expected. Her second attempt wasn't much better, but instead of becoming discouraged, it only made her more determined as she grew comfortable with the rifle. Her third attempt was less scattered, but on her fourth try, she went back to shooting like she was aiming with her eyes closed.

Now I see why she went for the automatic when she raided my cache. She didn't need as much control over her aim in order to kill.

"May I?" I asked after she took aim again, but immediately be-gan fussing with her adjustment. She licked her dried lips due to the wind and then nodded, so I stood behind her—probably closer than necessary—and brought my fingers to her chin. "This lovely face has uses beyond dazzling unsuspecting admirers, Hunter." I gently pushed her face toward the rifle until her right cheek rested against the stock and her dominant eye was properly aligned with the sight. "Better?" She nodded, so I smiled and kissed her soft but cold cheek, making her lips part on an exhale. "You've been forgetting your cheek weld," I instructed. "You won't get consistent shooting without it."

"Thank you."

"You're welcome." I let my hands rest on her voluptuous hips and kissed the corner of her pretty mouth. "Make me proud, Vengeance."

I stepped back.

Her fifth attempt to zero the rifle was successful. Hunter practiced for two more hours, switching to kneeling and then lying down with Abel's instruction before we were satisfied she'd gotten the hang of it.

Abel and I exchanged a look, and at his reluctant nod, I smiled victoriously and led Hunter back toward the building. She was too excited about her day of shooting and learning a new weapon to notice that we were walking hand in hand. She even let me help her into the back of the Denali, but we didn't speak the entire drive.

We were back at the cabin when she stopped before the door and turned to face me. "Thank you for today," she said sweetly. "I needed that. And I had fun."

"So did I."

It felt like the end of a first date—when the guy was standing on the girl's front porch, hoping she'd invite him in. I knew Hunter wouldn't, just like Hunter knew she wouldn't stop me if I asked.

"Did you know I'd enjoy it because you had me followed?"

"Yes," I confessed. It fired something inside me when Hunter didn't look away. There was nothing honorable about my obsession, but Coby and Hunter didn't run away from it. Instead, they embraced it on their own terms and brought me to heel with their own desires. "But I don't know what made you want to learn in the first place."

"You don't?" she asked me skeptically.

I swallowed, knowing the possible reason was an ugly one. "I have an idea."

Her father.

She learned how to shoot to protect herself from men like her fucking father. The one man Hunter should have been able to trust unconditionally.

"I'm sure you know I went to juvie, but you don't know the real reason why. No one does. Everyone thinks they know, and the ones who doubted didn't care enough to ask the hard questions." Hunter shifted uncomfortably, but she still didn't look away, letting me see her ugly parts, too. "Not one person stood up for me. Not even my court-appointed lawyer. My father's side of the story had more holes than Swiss cheese, but it made better headlines. Troubled Teen Stabs Father to Avoid Chores." She scoffed, and I felt her disgust because it mirrored my own. "Who cares that the truth rarely fits in one sentence? Lock her away."

"You pled guilty."

Hunter nodded, but her gaze was fixed on her hands as if she could see her father's blood staining them. "I did."

"Why?"

She squeezed her eyes closed and inhaled deeply. "Because I didn't look at those bars as keeping me in. To me, they were keeping my father out. When I was released, my forgiving father was there, waiting for his delinquent daughter with open arms." Hunter laughed, but it was a bitter sound. "So I ran. With the news cameras watching and anyone who bothered to remember my name, I ran from that monster, and I thought that was the end of it, but it wasn't. I thought I could move on, but I couldn't. Not while he was alive."

"That's when you burned his house down." She nodded. "But he got out, and you were caught."

"A month before I got out of juvie for stabbing him, my mother died. The same one who abandoned me when I was just a baby. Luck must have finally been on my side because I somehow got the only attorney in the world who could convince a jury that I actually mourned that bitch. I was sentenced to grief counseling and community service. That's when I met Coby."

"What did your father do to you, Hunter?"

"Nothing." She shrugged. "Not really. It's what he tried to make me do."

I inched closer but stopped just short of touching her. "What did he want you to do?"

"We were on the verge of losing the house because of my father's gambling habit. He was about to lose his job, so my father promised his boss something besides a good work ethic."

"What did he—" The answer hit me like a train before I could finish asking the question.

Hunter sighed, looking truly dejected. "I was supposed to fuck my father's boss, two of his best employees, and three golfing buddies so that my father could keep his minimum-wage job and his spot at his favorite poker table. Those were the *chores* the headlines unwittingly wrote about. I came home from school, and there they were—drinking my father's beer and waiting for his fourteen-year-old daughter to come home from school. I begged my dad not to give me to them, but he wouldn't listen. He said I would be fucking soon enough anyway, so he might as well get his fair share."

Hunter closed her eyes, and when she opened them again, they were brimming with tears. I pulled her into me and wrapped her in my embrace.

"I don't—" Her voice broke. "I don't remember picking up the knife. I could hear the disgusting things those men were saying about me in the other room. I was so scared of what they'd make me do. My father grabbed my hair, and I grabbed the knife I'd used to slice my bagel that morning. And then I stabbed him with it before running away." I felt her nails digging into my chest and welcomed the pain if it meant she didn't feel any. "I didn't get far before I was picked up as a runaway."

Hunter suddenly pushed away from me, and I gave her the space she needed.

"I tried, you know," she said as she stared at the ground. "I tried to tell the cops what happened, but my father got to them first. He had witnesses. Those men he brought home to fuck his underage daughter couldn't let the truth get out, so they backed the lie. They told the police that I stabbed my father unprovoked, and it was their word against mine, so I pled down to simple assault and did a year in juvie just to get away from him."

"And you've been training to protect yourself ever since."

It wasn't a question, but Hunter nodded anyway. "As long as my father lives, I will never feel safe. I'm sure he's forgotten about me by now, but I haven't forgotten him."

"Who else knows about this?" I asked while fighting to keep the violence out of my tone.

"Only Coby," she answered. Our gazes met. "And now you."

"You may not care to hear it, but I need to say it anyway. Your father is a dead man. I want names. Every single man who was there. I want their names, and if you can't give them to me, I'll find them anyway."

"I don't need you to protect me," she said weakly.

Losing my fight to be honorable, I pulled her into me. She didn't fight me as she stared up at me, looking so innocent and vulnerable. "Someone has to."

"I can take care of myself."

"I know you can, Vengeance, but I want that honor. Tell me I can have it," I pleaded.

"You're marrying my best friend," she reminded me.

"I am."

"How can you not see it? What you want will *never* work? I wouldn't mean as much to you as Coby. She would always own more of you than I ever could, and I know it's not a competition, but it doesn't seem fair. I've never done anything like this, but shouldn't there be a balance? If you tip the scales too much one way, wouldn't it all topple over? If I thought for one second that I could be the other woman and not let the jealousy consume me…"

She didn't let the rest fall from her lips.

"You would say yes," I finished for her.

"I would say yes."

"Hunter…" I felt my frustration bubble and forced it back down. "I have to marry. It has nothing to do with wanting Coby more than you. You wouldn't be the other woman, and I don't care what a piece of paper says. You would be my wife as much as Coby."

"But it's how I would eventually feel if you married each other. I would still feel on the outside." I felt her palm on my cheek; it was the first time she willingly touched me, so I closed my eyes to savor the moment. "Promise me you'll keep Coby safe and make her happy when I'm gone."

I turned my head to kiss her palm. "You don't have to leave, Hunter. Even if you don't stay for me, you can stay for Coby."

"I doubt Coby wants me to stay anymore. She hates me now."

"No, she doesn't. Not yet. But she will if you leave."

"Ocean, I told you I can't stay."

"I don't mean for that. We both want Coby safe, but as my wife and the woman I love, she'll be in more danger than ever. You've proved capable and willing to keep anything from happening to her. What if I gave you another reason to stay?"

Hunter's hand dropped from my face as she stared at me in disbelief. "What are you talking about?"

"I want to hire you."

The furrow in Hunter's brows deepened, and I forced myself to let her go. "To do what exactly?"

It seemed like the entire world had gone still, waiting for my answer. "I want you to protect my wife."

CHAPTER TWENTY-EIGHT

HUNTER

"*I* WANT YOU TO PROTECT MY WIFE."
My wife.
My wife.
Protect my wife.
"She's still sleeping."

The unexpected sound of Coby's voice in the cabin startled me awake, but the responding one with a deep Chicago accent had my eyes flying open.

Protect my wife.

I reached under my pillow where my Sig was hidden.

After I had accepted his offer to act as Coby's bodyguard, Ocean had given me some new and pretty toys to play with, which Coco kept mistaking for chew toys.

The floor was ice cold under my bare feet when I quietly climbed from the bed and pulled on my robe. Scooping Coco from the foot of the bed, I tiptoed to the door and peeked through the crack to see a man standing just a few feet away. His back was turned to me, but he still seemed annoyingly familiar. The blond hair, leather jacket, and cocky demeanor poked at my memory.

"Then wake her up, or I will. Her beauty sleep isn't my concern. She knows what she signed up for." I pushed open the door and slipped out with my gun aimed at the asshole's occipital. As soon as I did, he cocked his head like a predator who knows there's prey nearby. "Don't you, Hunter?" The man turned to face me before I could react. "You really thought I'd let you get the drop on me a second time?"

I lowered the gun with a roll of my eyes when I saw his face. "You should have drowned."

Kellan's green eyes twinkled with amusement. "I'm an exceptional swimmer."

I looked him over. "You look like shit," I remarked.

"So do you."

"You two know each other?" Coby asked.

"We've met," I replied without looking at her. She was right. I was a coward. I stepped around Kellan with Coco in my arms and walked to the door to shove my feet in my slippers.

Coby made a terrified squeak in the back of her voice when she saw him. I rolled my eyes because here we go. "Hunter, what the hell is that? Is it…is it a rat?"

"It's a Yorkshire Terrier. And from the looks of the pup, it's a runt," Kellan answered for me. "Don't tell me you're afraid."

Coby, the vegan who was afraid of animals, shuddered out a breath.

"Wow. Yeah, I totally get the fear," Kellan taunted. "A beast like that can totally gnaw your ankles to death."

"Don't tease her," I warned, taking up for my bestie.

Kellan rolled his eyes. Coby fled to the bathroom. I took the puppy outside.

After Coco relieved himself, I put him in the room and yelled out for Coby, who was still hiding in the bathroom.

"What are you doing here?" I directed at Kellan. I had the same question for Coby, who was staring at me now and anxiously chewing her bottom lip. It wasn't unusual for Coby and me to fight, but it was the first time it ever felt like it was the last one we'd ever have. Even while standing in the same room, it felt like there was a mountain between us.

"Your training starts today. Ocean's orders."

"Training?" Coby echoed before I could tell Kellan where to shove it. I guess Ocean never bothered to tell her about his job offer.

"The Strap offered me a job, and I took it," I answered.

"Please stop calling him that, Hunter. Doing what?"

"Protecting you."

Coby's eyes flared with horror. "No." She shook her head. "Absolutely not."

"Coby—"

"I said no! You're not doing it. It's dangerous!"

I squinted. "I remember telling you the same thing. You asked me to trust that you could take care of yourself, so now I'm asking the same of you. You wanted me to stay, remember? I'm staying."

"No, Hunter. I want you to want to stay."

"Maybe I should come back," Kellan said uncertainly. Despite being uncomfortable, he stayed where he was, his curious gaze swinging back and forth as Coby and I geared up for round two.

Instead of fighting with me again, Coby turned her fury on Kellan. "Where is he?"

Knowing exactly who she meant, Kellan answered, "In a meeting with the Boss."

"I thought his father was in Ireland until the wedding?" I asked.

"They have cell phone reception in Ireland."

"Take me to him," Coby demanded.

Kellan looked like he wanted to say no, but then he nodded and started for the door. "I'll be outside," he called over his shoulder. "You both have ten minutes."

"Hunter," Coby said as soon as the door closed behind Kellan. "Please don't do this." She started to follow me into my room, but then she remembered Coco and stayed in the living room. "What if someone hurts you?" she called out.

"Then try to imagine why I accepted Ocean's offer." I didn't know what constituted training, and I didn't have much to choose from, so I started dressing in the same outfit I wore to the shooting range. "I'm terrified someone will hurt *you*. You've seen how busy Ocean is, how often he's gone. You're in a treacherous world surrounded by strangers. You need someone who can be there when he can't. I was already willing to take a bullet for you, and I know you'd do the same for me, so what's really changing?"

Dressed now, I walked back into the main room with Coco warmly nestled inside my jacket to see Coby wringing her hands. "Does this mean you'll stay even after the wedding?"

I didn't trust that look in her eyes like she was hoping I might stay for other reasons, too, so I grabbed her hand and started for the door without answering. "We should probably hurry. I don't want to be late on my first day."

The main house was a vast, opulent maze that made me feel like a fish out of water. Coby and I followed Kellan through the long hallways while I tried my hardest to focus on creating a mental map and not gawking at the marble statues and busts, the high ceilings, and the glittering chandeliers. While we walked, Coby told me all about Glainne—Ocean's penthouse in the city, which was nestled at the top of that onyx tower she'd always wondered at.

Coby already seemed to be at home since she'd been basically living here. My brief encounters with Ocean's mom had been pleasant. Coby already loved her, so I told myself it was all that mattered. It's not like Effie was going to be my mother-in-law.

Our first stop was a room with tall, solid doors; behind them was a study. Kellan left Coby there to wait for Ocean before motioning me to follow him.

I thought the house had only two levels until we descended a spiral staircase into a sub-level too intricate to be a basement. The floor opened into a circular room with stone walls and low lighting. The air was dank and drafty with an earthy scent that said we were deep underground.

Perfect for a dungeon or torture chamber.

I followed Kellan through the doorless threshold and kept close when I noticed the floor was a maze of dark corridors, impossible to navigate without getting lost.

Eventually, we reached a gym of sorts, but it looked more like an underground dojo with black mats covering the floor and various equipment scattered throughout—striking shields, freestanding bags, ground bags, slip bags, teardrop bags, long bags, free weights, and other shit I couldn't name.

Abel was already waiting for us.

I couldn't deny how handsome he was. His deep, dark skin glowed beneath the fluorescent light, but his hazel eyes were watchful, without his usual distrust.

"You're late," he scolded.

"I don't own a watch."

Abel clenched his jaw and gestured for me to step on the mat.

I reached for Coco, who was still cradled in my jacket, and set him on the ground, but Kellan quickly scooped him up. "I'll take that. Have fun." With a grin and a wink, he was gone with Coco.

Exhaling, I slowly approached Abel, who cocked a brow at me. "You ready?"

"Sure."

Hours later, I was kneeling on the mat, breathing heavily, clutching my side, and dripping sweat.

And I'd never felt more alive.

The muscles in my arms trembled as I held up my hand for mercy I didn't want. It was just my natural self-preservation kicking in while the much darker, esoteric part of me that needed to be examined by a psychologist demanded more.

"Had enough?" Abel questioned.

"Not even close." I coughed and spat out blood. *Oh, Lord.* I hoped I still had all my teeth. "Just give me a minute."

"You can take a punch, and you're fast, but you have no endurance," he informed me coldly.

Abel hadn't warmed a single degree, not even when he was kicking my ass from one end of the room to the next. I could tell he was enjoying himself, too. At his request, our session started with me showing him what I knew.

Nothing.

I knew nothing.

And he wasted no time making that blatantly apparent.

For hours, Abel had me attack him repeatedly and hold nothing back, but each time, I'd quickly go from the offensive to the defensive until I was eager to learn everything he knew.

"You're done for today, Parrish."

"No—"

"You're no good to me tomorrow if I break you today. Clean yourself up, and I'll see you at five."

"A.m.?" I squawked, but he was already gone.

I collapsed with a tired groan and was still lying there, cheek to the mat, when I heard someone enter.

How long had I been lying here?

My eyes were the only thing I could move as they followed the direction the footsteps came from.

Ocean.

He was dressed in a suit today. This one was dark gray and tailored to accentuate his broad shoulders. Each of his strides that brought him closer to me spoke of confidence and power, and I was too transfixed to be on guard.

"Abel told me you might still be down here." Ocean crouched next to me but didn't touch me. I refused to read too much into why that felt disappointing.

I groaned again, feeling my stomach muscles spasm when I flopped onto my back. "That's all I got. Just leave me here and save yourself."

Ocean chuckled. "I told Abel not to take it easy on you." This time, he did touch me. I felt the sweep of his thumb under the tender part of my cheek. "Was I wrong?"

"No." What didn't kill me made me stronger, and I was done being a victim. I suspect Ocean knew that, too. I didn't realize I was nuzzling his hand until his thumb fell to my lips. "Thank you."

"You don't ever need to thank me, Vengeance." He scooped me from the floor, and I immediately felt horrible for ruining his expensive suit with my sweat—so horrible I lay my head on his shoulder while he carried me out.

"Coby's mad at you," I warned him groggily.

Ocean chuckled and gave me a squeeze. "I noticed when she yelled at me for half an hour, but thanks for the heads up, Vengeance."

"Don't be mean to her, okay? She just doesn't want me to get hurt."

He shook his head. "I would never mistreat her. And I don't want that either."

I lifted my head to stare at him in disbelief. "You hired me to protect her. The day will come when it's either me or her," I warned. "Coby's more important to you. She's more important to me."

I looked up in time to see Ocean shut his eyes and inhale. "Please stop saying that, Hunter. It's not true."

"But it has to be. Coby deserves to be the only thing that matters to you. As her best friend, I don't want anything less, so please believe I'm not saying this out of jealousy. I want you to understand that this marriage will be real for Coby and for you. Once you both say your vows, promise me you'll let go of whatever you want from me. Let me go... for Coby."

Ocean's teeth were clenched as he stared straight ahead. "Like you, Hunter, if I could promise that and mean it, I would," he said as he climbed the spiral staircase. "You deserve more than a lie. I will never let you go. I will never let Coby go. It's the only promise you're going to get from me."

"How can you be sure the three of us can work?"

"I'm not, Hunter. Love has never been a sure thing. It changes faces every day, and it's not always pretty. Coby and I took a leap of faith while you're still standing on that ledge waiting to see what happens. You're never going to stop being afraid of the fall. You just have to choose if you want to fall alone or with someone you love. With *people* you love," he corrected.

I stared at his profile. "Are you trying to tell me you love me?"

Ocean's gaze cut toward me before darting away. "I'm trying to tell you I've been falling ever since you first tried to kill me."

And now he was putting himself on the line, hoping I'd follow...

"The last man I trusted to love me unconditionally wanted to sell me for poker chips."

His grip on me tightened. "I know."

"And the last man I trusted to just be a friend tried to—"

Ocean's steps faltered. "What?"

I sighed heavily. "Let's just say that he wanted more than he was owed, and I found myself running again."

At least I hadn't been alone that time.

I'd taken Coby with me.

"Hunter—"

"Where are we?" I cut him off to change the subject as I looked around and frowned. "This isn't the way back to the cabin."

My mental map was already coming in handy.

Ocean was scowling now as he climbed another set of stairs to the second level without answering. I knew he wasn't upset with me, but the rage seeping from his skin gave me goosebumps anyway.

He didn't stop until we reached a wing tucked away from everything and a room with double doors facing a large window at the opposite end of the hallway. He set me on my feet once we were inside, and I didn't realize it wasn't just any bedroom until it was too late. The masculine decor gave it away, but when he shed his suit jacket and tossed it on the bed, it left no room for doubt.

"Ocean, what—"

"Hey, bestie!" a welcome voice called out. "Did you have fun?"

I followed the sound to the open balcony doors, where Coby was sitting at a small table set for three, the orange glow of the setting sun beyond her.

Relief carved its way into my chest at seeing her here.

It wasn't that I didn't trust Ocean to be on his best behavior. The problem was that I didn't trust myself. As exhausted and sore as I was, I still wanted to use and be used by him.

"I got my ass kicked," I confessed as I stepped onto the large balcony and dropped into the seat across from her. Ocean gallantly lifted the lid off my plate and then took the seat that faced us both with his back to the railing.

"You?" Coby said in disbelief.

We were both temporarily distracted when Ocean removed his cufflinks and began rolling up his sleeves to reveal muscle-corded forearms.

I cleared my throat and looked away from all that arm porn. "Abel's good."

"You'll be better," Coby said with total confidence. "And then you'll kick his ass, and I'll be there to watch."

That's why she was my bitch. It's too bad I wasn't shit, lusting after her fiancé.

My appetite fled as foreboding washed over me, but then my empty stomach gave a painful clench, reminding me I hadn't eaten today. It didn't help that the food looked amazing.

"What's wrong, Hunter?" Ocean was staring at me as if he'd read my mind.

I stared at my plate. "Is it possible to be hungry but too tired to eat?"

"I think so," Coby answered as she happily devoured her zucchini ravioli. She looked beautiful today in her sweater dress and fishnet tights, while I looked and felt beat to shit.

I felt my appetite waning again.

"Come here, Vengeance."

I looked up to see Ocean pushing back his chair, but not to stand. He sat there and waited for me to obey. I directed my confused frown in Coby's direction, who stared at me encouragingly while nibbling on a carrot. Standing on shaky legs, I went to him.

Ocean took my hand and pulled me into his lap.

As soon as I felt his hard thighs underneath my butt, my skittish gaze flew to Coby again.

She smiled softly at me, and it felt like I was dreaming.

"You two have to be the weirdest couple I've ever met," I grumbled.

Coby giggled, and Ocean snorted before lifting the silver dome off his plate. My mouth watered when I saw the braised short ribs on a bed of rice and carrots. He picked up his fork and knife, cut off a piece, and lifted the meat for me to eat.

I hesitated only a moment before leaning forward and accepting the offering. The flavors immediately exploded in my mouth, and I hummed my amazement.

"Oh, my God," I moaned.

"Good?" he asked me.

My skin flushed for some reason. "*Yes.*"

"Want some more?"

I greedily nodded, so he speared another piece for me. Bite after bite, he patiently fed me, and I was too hungry and exhausted to be embarrassed about it.

"What about you?" I asked after half the plate was almost gone.

"I'll eat when you're taken care of," he told me.

Coby finished eating, having gotten a head start while Ocean hunted me down, so she stood and announced she was going to shower.

I frowned after her as she left the balcony, leaving Ocean and me alone.

I stared off into the distance, so Ocean started eating from his plate and mine.

"Want some wine?" he offered between bites.

"Ocean," I shifted on his lap to face him when I heard the shower turn on inside the room. "What's going on?"

Sighing, he placed his fork and knife down. I actually felt a little guilty about not letting him finish, but not enough to deny myself the answers I needed. "You won't be staying in the cabin after tonight. There's a winter storm coming. You and Coco will be safer and more comfortable in the main house. Coby sleeps in my bed, but if you prefer, I can have a room prepared for you…"

If I prefer…

That meant it wasn't the first option being offered to me.

Curling his fingers with mine, Ocean lifted my hand from my lap and kissed the back of it. "Is that what you want?"

I didn't answer right away because I didn't know what I wanted. "You said if I prefer…"

"I did."

I gulped. "What's the alternative?"

Ocean sat back and rested his cheek on his fist as he stared at me. "My bed, Hunter."

My stomach dipped.

On cue, an off-key rendition of "We Belong Together" by Mariah Carey suddenly came from the direction of the bathroom.

Neither Ocean nor I reacted because it meant falling out of this bubble erected around us.

"You want me to sleep in your bed with you and Coby?"

"Yes. But only if you want it, too. I don't want to make you feel unsafe."

"I feel safe," I blurted. "I don't think you'll hurt me."

Ocean stiffened under me.

Oh, hell. What had I done?

"No, Vengeance. I won't," Ocean confirmed. And then he trailed a finger down my arm. "Not until you ask me to."

I squirmed in his lap, and all I could think was that it was a bad day to be going commando.

"What's the matter?" Before I could make some excuse, his hand slid up my thigh until it cupped my center. "Is it your pussy?"

"Yes." *What? What, what, WHAT?* "I think you know you're making me wet, Ocean."

"Kiss me, and I'll make it better, Vengeance."

I didn't give a damn why I shouldn't when I pressed my lips to his. I wasn't thinking at all. All I could do was bask in how wrong it didn't feel.

We kissed as if we had all the time in the world. We kissed as if we belonged. Coby was still singing in the shower while Ocean's middle finger massaged my slit through the leggings.

My best friend was happy with a man she should despise, a man neither of us should trust, but one we couldn't seem to resist.

We were screwed.

"Shit," he grunted. "You're making a mess, baby. I'd better check it." Ocean pulled his hand away and tapped my thigh. "Stand up."

I swallowed down the knot in my throat and obeyed. My legs were trembling as Ocean slowly peeled off my leggings like he was unwrapping a birthday gift. I felt my panic rising at how far over the line we'd crossed and grabbed his hand.

"It's okay," Ocean cooed as he gently pried my hand away. "It's okay. Let it happen."

Once my leggings were off, Ocean turned me around until I faced the table. I could feel my arousal soaking my inner thighs and had no clue what he planned until I felt his hands separating the plump cheeks of my ass. I could feel the warmth of his breath skating the lips of my pussy—and then he pushed his face between my ass and inhaled sharply through his nose.

My jaw dropped when he groaned and did it again.

Feeling my knees buckle, I reached behind me to grab the back of his head for balance.

He was scenting me.

It was so absurdly primal.

The bridge of his nose brushed my clit, and I lost all sense of who I was when I wiggled my ass on his face. "You like that?"

Ocean groaned…loudly…and inhaled again.

My wild gaze flew to the bathroom door. Steam poured out from underneath, and my best friend poured her heart out while I let her fiancée smell my pussy. Coby preferred bubble baths to showers.

She only took them when she was in a hurry, which meant we didn't have much time.

Finally, Ocean stood and roughly peeled off my shirt and sports bra until I was completely naked. I didn't feel the cold with him at my back. I felt so small this close to him—like he could break me in two if he wanted. The unspoken threat—the danger of it—sent a deep thrill rippling through me.

"What are you doing?"

He cupped my breasts with both hands and bent his head to whisper, "I'm done waiting, Hunter."

Heart racing, my lips parted to tell him we shouldn't, but it felt like a lie, so I closed them. I didn't want to wait, either. I wanted to feel him inside me.

But Ocean wasn't mine. He was Coby's.

This was wrong.

"Ocean—"

"Bend the fuck over."

I whimpered. "We can't do this to Coby."

Ocean's hands left my breasts, skimming my waist and belly until he reached my pussy. "Should I stop?" he whispered as he crudely cupped my cunt, his fingers sliding between my soaked lips. "You don't feel like you want me to stop."

"We can't," I weakly repeated.

"That's not what I asked you, Hunter."

"Please…" His hands left me, and I heard metal clinking as he opened his belt. "Ocean, please."

One of us had to be strong, and I knew it wouldn't be me.

"Tell me no," he urged as he tore open his pants. They dropped to the ground with an audible thud, and then I heard a condom wrapper tear open.

I glanced behind me to watch him roll the condom down his dick. It was so long, thick, and angry-looking with those thick veins, plum hue, and broad tip. A mournful sob ripped out of me at the gorgeous sight. There was no way I could say no to feeling that monster split me in two.

Ocean knew it, too.

I felt his hand on my back as he pressed me forward, and I didn't fight him. I submitted to his will, letting him bend me over the table, my hard nipples brushing the heavily starched cloth and adding another sensation.

I lifted onto the tips of my toes while he bent his knees. I was a little taller than Coby, but the height still wasn't quite right since Ocean was a freaking giant.

You can still stop this, the angel on my shoulder whispered when I felt the broad head of his dick probing my entrance. *It's not too late. He'll stop if you tell him to. Just say no.*

The devil on the other side had me reaching between my legs and shoving Ocean's hand aside to guide that big dick to my aching pussy. My lashes fluttered as soon as my warm walls parted to let him inside. There was only one problem...

"Open that pussy for me, Hunter."

"I'm trying," I whined. "You're too big."

It was Ocean's turn to push my hand away. Taking over, he slowly forced another inch inside me, and I cried out in ecstasy before remembering why I had to be quiet. I cast another frantic look at the bathroom door. The shower was still going, and Coby was still singing.

"Don't make this hard, Hunter," Ocean said with a frustrated growl. He roughly gripped the back of my knee and lifted it onto the table to open me up more. "Just give in." Shove. Grunt. "Just... give...in."

Finally, his thick pole broke through my tight wall's resistance, his groin clapping loudly with the heavy globes of my ass, and we both cried out in shock over how fucking good it felt.

Ocean braced his hands on the table on either side of me. "Such a tight little pussy. Such a good fucking girl," he praised. "Give me a kiss." Powerless to resist, I lifted onto my palms and tilted my head back to let him kiss me. "You okay?" he asked me once my lips were swollen and no longer fused with his.

I could feel the burn of my pussy from being stretched, but it felt fucking right. "More than okay."

"That's my girl." Ocean gave me another sensual kiss, his last tender act before his hand shifted to the deep crease where my wide hips met my narrow waist. "Hold on."

It was all the warning I got before he withdrew, leaving only the tip inside, and slammed forward again. His thrust was so forceful the table slid forward, but he didn't seem to care as he moaned and did it again…and again…and again.

This was no slow lovemaking or meeting of the minds. It was animalistic, unfettered, driven by instinct alone—it was pure *fucking*.

The wet clapping of our skin, his narrow hips bouncing off my round ass, the table scraping across the ground, the fine dishes rattling on top, my sharp cries, and his feral grunts had mixed in with the running water and Coby's cheerful singing, creating a sinful melody that I never wanted to end.

I was lost in Ocean's deadly vortex and didn't want to be free.

My heavy breasts swung wildly as he pounded in and out of me, and when my eyes drifted closed, a vision of Coby suckling my nipples while our captor drove his dick inside me invaded my mind.

Startled, my eyes flew open, but it wasn't because of the vision. Something far more terrifying had already grabbed my attention.

The shower had shut off.

And Ocean was still fucking me with no signs of stopping.

"Ocean," I warned. "The shower. Coby." I tried to pull away when he kept going, but I was trapped between him and the table. There was nowhere for me to go unless he let me. "Ocean, please." I reached behind me, placing my hand on his hard abs, but he grabbed my wrist and pinned my hand to the table.

"You ain't come for me yet," he demanded cruelly. And then he kissed me.

"She'll catch us," I whispered, horrified. Still, I kissed him back.

"So *come.*"

Tears pricked my eyes as panic rose in my chest. I didn't want to stop, but I didn't want to be caught either.

I had to hurry this crazy man up.

Sneaking my free hand between my legs, I found my swollen clit. I'd already been close, so it didn't take more than a few circles of the sensitive nub before I was coming harder than I ever had.

A cry tore out of my throat, but it was cut short when Ocean slapped a hand over my mouth and sank his teeth into my shoulder, flooding the condom with a harsh grunt.

It was eerily quiet after that.

No sound came from the bathroom.

The euphoria faded, and reality quickly came crashing down. How could I do this to her?

"What did I dooo?" I wailed.

Ocean said nothing as he slid out of me. The sound was a crude wet slurp that reminded me how much I'd loved what we'd done. I heard him remove the condom with a snap, and then he pulled up his pants and boxers.

"Look at me, Vengeance." I felt a tear roll down my face as I straightened and reluctantly faced him. "Stop this." He gently thumbed it away. "What we did was done with Coby's blessing." Shock rippled through me as my head whipped toward the bathroom door, but he gripped my jaw firmly, keeping my wide eyes on him. "But you will not tell her it happened."

My brows immediately drew down. "If Coby's okay with it, why can't I tell her?"

"Because she wants the three of us together as much as I do, and I promised her I would deliver. I will not get her hopes up in vain if you still plan on walking away, and you will not make me a liar."

"But it's okay if you make me one?" I ripped my face away from his hand and pushed him away. I could hear Coby moving around in the bathroom, so I quickly redressed.

"Do you really want to tell Coby you screwed her fiancé for the hell of it? Everything I do is to protect you both. I don't want you hurting Coby for your sake as much as hers."

"For the last time, I'm *not* your concern. *Coby* is."

Ire swam in sinful brown eyes. "As long as you are in my home, you belong to me, and I protect what's mine. That includes you, whether you like it or not."

The bathroom door opened.

I quickly put space between us when Coby stepped out, cloaked in a cloud of steam. I held my breath, certain she'd heard us. I didn't need to see Ocean's face to know he was, too. It didn't matter that we had her blessing—not telling her felt like deception.

But what if Ocean was right? What if the truth hurt Coby more?

Finally, the steam parted, revealing her pretty face.

My stomach sank.

This is so fucking awkward, I thought an hour later as I lay in bed staring at the vaulted ceiling and the exposed wooden beams while Coby talked my ear off.

For some reason, I'd chosen to follow my heart.

The only problem was that my head wouldn't stop screaming that this could never work. It was all I could do not to bolt out the door that I kept eyeing. I was already showered and dressed for bed in one of Ocean's T-shirts. I could already feel exhaustion creeping in, but I wouldn't allow myself to sleep. Not yet.

Ocean was currently in the shower while Coby and I waited for him.

In his bed.

"Hunter." Snapping out of my stupor, I looked over at Coby, who had slid over to lie next to me with her elbow propped up on the pillow and her head in her hand. "Are you okay?"

"Yes."

"Are you lying to me?"

"Yes."

"Hunter…I'll understand if you don't want to do this. We both will. I won't be mad. Promise."

I shook my head. "It's not that."

Coby frowned. "Then what's wrong?"

I made a sound of distress. "I can't tell you."

Coby searched my gaze before saying, "Ocean?"

Wordlessly, I nodded. Neither of us noticed the shower had shut off until Ocean left the bathroom, and we both jumped like we'd been caught with our hands in the cookie jar. He glanced at the bed on the way to the closet, and Coby scrambled back to her side.

"Why did you move?" I whispered.

Coby looked guilty all of a sudden as she avoided my gaze and drew hearts into the sheets. The long ribbon she wore around her ankle today was blue to match her nightie. "Because Ocean said I wasn't allowed to—not until you made up your mind."

I frowned. "Allowed to do what?"

Her eyes rose from the bed, but she didn't say a word. She didn't have to.

Ocean walked out of the closet just as I was about to spill our secret and expose what a hypocrite he was, but one meaningful look exchanged between us, and all I wanted to do was follow his lead.

Ocean climbed into the middle of the bed, and Coby immediately went to him while I stayed frozen where I was, content to watch him grip her ass beneath the blue nightie and kiss her senseless. Their size difference was crazy. I couldn't tell if she was just that small or he was just that tall. Even with Coby on top, it was clear who was in control. They were obviously used to sharing a bed, and so were Coby and I, but *this*…this was new.

"We should probably stop," Coby teased after ending the kiss and falling to Ocean's side. She rested her head on his chest and stared at me. "I think we're scaring Hunter."

"Vengeance," Ocean called his pet name for me in a deep rumble. "Come here."

I felt the back of my neck grow hot as I let myself slide across the bed until I was curved around Ocean's other side with my hand resting on his abs. I wasn't prepared for Ocean to roll me onto my back and kiss me as deeply as he kissed Coby. His body on top of me felt so good, I forgot to be afraid of how much I wanted it as I clutched his side and wrapped my legs around his waist. I moaned, feeling Ocean's big dick harden against my pussy, and then a moment later, the kiss ended.

"You good?" he asked, checking in with me.

I nodded when I couldn't quite catch my breath, and then his heavy weight was gone. Ocean returned to Coby, who was watching us with a victorious smile she tried to hide, and then he dragged me against him.

"Good night, *mo aingeal.*"

"Good night."

Ocean closed his eyes and settled in for the night before saying, "Good night, Vengeance."

My eyes were already drifting closed when I mumbled, "Good night."

CHAPTER TWENTY-NINE

COBY

I LIFTED THE HEAVY ARM LOCKED AROUND MY WAIST AND exhaled quietly when it dropped like dead weight on the mattress behind me. Ocean had come in late, showered, fucked me, and then collapsed next to me with a gentle kiss goodnight before he succumbed to exhaustion.

He was traveling to the city a lot. And when he was home, Ocean was locked away in secret meetings with his father's *capteans*. I knew what he was doing and why, but it didn't make me feel any better because I knew shit was about to get real.

Ocean was preparing for war.

Our wedding was in a week, and his father would be back any day now.

I locked away thoughts of the mysterious Boss of the *Fola*—who would kill me the moment he discovered I was marrying his son—and slipped from the bedroom.

It was almost midnight, and I didn't want to be late.

Two weeks ago, Ocean moved Hunter and Coco into the main house, and not a moment too soon, because the lake was permanently frozen now until spring. The first real snow had left the thirty acres of the Kilpatrick's estate under a thick, white blanket. I could see the cabin from the main house—or at least the parts that weren't covered under a white blanket—and was glad that Hunter wasn't trapped inside.

My toes were warm against the heated floors as I tiptoed around the enormous house, but after several wrong turns, I reached my destination a few minutes before the hour turned.

Hunter stood at the kitchen island in her pale pink robe and matching house slippers.

There was a match in her hand.

Her expression was despondent until she heard me arrive. Seeing me, the look faded, and she smiled softly. "I was starting to think you forgot."

"That would be pretty impressive since this tradition was my idea."

"Where's The Strap?"

"He's sleep—Hunter…"

She smiled conspiratorially, lit the match, and brought the flame to the kindling.

One by one, twenty-six tapers ignited until the small flames danced in the dark, illuminating the blue or maybe purple cream they were embedded in.

"I'm not singing," she warned, just as she did every year.

I smiled and moved over to the island to stand next to her. "Of course not. Someone might actually think you're all mushy inside."

"Happy Birthday, bestie," Hunter whispered.

"Thank you." I kept my gaze on the tiered cake as my lips twitched. "Two layers this year. Is this how the other side lives?"

Hunter snorted with a close-lipped smile. "You can thank your future husband for sponsoring the extra batter. We're fancy now."

I laughed. "What kind of frosting did you use?"

"Blueberry." Hunter wrinkled her nose, and I sighed.

"This should be interesting."

"Any time you want to return to the dark side, just say the word. I can have a juicy, delicious, guilt-free fat-as-fuck cow waiting for you like that." She snapped her fingers, and it was my turn to snort. "Ooh!

It's midnight!" Hunter said after glancing over her shoulder to check the oven for the time. "Make your wish."

Instead of blowing out the candles, I thumbed away the white dusting on her cheek. Hunter and the kitchen were a mess of flour, sugar, and frosting.

Every birthday, there was a cake. Always homemade and never store-bought. We didn't always have money for gifts, so we chose a tradition paid for with love and whatever ingredients we could find around the house. Or steal, in Hunter's case.

I held her gaze and licked the flour from my thumb without thinking much about it. I didn't realize how it might be interpreted until Hunter's lips parted and her pupils dilated. The moment ended abruptly when we heard a door slam somewhere in the house.

Hunter cleared her throat and moved away.

"I almost forgot," she said while I stared at the countertop. What the hell did I just do? I didn't blink or breathe until Hunter returned and slammed a bottle of tequila and two mini tumblers down. "Shots!"

I forced a grin and snatched the bottle. "Fuck it. Let's do it."

"Your candles!" Hunter screeched when she noticed the wax melting into the frosting.

I'd completely forgotten. "Oh, shit. Help me."

Together, we leaned over and blew out the candles, and then, per tradition, we skipped the formalities of knives, forks, and plates and dug in with our hands.

I was delighted to see she'd gone with a dark chocolate cake.

An hour later, we were smeared in cake and blue frosting and on our way to being drunk. We were sitting on the cold kitchen floor, shoulder to shoulder, and gossiping like we often did in our apartment when it was just us.

"Oh, my God." I giggled and then hiccupped, which Hunter found hilarious thanks to the tequila. "Remember that guy you dated who wanted you to pretend he was a dog while you screwed him?"

"I try not to," Hunter said with a groan. "Do you remember the guy *you* dated who liked to walk around bare assed all the time?"

"The weirdest part was that he kept his shirt and socks on."

Hunter and I cackled at the memory of Tommy's peeping pecker. We continued trading dating horror stories until I made the mistake of mentioning Darius. He wasn't the first of our exes to try to come between Hunter and me, but he was the only one to almost succeed. It hadn't been while we were dating either.

It happened during the aftermath.

"I still can't believe he said I didn't need a man since I had you."

"Fuck him," Hunter snarled. "Darius didn't know shit."

"Yeah, but he wasn't the only one. What about Justin? He broke up with you because he thought I was around too much."

"Insecure little bitch. He's lucky I didn't shoot him when I had the chance."

"And Levi?" I challenged. "You broke up with him because he wanted to move in."

"It was too soon."

"You dated for over a year." Hunter rolled her eyes but didn't reply. "I'm just wondering…"

"What?" she snapped.

"I'm just wondering if they had a point? Our relationships crashed and burned because we were too close. Closer than best friends should be."

Hunter sighed. "What's your point, Coby?"

I looked down at my hands smeared with blueberry frosting and clenched tightly around the T-shirt I'd worn to bed.

Ocean's T-shirt.

It smelled like him, so I'd worn it to bed. His expensive cologne gave me courage even now, as if he were wrapped around me, ready to protect me from anything.

"What if we were meant for more? What if we just needed someone who wouldn't mind having both of us around?"

Hunter leaned her head back, resting it against the side of the island as she stared at the ceiling. "Here we go," she grumbled. "Why are you pushing this, Coby?"

"Why have you been walking funny all week?" I shot back.

Hunter's gaze pinged around the kitchen while avoiding mine. "Abel is an asshole," she answered after a while. "And he knows his shit. I'm learning a lot."

"Training?" I mocked. "Is that the only reason?"

Her head swung toward me this time, and she stared me down with a furrow between her brows. But the worry in her eyes made the knot in my stomach tighten. "What other reason would there be?"

I shook my head and decided to let it go. "Forget it."

Something big had happened between Ocean and Hunter, and they were both trying like hell to keep me from knowing. I could see it all over their faces after the three of us had dinner together for the first time.

I guess it was our bedroom now.

"Coby—"

"I said forget it." I stood and started to leave the kitchen when Hunter grabbed my hand and forced me stop.

"Tell me what the fuck you meant by that," she demanded.

"You want to know what I meant?" Hunter didn't get to respond because I shoved her into the kitchen island behind her, but instead of slapping her for lying to me, I trapped her there with my body and pressed my lips against hers.

Hunter's eyes were wide, and her lips were unmoving as I kissed her—as I broke the rules.

The boundaries we set after Darius broke up with me. And then Hunter, desperately seeking to comfort a friend out of guilt, had thrown us into murky waters. Later, when I tried to tell her how I felt, she made me swear we wouldn't let it happen again. She said we had to protect our friendship no matter the cost.

And now here I was, shattering that promise with one reckless kiss.

Finally, Hunter's eyes lowered. I felt her lips moving under mine and my hand drifting between us to untie her robe. She moaned into my mouth while I curved a hand around her breast, smearing her dark nipples with blueberry frosting before bending my head to lick them clean. All I could think about was doing the same to her pussy. I wanted it more than air. Instead, I forced myself to end the kiss and rest my forehead against hers.

"Maybe you were right, Hunter."

She was still panting with her eyes closed when she asked, "About what?"

"If you hadn't fucked me and then broken my heart two years ago, I never would have met Ocean. I never would've known what it felt like to be owned by him." I shifted my head to kiss her again. "And neither would you."

Moving my hand down her belly and between her thick thighs, Hunter made a sound of shock when I circled her swollen clit.

"Coby... what are you doing? You can't."

"Can't I? I know your pussy is as sore as mine right now, and I know that *training* didn't do it." Holding her gaze, I swished my fingers through her fat lips and her wetness, knowing it wasn't just her arousal I was feeling. "You're hoarding my husband's cum in your pussy. I can do whatever I want with it." Bringing my fingers coated in Hunter, Ocean, and blueberry frosting to my lips, I licked them clean.

"I'm sorry," Hunter said as she watched me taste her. Taste them. "He...we—"

Dropping my hand with a scoff, I backed away and drank in the sight of Hunter, dazed and undone. She stared at me as if I had slapped her. "I know exactly what you two have been doing, Hunter. No need to explain. You can fuck Ocean. You can fuck me. But you can't be with either of us, right?"

"Coby, wait," she pleaded.

I turned to go. "Thanks for the cake."

I stood on a dais in the bridal boutique in Black Veil, staring into the wall-length mirror but not seeing myself. The gold and crystal chandelier above me glittered, showing off my glowing skin.

I only wish I felt the same inside.

I wore a satin-and-lace number with a sweetheart neckline, a firm bodice, a long train, and an oversized bow at the back. I looked like a princess—like the angel Ocean called me—but today...

Today, I felt truly wicked.

It was a little late for a final fitting, but money talked, and bullshit walked. With the help of Ocean's cousins, I'd found the perfect wedding dress weeks ago. But I couldn't stop reliving last night to care. I couldn't stop missing my mom and wishing she were here to help.

No one could ever replace her, but at least I wasn't alone.

"Some girls dream about this day, but your mind seems a million miles away," Effie noted as she gently touched my hand. "You're thinking about your mother, aren't you?"

Tearing up, I looked down at Ocean's mom and saw her son's eyes staring back at me.

They looked a lot alike.

Just picture a softer, tinier, feminine version of Ocean, and you have Euphemia Kilpatrick.

She was breathtaking, and her kindness made her even more so. The only thing Ocean had inherited from his father was his power, money, and penchant for cruelty.

Except Ocean wielded his for good. He used it to protect, not to crush those around him indiscriminately.

"Yes," I answered plainly, not wanting to say more and risk sobbing like a baby all over my future mother-in-law. "And I haven't been getting much sleep lately."

"This life," she stated knowingly. "It can be a lot. I know."

"Yeah," I agreed, because blaming my sorrow on being in a whole new world was an easy scapegoat.

"My son can be demanding, too," Effie stated with a sigh. "He'll roll right over you if you let him." And then she eyed me. "You're not, are you? I hope he's been good to you."

"Oh, yes. He's um… Ocean's not what I expected."

"I'm sure he feels the same way with you. Ocean's kindness and generosity often surprise even himself. He runs from it because of his father, but I'm hoping that you can help him with that. You and that brave young lady you both speak so highly of."

My eyes flared as I met Effie's in the mirror.

She smiled knowingly as she strutted away, sipping her third glass of champagne.

Suddenly, the heavy curtain shielding one of the dressing rooms parted, and Hunter stepped out wearing her maid-of-honor gown. It was a champagne number with a low scooped neckline and high split that showed off the curve of her thigh. Priscilla had shown me a number of bridal party gowns, and I remembered choosing this one weeks ago because I knew that Hunter would love it.

The rest of the room faded away as I admired how her hips pulled at the crystal satin. It was a good thing Effie was no longer standing there because I couldn't hide my attraction to Hunter anymore if I tried.

"Damn, Coby." Hunter rushed to my side as fast as she could in the mermaid-style gown. "You look so beautiful. This dress is so you." And then I realized it was Hunter's first time seeing my wedding dress. In a perfect world, she would have been there to help me choose it. In fact, I never imagined it going any other way.

"Thanks," I said quietly.

"And Hunter, you also look stunning, baby," Effie complimented.

Hunter beamed. "Thank you, Mrs. K."

"I told you," my future mother-in-law gently reminded her. "Call me Effie."

Hunter glanced at me, probably feeling like she was encroaching on my future mother-in-law. Seeing that I wasn't going to descend into a jealous rage, she conceded with a shy smile. "Okay. Effie."

"This was such a great choice, Coby," Ocean's mom praised while studying Hunter more closely. "I think the color goes beautifully with the theme you chose."

My gaze slowly met Hunter's in the mirror. "Yeah… I think she looks beautiful."

It didn't occur to me until I saw Hunter look away that Effie had asked how I felt about the dress, not how it looked on Hunter.

Officially embarrassed and unable to trust myself around anyone right now, I excused myself and hurried off the dais. I had to lift the ample skirt of my gown to move as quickly as the satin and crystal Christian Louboutin pumps would allow.

The bridal dressing room was the size of an oversized closet to accommodate all the extra material in the wedding gowns. It even had mirrors with built-in LED lighting to taunt me with the glimmer of the tears I had yet to shed. I put my face in my hands, my shoulders trembling with the effort it took to hold them back.

Eventually, I collapsed into a sea of white satin and lace, and that's where I stayed. I stewed in my misery until the curtains were ripped back without warning. Fearing it was Effie, I snatched my hands away and stood with some excuse ready on my lips, but it was worse.

It wasn't my future mother-in-law who had snuck in while my wounds were wide open.

It was the one who'd dealt them. My best friend. My ride or die. The one person I would let hurt me over and over.

Hunter.

Today was her debut as my new bodyguard, so she was dressed once again in her all-black uniform—skin-tight cargo pants, boots, and a shoulder holster over her shirt. She was armed to the teeth with her long braid cascading down her back and her baby hairs laid.

The moment I finished eye-fucking her through my tears, she shoved me against the mirrored wall—much like I'd done to her last night in Glamis's lavish kitchen—and got in my face. "What is it with you, Coby? You're either being stolen away from me or running away all on your own. I'm getting sick of it."

"I'm sorry," I said pathetically. "I fucked up."

"Shut up already." Hunter gave me no option but to obey when she pressed her soft lips against mine, hard enough to steal my breath. Ocean's kisses always felt like the stars were aligning. With Hunter, I heard them sing. Her hands glided over my bare shoulders, down my arms, and circled my wrists. "If you don't know that I never stopped wanting you," she whispered between kisses, "you're not as smart as I thought."

"You said we had to stop. You said we couldn't be like that because one day it might end and we'd lose each other forever."

"I know." Hunter ended the kiss and exhaled heavily as she shook her head. "I'm not very smart either."

Was I dreaming? Or was this really happening, meaning I'd died and gone to heaven?

Hunter kissed me again as if she'd heard my thoughts and wanted to prove that it wouldn't be like last time. I waited for this to feel awkward or wrong, but it didn't. Not now and not then.

When Hunter applied pressure to deepen the kiss, I didn't back down this time. I granted the access she demanded and sighed into her mouth when I felt the tip of her tongue lick mine.

"Hunter," I moaned. "What do we do now?"

Her hands grabbed the skirt of my gown and lifted it, gathering the satin around my waist. Knowing what she was after, I reached down and held my dress up for her to free her hands. Her fingers began tracing the hem of my panties, and I parted my thighs, moaning when she bent and nipped the swell of my breasts spilling from the tight bodice.

"What do you want to do?" she returned coyly.

"I want you to touch me."

I needed so much more than that, but for now, this would have to do. Hunter was still a flight risk. She always had been. The trail of broken hearts she'd left behind whenever things got too deep spoke for themselves. I'd been the only one Hunter had ever let stay once in, but then she'd torn her own heart apart just to keep it from ruining me.

"Do you remember when I used to sneak into your room and play with you?" she asked, lowering my panties down my legs and following them until she was crouched.

"Yes."

"I'd touch and kiss you here," she whispered, brushing her knuckle against my warm slit. "You squirmed for me. Remember that?"

"Yes, Hunter," I whined. "I remember. Stop teasing me. Please." Hunter shifted her hand and slid two fingers deep. My lashes fluttered as I leaned against the mirror. My head fell to the side, and one glance in the mirror showed Hunter's hand hidden underneath the heavy skirt of my wedding dress. "God, yes," I moaned as I rode her fingers. "Don't stop, Hunter."

"Why shouldn't I?" she taunted. "You squirm for him now. Not for me."

I opened my eyes enough to see jealousy and guilt warring within her own as she played with my pussy. "And you don't?"

Hunter shoved to her feet and pushed her chest against mine, fucking her fingers in and out of me harder and faster. I could hear the proof of my want echoing around the small room. The wet slap of her fingers tunneling in and out. Even her warm breath on my hot skin was an aphrodisiac.

"Just say it, Coby." Her eyes were dark and vengeful now, like she wanted to punish us both for falling for the same man. "I know you know."

"You fucked him," I accused.

"Yes."

I came, my walls squeezing Hunter's digits as she ground her heel against my clit to prolong it. My hips moved without any discernible rhythm, the rustle of the satin swishing as I chased my orgasm to the very end.

"Would you like to know how it happened?" Hunter teased as her fingers kept going.

My eyes drifted closed. Lord, help me. I nodded.

"Ocean undressed me, sniffed me, teased me…and then he bent me over the table while you were in the shower," she told me. I could already feel a second orgasm rushing to meet the first as she tormented me with her betrayal. "My pussy was so tight, but he made me take it anyway. I wish you could have seen how hard he fucked me. How much he wanted it. I thought about you while your man was inside me. I fantasized about what it would be like if you had touched me, too. I came so hard for him, Coby. I left my cream all over his big, black dick, and I wanted so much for you to taste it. Taste *us*."

"Oh, Hunterrrrrr. Oh, fuuuuck."

"I know," she cooed. "Come for me, bestie. Please?"

My lips parted to cry out, but Hunter kissed me, swallowing my scream as I came even harder than the first time.

I'd forgotten my future mother-in-law was waiting on the other side of the curtain for us—possibly hearing every word, every sound.

I swore and pushed Hunter away.

She was breathing too heavily to say it, but her eyes told me we weren't done yet.

My dress was still bunched around my waist, my expensive lace panties discarded and forever ruined. I let the hem of the gown fall, but I could still feel the evidence of what we'd done running down my thigh. My pussy was throbbing like it had a pulse, and I wanted more.

Hunter lifted her hand and held my gaze as she repeated my lewd actions from the night before and slipped both fingers in her mouth. "Mmmh," she moaned. "Still as sweet as I remembered, bestie."

I felt like I was tied in so many knots—Ocean, Hunter, the wedding, my brother…

When had life become so complicated?

Standing there, feeling thoroughly fucked, all I wanted to do was unravel.

It was the only explanation for why I rucked up my wedding gown again and pushed my best friend to her knees. Hunter didn't fight or question what I wanted as I desperately straddled her face without a word. She simply watched me with possession in her eyes as her tongue darted out and began lashing my sensitive pussy. The mirrors all around us made it impossible for us to hide from the lines we were blurring once more, but that was okay because I was done denying myself what I wanted.

Instead, I reveled in the sight of how we looked together.

Hunter dressed to kill with my pussy in her mouth. And me, dressed to offer my hand in marriage to the man who had stamped his ownership over it. I was very much aware that Ocean wouldn't like me disobeying him, but I couldn't bring myself to care as I swiveled my hips and rode my best friend's face.

With tears streaming down my face, I stared at the scandalous vision we made as Hunter moaned and licked me into a third orgasm. I was still mid-scream—muffled by my own hand over my mouth—when I heard a polite knock on the wall next to the dressing room and then the bridal stylist's high-pitched voice penetrating my post-orgasmic bliss.

"Um, sorry to bother you. Mrs. Kilpatrick had to step out, but *Mr.* Kilpatrick is waiting for you in the lobby." There was a pause and then. "He'd like to speak to you both."

The stylist's footsteps quickly hurried away.

"Shit," I swore as Hunter's head popped from underneath my dress. "Do you think they heard us?" Hunter's face was blank as she gave a careless shrug. "Shit!" I cursed again. "Ocean can't see me in my wedding dress." Assuming there would even be a wedding after this. "Help me."

I turned around to face the wall.

I waited several agonizing moments before Hunter stepped forward and helped me.

The gown fell to the floor with a heavy thud, and I quickly re-dressed in the clothes I came in. Before we left the dressing room, though, I couldn't resist kissing Hunter one last time, tasting myself on her lips that were still glistening with my juices.

"I love you," I whispered.

It wasn't the first time I'd told her so, but it was the first time I'd meant it as anything but a friend. I didn't give her time to reject me before I hurried out of the dressing room.

Hunter fell three steps behind me like Abel had reminded her before we left Glamis this morning. I was careful not to meet any of the stylists' and seamstresses' eyes just in case they'd heard us. It was eerily quiet in the boutique, adding to my nervousness, and I realized why when Hunter and I reached the lobby.

A tree-trunk of a man in an expensive suit towered by the door with two armed men guarding it, but it wasn't Ocean waiting for us as we expected.

It was Malcolm Kilpatrick.

Ocean's father.

CHAPTER THIRTY

HUNTER

"MY APOLOGIES FOR THE INTERRUPTION," THE BOSS OF the *Fola* greeted as he regarded Coby. "But considering what my son has been planning right under my nose, I'm afraid it just couldn't wait."

He smiled, and I stretched my fingers toward my gun.

It was my first time being in the same room with Malcolm Kilpatrick, but Coby had already warned me that he and Ocean were not on good terms. That was putting it lightly. It made me question why we were living in the man's house if he was such a threat to us—that is, until I caught on to what Ocean was doing. And why he's been so busy the last couple of weeks.

He was seizing the throne while his father was away.

Marrying Coby was just insurance—to make sure the rest of his family didn't have a reason to challenge him once he was Boss.

It would have been the perfect plan if Malcolm hadn't caught wind of it.

He glowered at Coby now like she was the ruin of his kingdom, and I wondered how mad Ocean would be if I shot his father in the face.

"If you're done here," Malcom said in a polite tone that I didn't buy for a moment, "I'd like to escort you back to my home so I can have a chat with my son."

"I'm sorry, but we're not allowed to get in the car with strangers," Coby said with equally false sweetness. I swallowed my snort.

Malcolm clearly didn't find Coby as funny and clever as I did because his polite expression darkened with displeasure.

I didn't care if it was wise to threaten the mafia don. I unholstered my gun.

Malcom's men did the same.

"I'm afraid I wasn't asking. If you want to marry my son, you're going to have to learn that refusing an order from me comes with severe consequences. Starting with *her*." Malcolm jammed a thick finger at me.

Ocean had carefully chosen Coby's bodyguards—men only loyal to him, which meant they could only be dead. I was only still alive because I'd been in the dressing room eating his bride's pussy.

Coby must have come to the same conclusion because she gave the man a gracious nod that threw me off guard. I'd been so focused on Malcolm that I hadn't noticed her posture. Her spine was ramrod straight, her shoulders thrown back, and her hands were clasped dutifully in front of her. Coby's poised but meek pose made my gaze narrow.

Someone had been in her ear, and I had a good guess who.

Effie.

She carried herself the same way.

"In that case," Coby said, "lead the way, sir."

Some of the violence rolled off Malcolm as if he was pleased with her sudden submission. Not having received the same lesson in surviving Malcom, I stepped forward to tell her she wasn't going anywhere with this man when Coby cut me off with a quick, pleading glance.

"Trust me," she whispered.

Coby started forward before I could argue, leaving me with no choice but to follow her and the Boss of the *Fola* out the door.

A black and chrome Bentley Mulsanne was waiting at the curb when we stepped out. The sidewalk on the far side of the street seemed overcrowded, while the one we occupied was terrifyingly deserted. Eight more goons kept a perimeter, their faces grim as they watched for threats. At least half those eyes were locked on me.

I forced myself to appear unthreatening as I waited for Coby to climb into the chauffeured car. Malcolm hadn't killed me yet when I should have been just as expendable as the others. It meant Ocean's father knew more than he let on, so I calmly walked around to the other side of the car, but my steps faltered when I spotted a familiar figure lingering in the crowd.

Kellan had a phone plastered to his ear, and I could see the tense lines around his mouth from here as he spoke. Our eyes met, and for once, he didn't look smug or amused as he blended back into the crowd.

The sheer alarm in his eyes told me that Ocean had no idea his father was back in town. Malcolm had clearly flown back from Ireland and immediately sought out Coby and me.

Exhaling, I climbed into the car and steeled myself.

I could do this. I could get Coby out alive. Nothing else mattered.

The Bentley had rear-facing seating with diamond-quilted leather hand-crafted to make you feel like royalty. I felt like dog poo, and it only made me think of Coco, who was at Glamis waiting for me to come home.

I knew as soon as the car door closed behind me that I never would.

"Coby, what the hell was that?" I whispered. We only had seconds before Malcolm joined us.

"Just trust me," Coby whispered back. "He's dangerous."

"So am I." I didn't mean that arrogantly. It was just a fact. I could and would protect her from that man.

Coby's eyes were wide with horror as she shook her head. "Not like him. You're not a monster."

Malcolm was suddenly filling the seat across from me.

The remaining seat across from Coby became occupied as well,

and I sized up the grim-faced guard before glancing at Coby, who
was doing the same.

The air was alive with Malcolm Kilpatrick's poison as the limo
promptly drove away.

"You must forgive my bad manners," Malcolm said as he cut the
end of a cigar and lit it. "My son has always been defiant, but I believe I underestimated the lengths he'd go to challenge my patience."
With his gaze pinned on Coby, who was shrinking against the seat,
he said, "I'm afraid he's misled you."

"Misled me?" Coby parroted.

"My son is already engaged to marry someone of my choosing—
someone *den fhuil*[8]. So you see… You cannot be allowed to marry
my son. He will wed Niamh next week, and I'm afraid you will be
used to set an example."

"Last we checked, your son is a grown man," I said. "I'm sure he
can marry whoever he wants."

"My son's *pet* will not speak unless spoken to," Malcolm barked.

"Who the hell is Niamh?" I asked as if he hadn't spoken.

"His cousin," Coby said hoarsely. Horror was written all over her
face, which had paled. "Niamh is his cousin. She's just a fucking kid."
Ewwwww.

Suddenly, it felt as if I had just landed in the middle of a trailer
park soap opera.

It was too disturbing to watch.

"Wow, you're even nuttier than I thought," I taunted. I whipped
my head toward his goon. "And what the fuck are you looking at?"

The henchman lunged for me.

Unfortunately, I didn't get to use the super cool defensive move
that Abel had taught me.

Because Coby was there.

I marveled at how fast she had to move to get one of her heels
in hand before he could grab me. The goon screamed as Coby embedded the sharp five-inch heel into his ear. I felt the warm spray of

---

8   Of the blood.

his blood after I unsheathed my knife and drove it through his chin to shut him up.

The divider behind us lowered, and a gun appeared, but I quickly disarmed the goon in the front seat by snapping his wrist in two moves.

Thanks, Abel.

I was still holding on to the henchman's arm when my gaze met Malcolm's thunderous one. I only hesitated the second it took me to remember that he was Ocean's father. And *then* I remembered the disgusting shit he was trying to force his son into.

Fuck it.

I kicked out and drove my boot into his stupid face. Malcolm's head snapped back, and his old ass slumped against the seat. Blood gushed from his crooked nose, but he was knocked out cold.

The limo suddenly swerved, and the driver slammed on the brakes. I didn't have to question whether he was armed, too.

I was reaching for my gun to take care of him when Coby screamed my name. "Hunter!" She flung open the door and grabbed my hand. "Forget it! Let's go!"

Even though I really wanted to spill more Fola blood, I didn't fight her as she pulled me from the car.

Together, we darted down the street, but we weren't alone.

Tires squealed behind us. When I looked back, it was a familiar lone Denali cutting away from the rest of the traffic to race after us. The rest of Malcolm's goons were too busy rushing toward the limo to check on the Boss to bother with us.

Cutting down a side street, I pulled Coby behind me, but that damn SUV was closing in fast as I led us both down a narrow alley. It was wide enough for the Denali to fit un-fucking-fortunately, so I picked up the pace. Believing we were pinned, the truck slowed as Coby and I approached what appeared to be a dead end.

I knew better.

The Blood mafia might have ruled Black Veil, but the streets were my playground.

Coby and I barreled full speed ahead, aiming for the hairline crack in the fence. If you didn't know it was there, you'd miss it. It was a favored escape route amongst my fellow degenerates, but it was the first time I'd used it to evade someone other than the cops.

The driver of the Denali beeped the horn to get our attention, and I could feel Coby's steps slowing from her confusion.

Cursing, I tugged her forward before she could stop.

Pushing aside the broken chain link, I didn't realize I was holding my breath until Coby slipped through the fence without looking behind her.

"Keep going!" I shouted when she stopped to wait for me.

Coby's adrenaline was rushing too fast to question my reasons. She kept going, and I watched her round the corner before following.

"Hunter! Stop!" a familiar voice shouted once I stood on the other side.

Fucking Kellan.

I straightened and paused to flip off Ocean's associate, and then I was gone. I knew Kellan would report to Ocean that I'd run from him. I just hoped Coby could forgive my deceit. Penniless, we raced through the city on foot, and we didn't stop until we reached the unlikeliest havens.

"You couldn't help yourself, could you?" Coby snapped as soon as the front door slammed shut behind us.

"Coby, not now." I wasn't ready to have this argument, not just because I hadn't caught my breath yet. Abel had been right. My stamina was shit. And we weren't out of the woods yet. "Let's just get what we need and go before your brother comes home."

"Go? Why? We can just stay here. Roshaun won't mind."

"No. Not happening," I barked. Coby gave me an exasperated look, like now was not the time to be beefing with her brother. She knew her brother had sold her to Ocean, and it didn't matter. She still loved Roshaun—still felt an incredible amount of guilt over "stealing his life" from him. "They'll know to look for us here," I explained. "We can't stay, and we can't go home."

Coby began to pace. "We should just call Ocean. He'll understand why we ran. His father was going to kill us."

Feeling the back of my neck grow hot, I blew out a breath and winced. Yeah, about that..."

Reading me like a book, Coby closed her eyes and tilted her head back. "Hunter, what did you do?"

"The SUV that chased us wasn't one of Malcolm's. It was Kellan. I think he was trying to help us." I swallowed nervously. "I *know* he was. I saw him, but I made you keep running anyway because of what happened between us last night and at the boutique. I wasn't ready to go back, and it's not just because I'm jealous as hell that he gets you. It's because I'm scared of saying yes. I need more time, and if I see him..." Coby's eyes opened, and I lost my nerve to admit my feelings. "Call Ocean if you want, but I can't go back. Not yet."

Moving toward the stairs, I jogged to the second floor and went straight for Roshaun's bedroom. The urge to burn it all down as soon as I entered nearly overcame me until I remembered that this place wasn't just another source of my trauma. It was also where Coby grew up. It was the home she shared with her parents. And she loved them, unlike me. She loved them so much that she'd turned herself into a remembrance. It's why she wore a ribbon every day. To remind herself that though they might be gone, they lived on through her.

When Roshaun moved me in, I think he'd been relieved to have someone else emotionally available for his sister, so he didn't have to be. He moved me in, and I endured his leering because it meant I could be close to Coby, but my gravest mistake had been assuming he was content to look but not touch.

Eventually, my body became the price I paid to be with her.

She still didn't know what a dirty dog her brother was, and if I had my way, she'd never find out.

I scrunched my nose at a pair of Roshaun's worn boxers sitting on the floor and beelined for the nightstand.

Roshaun couldn't be that stupid, could he?

I slid open the top drawer and lifted the false bottom, grinning at the thick roll of green with rubber bands around the wad to hold it.

Roshaun was a fucking idiot.

Who doesn't move their secret stash once someone else knows about it? I grabbed the cash and tucked it into my bra. I knew from experience that it was at least ten grand. The same amount of hush money that he paid me when I finally moved out and took Coby with me. I would have kept my mouth shut anyway—for Coby—but Roshaun didn't need to know that. The money had funded my new life with his sister, away from him.

The house was quiet when I left the bedroom. My steps grew heavier as I returned downstairs, where I left Coby.

She wasn't there.

Feeling like my legs would give out at any moment, I sat on the stairs and stared at the floor.

Coby had chosen to return to Ocean without me, and while my heart was tugging me in that direction, too, I couldn't bring my feet to move. I was so afraid of the things he made me feel. The things he made me want.

I needed more time. I needed to think. I—

"Why so glum, bubble gum?"

My head darted up, and I felt my chest cave with the crushing weight of exhilaration when I saw Coby standing with her hands on her hips.

"I thought—" I swallowed past the knot in my throat. "I thought you left."

Coby's gaze softened, and then she fell to her knees in front of me and placed her hands on my spread thighs.

"Ride or die, bestie. Remember? Either we both go back together, or we don't go back at all."

Unable to speak, I nodded.

Coby looked unsure momentarily, biting her bottom lip before she stretched forward and kissed me. A wave of warmth washed
over me, along with gut-wrenching hunger when I felt her soft lips
against mine. She pulled away too soon and blushed. "So, are you
coming or what?"

I nodded. Coby rose.

Reaching out, I grabbed her hand, but not to stand. "I'm sorry
that I fucked Ocean."

"Hunter," Coby said with a long-suffering sigh that made me
frown. "I *told* Ocean to seduce you. I told him to do all the things
you're feeling guilty about, so maybe it's me who can't be trusted. I
don't know, and I don't care. We've both made mistakes, so maybe we
should stop repeating them and be a team again. You need time, and
I'm not going anywhere without you, so get your ass up and let's go."
She held up her hand, and I finally noticed the keys in her hand. "I
know where Roshaun keeps the spare car he uses for dirt." She gave
me an expectant look. "Did you find his stash?"

Reaching inside my bra, I tugged out the fat knot, tossed it in
the air, and caught it. "Got it."

"Then let's not waste any more time." She grabbed my hand and
pulled me up.

Coby and I shared a grin once I stood, but that faded with the
knock at the door.

I didn't hesitate to pull my gun and let my voice deepen to sound
like Roshaun when I spoke. "Who is it?"

Okay, that was terrible. Coby snorted despite the possible danger while I made a silly face and then shushed her.

"Seriously?" Kellan called through the door. Coby and I groaned.
"You really think that voice is fooling anyone? We all know you've
got balls, Parrish, but they're metaphorical, yeah?"

I rushed forward and snatched open the door. "How the hell
did you find us?"

"Again… seriously?" He quirked a pierced brow. "I'm actually disappointed you were dumb enough to hide out *here*. It's the closest known location we have on file for you."

I crossed my arms and popped a hip. "You really have a file?"

"Yup. Everyone does. Yours is as thick as my—"

"Ew. Don't say it," I cut him off.

Kellan gave me a withering look. "I was going to say thumb."

"Sure, buddy." I blindly reached behind me, and Coby slipped her hand into mine again. "Now, if you'll fuck off. Coby and I have some disappearing to do." I tried to pass him, but he blocked me with his arm and grinned when I glared.

Behind me, Coby sighed after our silent battle of wills dragged on.

"Where is he?" she asked Kellan. Coby already seemed resigned to our fate while I was still plotting a way out of here. I dodged Kellan once. I could do it again.

Kellan didn't look away from me when he answered smugly. "Eager for you to join him at Glainne." Kellan retreated a step, probably in case I thought about hitting him. "Now if you're done stalling, let's go. We both know you're not getting away a second time."

"Fine," I agreed to everyone's surprise, including my own. We followed Kellan to the Denali, where Paul was waiting.

Coby stopped me before I could climb inside. "Are you sure?"

"No," I mumbled. "But look how fast Ocean found us. There's no reason to believe Malcolm couldn't find us just as fast. Where else are we going to go?" Coby's worried gaze searched mine, so I smiled to assure her that I was okay with this before we climbed in. "Hey, Paul," I greeted with false cheer.

He chuckled good-naturedly while watching me warily through the rearview. My reputation had been well earned. "Hunter."

We rode silently until we reached the onyx tower in the city's center. I looked around in awe as Coby and I followed Kellan up to the penthouse, which conveniently had a private elevator. Once we reached the top floor, the elevator opened directly into an apartment that called me 'poor' and 'peasant' in five languages.

As soon as we stepped inside, I spotted Ocean standing in front of one of the many windows with his back to us. The muscles were coiled tightly, and I knew even before he turned around that he was angry. When he did, I saw that the dress shirt was unbuttoned, showing off his sculpted abs and chest, but it was the blood staining the crisp white linen that held all my attention.

Ocean's unguarded expression was hard as stone, the tension in his broad shoulders taut. When he spotted us, I could have sworn he softened a little.

"I found them at her brother's house just like you said," the ass-kisser snitched. He didn't mention that we had been getting ready to run again.

"Thank you, Kellan."

The associate turned to go, but he surprised me when he reached out and squeezed my arm reassuringly as he passed. It worked to settle my nervous gut a little. I didn't want to like his meddling ass, but he was slowly becoming my friend.

Kellan stepped back into the elevator, and then he was gone.

Still, Ocean said nothing to either of us as he stalked to the fully stocked bar.

I peeked over my shoulder.

Water from the small sink ran as he cleaned his hands. When he looked up, I faced forward again like an errant child awaiting punishment. I listened as he dropped ice into a glass before pouring himself what was probably a stiff drink. A few more seconds passed as he gulped it down, and then the glass slammed on the bar loud enough to make Coby and me jump.

Ocean finally spoke, his voice a dark promise of blood and vengeance. "Are you hurt?" he asked without making it clear who he was speaking to.

"No," Coby and I chorused.

Suddenly, Ocean was standing in front of us, raking his gaze over every inch of me and then Coby before he seemed satisfied with our answer. Coby was staring up at him like he was her god, and he was staring down at her like he wanted to worship at her altar. I looked away and reminded myself they'd be married in a week (assuming that was still happening). They had every right to look at one another as if they couldn't live without the other.

I stubbornly kept my gaze on the wall when I heard them kiss moments later.

For every second that passed, I felt my control slipping.

The kiss continued until I thought I might snap, and then I heard Ocean say, "Come with me." They moved together toward the stairs while I stayed put near the elevator. I was contemplating riding it down and quietly disappearing to let them live happily ever after together when Ocean called out to me without turning around. "Hunter." My gaze snapped to his strong back. "That means you, too," he ordered sternly.

CHAPTER THIRTY-ONE

OCEAN

"WHOSE BLOOD IS THAT?" COBY ASKED THE MOMENT THE three of us were shut inside her bedroom. Hunter was looking around the room, which looked like a palace, and I could tell she was impressed but didn't want to show it.

"Someone who got in my way," I answered.

My father's men had tried to ambush me on the way from Glamis to Glainne, but it hadn't gone so well for his men. Abel and I narrowly escaped, and my rage over the delay in getting to Coby and Hunter had me eager to go back out there and paint the streets red.

"Are you okay?"

"I'm fine, *mo aingeal*." I moved to sit on one of those ridiculous pink and gold chaises, and Coby and Hunter followed once I waved them over to join. They were both acting jittery and nervous as they sat beside each other on the opposite chaise. I'm sure my dark mood wasn't helping. By coming for them, my father had severed the last of the tattered bond between us, and now I was going to kill his ass. "Tell me what happened."

"What happened isn't as important as what *didn't* happen," Coby snapped. "Why didn't you tell us the woman your father wanted you to marry was *Niamh*?"

I winced and for good reason. The way they were both looking at me matched the feeling of a million fucking bugs crawling all over me.

"It wasn't relevant because there was no force on earth and no pun-ishment my father could enact to make me go through with that shit."

"Does Niamh know?" Coby asked. When I nodded, she didn't look surprised, but I wasn't hung up on it, and neither was Coby. "That's why you were going to force me to marry you. You were try-ing to save Niamh."

"Don't romanticize what I did, *mo aingeal*. I was giving Niamh a choice by taking away yours.

"Yes, but…Ocean, I saw the way she looked when I told her we were getting married. She looked so scared and vulnerable, but there was hope, too. You gave that to her. And now I know why she kept thanking me every time we saw each other." Coby wrinkled her nose like my cousin's unexplained gratitude had been nothing more than a nuisance.

"And you?" I challenged, wanting her to never forget that I might not have been insane like my father, but I was still no hero.

"Me?" Coby shook her head when she caught on to what I was asking. "I was never afraid to marry you. You never gave me any rea-son to. I could have done without the kidnapping, but it is what it is."

My gaze traveled over to Hunter, who had been unnervingly si-lent. Her ass had fallen asleep with her head on her fist—as if today had been just another day—I chuckled and held my finger up to my lips when Coby started to call her name.

Standing, I lifted Hunter from the chaise, and she barely stirred as I carried her over to the bed and laid her on it. I then got to work removing her boots and weapons.

Behind me, Coby gasped. "Oh no." When I peeked over my shoulder, she asked. "Where's Coco?"

"He's in my room." I'm glad I had the forethought to grab the little rat before I left Glamis. I had no doubt that Hunter would have risked her life going to rescue him.

I was having similar thoughts about my mom, who was currently trapped there with him. There was nothing I could do about it now, so I pushed it from my mind. If anyone could successfully navigate my father's rage unscathed, it was her.

Once Hunter was stripped down to just her clothes, I took Coby into the bathroom with me. I lifted her onto the sink and pulled off her ruined heels. As I suspected, her tiny feet were red and swollen from running through the city on foot, so I pulled her right foot in my hand and gently massaged it.

"Anything else happen today?" Coby didn't answer right away. She was already leaning back with her eyes closed and moaning as I kneaded the sore muscles in her feet. "Coby." Her eyes slowly opened when I released her foot. "Anything you want to tell me?"

After thinking about it for a while, she nodded. "Something else happened, something with Hunter and me, but I'm not ready to tell you. Is-is that okay?"

"Of course." Grabbing her left foot, I repeated my ministration, and Coby's eyes fluttered.

After thoroughly working the muscles in her foot, I helped her stand and then undressed us both before we got in the shower. I kept my arm around her small waist since she looked too exhausted to stay on her feet.

I wouldn't ever stop reminding myself that I'd almost lost them both today. I wouldn't let myself forget so that it never happened again. They had been right to run. My father would have used them to bring me to heel, and then he would have slaughtered them anyway as a warning to the rest of the family.

The shower water was beating down on us, and Coby was squirming in my arms minutes later as I cleaned her perfect pussy. Her soft moans were driving me up the wall and steering my mind into the gutter, but I was still aware of the bathroom door opening just a crack.

Hunter was awake.

I could feel her eyes on us, so I waited, enjoying the anticipation of her joining us.

She didn't come in.

Hunter wanted a show, and it just so happened I was in the mood give her one. Coby said something had happened between them today, but it had only been a matter of time.

Did I feel threatened? Not at fucking all.

Was I jealous? Most definitely.

But whatever they felt for each other, they both still belonged to *me*.

My lips moved across Coby's shoulders as I drove my hips forward. My goddamn dick was harder than a brick. "You want it?"

Coby responded by pushing her ass back against me. "Yeah," she moaned.

I pecked the soft skin of Coby's shoulder. "Good. I want you to get on your knees, sweet girl."

I turned us so that my back took the brunt of the steaming shower water, and then I gently pushed Coby to the ground. I was facing the door now, but I didn't allow my gaze to shift that way. I focused on Coby as I grabbed her nape with one hand and my dick with the other. In this moment, I had eyes only for Coby, staring into her beautiful, trusting brown ones as I began to pump. *Up, down. Up, down.* I squeezed the head on my upstroke, and pre-cum leaked from the tip. It landed on the deep bow-shaped curve of her upper lip, and I watched her pink tongue dart out. I could feel my balls tightening when she curiously licked the drop from her lip.

Her eyes became hungry, and then she lurched forward, mouth parted and ready to swallow me whole. My hand tightened around her nape to keep her still.

"You don't want me to suck you?"

"Yeah, baby," I answered with a grunt. I was pumping harder and faster now. "You're going to suck me."

Coby squirmed impatiently, and I could still feel Hunter watching, wanting, but she refused to join us.

A part of me was thrilled for the hunt. But my patience was wearing thin.

I grunted again when my balls drew up, so I thumbed Coby's

lips open. The moment she eagerly opened wide, I shoved my dick inside with a groan and only managed to fuck her mouth twice before spilling down her throat.

Coby didn't miss a beat, deep-throating my dick while I locked gazes with Hunter through the crack in the door. Did she like what she saw? Was she touching herself? My toes curled against the shower floor when it felt like I wouldn't stop coming.

After what felt like forever, I reluctantly pulled my dick from Coby's mouth before helping her stand. I felt Hunter leave as I shoved Coby against the glass wall and kissed her.

Once we left the shower and finished our nightly hygiene, I carried Coby to bed and tucked her in.

"What are you going to do?" she whispered in the dark once I lay down next to her. She was curled up against my side with her hand on my chest while I stared at the ceiling with my arm under my head.

"I'm going to kill my father."

"No. I mean… about Hunter. I know you know."

That they ran from me? Yeah. Kellan told me what happened when he tried to help them.

"Don't be mad at her. None of this is easy for Hunter. She has a hard time letting people in. *We* didn't even like each other the first time we met," she whispered with a yawn. "She thought I was sheltered and naive, and I thought she was bitter and a bitch." The news surprised me, but I said nothing as Coby got what she needed to say off her chest. "Hunter faced down the head of the mob today, and she wasn't afraid. Her heart is a different story. She's terrified of trusting it, so be patient with her. Just a little while longer. Hunter's worth it."

"I will," I promised. "And I know. I'm not angry with either of you. I promise."

"Good," she said with another yawn. "I'd hate for us to jump you, too." I laughed while Coby giggled. I had no doubt they would. "So I guess this means the wedding is off?"

My head snapped toward her as I frowned so hard it was a wonder my face didn't break. "Why would you say that?"

Coby worriedly chewed on her lip. "Your father knows."

Leaning over, I kissed the top of her head. "*Mo aingeal*, my father isn't stopping shit. He's only delaying it for a while. My pops will be lucky if he makes it another week after what he did today."

"Your mom might be mad."

"My mother hates him more than I do." I rolled Coby onto her back and climbed on top of her before she could say another word. "No more worrying about other people's thoughts. You're my queen, Coby. Anyone who doesn't bow down will get put down. Understand?"

Even through the dark, I could see her blushing. "I don't want you killing anyone for me."

"Too bad." I tickled her sides, which made her squeal, and then I rolled away before pulling her into my arms. "Now go to sleep for me, sweetheart."

"Okay." Coby snuggled deeper into me. "Night."

I waited until I was sure she was sleeping deeply before kissing her cheek and leaving the room. I went to my room, dressed in jeans and a hoodie, and strapped a few weapons to me.

I found Hunter downstairs, sitting on the couch in the living room as if she hadn't been spying on us in the shower. I walked over and sat on the low coffee table in front of her while she stared at her lap, twiddling her thumbs. It was the most vulnerable I'd ever seen Hunter Parrish, and it was all I could do not to touch her. I wasn't sure she would welcome it, so I kept my hands to myself.

"Look at me, Vengeance."

She sucked in a breath before lifting her head and letting me see the uncertainty in her eyes. I wasted no time putting her out of her misery.

"You did nothing I wouldn't have done myself," I told her.

The tension left her shoulders all at once. "So what happens now?"

"I go to war with my father."

Her surprise was palpable. "Are you serious?" I gave a grave nod. I would be digging a lot of them before the end. "And then?"

I reached for her and took her place on the couch before pulling her into my lap.

"You don't need to be afraid of me," I assured her because I felt like I needed to. Hopefully, for the last time.

Hunter surprised me when she snorted and curled against me. "I'm not afraid of you. I'm pretty sure I could take you, pretty boy."

"Oh, yeah?" I laughed as I toyed with her delicate fingers. Coby had implied something similar. "Maybe I should visit next time you're training with Abel. We could go a few rounds on the mat. See who takes who."

Hunter squirmed in my lap, probably at the thought of me taking her in a different way. "You still haven't answered my question. What happens if you win and become Boss?"

"*When* I become Boss," I corrected as I rubbed her thigh, "I change the rules, and I make you my queen. You…and Coby."

Hunter stuck her nose in the air and looked away so I wouldn't see how much she liked that idea. "Well, don't expect me to mourn you if you die."

"Brat." I smiled as I slipped a hand under her shirt. My thumb absently swept the small pudge on her lower belly as I watched her. "Not even a little?" Hunter shook her head, and I kissed her arm. "Well, it's a good thing I have no intention of failing."

Hunter scoffed while her nostrils flared. "No one ever intends to fail, Ocean."

"Look at me." She met my gaze as I brought her hand to my lips and kissed the back of it. "I won't fail," I assured her. I knew the real reason she was pouting. "I won't die."

Hunter searched my gaze and surprised us both when she leaned down and pecked my lips. "You better not," she whispered.

The last thread of my control snapped.

"Hunter." I pleaded against her lips as I kissed her deeply.

I felt her soft hands framing my face as she chased my tongue. "Yes, Ocean?"

"You know I'm not letting you go to sleep without beating that pussy, right?"

Her breathing quickened as she eagerly nodded. "Please do."

"Lay down."

Hunter quickly obeyed, shoving her pants down her legs as she went. I ripped open my jeans with the same urgency, but froze when she gaped her legs open to show me her pussy. My hand trembled as I shoved aside the one she used to play with her clit and reverently slid a finger through her glistening lower lips.

"You touched yourself while you watched us?" I asked. I wanted to hear her say it.

"Yes."

"Did you come?"

Hunter's face was pinched as she circled her hips like she was on the verge of doing it again. "So hard."

I leaned over to steal a taste of her pussy, kissing and licking her perfect lips until she was writhing and mindless and dripping down her thighs and onto the couch. I brought Hunter to the edge, and she cursed me out when I stopped right before she tumbled over.

Holding her gaze, I shoved my jeans and boxers down just enough to free my dick.

"I have to go. This has to be quick," I warned as I climbed between her thighs. "I'm sorry, Vengeance."

"I'm not. *Please, please.*" Hunter gripped my dark blue hoodie tighter while pulling me closer. "I need you."

"Fuck, I need you too."

I swallowed her cry as I granted her wish and slid inside her warmth. I didn't stop until I was balls deep and felt her walls hugging every inch. Hunter's heels dug into my ass while I pounded in and out of her, fucking her into the couch cushions without mercy or thought.

They both ran from me today, so I made it my mission to show

them why they couldn't run forever. I'd chase them to the ends of
the earth, and they'd keep coming back. This invisible pull that held
us captive left no room for rationality. Nothing else made sense but
the three of us. Nothing else mattered.

I threw her legs over my shoulders, locking her place as I increased my pace, hitting her spot like a battering ram. Hunter gripped
the couch arm above her head with one hand and my hoodie with
the other as she tried like hell to hold on.

"Ocean, Ocean… fuuuuuuck meeee!"

I clapped my hand over her mouth to keep her quiet. I didn't
want to wake Coby and start this process of putting them both
to sleep all over again. "Come for me, baby," I demanded quietly.
"Squeeze my dick and squirt all over it. Fucking drown me. Please?"

She did just that.

It was only after I was already spilling inside Hunter's pussy that
I realized I'd forgotten to wear a condom again. Even if I wanted to,
I couldn't stop now, so I lodged my dick deeper, making her cry out
behind my hand. I muffled my groan in her shoulder as I emptied
my balls and then collapsed on her, giving her only as much of my
weight as she could take.

"Are you on birth control?" I asked after I caught my breath. My
heart was still racing, but at least I wasn't still seeing stars.

"No." Her gaze widened as sheer panic took over when she realized why I'd asked. "Oh, my God."

"Good." With one last searing kiss, I climbed off her and redid
my jeans while Hunter gaped at me like I was crazy. I grabbed one of
the throw pillows and tucked it under her hips to keep them propped
before leaning over and staring into her torn gaze. "Tell me you're
mine, Vengeance."

"You haven't earned me yet," she said before turning her head
away. She could pretend to be mad all she wanted, but I didn't hear
her objecting to having my baby.

I placed a kiss on her cheek before standing. "I will."

Hunter stubbornly didn't respond, closing her eyes and turning away from me.

I covered her with a blanket and then sat on the table and watched her until her breathing slowed and she fell asleep.

Standing, I quietly stalked for the elevator and rode it down to the lobby, where Abel was waiting. The last place I wanted to be was in the streets when I could be with Hunter and Coby instead, but my father had forced my hand, which meant I still had moves to make before I could even think about sleep.

Abel was never without his game face, so I didn't have to ask if he was ready. Still, I could see his concern for Hunter and Coby bleeding through. They were growing on him, especially Hunter, though he'd never let her know. "Are they good?"

I nodded and said a silent prayer to God for Hunter and Coby's instincts and ferocity when it came to each other.

My pops made his move, and now it was my turn.

I was going to kill the head of the *Fola,* and after, I'd deliver his head to my queens as a wedding gift.

CHAPTER THIRTY-TWO

COBY

TODAY WAS SUPPOSED TO BE MY WEDDING DAY, BUT I HAVEN'T seen Ocean in a week. He hadn't returned to Glainne since the day his father tried to make Hunter and me disappear. For good reason, the wedding was postponed until after the war (unless the world wanted a repeat of the Red Wedding). Hunter and I have been busying ourselves making the huge penthouse festive for Christmas. Or rather, I decorated with the help of the staff, while Hunter the Scrooge complained that it was pointless.

I was starting to think I would get through the holiday unscathed when I woke up to a disturbing text this morning.

Shaun: I'm still your brother…

It had been a few hours since he sent that obvious attempt at guilt, so I sighed and finally texted back.

What do you want, Shaun?

The bubbles that told me he was typing appeared immediately.

Shaun: We need to talk. Can u meet me?

I can't, I texted back. *Ocean will kill you.*

Shaun: Ain't nobody afraid of his bitch ass!

As usual, my brother's temper made him a damn fool. We both knew Ocean was far from a bitch. When I didn't respond right away, Shaun texted again.

> **Shaun: Just for a few minutes. He won't know.**
> **Just tell me where u r. I'll come to u.**

> **Shaun: U owe me that much...**

I nibbled on my lip as guilt finally clawed its way inside my belly. I heard everything he didn't say. It wasn't just about what he did for me after our parents died. I left him in the hospital to die. I should have fought harder to be there for him while he was injured. Ocean had turned me down whenever I asked until it became a sore subject between us. I couldn't even mention my brother's name in his presence without putting Ocean in a foul mood. It was more than just Roshaun stealing from him. Ocean didn't respect how Roshaun didn't do more to protect me. Ocean had every right to hate him, but Roshaun was still my brother.

Okay, I texted back.

And then I told him where we were.

It took another hour before I had my opening.

It came after dinner when Hunter was knocked out on the couch. Ocean was still gone, and he'd taken all of his guards with him because there was no way up to this floor without access. It went unspoken that Hunter and I weren't allowed to leave Glainne, but I couldn't turn my back on my brother anymore than I could stop my heart from beating.

I wasn't going far, and I wouldn't be long.

Ocean doesn't have to know.

After pulling on a pair of jeans, a sweater, and tall silver sequin UGGs, I snatched the extra keycard off the counter that Ocean gave us for emergencies only—like the building being on fire—but my brother sounded desperate, so close enough.

I glanced at Hunter to ensure she was still sleeping before taking a deep breath and quietly leaving the suite. I knew she wouldn't understand any more than Ocean since she hated Shaun, so I'd decided against telling her.

It's not like my brother would hurt me.

I took the stairs because I didn't want to risk running into Ocean in the elevator, in case he decided today was a good day to show his face. Over forty floors later, I was panting as I entered the underground parking garage and looked around for Shaun, who had already texted that he was there.

"Coby."

I gasped and jumped with my hand on my chest as I spun around to see who had snuck up on me. "Goddamn it, Shaun. You scared me!"

"My bad." Even though he looked different—the curly hair on top of his head was now braided with the sides shaved into a fade— he gave me his signature crooked grin and then opened his arms. I felt a surge of joy at seeing my big brother alive as I rushed to hug him. He winced a little when I slammed into him, and I remembered he was still recovering.

"Sorry!"

"I'll survive." Chuckling, he hugged me back. "How are you? Did he hurt you?"

"No, of course not," I rushed to say, realizing too late how that must sound to him. Ocean hadn't obtained me peacefully, so how did I explain to my brother that the last two months had been the happiest of my life?

Roshaun looked around warily and then grabbed my hand before walking off. "Come on. Let's talk in the car, where it's private." Nodding, I followed him to his car and climbed into the passenger seat. As soon as both doors were closed, Shaun spoke. "So I've been hearing some wild shit on the streets, little sis."

"Wild?" I frowned as I ran my sweaty palms down my jeans. Why was I nervous? It was just Shaun. "Like what?"

"You're engaged to Ocean," he announced. The way Roshaun stared me down had me feeling like a teenage girl again—back when he had to step out of his big brother role to parent me. "Tell me that's not true."

I unconsciously reached for my ring, twisting it around my finger to assure myself it was still there. I refused to feel ashamed now that I'd fallen for Ocean, so I held my head high and met my brother's gaze. "Why would you care? Are you not the one who gave me to him to do whatever he wanted?"

"That's not the fucking point!" Roshaun punched the steering wheel, making me jump. "Have you lost your goddamn mind?" he roared.

"Calm down, Shaun. You don't know the whole story."

"I don't need to know shit! You're not marrying him!"

"You don't get a say in what I do! I'm grown!"

"I don't give a fuck if you were a hundred years old! I raised you! You owe me more than fucking the opp!"

"He's only your enemy because you stole from him!"

"So!"

I gaped at him.

He did not just say that.

"Are you serious?" I screamed back. "*I'm* the one who's cleaning up *your* mess, Roshaun, so I'd say we're about even. And by the way, you didn't raise me. I appreciate what you did for me, but I was fifteen when our parents died and barely eighteen when I moved out. I am who I am because of *them*, not you. Get over yourself."

Shaun's arm whipped out faster than a snake. His hand was like a hot brand on my cheek as he slapped fire out of me—hard enough to knock my head into the window. The blow dazed me for a moment, so I couldn't hit him back or get the hell away from him immediately.

The stars I was seeing had barely begun to dissipate when the glass in his window shattered. My eyes widened in horror when I saw two gloved hands reach inside and pull my brother through the broken window.

The jagged edges of the remaining glass sliced into his skin, making Roshaun scream in pain before he was thrown to the ground.

"Wait! Stop!" I opened my door and scrambled out to help my brother, but I didn't get far before I was lifted off my feet and forced to watch as my brother was beaten to a pulp.

"You don't want to do that," a familiar voice warned. "The last thing he'll forgive is you defending that piece of shit right now."

Knowing Abel was right, I slumped in his hold and watched helplessly as my brother got his shit rocked. It wasn't even a fight. Roshaun had long since stopped fighting and had curled into a ball, but Ocean kept going, viciously stomping my brother into the pavement.

I couldn't see his face, but I knew it was him.

He wore a hood, and his back was turned to me, but his muscular build and the line of his shoulders were all too familiar to me. After an eternity, he finally stopped, but Roshaun didn't move again. Ocean turned to me, and I gasped when I saw the blood all over him. There was no way it all belonged to my brother.

Ocean had been busy.

CHAPTER THIRTY-THREE

HUNTER

THE BEDROOM DOOR SLAMMING CLOSED STARTLED ME OUT of my pre-bed warmup. I lifted my head, ready to cuss whoever was responsible for ruining my nap, when my gaze collided with Coby's. Coco left his bed and went over to sniff Coby out of concern, but she was so upset that for once she barely noticed him.

"What the fuck?" I croaked as I sat up, seeing she was dressed and crying. "Did you just come in?"

It wasn't until she ran over to the bed to sit next to me with her hands clenched tightly in her lap that I saw the terror in her eyes. "I think I'm in trouble," she said while staring at the door like she was expecting someone to come barreling through.

"What do you mean? For what?" *I take one nap and look what happens.* "Did you leave the apartment?" Coby only nodded. "Why? Where did you go?" The questions just kept pouring out until I saw her eyes becoming glossy.

"Shaun texted me."

I may have turned to ice after hearing that. "What did he want?"

"He wanted to know where I was so we could talk."

I shot to my feet. "Please tell me you told that fool to kiss your ass."

Coby only looked up at me with such hopelessness. "He's my brother, Hunter."

Biting my tongue, I turned away under the guise of pacing to keep from telling my best friend that the bitch was not her brother. Roshaun didn't give a fuck about her. It may be true, but I knew Coby wasn't ready to hear it.

She knew Roshaun had sold her to Ocean and still wouldn't let his ass go.

What would it take?

Coby wouldn't even let herself believe the truth about her inheritance and that Roshaun had obviously stolen it. I knew her brother was the only thing she had left of her parents, but it was time for her to wake the fuck up.

"Tell me what happened," I gently demanded.

And so Coby did.

By the time she finished vomiting all the drama that had happened right under my nose, I knew two things for sure.

One, I was so fired as Coby's bodyguard.

Two, she wasn't telling me everything.

Ocean wasn't a hothead who only thought with his fists. I seriously doubted that Coby talking to her brother would have driven Ocean to smash his fist...*through a window.* The rage it would have taken to fuel that much power...

"Is Ocean okay?"

Coby shook her head. "I think he broke his hand. Abel took him to get it checked."

"That's not good." A broken hand would weaken him, but I'd be a damn fool to think it would render Ocean completely incapable.

"No," Coby agreed. "And Ocean had his goons take Roshaun, but I don't know where."

I kept my face blank as I nodded. Coby didn't seem to notice how little I cared anyway as she exhaled and placed her face in her hands. She shook her head mournfully. "He probably thinks I betrayed him. I don't think he's ever going to forgive me."

I just barely kept from rolling my eyes. "Roshaun will get over it."

Coby slowly lowered her hands and looked at me like I was daft. "I was talking about Ocean."

Exhaling, I grabbed my phone from the table and dialed his number. It rang until the voicemail picked up. Swallowing my pride, I tried twice more. When my back-to-back calls went ignored, I sent a text.

This is why I don't do relationships.

Too. Fucking. Complicated.

"Well, if he doesn't, fuck him too," I said, pissed at Ocean myself now.

Coby nodded absently while typing on her phone. I snuck a peek and saw Ocean's name saved as 'Hubby' at the top of the thread she was texting. "Yeah, fuck him," she mumbled.

We were both some lying ass bitches.

I convinced Coby to lie down after she grew increasingly frustrated having her texts and calls ignored, but then, of course, she became super clingy and didn't want me leaving her alone.

Crawling under the covers with her, we both drifted toward the center until we were curled around each other, my leg tucked between hers, the heat from her pussy warming my thigh, and the front of our bodies pressed together underneath the duvet.

It was hard to pretend we were normal best friends when you've had said friend's pussy on your mouth and her juices dripping down your chin. We still haven't discussed what had happened, but what more was there to say?

I loved her.

She loved me.

We both loved Ocean.

Coby refused to give up and tried calling Ocean again once we were settled, but he still wouldn't answer. I even tried Abel, who at least texted me back and assured me that Ocean was fine and was cooling off before he came back to Glainne.

I showed the text to Coby.

"Do you think we should leave?" she whispered in the dark.

"Why should we leave? Ocean hasn't been here in a week. I say we invoke squatter's rights," I teased. "This place is ours now." I grinned, but Coby just stared at me sadly, so I sighed and began playing in her short curls. (The ones on her head. Get your minds out of the gutter, nasty.) Massaging her scalp always helped her relax. "Do you want to leave?" I whispered after a few minutes.

"No, but what if my brother is something he can't get past?"

I shrugged, not believing for a second that Ocean would let Roshaun or anyone else tear them apart. "He will. I can easily think of five different occasions you've made me homicidal, and not one of those times did I think I would be better off without you," I told her. "But if Ocean can't get his shit together, just say the word, and we're gone."

Coby gave me a skeptical look. "You really think it will be that easy for us to walk away?"

No. "I don't know."

Coby inhaled. "I love him so much."

"You think?" I mocked sarcastically.

She looked a little sheepish as she shrugged. "Isn't it too soon for me to be sure?"

"Love doesn't abide rules, Coby. It's disrespectful like that. It comes when it wants, infects who it wants, and doesn't care about our reasons for denying it."

Coby released a huge yawn and let her eyes drift closed. "Mkay. Sounds good."

I yawned too as I rubbed her feet with mine under the warm covers. "Try to sleep. You can be lovesick and dick dizzy tomorrow."

"'Kay."

Coby blindly moved to kiss my cheek at the same time I moved to kiss hers. That's how I ended up feeling the weight and curve of her mouth, tasting the mint from the toothpaste on her lips, and seeing her eyes widen to mirror mine when we realized our blunder.

She was the first to surrender, her lashes lowering right before my fingers tightened in her hair. Neither of us attempted to end the kiss. She pressed harder, and then I licked the seam of her lips—a gentle demand. Coby parted them with a moan that I immediately swallowed as I yanked her closer.

Hearing that my best friend was in love with someone else had ripped me in two. Hearing that she was still in love with me and that we were in love with the same man…? Tyler Perry couldn't write this level of messy.

"Hunter," Coby gasped and pulled away suddenly. I started to apologize when the words halted on my lips as she touched her cheek. She frowned at the wetness on her fingertips before looking at me. "You're crying." *What?* Coby thumbed away the tear on my cheek and then looked at me sadly. "I didn't mean to make you cry."

I stared at her before rolling onto my back to stare at the ceiling. "Didn't you?"

"No." Coby followed me until she was lying half on top of me. She kissed down my neck, pulling the straps of Ocean's white, ribbed tank off my shoulders as she went. It was long on me, covering my ass and nothing more.

I didn't stop her as she shoved the material down my torso until my breasts were bared. Her eyes were hungry as she palmed them and licked my nipples. My back arched, and I cried out, feeling my pussy gush and ruin the sheets when she retreated with my nipple trapped between her lips, pulling it past its stretching point before releasing it with a pop.

She moved over to the other, her gaze on me as she showed it the same attention, switching back and forth until I was a squirming, blubbering mess. I loved having my nipples stimulated, and she knew it.

She knew everything about me.

I didn't even realize her hand was on my thigh, sliding upward, until she spoke. "Do you remember how you made me feel better whenever I was sad?"

"Yes," I moaned when her hand disappeared under the tank.

I wasn't wearing panties, so there was no barrier between her fingers and my pussy. Coby found my hole right away, pushing two fingers inside while she reminded me of sweeter, sinful times.

"You were so good to me," she cooed as she played in my pussy. "No one had ever made me come as hard as you did. After we stopped messing around, I'd touched myself at night. I'd stare at the door while my fingers were stuffed in my pussy—just like they're stuffed in yours now. I'd wait for the door to open, for you to come inside and finish the job." Our gazes met, and I saw all the hurt she'd hidden from me before in her eyes. "But you never did."

"I know," I confessed with a gasp when the heel of her palm brushed my clit. "There were nights...when I wasn't strong enough... to stay away. Oh, fuck, Coby. Just like that. Please." Coby shifted to lie on her side next to me so she could watch her fingers disappear in and out of my pussy. "I'd stand outside your door...listening to you say my name...when you came. I knew if I came inside, I'd touch you."

Coby leaned over, and I met her halfway for a kiss so hot, I thought I'd melt into the bed. Ocean's bed...where we waited for him to find us when he returned. What would happen if he did? Would he be upset? Would he watch us? Join us?

"Do you want to touch me now?" Coby asked, interrupting my thoughts.

"Please"

Coby broke the kiss, slipping her fingers out of me as she sat up to tear Ocean's t-shirt off her body.

She wasn't wearing panties either.

It was as if we both knew this would happen.

I let my thighs fall open, but Coby surprised me when she lay back down and motioned me on top. "I want to taste you first."

She didn't have to tell me twice.

Sitting up, I removed Ocean's tank from around my waist and threw my leg over Coby's shoulder, straddling her face in a crouch and lowering my pussy onto her waiting tongue.

The first swipe had me digging my fingers into my thick thighs as I threw my head back and groaned. I was already so close. My arousal was a fountain at this point, making a mess of Coby's lips and chin as I rocked my hips. The only other person I ever felt this insatiable with was Ocean.

I looked over my shoulder where the armchair sat in the corner. I pictured him sprawled in it, stoically watching his angel devour my wicked little pussy. The only sign that he enjoyed being cuckolded would be the hand stroking his dick while he waited for his turn.

"Oh, my God, bestie," I cried as my hips kicked into overdrive.

Coby hummed as she lashed my clit, and then her hands found my ass, spreading the heavy globes apart and opening me up for her tongue to travel through my folds. The moment her tongue circled my opening, I knew I was going to come. Coby must have known it, too, because she promptly returned to my clit, and that was all she fucking wrote.

I was done for.

My legs shook as I threw my head back and released in her mouth. Coby, like the deceptively innocent little freak she was, greedily slurped it all up. I was too spent to trust that I could stay upright, so I collapsed on the bed next to her to catch my breath.

Coby had other plans.

My pussy was still a throbbing wet mess when Coby nudged my thighs apart and climbed between them. I cracked my eyes open in time to see her straddling me sideways, lowering all that glistening pink...

"Shit, Coby," I cried when I felt our pussies kiss. My clit gave an excited twitch that Coby no doubt felt since ours were lined up perfectly to stimulate one another.

"It can always be like this," she moaned as she began to rock her hips while holding onto my raised thigh. I could feel the wet friction of her pussy massaging mine as she rode me. Used me. "If you stayed...we could spend the day playing together while Ocean was away. And when he came home, he'd use us again. We would be safe, loved, and free to love. We would never want for anything. Our kids would even be siblings. We could be together. Happy. Never having to part or be too busy with our separate families to see each other as much as we used to. We'd be a family. It would be all of us against the world. We could sleep in the same bed and wake up together every morning. All you have to do is say yes. Say yes, and we're yours. Forever."

I saw the picture Coby painted clear as day in my mind as I held onto her hip and fucked her pussy from below.

Ocean would forbid us from playing without him because he was cruel and jealous. Coby and I would break the rules anyway to make him hurry home to punish us. I imagined him coming in after a long day and taking one of us before he went to sleep, and using the other in the morning before he left for work. I imagined how much more merry the holidays would be with three, never feeling alone or unloved with Ocean and Coby always around. I pictured Coby and my kids growing up together as real siblings and not just pretend. I'd never have to worry about her moving away because her husband got a new job on the other side of the country.

In my fantasy, we both wore Ocean's ring, and it meant something.

But in reality, only Coby did.

I'd like to say it didn't matter to me, but it did—because no matter what they promised, Ocean and Coby would always have a higher claim on each other than I ever could. I'd just be the mistress times two.

"Hunter… I'm going to come." Coby gasped before I could break her heart all over again by saying no. "You feel so fucking good."

My lids lowered even more as I wound my hips and lost myself to the sensation we created.

Somehow, this always felt twice as intimate as anything else we'd done. Fused together like this, I couldn't tell where I ended and Coby began. I didn't care about right or wrong, hearts and souls, or who belonged to whom. All I could do was fuck.

"You're so fucking sexy," I praised. "Come on my pussy, bestie. I want to feel you squirt."

If Ocean walked into the apartment right now, there would be no denying what we were up to as our cries rose and mingled to create a sinful harmony with the wet glide of our pussies rubbing and grinding together as backup. It was messy, electric, and filthy.

It was almost too much to handle.

I felt my toes curl as my orgasm swiftly rose.

The only thing that could make this even more explosive was knowing I had a good, stiff dick waiting to fill me up after.

As if thinking the same and racing to finish so we could both be stuffed with dick, Coby was the first to break. Her hips lost their rhythm as her muscles tensed, and then she screamed.

Coby's release triggered my own, and I came barely a breath behind her.

She collapsed on top of me, and I held her as she hid her face in my neck with the front of our naked bodies lined up. It was quiet for so long that I assumed she'd fallen asleep until she lifted her head sometime later to stare at me. "You never answered me earlier."

"About what? I was a little busy," I teased groggily.

Coby rolled off me to sit against the headboard with her knees tucked against her chest. "Why didn't you want to be with me?"

I sighed as I pulled myself up, grabbed our discarded shirts, and handed Coby hers. I waited the ten seconds it took us to redress to respond. "I did. I still do. I just… can't."

"But why?"

Post orgasmic bliss over, I climbed off the bed. "I don't want to talk about this. I'm going to shower."

Coby followed me, running around the bed to cut off my path to the bathroom. "No!" she yelled as she pushed me back. I stumbled but caught myself. "I'm sick of you running away from me. We're going to talk about this, and we're going to do it now! Tell me why we can't be together."

"You mean besides the obvious fact that you just told me you're in love with someone else and you're marrying him?" I pushed her back, but she caught my wrists to keep me from going anywhere.

Coby was a lot stronger than she looked. The only way I was going to shake the bitch loose was to fight her ass off.

"That's not good enough!"

"Fuck it. You want to know why?" I grabbed her arms since they were all I could reach and yanked her close until her chest was pressed into mine. I could feel her heart pounding. "Because you were the first to ever last. The first one who didn't hurt me. I wasn't going to risk losing you by getting greedy. If it didn't work out, we could never return to being friends. Did you think about that? I'd be alone. No... actually, I wouldn't be. If you ever walked away like everyone else, I would die, Coby, and I don't mean in my heart. I would literally throw myself into the sound and cease to exist. The only way I could survive losing you is to not survive at all. You get it? Are you happy now? Can I go wash you off me now and forget this ever happened?"

Coby's grip loosened from the shock of my admission. "Oh, my God, Hunter," she wailed. "Why didn't you tell me?"

"Because later, when you wanted to break it off, you'd remember. You'd try to make it work even if it cost you everything. I wasn't going to let you sacrifice your happiness for mine. I love you too much."

She gave me a sad smile. "But only as a friend, right?"

"No," I heard myself say. "*Not* as a friend."

Coby sniffled and then took cautious steps toward me. "Then be with me. Be with us," she quickly amended. "Ocean loves you as much as I do, and I know you love him."

"Coby...*think*. What if one of us gets jealous or feels like the other is getting more attention?"

"Jealousy wouldn't be anything new for us, don't you think? I don't know about Ocean, but it's like foreplay for us now. And when have you or I ever been callow enough to cry about not getting enough attention? This isn't a competition. It's a relationship. It's love. For this to work, you need to have your own connection with Ocean, just as I do, and just as we already do. I'll respect yours if you respect mine. Otherwise, we'll all just end up feeling like a third wheel. I'm not saying this arrangement can work for anyone. I'm saying it can work for *us*. We're the exception, not the rule."

"I hear you," I returned. But I still wasn't quite convinced, and Coby knew it.

"Hunter, I'm not saying it will be easy. It won't be a normal relationship because none of us is normal. You think there's anyone more perfect out there for you? For Ocean? For me? Yes, I get jealous whenever I think of you together, but I love the way it feels. I love the bitter burn. I've fantasized about the things you told me he did to you. I crave the day when I can watch you two together, but it's not just about sex. Ocean would do anything for me, and nothing makes me happier than knowing he would do the same for you. I never wanted to be without you, and to know I don't have to be feels right. If there was ever anything worth fighting for, it's this. It's us. Ocean isn't the knife to tear us apart. He's the glue. Tell me you don't feel it."

I stared at her, but I couldn't make the words come. I've lived my whole life afraid of giving my heart away, and now it was in danger of being stolen twice.

"You can't run forever," Coby said as if she'd read my mind. "I won't hurt you, Hunter, and I'd never let Ocean either."

"But what if I hurt you?"

"You'll do that anyway if you leave, so what do you have to lose?"

"You."

When Coby shook her head, I already knew what she would say. I knew it because my heart was telling me I'd already made a choice. I just had to make my lips say it. *Yes. Yes, yes, yes.* "You don't see it, do you? Maybe you do, but you're too stubborn to admit it." She huffed and shook her head as if I were being purposely dense. "It's already too late, Hunter. We've said too much. Done too much. There's no going back for us. No matter what, we will never be just friends again."

As the truth of her words sank in, breathing became a challenge. The room began to spin, so to keep from passing out, I focused on the dark shadow lingering by the open door.

"Hunter?" Coby reached out as if ready to save me from the floor if I fainted. "What—?" Noticing my attention, she spun around to see what had stolen it.

Ocean was standing there with a cast around his right hand, listening to every word.

CHAPTER THIRTY-FOUR

OCEAN

M Y HAND WAS FUCKING KILLING ME.
I'd refused the pain medication because I wanted to remain lucid and had opted for whisky instead.

Right now, I needed a drink for a different reason.

"What did you do to my brother?" Coby demanded as I was taking a piss. She stood inside the bathroom with her arms crossed, ready for a fight after I iced her out all night.

"Nothing yet." I moved over to the sink to wash my hands. It was awkward as fuck doing everything with my left hand. I still had use of the fingers on my right hand, but that was it.

I waited for Coby to plead for her brother's life, but she was surprisingly silent as I shut off the water and moved over to the running shower, dropping the shorts I'd slept in while I went.

"Don't kill him," she finally begged once I was naked. *There it is.*

I stepped into the shower without a word. Coby flung her arms up and tried to storm out, but I reached out and grabbed her wrist, forcing her into the shower with me. Thankfully, my cast was made of fiberglass, so it was waterproof.

"Ocean, my hair!" Coby squealed.

Cursing, I leaned out to grab her shower cap from the hook by the glass door and quickly covered her short ginger curls.

The hot water had already soaked through the t-shirt that she was wearing. I could see her nipples and taut stomach clinging to the cotton. She smelled like her usual green apple perfume, but another, *heavier* scent clung to her wet skin, too.

It was jasmine.

"Ocean—"

I shoved my sponge in her hand, and Coby pursed her lips into a pout and grabbed my body wash. Once it was good and lathered, she started washing my chest, so I curved my hands around her hips as I watched her. "So, what did you and Hunter get up to last night?"

The sponge paused on my chest as Coby looked up at me. "Not much. Why?"

"*Because I smell her on you.*"

Coby dropped the sponge and then rushed to pick it up from the shower floor. "What are you asking me, Ocean?"

I placed my hand around her neck and drove her into the wall. "Did you fuck her?"

"Yup!" she said, popping the p with her smart ass. "I got all up in that pussy just like you did, and it was the best I ever had. Of course, I've only had hers, but who's counting?" Finally, she met my gaze and smiled, but it wasn't a nice one. "Want to compare notes?"

"Sure." I smirked back. "You start."

Coby rolled her eyes at me for not taking the bait. She still wanted to fight because she thought it would save her brother, but I was done with all that.

Once Coby and I finished showering, we went downstairs to eat the breakfast the chef had prepared. Hunter was nowhere to be found, which meant she was blowing off steam with Abel in the gym.

"Why did you risk your life going to see him?" I asked.

We hadn't talked about it last night. I just told Coby and Hunter I'd deal with them in the morning before passing out from the pain and booze.

"Because he's the only family I have left and I wanted to see for myself that he was still in one piece."

Not anymore.

When Roshaun eventually woke up, he was going to find himself without the hand he used to slap my wife. I didn't kill him. Not yet. But I had taken great pleasure in causing him a shitload of pain.

"You're wrong, *mo aingeal*. He's not your only family. You have people who love and adore you so much that they'd *never* raise a hand to you."

"Like you?" she said with no real ire.

"Exactly."

Coby sighed but didn't agree with my point. How could she?

"I think…" Coby mused out loud, drawing my attention. My eyes fell to her left hand resting on the table. She was deep in thought as she toyed with her custom engagement ring. "I think if we get married, Hunter will leave. She won't stay." When I simply stared at Coby for an explanation, she obliged. "Last night, she kept talking about balance—about jealousy, ownership, and making things fair. I think if we want her to be with us, you and I can't get married. I know the position this puts you in, so what I guess I'm saying is…give it some thought because you may have to choose."

I frowned at that. "Between you and Hunter?"

Coby shook her head and then squared her shoulders. "Between being Boss or being with us."

Staring off, I didn't say anything for a long while as I considered all that Coby had said. I felt her gaze on me, and she looked sort of desperate for an answer that I wasn't ready to give. It's not that I wanted to be Boss that badly. It's that I knew in my gut there had to be a way I could have both, so I nodded. "Thanks for letting me know."

Coby sighed and pouted, resigned to having to wait for my answer. I almost smiled because her brattiness had always amused me. We finished eating, and then I pulled her into my arms to say goodbye properly before I headed out.

"I almost had her, you know," Coby said after we finished kissing slowly like we had all the time in the world. "She was about to say yes before you came in with your moodiness and fucked everything up."

I snorted. "You did not."

"I did!" she squealed in delight.

I pursed my lips skeptically, and she punched my arm.

"She's not coming," Abel grumbled for the third time.

"She's fucking coming," I snapped back as we stood by the elevators dressed in all black.

"I don't know what you said or did, but she actually almost kicked my ass this morning. She's not coming."

I didn't respond as I stared at the stairs, waiting for her to appear. I didn't want to admit that Abel might be right. I'd texted Hunter the time and place to meet tonight, but I didn't tell her why.

Another five minutes rolled by—three minutes past our meeting time—and still no Hunter. She was supposed to meet us at midnight, and she was always prompt, so I knew there was a good chance she wouldn't show.

I grappled with either leaving without her or dragging her out of bed, but since waking Coby would ruin the mission before it started, I refrained.

Just as I was about to say fuck it and leave without her, Hunter appeared at the top of the stairs dressed in dark clothing as I'd instructed. Her long hair was braided back, and her face was blank as she approached us.

"You're late," Abel couldn't help complaining.

"Sorry, I thought you'd learned how to change your own diaper by now," Hunter retorted.

"Ignore him," I said as I stabbed the button for the elevator.

Hunter chose not to speak to either of us as we climbed inside and rode it down. Abel found that hilarious, silently laughing at my expense behind Hunter's back.

I swear to God, I almost shot him.

I'd given Paul the night off, wanting as few witnesses to what we were about to do as possible, so Abel hopped into the front seat of the Denali while Hunter and I climbed into the back.

I watched her while she stared out the window.

We rode south for an hour until we reached a secluded road, where we found a fleet of cars blocking our path. Abel flicked his lights so we wouldn't be shot the fuck up as soon as we stepped out.

"This feels familiar," Hunter said, the first words she'd spoken since we left.

"Yeah, well, it'll feel even realer in a second."

The three of us climbed out and walked toward the cars parked up ahead. I stopped Hunter just before we reached them while Abel kept walking, leaving us to talk alone.

"What's up?" Hunter asked me.

"You once mentioned a friend you trusted who tried to take more from you than you were willing to give. Tell me who he was."

Her brows rose as she cut her gaze toward all the men waiting for us a few feet away. "You want to talk about this now?"

"A name," I demanded.

Still resistant as ever, Hunter sighed. "Why does it matter, Ocean?"

"Because tonight will go one of two ways. Your answer will determine which path we take, but only one of them is irreversible. The other has lasting consequences."

"Wow, so mysterious." She looked toward the cars, all facing one way and blocking her view. I swear she paled a little when it dawned on her why I brought her here. "And what if I don't want that? Whatever it is?"

Using my good hand, I pulled her closer until she had no choice but to lean into me. "Don't you?"

Hunter gulped and then squeezed her eyes closed. "It was so long ago, Ocean. I'm fine now."

"But it still happened, Hunter. Who. Was. He?"

"I can't." Her eyes flew open as her breathing increased until she was hyperventilating. "I can't kill him. I can't. She'll never forgive me."

"Shhh. Calm, Vengeance. Calm." I tucked her face into my chest and rubbed her back, whispering sweet nothings until she went lax against me. "What do you want to do? I'll take your lead, but Hunter… he can't come anywhere near you or Coby again. One way or another, Roshaun has to go."

"Not that I'm torn up about it, but why can't he see Coby? He's a piece of shit, but he is her brother."

I released a heavy sigh. Of course, Coby hadn't told her.

"Because he put his fucking hands on her. He slapped her so hard, her fucking head hit the window. I'm not giving him a chance to do something like that ever again."

Hunter stiffened, and then she slowly lifted her head from my chest.

The last time I'd seen that look in her eyes was when she nearly succeeded in sticking a hunting knife in my heart.

One moment, I was holding her.

Next, she was gone.

CHAPTER THIRTY-FIVE

HUNTER

OR THE FIRST TIME SINCE I WAS A SNOT-NOSED KID, IT TRULY felt like Christmas morning.

"Hunter?" Roshaun peered through the dark, the mist spilling from the trees onto the road. The eye that wasn't swollen shut widened briefly when I stopped before him. "Shit, it is you. Aye..." He shifted anxiously on his knees. "Listen, you got to help me. My sister—"

"You hit her."

Roshaun paused and then blinked like he didn't know what I was talking about. It made me wonder if this wasn't the first time he hurt her, and Coby had kept it from me. "What?"

"You. Hit. Her."

Seeing that playing dumb wouldn't work on me (I knew too much about him), he sucked his teeth and looked away dismissively. "Bitch, I ain't hit nobody. If she told you that shit, she's lying."

It was all I needed to hear as I reached for my knife.

"Whoa, whoa, what the fuck are you doing?" Roshaun screamed as he scrambled to get away from me. He only made it as far as his ass since his hands were bound behind his back.

Several goons looked at each other, not knowing whether to kill us both when I walked around him and cut through the cable tie, freeing him. Roshaun—wary, injured, and close to pissing his pants—was slow to stand, and I remembered he was still healing from his broken ribs.

It was the first place I struck when I sent him back to his knees.

I watched coldly as he leaned over and spat up blood before wheezing for air. "I knew you were a piece of shit, but I didn't know you were pathetic too," I grumbled. This was so disappointing. I wanted to beat him up, show him I wasn't afraid anymore, and that if he came for me, I could protect myself. But Ocean had already worked him over pretty well, so there wasn't much fun in it for me. "Get up."

"I can't."

"Get up!" I roared.

"The fuck…the fuck…the fuck are you doing," Roshaun struggled to get out as he rose off his hands and sat back on his heels.

"I trusted you. Coby trusted you!" I drove my knee up, hitting him under his chin and knocking him back.

"Push off the ground with your opposite foot for more power and keep that leg straight," Abel instructed. And then he sighed tiredly, like I was a disappointing pupil. "We've gone over this."

Ignoring him, I placed my foot on Roshaun's dick and pressed until he released a blood-curdling scream. Several of Ocean's men flinched. "Don't be so fucking dramatic," I teased. And then I shifted more of my weight onto him, making him scream again. "How many girls have you forced this thing on?"

"Hunter, p-please."

"I said please, too. Did you listen?" When I was sixteen and begged him not to kick me out, he said if I wanted to stay with Coby, I knew what I had to do. Roshaun didn't answer, so I shifted my foot to his throat. He made a gargling sound when I cut off his ability to breathe or swallow. "Did you?" The fear in his eyes, knowing his life was at my mercy, was more satisfying than tiring myself out by besting him in a fight.

Only it wasn't Roshaun's face staring back at me.

It was my father's.

And then it was Roshaun's again.

Back and forth, the face of the man who hurt me switched.

One moment, I felt Roshaun's hands on me after watching me strip. Next, I heard my father's voice ordering me to fuck his boss. Eventually, the two men melted into one.

I pressed harder, taking away my abusers' ability to breathe just as they'd taken away my ability to feel safe, to feel loved, and to trust. No matter whose visage appeared before me, the anger and betrayal felt the same.

The loss felt the same.

I didn't realize I'd blacked out, and so had Roshaun. He'd stopped struggling long before I felt Ocean's hands pulling me away. I knew it was him because of his cologne.

No one on Earth smelled as sinful as Ocean Kilpatrick.

He locked his arm around my chest, kissing the side of my face and bringing me back from the rage that had taken over me. Roshaun and my father didn't get to decide who I was anymore.

As for the latter, I had no idea if that bastard was even still alive.

"He won't be for long," Ocean promised, and I realized I'd spoken out loud.

"I don't care," I lied. "Thank you for this, but I can't." I inhaled deeply because the effort it took—the weight of it—not to give in and end Roshaun Perry once and for all nearly crushed me.

But there was something else I needed more.

Something else I couldn't live without.

"If I kill him, Coby will hate me forever. If I lose her, he wins." It didn't matter that I'd pictured this moment a thousand times, and in none of them did I fantasize about walking away, but I needed Coby more than I needed revenge. "I'm making a choice not to think about him or my sperm donor ever again."

"And you won't have to."

With one last kiss to my temple, Ocean led me away, back to the Denali. I didn't even look back as I let him. It was just the two of us when we drove back to the city. Abel had stayed behind to take care of Roshaun. I didn't want to ask what Ocean would do with him because I didn't want to lie to Coby. The second reason is that I just didn't care anymore. Roshaun had no power over me.

Staring out the window, I was lost in my thoughts until I felt Ocean's hand curving around my thigh. I looked down at it, and then I did something crazy.

I laced my fingers through his, and when he squeezed, I squeezed back.

Ocean didn't drive us back to Glainne.

It was the wee hours of the morning, and even on Christmas, the city was still asleep.

The drive-in theater Ocean took us to was miraculously open, though no one else was around. I tried to hide my excitement and curiosity since I'd always wanted to go to one of these. I eyed Ocean suspiciously as he backed the Denali into the perfect spot so that the tailgate faced the screen. Once parked, Ocean told me to stay put before climbing out.

I checked my phone to ensure I didn't have any messages from Coby in case she'd woken up while Ocean messed with something in the trunk. I was starting to wonder if he had a dead body back there or something. He was swearing viciously as he shifted things around. Whatever he was doing, it took him twice as long since he only had one working hand.

I offered to help, but he ordered me to stay my ass right where I was, so I did. The last movie of the night/morning was about to start, and I didn't care what it was. I was just excited to be here.

Wish I had some snacks.

Ocean finished with whatever he was doing back there and came to my door to help me out before leading me to the back of the Denali.

As soon as I saw what had kept him, my heart skipped a beat.

A thick blanket had been laid out where the third row of seats had been stored inside the floor to make room. There were pillows propped against the back of the second row of seats to make it extra cozy and electric candles to add ambiance. The picnic basket, centered on the blanket, caught my eye, along with the large tin can of popcorn. It was filled to the brim with three different flavors—cheddar, caramel, and butter. There was also a wooden board filled with an assortment of sugary sweets.

I felt the heat of Ocean's body at my back, watching me take it all in. I'd love to say I was a wall, giving nothing away, but it would be a lie. My skin prickled with all the emotions pushing to be free.

"You did all this?"

I felt Ocean nod against my shoulder. "Climb in," he whispered. "I won't bite."

I didn't believe that at all.

My cheeks were warm despite the biting cold as I crawled into the back of the Denali. The engine was still running, so there was heat blowing through the vents, but it wasn't enough to combat the northern winter coming in through the open hatch. Once Ocean climbed in with me, I found myself inching closer to him while he pulled two large thermoses out of the basket and handed me one.

Steam poured out once I opened the top.

I sniffed at the contents, and my stomach growled when I smelled the hot soup. I poured some into the lid that doubled as a bowl and greedily slurped at it. Heat immediately flooded my veins and thawed my blood while I moaned in pleasure.

Ocean lounged against the pillows before pulling me between his legs, and I didn't fight him. I leaned against his chest while he covered my legs with another blanket, and I sighed contentedly.

I'm not sure what came over me, but I grabbed my phone and opened the camera app.

"Say cheese," I teased, not expecting him to comply.

Ocean surprised me when he leaned over my shoulder and flashed an adorable smile at the camera. I snapped the picture and then took more of our little nook. I studied them for a while, ago-nizing over whether to send them to Coby when I usually would if Ocean were anyone else. Fuck it. I sent the photos with a text.

You told him. I'm going to kill you.

My idea of a perfect date *and* my favorite snacks? This had Coby written all over it. It was obvious by now that Ocean and Coby had teamed up to wear me down. I knew my text wouldn't wake her up since Coby kept her phone on silent at night, so I tucked it away as the movie started to play on the mega screen.

It was *Die Hard*.

"I was hoping they played this," he said.

My brows immediately lowered as I turned my head to glower up at him. "Please tell me you're not one of those nut cases who think *Die Hard* is a Christmas movie."

"You don't?"

I groaned dramatically as I turned my attention back to the open-ing scene of Bruce on a plane. There was no way I could enjoy this movie as much as I did if it filled me with holiday cheer.

"Why don't you like Christmas?" Ocean asked after we watched nearly half the movie and ate our soup silently.

My appetite fled, so I capped my thermos and set it aside with a shrug. "I wanted to. I tried, but it was never in the cards for me."

"Why?"

I almost didn't answer.

I'd never told anyone why—not even Coby. She loved Christmas, and I never wanted to sour her joy for the holiday with my bitter memories. She was too empathetic and loyal not to hate Christmas with a fiery passion if she'd known.

But I figured if anyone could relate without pitying me, it would be Ocean.

"Believe it or not, everything bad that's ever happened to me since I was a child occurred during this cursed holiday, starting with my mother leaving and ending with Coby almost marrying you on Christmas Eve. I don't know if it's a coincidence or if ol' Saint Nick has it out for me, but I've learned to anticipate the worst during this time of year."

"I'm sorry."

"Don't be. It's just a season. A few bad days lumped together, and then it's over."

I shivered, and since I was pressed against him, Ocean felt it. "Cold?"

"No," I lied.

Ocean reached inside the basket and handed me another thermos anyway. As soon as I smelled the hot cocoa, I looked at him hopefully. "Marshmallows?"

"Nice try," he said dryly. "You hate marshmallows."

I smirked and took my first sip of the cocoa. "Just checking."

He held me tighter, and I stroked his cast. "The hot chocolate or how well I'm paying attention to you?"

I hummed happily as I took another sip. "Both."

"Stop looking for holes in my strategy, Vengeance. You won't find any."

"I already did."

"Yeah? Tell me." He nipped my ear. "Where did I fuck up, Hunter?"

I sighed. "At the end of the day, whether you *want or need* to be married, you still chose Coby to fill that role, and I don't blame you, but you can't ask me to be in this throuple with you and be okay with that. To everyone who sees us, it will be Mr. and Mrs. Kilpatrick and their jezebel mistress."

"And that would matter more to you than the truth?"

"Well...you and Coby really would be married, so it would be the truth no matter what any of us felt."

Ocean was silent for a while before he took my thermos full of yummy hot chocolate away. I whined at the loss. He rolled us over and shifted until he got me beneath him, and I forgot all about that damn cocoa when I felt his hard body on top of mine.

"We can't control what other people think, so you shouldn't

worry so much about it. But I care what *you* think, so what if I found a way to make you believe we can work and not just for a little while. Forever."

What he was suggesting was impossible. "You can't."

"I can."

"Why are you so sure?"

"Because I love you, Hunter. A man can move mountains when he's in love. Don't let anyone tell you different." Ocean rested his forehead against mine and sighed. "Say yes," he urged. "Trust that I can make you both feel safe, cherished, and loved. But even more, believe that you deserve it." He kissed me sweetly. "Because that's all I want to do, Hunter. I want to take care of you."

"And Coby?"

"Hell, yeah."

I moaned when he deepened the kiss. It was always so drugging. "We're kind of a lot. Are you sure you can handle us?" I teased between kisses.

Ocean wrangled his lips from mine and looked down at me like I was crazy for even suggesting it. "Fuck no," he barked, making us both laugh. "But I don't give a shit. I need you. I need her."

I hid my smile and shrugged. "It's your funeral."

Ocean froze, and then his eyes widened when he caught on to what I was saying. "Is that a yes?"

My stomach was suddenly attacked by a thousand butterflies as I stared up at him. The sheer hope in his eyes that I might surrender… I'd never felt more powerful or desired. All I wanted to do was chase that feeling. "Yes."

Rolling off me, Ocean pulled me into him. His hold was crushing, as if he thought I might change my mind or poof out of existence. We cuddled and gorged ourselves on popcorn and candy like two teenagers while watching the rest of *Die Hard*. I don't think either of us made it to the end before falling asleep.

I woke first while the ending credits were still rolling.

For a while, I just watched Ocean as he slept.

I never realized how long his lashes were until now. I lightly played with his beard so that I wouldn't wake him, and after, when I could no longer ignore how fucking cold it was, I searched through the mountain of pillows and extra blankets for my phone.

Waking the screen, I cursed after seeing what time it was.

"Ocean." I pecked his lips several times until he finally opened his eyes. "We've got to go." I had to shake his ass awake again when it looked like he would fall asleep again. I almost felt bad for waking him, knowing he hadn't been getting much sleep lately. "Coby will be up soon."

He blinked and then checked his watch before frowning, sucking his teeth, and rolling away from me to slip back into sleep. "Hunter, please," he groaned when I shook him again. "It's barely five in the morning. Coby's sleeping. I'm sleeping. Go to sleep."

"No," I whined. "I'm cold, and it's Christmas morning. Coby's always up before the sun because she's so obnoxiously happy about Christmas that she can barely sleep the night before."

Unconvinced that anyone would willingly wake up this hour, Ocean lazily reached for his phone. I thought it was to call Coby, but after staring at the screen for a while, I realized he was watching something.

I peered over his shoulder, and my jaw dropped when I saw a video feed of Coby's room at Glainne. On the screen was a live recording of the bedroom and Coby stirring. "Is that—have you been watching us?"

"Of course," Ocean said casually as if that wasn't a huge invasion of privacy.

That meant he knew everything.

Saw everything.

As if reading my thoughts, Ocean looked over his shoulder at me and smirked. He rose and tucked his phone away before kissing my lips. "You're right. We should go."

I was a ball of confused emotions as I helped him clean up. I was sad to see our little nook go, but I was more torn over what the hell

Ocean might have seen or heard and what he planned to do about it. I knew he wanted us all together, but how did he feel about Coby and me having our own thing?

Ocean drove us back to Glainne while I worked up the courage to ask.

The words still hadn't come when we reached the glittering onyx tower. We dropped the Denali off with the valet just as Abel seemingly materialized out of nowhere. I wasn't surprised. Ocean had been too at ease at the drive-in while in the middle of an open war with his far, which meant we hadn't been alone after all.

We held hands as we rode the private elevators up to the penthouse. As soon as the doors slid open, I could hear Coby's favorite Christmas carol blaring through the speakers, and for the first time in years, I wasn't completely dreading the day.

CHAPTER THIRTY-SIX

COBY

I STARED AT THE PHOTO OF HUNTER AND OCEAN ON THEIR movie date and saved it to my phone before making it my wallpaper. If a picture said a thousand words, this one only needed to say three.

Hunter was in.

Nervous butterflies fluttered in my stomach at the thought of sharing my soulmate with the man who owned my heart. I was so excited, I found myself slipping out of bed before my alarm could go off.

Waking up early on Christmas morning was my ritual, but I'd never been this restless. I was eager to see if what Hunter had secretly conveyed in her text was real or imagined. I needed to know that I hadn't read too much into it—that it wasn't just wishful thinking.

They must have left the penthouse after I fell asleep last night. It seemed like an odd time for a date, but nothing about Ocean was conventional, so I didn't question it too much.

After connecting my phone to the speakers and opening my Christmas playlist, I sang along to the carols as I started a new group chat.

Coming home soon?

Hunter was the first to respond.

Mine: Otw. Ocean's driving, so he can't respond.

K. I'll get breakfast started. :)

Mine: French toast, pls! And none of that vegan crap.

Lmao - I got u.

The bubbles appeared before I could back out of the thread, so I waited. They disappeared again, only to reappear seconds later. This went on a few more times, so I darkened my screen and went into the kitchen to get started.

Setting my phone on the counter, I gathered the ingredients for vegan French toast. Hunter claimed she could tell the difference, but she never did.

I was whisking the cornstarch and soy milk together when my phone chimed moments later. I glanced at the text on the locked screen, but it wasn't from Hunter.

It had come from an unknown number.

Unknown: Just thought you should know who you're marrying…

Wondering if an old girlfriend of Ocean's had somehow gotten hold of my number, I snatched up my phone and opened the text without hesitation.

The last thing I expected to pop up a second later was a picture of my brother. The camera had been zoomed in, so only his face was visible, but I knew it was him. I could see the familiar faint scar near his hairline from when he fell out of a tree when he was six. His eyes were open and staring back at me, but something was off. They seemed dull. Lifeless.

Roshaun was staring at the camera, but there was no awareness.

Noticing the white target symbol in the upper left-hand corner, I tapped it, and the photo came to life, showing me what had happened two seconds before the picture was taken.

A gloved hand speckled with crimson.

My brother's braids trapped in its grasp.

Roshaun's mouth twisted and forever frozen mid-scream.

His neck was nothing more than mangled flesh, blood, and tissue.

In the background, I could see the rest of him wearing the clothes I last saw him in. His body was slumped against the wall in the background.

Headless.

The photo reverted to a close-up of his eyes, forehead, and nose, but it was too late.

I was already screaming.

My wails joined the jaunty Christmas carol blasting through the suite and mocking my pain.

And then my phone chimed again, and another text came through.

Unknown: Merry Christmas.

Dropping the phone, I darted over to the kitchen sink. I heard someone running up behind me, but I was too busy spilling my guts inside to care who.

"Coby?" Kellan called out. "I heard you scream. What happened?"

An image of my brother's mutilated body flashed in my mind, and my throat jumped. This time, when I heaved, nothing came out.

Roshaun was *gone*.

My legs gave out, and I collapsed to the ground, another wail tearing from me when my gaze landed on my phone and Roshaun's lifeless eyes staring back at me just before the screen went dark.

I crawled across the cold tile and picked it up with shaking hands.

This couldn't be real.

It had to be a trick.

A cruel fucking joke.

"Please, God."

"Coby, tell me what's going on, or I'm calling Ocean," Kellan warned.

Ignoring him, I unlocked my phone and dialed my brother's number.

It rang and rang and rang, but he didn't answer. Breathing became impossible as I tried three more times in vain.

"Coby…"

"C-c-can you p-p-please take me to my brother?" I begged Kellan once I accepted the fact that Roshaun wasn't going to answer. "I th-think he's in tr-trouble. Please."

Kellan shook his head, his green eyes filled with pity. "You know I can't do that. Tell me what happened. Maybe I can help without getting killed. Start from the beginning."

I couldn't because it all led back to Ocean.

Ocean had killed my brother.

"Oh, God." I held my stomach with one hand and my mouth with the other when it felt like I'd throw up again.

"Fuck," Kellan cursed when he saw a fresh wave of tears spill from my eyes. "Just let me call Ocean."

"There's no need to call me," a deep voice interrupted. "I'm right here."

Kellan and I turned toward the elevator and saw him standing there with Abel and Hunter. My bestie took one look at me and let Ocean's hand go to rush over.

"What's wrong?" Hunter demanded. She touched my arms, and I broke, throwing myself around her and sobbing like a baby. My big brother was dead. "You're shaking, Coby. Come sit down."

I let her lead me to the couch while Kellan whispered his report to Ocean. I glared at the latter, but he kept his face carefully blank while listening to Kellan and staring right at me.

The man I loved killed my brother. Where did we go from here?

I leaned forward. Hunter mirrored me, tilting her head to give me her ear. "Can I borrow your gun?"

Hunter reared back, searching my gaze as if she didn't recognize me. "Coby, talk to me," she pleaded. "You're scaring me."

I was scaring myself.

Ocean killed my brother.

But if I could still love Roshaun this much after he was gone, I could do the same for Ocean.

"Roshaun's dead. Ocean killed him."

Hunter visibly tensed. "What? How do you know?"

I handed Hunter my phone. Since she knew my code, she was able to get in. "Check the last text."

Overhearing, Ocean wandered over, unperturbed by my glare, warning him to stay away.

"What the fuck?" Hunter spat.

"Let me see," Ocean demanded.

Hunter stood and handed over my phone before I could tell him what a murderous bastard he was. I watched Ocean admire his handiwork, but his brows dipped like he was confused.

When he looked up to study me, I could smell the lies coming a mile away.

A moment later, his expression became unreadable as he called to his bodyguard. "Abel."

Abel took one look at the photo, swore, removed his own cell phone, and stormed from the room.

Ocean's attention returned to me, and one look decimated the wall he'd put up. Kneeling before me, he took my face in his hands when I bent my head to hide the fresh wave of tears.

"Coby, look at me, please. I didn't do this," he swore when I obeyed.

Before Ocean could tell more lies, Hunter jumped in. "Now let's get one thing straight. I won't stand here and listen to you lie to her. I told you she wouldn't understand why Roshaun had to die."

An invisible hand punched inside my chest and ripped my still-beating heart free.

Hunter knew.

She was probably there when it happened. I knew she hated him, but I never imagined it could be that much.

"Which is why I didn't kill him," Ocean denied. He was speaking to Hunter but looking at me. "I told you I would follow your lead, Vengeance. Last night, when you walked away for Coby's sake, I did too. I swear to you, Abel dropped Roshaun off outside the city, warned him never to return, and left him there. This wasn't us." His pleading gaze turned to me. "This wasn't me, Coby. I swear to God."

"But you were going to kill him," I said. "You both were, and now he's dead. It doesn't matter who dealt the blow. He's dead because of both of you! How could you?"

I made the mistake of directing the question at Hunter. Her betrayal hurt worse.

Roshaun had taken her in. He'd given her shelter when no one else would and never asked for anything. I didn't know what happened to make them hate each other, but I knew my brother. He wasn't perfect, but he didn't deserve to die like that.

Ocean's tone was full of ice when he echoed, "How could she? No, *mo aingeal.* How could she *not* was the real question. Your brother is dead, and I'm sorry that you're hurting, but Roshaun still got off way too easily. You were sheltered from who he was for way too long, and it ends *now.*"

"What are you talking about?"

Hunter was clutching her neck and staring out the window like she was considering throwing herself through it.

"I didn't force Roshaun to give you up," Ocean confessed. "I hadn't even mentioned your name."

My mouth fell open. I already knew Roshaun had sold me out, but what Ocean was implying… My gaze narrowed. "What are you talking about? You…you broke his ribs."

"And I had three million reasons to do so," Ocean confirmed, "but I only needed one." His gaze softened. "I only needed you."

"You're saying it was his idea to use me?"

"Roshaun promised to repay every penny and offered you as

collateral. I warned him that I had no intention of ever returning you if I accepted. I described exactly how I'd use you—how much I'd enjoy breaking you until I got bored and passed you along to be used some more. I had to get my money's worth after all. Do you know what your brother did? He laughed, Coby. He actually fucking laughed and told me to consider you interest. *That's* when I broke his ribs."

Shame that I could be reduced to so little by my brother washed over me.

Hunter had been trying to tell me since we were sixteen that Roshaun hated me, and I hadn't listened. It made me wonder if there was more she *wasn't* telling me.

"Hunter?"

She seemed to know what I was asking, the tension in her shoulders deflating as she crumpled before my eyes. Her gaze slowly drifted over to meet mine. In my peripheral vision, Kellan discreetly left the room to give us privacy.

Even though Hunter's voice was robotic when she spoke, I could finally see the other half of her pain—the hurt she'd been hiding from me because the person who'd caused it was someone I loved.

"Your brother forced me to have sex with him while we lived together."

"What?" I slowly stood from the couch because I didn't trust my legs, but Hunter seemed like she needed the space to get this out, so I forced myself to stay put.

"He started small," Hunter explained. "Looks and grazes that I could brush off as harmless and accidental. I didn't realize he was testing the water until it escalated into outright assault."

Tears ran down my cheeks, but I no longer grieved Roshaun.

I only mourned that I ever let him near Hunter at all. I'd offered her shelter in my parents' home, thinking she would be safe with me. Little did I know, my protection had led her into the maw of another monster.

"Why didn't you tell me?" I cried.

Hunter shrugged, but it was weak. She was hurting, and it was my fault. I was blind to it because I didn't want to see it. "Roshaun promised that if I said anything, he wouldn't just kick me out, which I could handle. I was still underage and technically a runaway. All he had to do was make a phone call, and I'd never see you again, so I did what he wanted because losing you was worse."

I took a chance and grabbed Hunter's hand.

She was cold as ice.

"I would have run with you," I promised too late.

The damage my brother wrought had already been done, and I'd unknowingly furthered Hunter's pain by mourning him. If I could kill him twice, I would without hesitation.

"I know," Hunter whispered.

Glancing at Ocean, who had taken my spot on the couch, I could tell he was once again regretting showing my brother mercy.

Needing her close to touch and comfort her just as I needed to—Ocean pawed at Hunter's hip and pulled her into his lap. Even more miraculous was that she let him. Hunter curled into his lap and closed her eyes, resting her head on his shoulder.

I collapsed onto the couch next to them, and Hunter blindly reached out for me, taking my hand. The epiphany came as soon as I rested my head on Ocean's other shoulder.

The only way for the three of us to survive this and anything else thrown at us was together.

"You should have killed him," I said to no one in particular.

Hunter nodded but still didn't open her eyes or speak.

It was Ocean who answered, his voice gruff over the missed opportunity to avenge her honor. "You're right. I should have."

CHAPTER THIRTY-SEVEN

COBY

Three months later…

"COBY." IT WASN'T MY NAME THAT CONVINCED ME TO WAKE up. It was the frantic breaths against that sensitive spot behind my ear. It was the hard chest pressed against my back. The fingers skating underneath the t-shirt I'd worn to bed. The hard, demanding ridge lodged against my ass. "Lift your leg, baby. I got to go."

I complied without opening my eyes.

It was still early. I could feel it in my exhaustion.

But I couldn't do without this.

Ocean had woken Hunter and fucked her to within an inch of her life when he came home late last night. I'd woken in the middle of it, her choked cries, the rough jostling of the bed, and Ocean's gruff and filthy commands briefly piercing my sleep.

Now it was my turn.

My panties were shoved aside, and I felt the coolness of the air against my warm, wet pussy before his dick was there, slowly filling me up. I'd been plagued with dreams of this before Ocean woke me, so I was more than ready to be fucked.

This had become our unspoken routine. Ocean would take one or both of us before he started and ended his day. My personal favorite was when he tracked down one of us during the day. Those secret rendezvous were rare since he was hardly home.

The war with his father was still ongoing, neither side making much progress. Some days, Ocean didn't come home at all, but at least Hunter and I had each other.

I knew that's what would happen now.

Ocean would fuck me and then leave me here, spent and dripping to curl against Hunter for warmth while he left us safe and sound to put himself in danger again.

Ocean flexed his hips when my thoughts caused my pussy to resist him a little, and then we both let out a moan when he finally sank that last impossible inch inside.

I loved these slow, leisurely morning fucks.

No matter how busy Ocean's schedule was, he always made time to show me how much he needed me. Sometimes, we'd make love. Other times, he'd take me on a hike, teach me how to play chess, or sit and let me read to him until I fell asleep in the middle of a chapter.

Feeling my need grow, I pushed my ass back against him, and Ocean responded with a thrust of his own.

"So fucking tight," he groaned hoarsely.

Together, as if we had all the time in the world, we moved under the sheets as one, our heavy breathing penetrating the early morning quiet and the scent of our sex mingling with his and Hunter's.

It was perfect.

Exactly how it was always meant to be.

Hunter and I were never meant to be apart; Ocean and I wouldn't have been able to resist each other forever, which meant the two of them would have destroyed each other over their shared obsession.

Feeling my orgasm rise, I reached out for something to hold onto, to anchor me to this plane so that I didn't float off from the ecstasy, but instead of the bedsheet, my fingers met soft skin.

Hunter.

The princess palace, where we'd gone to bed last night without Ocean, was still cloaked in shadows when I finally opened my eyes.

The first rays of morning light had already begun to penetrate the dark, so I could just make out Hunter's sleeping form. She was lying on her back with her thick thighs still gapped open, the slip she'd worn to bed bunched around her soft middle, leaving her pussy and breasts bared.

Her hands were still bound and stretched above her head with the rope tying her wrists together. I shivered at the sight of her splayed out and vulnerable with her pussy on display and Ocean's nut still drying on her thighs.

How long had they gone at it while I slept beside them, an unconscious witness to it all? They had obviously only just finished, but still, Ocean needed more.

Hunter's heavy tits bounced with our movements, but she didn't wake. My pussy tightened around Ocean as I reached for her, but Ocean yanked me back with a growl, possessive of both of his spoils. Wrapping his hand around my neck, my mouth fell open when he tightened his grip and picked up the pace, fucking me harder and staking his claim.

I knew it was coming.

Ocean always got like this whenever Hunter and I fooled around. The jealousy between the three of us excited me to the point that I'd find myself giving in to it more often than not.

Like now.

Poking the bear, I moaned, "Oh, God. Hunter."

Ocean cursed before flipping me onto my stomach and yanking my ass in the air. "Who?"

I could feel his monster dick looming near my entrance like a threat.

"Ocean," I moaned shyly this time.

My fingers and toes curled into the sheets when he re-entered me, digging his fingers into my hips to keep me still as he used me.

Resting my head on my arms with a smile, I happily let him.

After Roshaun was murdered, Ocean moved us far away from the city and into this beautiful ranch home in the middle of nowhere. This large plot of land was only a short hike from one of the many bluffs overlooking a massive lake, and I couldn't love it more.

Ocean was out again while Hunter and I were on the back patio overlooking the pool and open fields. We were sharing a bag of grapes and gossiping about one of the bitches we used to work with.

Apparently, Cadence was getting married to Will, a former co-worker who had gone all *Fatal Attraction* on Hunter after she let him eat her ass for lunch a few times. Needless to say, Cadence couldn't stand Hunter.

It had been months since we literally disappeared off the face of the earth, but the girl was still keeping it up like she had nothing better to do than think about Hunter.

"I'm going to comment," my bestie warned.

I lunged for her phone because I knew she meant it, but she held it out of reach. Damn, my short arms! "You better not, Hunter."

"Why not?" she tossed back while tapping on the comment section of the picture we'd been looking at.

"Because it's their engagement photo!"

Cadence and Will had just announced they were getting married, yet Cadence was still taking shots at Hunter in the post.

It made no sense.

Hunter could not care less about either of them. Will had been unequivocally single when they messed around. And we'd even quit that job to get away from him, but Cadence was still convinced that Hunter wanted her man. She must have been bored with him and needed the drama to make their relationship feel alive. And because Will never stopped liking and leaving heart eyes under Hunter's old pics. She obviously hadn't posted anything since we were in hiding, but she still checked it regularly. Hell, Will had even DM'd her a few days ago.

"Fuck that hoe," Hunter spat. "She wants to talk out of her ass? I'm going to ask her how mine tastes."

"Hunter!" She didn't respond as she quickly typed a comment and hit send. I stole a peek at what she wrote and saw that she'd written precisely that. "Bitch, you hell!" I said, cackling.

An hour after her comment, Will was on live, calling Hunter every name but a child of God. Hunter and I thought it was pure comedy, knowing he was trying to save face and appease his horse-faced fiancée.

A notification for a post that Hunter was tagged in popped up while we were watching Will go off. She rolled her eyes when she saw the name, but clicked on it nonetheless.

The post was from a distant relative of Hunter's, announcing the memorial service of Lester Parrish.

Hunter's father.

The bastard had died tragically in his sleep during a house fire. In his fucking sleep.

The grape I was chewing turned to ash in my mouth. "Oh, Hunter, I'm—"

"It's fine," she cut me off. Hunter darkened her phone without responding to the post.

I sent a text to Ocean anyway, who dropped whatever he was doing and rushed home.

Three days later, Hunter had still barely spoken a word to anyone. We found her alone in the training room that morning, taking her frustrations out on a punching bag.

Ocean had come prepared, though.

I took a seat on one of the benches and hugged my legs as I watched Ocean slowly approach Hunter like he would an injured animal.

And just as any would when cornered, Hunter attacked.

For what felt like hours, Ocean and Hunter battled it out until

Ocean managed to pin Hunter to the mat. "It's a lie. He suffered," Ocean swore as Hunter thrashed violently underneath him. "I promise you, baby. He fucking suffered."

Hunter suddenly went still, and so did I at the realization that, *of course,* Ocean killed her father. He wasn't going to make the same mistake as he did with Roshaun. I never in a million years would have thought I'd actually smile at the thought of someone being brutally murdered.

One by one, our enemies fell until there was only one.

Malcolm.

Ocean was still hanging out at home a week later.

Back to herself again, Hunter kept rolling her eyes at our insistence on coddling her.

If only she knew…

Draping his arm over my shoulder, Ocean kissed the top of my head as we waited for Hunter to finish putting her makeup on. "Ready?" he whispered so Hunter wouldn't overhear.

I nodded eagerly as I bounced up and down on my toes. "Hunter, go outside!" I squealed when my excitement became too much to bear.

She turned from the mirror at the vanity table in our bedroom and gave us both a weird look. Ocean was better at keeping a straight face than I was. I was grinning like a maniac because it was Hunter's birthday today, and Ocean had pulled off the mother of all surprises.

After trying unsuccessfully to get us to spill the beans, we followed Hunter and Coco through the house and out the massive front doors. Just as she stepped out from under the portico, her birthday surprise appeared.

An off-white 1993 Ford Thunderbird.

Abel was behind the wheel as he parked the old car in front of Hunter, who had gone utterly still.

It seemed impossible for my smile to get wider as I watched the shock play out on Hunter's face.

Abel climbed out of the car after killing the engine, which didn't knock or sputter like it had before the car went into the pond. She even had a fresh paint job and a new interior.

It had taken a while to repair the extensive water damage and find all the genuine parts needed to restore the old Thunderbird to her former glory. She was in even better shape than when Hunter found her, but still a cranky old bitch.

Honestly, it would have been cheaper and easier to just buy Hunter a new car, but she'd never love another car the way she loved Deb.

Before the three of us came together, this car had been the only place that ever truly felt like home to Hunter. And she'd sacrificed Deb to save me.

Abel nodded in deference to Hunter and me before tossing something to Ocean.

It was a long platinum chain with two silver keys hanging from it.

Ocean stepped forward and draped it over Hunter's neck. I watched him kiss her cheek, and then I did the same. Hunter's hand trembled when she reached for the chain.

Once she felt the car keys resting against her heart, she dropped to her knees and sobbed. "Debbiiieeeeeee!"

A moment later, Kellan burst through the front door behind us. "Is it here? Did I miss it?"

No one answered him as Hunter sobbed.

This time, they were happy tears.

Deborah was back, bitches.

CHAPTER THIRTY-EIGHT

OCEAN

My father's failed attempt to frame me for Roshaun's death had forced me into the offense just as he wanted. Instead of cutting down everyone in my path to get to him and dying in the process, I started by cutting off his cash flow. It had taken months and copious amounts of bloodshed, but I'd finally weakened my father enough that he'd lowered himself to request a meeting.

For days, I'd been keeping him on ice.

Now that my plan B and leverage—Michael fucking Black—was stripped, gagged, and bound to a chair in my basement, I extended my father an invitation of my own. If he wanted to meet, it would be on my terms.

It had taken a lot of time and manpower to hunt the shady pimp down since he was under my father's protection. I thought it was dirt Black had on him, but my father would have simply killed him and been done with it. Instead, he'd been protecting him.

It meant Michael had something my father wanted.

And what my father wanted above all was Chicago. Michael's old stomping grounds.

It was currently in control of the Knights.

They weren't mafia. They were a force far worse. A family twice as old as ours, who only dealt in secrets and blackmail and couldn't be bought. The Knights did the jobs that no one else had the stomach for and had toppled organizations like the *Fola* as easily as snapping a twig. It pissed my father off to no end that he couldn't run them out.

Securing Black had become even more vital after learning how he planned to help my father take over Chicago. It would be an act of war and one we couldn't win.

My phone rang, and seeing who it was, I cursed and checked my watch before standing and leaving the floor. Ignoring the call was not an option, but so was answering it. I pretended not to feel Abel's frustration at my lack of focus as he shadowed me down the dark hall.

I closed myself inside Roshaun's old office at the Diamond Lounge and sat at his desk. I'd still been his silent partner at the time of his death, so shutting the club down for fumigation had been easy. Roshaun's share had already been transferred to Coby. I planned to gift her mine as well, giving her full ownership to do whatever she wanted with it, including burning it down if she chose.

"What's the matter, sweetheart?" I asked after answering the video call.

"Nothing," Coby mumbled with a fist on her cheek. She was pouting as I knew she would be. "Just bored."

I hummed. "Where's Hunter?"

"Playing cards with Kellan. Where are you?"

"Around," I said, not wanting to reveal too much on the phone.

"You're safe?" she asked absently. Her gaze was busy searching my background for clues, so I brought the phone closer to my face.

"Always."

"We haven't seen you in days," she whispered while pouting still. "So, how would I know?"

We'd finally gotten to the crux of this phone call.

I kept Hunter and Coby updated whenever I was in the streets as promised, but Coby was spoiled as fuck. Anything less than seeing me every day was unacceptable. I couldn't fault her, since I felt the same way. "I know, baby. I miss you both, too. Did you get my gifts?"

She rolled her eyes. "Gifts aren't you."

I grinned at that. "I know. Diamonds can't fuck you like I can. Can they, pretty girl?"

Coby blushed and fingered a ginger curl behind her ear to slyly show me that she was wearing them now. Her hair had grown a lot in the last few months, reaching toward her shoulders. I could even see the natural light brown color taking over the copper. "That's not what I meant, nasty."

"Sure."

Coby changed the subject, and I gave her my undivided attention as she talked a mile a minute, her brown eyes glowing as she updated me on the rest of our secret plans. I was content to listen, even though I hadn't caught most of it because I was more fixated on watching how her pink mouth moved as she talked.

When Coby mentioned making a trip into the city tomorrow to meet with the caterer, it snapped me right the fuck out of my trance. I told her it would have to wait until I returned, which sparked an immediate argument.

"Well, when will you be back?" she whined.

Before I could answer, there was a knock on the door. I glanced up to see Abel poking his head inside the office.

"He's here," Abel informed me.

"Who's there?" Coby's nosy ass questioned.

I looked down at the screen. "Baby, I got to go."

"Why?"

"Coby."

She hung up the phone without saying goodbye, I love you, fuck you…nothing. I made a mental note to check her little ass about it later.

Right now, I had a meeting with my father.

"He's alone," Abel announced as soon as I stepped out of the office, and we started back down the hall.

I stopped in my tracks. "What?"

"The smug fuck actually came alone. No guards. And he wasn't armed when my men checked him."

Sure enough, my father was sitting alone at one of the VIP tables with a drink already in his hand.

My men were visibly nervous to be in the same room as the Boss of the *Fola*, which only pissed Abel's cantankerous ass off even more. Most of these guys were newly made and hadn't been hardened to the life yet, but under my head of security's guidance, they would be soon.

I could see my reflection in the glass partition behind my father, which separated this booth from the next one. He was wearing a brown suit, one of his finest, and his eyes were surprisingly subdued.

I relaxed my body into a lazy lounge when I sat across from him because I knew it would offend him.

"Son," my father greeted first.

"Why are you here?"

"You were trying to get my attention, were you not?" He waved his hand. "Now you have it."

"So you consider commandeering sixty percent of your operations in a matter of months, *wanting your attention*?"

My father visibly bristled at the reminder of how easily I'd cut off his nuts. "Don't get cute, boy. You think still being alive is your doing? You think you're protected? Careful? Hidden? I could have walked into your little love nest at *Glainne* and ended you and those whores anytime I wanted."

I perked a brow as I sat back and signaled one of my associates for a drink. Kellan was my usual go-to, but right now, he was the only one besides Abel that I trusted with my girls. "So why didn't you?"

"You are my heir," he answered, glowering into his drink. "And I'm too old to make another." When I said nothing, he lifted his glass before swallowing the last of the contents and slamming the tumbler back down. "Enough. Let's get this over with."

"Get what over with?" I still didn't know why he requested this meeting. Malcolm Kilpatrick was not one to beg for mercy or make deals.

"You were more ruthless these last months than you've ever

been your entire disappointing life," he said instead of answering my question. "You didn't let familial attachment get in the way of seizing strength. Watching you destroy me has been the only time since you were pulled from your mother that I've been proud to call you my son."

I scratched my chin and merely said, "I had plenty of motivation. You met them once when you tried to take them from me."

"Then you should have no problem killing me."

I didn't think it was possible for my father to stun me. "Excuse me?"

"I'm offering myself up for execution on one condition."

"And that is?"

"You rid yourself of those whores. They are your weakness and a distraction. Walton's daughter," he said, referring to the oldest *captean* of the Torrance family, "is young, fertile, and knows her place. Marry her."

"Not happening."

"This isn't a negotiation," my father snapped.

"You're right. It's not," I said, pulling my gun. "Because living without Hunter and Coby for one moment is not up for discussion. You came here for nothing. You were a dead man regardless, but at least you would have gone down swinging."

"I didn't come for nothing. Regardless of what happens here, my wishes will be carried out."

A cold like nothing I'd ever felt washed over me as I stared at my father across the table. Malcolm Kilpatrick wasn't one to mince words, which meant he was stalling. I didn't have to question why.

"What did you do?"

"I sent someone to take care of the problem."

I shot to my feet, but my father wasn't done. Luckily, Abel had overheard every word and was already calling for a charter. It would take hours by car to reach them.

And even then, it might be too late.

"My final act as Boss will be to rid this family of its greatest threat. I gave you a chance to send them back to that hovel they came from, and you refused. You have only yourself to blame."

I had my gun to his head before he even finished speaking. "Call them off."

He slammed his fist on the table. "You think death scares me, boy? I came here to die. This was always how it was going to be. It's been our legacy since James killed Rory."

"Rory was hanged by a lynch mob," I said through clenched teeth.

"He was murdered by his brother because even James knew love was for the weak. Your great-grandfather turned his grief into power, and his sacrifice is why we've thrived."

"So everything I've been told about the Brothers of Rory—"

"Was a lie. I killed my father for the throne, and my father killed his. One day, your son will do the same and kill you," he said with no small amount of glee.

My punishment for committing patricide would one day be meted out by my own child, and he wouldn't know the vicious cycle he'd been born into until it was too late.

Until I gave him no choice.

"Blood in, blood out," my father roared when I hesitated. "Now make your sacrifice!"

They were the last words he ever spoke. My face was the last he ever saw. And my growled, "Never," was the last thing my father ever heard.

CHAPTER THIRTY-NINE

HUNTER

"**L**EFT HAND, BLUE."

I gritted my teeth and twisted my torso, stretching my right arm until my hand landed on the closest available circle—between Kellan's legs. It was funny as hell to watch him grow increasingly agitated with each round that brought us closer and put us in compromising positions.

He was in an impressive back bend that lifted his shirt a little, showing off his Adonis belt and the dark trail of hair that disappeared inside his jeans. If I hadn't already seen the dark hair peeking through his roots, I'd be shocked to learn that Kellan wasn't a true blond.

He kept muttering about losing his hands and feet over a childish game. The laugh I was holding in broke free and nearly sent me to my ass when Coby spun the spinner and called for him to put his left foot on red. I was already straining to hold this impossible position, but thanks to Ocean, I hadn't been eliminated yet. After a season of sexual gymnastics, my body was now accustomed to being twisted into a pretzel for an extended period.

Cursing, Kellan moved his bare foot to the red circle above my head, widening his legs and putting his crotch in my face.

"Why, Kellz, so soon? We hardly know each other," I teased.

Coby and I laughed uncontrollably while Kellan groaned.

Coby took pity on him and flicked the spinner again, calling for me to move my right hand to yellow. I fell on my face, and Coco barked before running over with a click of his nails on the hardwood floor. I lay still while he sniffed my hair to make sure I wasn't dead and then bossily barked for me to get my ass up and stop faking. Some of his black fur was already giving way to the brown, but he still looked like an asshole.

"Thank fucking fuck," Kellan huffed as he straightened and stood. He held out his hand to help me up.

"What's so scary about a harmless game of Twister?" Coby asked as she stood from the couch with a wary glance thrown at the barely three-pound puppy. She tossed the spinner into the box, grumbling about sharp teeth and rabies.

"Your fiancé," Kellan retorted. "Do we have a deal? I played your dumb game. Now, you two agree not to sneak out again and give me a heart attack."

Coby pouted. "We were bored."

Last night, Coby, Deborah, and I had snuck out for a test drive that ended way too short once Kellan caught up to us and dragged us back here.

"What's the big deal anyway?" I griped. "We're out here in the middle of nowhere."

There was also a lot of land and a long, private road between the rest of the human population and us.

After Roshaun had been executed, the three of us left Glainne and retreated here when Ocean decided to take the offensive. Apparently, he had this six-thousand-square-foot ranch house just waiting on standby.

This house was half the size of Glamis, which suited me perfectly. There were enough rooms to retreat when one of us needed space, but not so big that you could hide for long.

The only problem? Ocean was gone most of the time.

The war against his father had gotten ugly, and Ocean had wanted us as far away from it as possible.

I hated that.

I hated sitting here wringing my hands like a damsel.

I hated not being there to watch his back.

I hated that tomorrow I might wake up to another morning without Ocean between us.

And I knew Coby hated it all, too.

He'd kept his promise and checked in regularly, but it wasn't enough. It wasn't him.

"Malcom's power reaches further than you think," Kellan warned. "He has eyes and ears everywhere. What happened to Roshaun should have told you as much. If you were captured or killed during your frolic through town, what happened to your brother would look like a kiss on the fucking cheek compared to what Ocean would do to me."

"He wouldn't hurt you," Coby denied. "You're his friend."

Kellan shook his head, but his voice held no bitterness when he spoke. There was only respect. "In another life, maybe. In this life, Ocean is my boss. He's…" Kellan trailed off before abandoning that train of thought with a shake of his head. "Let's just say I grew up with someone just like him. Someone I called a brother, and when I had to walk away, it was the hardest thing I ever had to do. I'd rather not form attachments this time."

"It sounds like you have no intention of sticking around," I said, letting suspicion ride my tone.

Kellan merely shrugged. "I'm a drifter," he explained simply. "It's what we do."

"Hmm."

An hour later, Kellan surprised us with dinner. Afterward, Coby disappeared to make a few phone calls. She's been doing that a lot lately. I frowned at her retreating back as I wondered what she was up to.

She and Ocean were both little schemers.

Kellan got bored enough to ask if I wanted to play cards, so I agreed. After winning the first hand, I decided that I was entitled to a truth. "How did you and Ocean meet?" I asked while we took turns drawing a card.

I didn't expect the answer to come so readily.

"He saved my life. I had just left Chicago and was new in town. I didn't know all the players yet and pissed off the wrong people. Ocean stepped in, threw his weight around, and I got to keep breathing."

"That was nice of him."

Kellan laughed and shook his head. "Not really. Nothing in this town comes without a price."

"That's when you started working for him, huh?" Kellan nodded and tossed seven of clubs on the table. I threw a nine of the same suit and scooped up the cards. "Why do you think he saved you?"

"My sparkling personality and devastating good looks?"

"Kellan." I gave him a reproachful glance and threw down a king of hearts.

He blew out a breath and then tossed a two of spades down before taking the trick. "I think Ocean wanted someone in his camp who had no connections or shred of loyalty to his father. Who better than a stranger in his debt?"

"So you really don't think he cares about you?"

"I didn't say that. Ocean is a good man. I wouldn't work for him if he wasn't, but I don't let things get personal anymore."

"Ah, right. Because of your *real* friends waiting for you back home," I teased.

"You know I knew a headstrong girl like you once." A fond smile appeared on his lips before he said, "You'd like her. She had a knack for driving me up the wall, too."

"You loved her?"

Kellan shook his head. "Only as a sister. I mentioned that the *Fola* isn't the first family I've served and survived, but what I *didn't* say was that Ocean isn't the first heir I've known to burn down his entire world for the woman he loves. Or in Ocean's case, the wom*en* he loves." Kellan waggled his brows.

"So…how did it end?"

The knot in Kellan's throat bobbed as he swallowed, and the cards crumbled a little in his fist. "He sacrificed himself for her."

"Oh…" Well, that doesn't sound promising. I placed my hand on Kellan's arm. Considering how lean he appeared, I was surprised to feel so much muscle there. "He died?"

Kellan's lips flattened as he pondered his cards. "Worse. Prison."

I wanted to pry some more, but talking about it didn't seem to be helping Kellan, so I forced myself to let it drop and tossed down three of spades. "So…he's the friend you mentioned?"

"They both are." It was Kellan's turn to play a card, but he didn't notice. His mind had already drifted off somewhere far away—to home.

"You miss them."

He blinked as if startled and then answered hoarsely, "Yeah."

"So why don't you do something about it?" I gave him a gentle nudge. "I'm sure they miss you, too."

"Because I left Chicago for a reason," Kellan answered. "I'm not going back until I find what I'm looking for."

"And what is that?"

His green eyes turned hard as he stared down at his cards. "Revenge," he answered coldly.

Whoa. Kellan's blond-dyed hair swung in his face, so he cursed and ripped off the rubber band around his wrist. I watched him pull his hair, which had grown to a considerable length since I met him, into a messy top knot.

"The douchey man bun look suits you," I remarked.

Kellan snorted and tossed down a card. "Thanks."

We played another round before my eyes started to grow heavy. I told Kellan I was calling it a night and stood from the stool. He nodded, shrugged on his leather jacket, and then left the house to do his usual patrol around the grounds since it was just us.

No guards.

Ocean had been too paranoid after Roshaun to trust that any one of them wasn't feeding information back to his father.

We weren't completely helpless, though. I've been keeping up with my training with Abel, so if anything popped off, I'd be more than ready.

I heard the mudroom door slam behind Kellan as I left the kitchen—Coco weaving between my ankles—and walked down the gallery beneath the skylight and vaulted ceiling. The house was massive and all on one level, excluding the basement Ocean had deemed off-limits to Coby and me.

Searching for Coby, I headed to the master bedroom when I couldn't find her anywhere else and stepped inside to find her without a stitch of clothing on. She was lying on her stomach across the four-poster bed with a sensual smile on her lips, and I knew without a doubt that she'd been waiting for me.

"I thought for dessert you could have me," she invited sweetly.

Smiling, I reached for my shirt to pull it over my head as I took one eager step toward the bed.

Before I could reach her, though, the lights went out.

CHAPTER FORTY

COBY

"WHAT THE HELL?" I SAT UP WHEN THE ROOM WAS suddenly plunged into darkness. It took a few seconds for my eyes to adjust to the pitch black. Hunter cursed as she yanked her shirt back down. "What's going on?"

"I don't know, but we're not sticking around to find out. Get dressed."

"Whoa, wait," I said when I heard her strapping as many weapons to her as she could. "It's probably just an outage."

"Coby, when you're in bed with the mafia, it's never just an outage. Malcolm's found us."

"But how?"

Hunter shook her head. "I don't know, but I think Kellan's involved."

"What?"

Hunter didn't bother to explain as she threw me a pair of sweats and a hoodie. I felt my heart beating fast as I quickly dressed. She then ushered Coco into his carrier and locked the cage door, thank God. A moment later, she shoved the carrier into my chest, and I squeaked at the same time Coco whined. Hunter then moved over to the bedroom door and pressed her ear against it.

"Hunter, talk to me," I pleaded. "Why would Kellan betray Ocean?"

"Because after he made it *very* clear he and Ocean weren't friends, he told me he used to work for another family like the *Fola* back in Chicago. Kellan also told me he came to Black Veil specifically looking for revenge, and through a stroke of fucking luck, he just happened to land a job working right at Ocean's side."

I thought about it until it started to make sense. Kellan was the only one who was never constantly with Ocean. He was the only one without family or friends here, and absences he couldn't explain. I always just assumed he was out doing something for Ocean, but maybe not.

"I don't know," I said slowly. "It makes sense, but it doesn't fit, Hunter. We like Kellan."

Hunter was visibly frustrated when she grabbed my hand and started tugging me toward the door. "Well, we're not sticking around to find out if I'm right or wrong. Let's go."

"Hunter, wait." Before I could say more, a bullet pierced the window and lodged in the wall next to the door. A barrage of them quickly followed, forcing us to the floor. "Never mind! Let's go!" We hurried out of the bedroom while bullets tore it apart. Once out of range, we sat on the floor with our backs to the wall. "Where do we go?" I whispered.

"Basement."

I nodded. We could barricade ourselves until Ocean arrived, but there was no telling when he'd return. Stupidly, I'd left my phone on the nightstand, so I couldn't call him.

I stayed put while Hunter slowly peered around the wall.

Two stairs led down to the basement. Luckily, the first was on this side of the house. The other was a cellar door that led outside on the opposite end. We'd still have to cross the gallery—that extremely long corridor that connected the west and east wings—to get to the closet one.

Satisfied that the coast was clear, Hunter removed one of her guns from a holster. "Do you remember what I taught you?" she asked while handing me the Sig.

"Firm grip. Safety. Aim. Fire. Piece of cake."

Coco whined again like he knew we were doomed.

The shooting behind us ceased, and the house was eerily quiet now when Hunter peered around the wall and gestured me forward while keeping watch. I wasted no time darting the gallery's ten-or eleven-foot width. As soon as I was clear, I peered around the corner to keep watch for Hunter.

She was halfway across when I saw them.

Up ahead, moving stealthily under the skylight between the living room and foyer, were two masked men. They were bathed in shadows and moonlight and bearing scary-looking rifles. They hadn't spotted Hunter yet—or at least that's what I thought until one of them raised their weapon.

"Hunter!" I didn't think about the fact that I might be giving away our position. I just reacted, flipping off the safety and shooting blindly in the dark. It gave Hunter the cover she needed to dive the rest of the way across.

She deftly regained her feet just as I ran out of bullets.

Together, we sprinted for the basement door while Coco barked his ass off.

I went through first, and just as I stopped to wait for Hunter, the door slammed shut in my face—with Hunter still on the other side.

I heard something heavy scraping across the floor and lunged for the handle. The door wouldn't budge. "Hunter?" I slammed my fist against the door when she didn't answer. "Hunter!"

"Keep quiet, bestie," I heard her muffled voice say. "I'll be back."

And then she was gone.

No matter how much I called her name, she didn't answer. I shoved and kicked at the door until my shoulder throbbed and I was forced to give up.

I descended the stairs into a wine cellar, but as I quickly found out, the only way forward was locked. With the help of the flashlight I'd found, I tore apart the cellar, searching for a spare key until I struck gold.

With only this flashlight to light the way, I slowly made my way to the east wing with Coco, searching for that cellar door near the room Abel and Hunter used for sparring. I was somewhere beneath the garage when I tripped and landed in a puddle of water.

It was warm.

Thicker than water should have been.

And it smelled strongly of copper.

I reached out, looking for Coco, whose carrier had skated off into the dark when I fell, but my hand met bare skin instead. I screamed, and Coco barked from somewhere close while I lunged for my fallen flashlight, swinging the light over whatever the hell I'd touched.

I could barely make out what was left of the man's face. He looked as if he'd been stabbed a thousand times. His naked body was still bound to the chair that had toppled over, either by my doing or whoever had killed him. I was no expert, but it looked as if the bound man had been killed recently when Ocean hadn't been home in days.

At least, now I knew why Ocean hadn't wanted us down here. I was going to have a serious talk with my husband about keeping dead bodies in our basement. For now, I found an old blanket and covered the man up before leaving him behind.

Hunter needed me.

Collecting Coco and as if I hadn't just found a dead body in my own home, I ran full speed for the east wing. The ranch house was shaped like a broad X, so it was easy to get turned around, especially down here.

It took some time, but I eventually found the steps to the cellar door.

I barely noticed the rain when I climbed out. It quickly soaked through my clothes as I ran around back and re-entered the house through the game room. Tiptoeing through the family room, I was about to enter the kitchen when I saw a dark figure step inside from the other end.

Before I could hide, a hand that smelled like blood and rain covered my mouth and yanked me back just as the masked man ahead turned, his eyes landing on the spot where I'd been.

I struggled against my captor, who was definitely not Hunter, as he lifted me off my feet and carried me back toward the game room.

"Quiet!" he ordered.

Too late.

I'd already kicked out, knocking over a vase. As soon as it shattered, I heard footsteps rushing from the kitchen. I was quickly pulled back through the sliding door I'd come through and out onto the roofed portion of the patio.

It was still dark, but I recognized the sharp angles of Kellan's face and his shoulder-length blond hair secured into a top knot as he pushed me against the wall.

Coco whined just as the masked man stepped out onto the patio, but Kellan moved fast. He made quick work of disarming the assassin and then snapping his neck like it was a twig.

I gulped.

This was not the playful associate I'd come to know.

"Where's Hunter?" he asked as he peered into the dark house to ensure there weren't more.

I didn't respond, didn't breathe, didn't hesitate as I set Coco down and moved toward the dead man at my feet, and slowly bent. When Kellan turned around, he found himself staring down the barrel of the rifle. "What the fuck?"

"Did you do this?"

He stared back at me incredulously. "Do what?"

"Are you trying to kill us?" I yelled.

"Keep your fucking voice down," he whispered. When I didn't respond or lower the gun, he swore. "Tell me what the fuck is going on."

"You first."

Hunter hadn't been making a ton of sense earlier, but that was my bitch, so her word was the only one besides Ocean's that I took blindly.

"My guess?" Kellan retorted sarcastically. "Malcolm found out where you were and sent out a hit on you and Hunter. I've counted eight of them so far. Two of them I found dead, and this guy makes three." He nudged the dead body with his boot.

"Four," I corrected. At his questioning look, I added. "There's a dead body in the basement, but he definitely wasn't one of them."

"He's not. His name is Michael Black," Kellan informed me.

"Who is he?"

With deep-seeding hatred spilling from every word, he said, "A pimp with a knack for destroying everything he touches. Young women, most especially. He's also a heartless fucking deadbeat. Ocean had some questions for him, but..." Kellan gave a lazy shrug while staring down at his bloody hands. "I got to him first."

Oh God.

Kellan had killed the man in the basement.

He looked up, and I could see that the bloodlust hadn't entirely left him. "Your turn for honesty." Kellan's green stare was uncomfortably piercing, and I realized Hunter's instincts had been on point. It wasn't just his eyes, which no longer held the playful twinkle that made him easy to trust. Kellan's entire demeanor had changed. "Why do you think I want to kill you?"

"Because Hunter thinks you're Malcolm's spy."

Laughing at that, he shook his head. "Of course she does. Malcolm has many spies, but I'm not one of them."

"Then why are you really here, Kellan? Or is that even your real name?"

Suddenly, I heard movement nearby. Judging by the way Kellan's jaw clenched, he'd heard it too. He looked around, searching for the next threat, but the only one I cared about right now was the one standing in front of me.

"We need to find Hunter and get the fuck out of here. More may come."

"I'm not going anywhere with you," I replied. "But feel free to leave. I'll find Hunter on my own." I kept the gun on him as I put more distance between us.

Kellan looked like he was considering doing just that.

Hunter had said he'd come to Black Veil looking for revenge, and now he'd found it. Nothing was keeping him here anymore.

"Sorry. Not happening," he said while following me across the patio. I placed my finger on the trigger, but he didn't slow his pace. "I'm a liar, not an asshole. I won't leave until I know you and Hunter are safe."

Gunshots erupted nearby, sounding like they had come from the living room.

"Hunter!" Heart plummeting, I ran across the patio with Kellan hot on my heels. We'd made it within steps of the doors overlooking the pool when the glass suddenly shattered from the masked man falling through it.

He was dead before he hit the ground.

Hunter was inside, already fighting another and winning, but she didn't see the others pouring into the room.

A whole lot fucking more than eight.

I raised the rifle and started laying down fire.

Too many.

There were too many of them.

Kellan barreled into the first of those who'd escaped my un-trained aim, neutralizing him and then picking off the rest. Meanwhile, Hunter took down the goon she was fighting and immediately turned to the next. I was amazed at her speed and skill as she tore through one after the other before they could get a shot off.

Still, it wasn't enough.

The room was quickly overrun, and Kellan and Hunter were surrounded.

Still shooting, my lips parted to scream for Hunter, but the sound never made it out because I spotted something being tossed inside the room. I was forced to lay off the trigger when thick, white smoke began to fill the room, and I lost sight of Hunter and Kellan.

The hitters began to panic, while some even ran.

I couldn't think about that as I searched blindly for Hunter through the smoke, ignoring the screams of the masked men as they fell around me like flies.

Crouching, I made it to the open archway by the kitchen where the smoke was thinnest when I was yanked backward by my hair, my scalp screaming in pain as I was forced to my feet.

"Hurry! Shoot her!"

Another hitter whirled to take aim, but I was faster. I raised the stolen rifle and shot him in the foot. The goon screamed in pain and hopped around while the one holding my hair ripped the gun from my hands and tossed me to the floor.

He raised the rifle, and I glanced past his shoulder before quickly closing my eyes and waiting for death to collect. A moment later, I felt the warm, thick spray of blood, and the wet sound of flesh tearing open. When I opened my eyes again, Ocean stood between us like an avenging knight.

The goon was staring down at what was left of his stomach, his intestines spilling onto the floor faster than he could futilely stuff them back in. When I felt a laugh bubbling up at the sight, I clapped a hand over my mouth and started to fear for my sanity.

And then Hunter appeared out of nowhere, the smoke parting and her face blank as she approached.

If Ocean was an avenging knight, Hunter was a dark angel.

Lifting her favorite knife, she coldly swiped the serrated edge across the disemboweled goon's throat. *Excessive.* Blood gushed from his neck, but he was somehow still standing when Ocean and Hunter walked away. Hunter held out her blood-caked hand for me, and I slipped my equally bloody one into hers.

As soon as I was on my feet, she grabbed my face and kissed me hard.

At the edge of our kiss, I heard a body drop. The sound of death, screams, and more bullets flying faded into the background, and by the time Hunter pulled away, the house was hauntingly silent again.

"Are you okay?" she asked softly.

I glanced at Ocean and saw him waiting for my answer, too, so I nodded, and then he pulled Hunter and me out of the room. Abel was methodically walking from room to room, putting a bullet in the fallen hitters' heads to make sure none survived.

In the gallery, Ocean backed Hunter against the wall first, ignoring the dead bodies strewn around us as he checked her for injuries. Hunter silently endured it since she was doing the same to him. She had a few wounds that would need care, but her lips trembled at seeing that she was okay. When Ocean kissed her, his relief and anger were palpable. He poured it all into their kiss. I watched him whisper something to her when they came up for air, and whatever Hunter whispered back made him squeeze his eyes closed.

He barely collected himself before he was on me, checking me over as thoroughly as he had Hunter. I ran my hands all over his body, not caring how crazy it looked. I needed to see and feel for myself that we would all walk away from this night. Afterward, he kissed me with all the sorrow and unrest of a man who'd almost lost everything.

If Hunter and I had died, Ocean would be alone again. I would never let that happen, and I conveyed that promise through our kiss. Pulling back just enough to see his face, I whispered, "I love you."

The knot in his throat bobbed and then kissed me hard one last time. "I love you more. Are you sure you're okay?"

"Mhmm. Thanks to Hunter. She kicked their asses. Kellan, Coco, and I helped. Oh, my God! Coco!" I'd left him outside with a dead body. Hunter was going to kill me.

"I found him right before I found you. He's fine," Hunter assured me.

"Oh, good," I said while trying and failing to sound relieved. "*So* happy the little rat survived."

And then I froze, remembering I hadn't seen Kellan either since Ocean or Abel arrived in the nick of time to save our asses.

"What's the matter?" Hunter asked, noticing my worry.

"Has anyone seen Kellan?"

Hunter shrugged and then leaned against the wall. I had no doubt she was exhausted, but she was trying too hard to appear casual. Oh God… she killed him, didn't she? "We got separated in the smoke. I'm sure he's fine, though."

Unwilling to take that chance, I walked back into the living room with Ocean and Hunter trailing me like two mother hens. I searched the carnage for a familiar face and prayed I didn't find one. Behind me, I overheard Ocean asking Abel if he'd see Kellan.

The four of us searched the house and grounds that night, but there was no sign of Kellan.

He wasn't the only one missing, either.

Deborah was, too.

Everyone assumed Kellan had stolen the car and taken off during the chaos, but the single key now hanging around Hunter's neck told me differently.

CHAPTER FORTY-ONE

HUNTER

COBY REALLY DID MAKE A BEAUTIFUL BRIDE. AND AS IT turned out, so did I.

Our wedding was small and intimate, with only Abel, Effie, and Ocean as witnesses.

This came two months after Coby and Ocean's glamorous—and completely fake—wedding, with an even faker priest performing in front of the entire *Fola*.

And what a performance it was.

The only thing real about it had been our vows to one another.

Of course, all it would take to uncover our duplicity was for someone to look for the nonexistent marriage record between them. Ocean was confident that no one would ever think to since his family had seen them marry with their own eyes.

As for my secret, legal marriage to Coby, Ocean bribed a judge to seal the record, so no one would ever find proof of it either. If anyone ever went digging, we could simply say there must have been some mix-up at the court.

Word had gotten around about our unconventional relationship, so there had been plenty of whispers, but no one dared let the new Boss of the *Fola* hear them. People were far more scandalized by the undoing of Malcolm Kilpatrick and the fact that Ocean had left him alive to wish he were dead.

Malcolm would live to break the vicious cycle he promised Ocean would continue with his own son one day.

So Ocean chose another path. He chose to keep him alive, but it was far from an act of mercy.

It was unheard of for a former Boss to survive his succession, and it left us all vulnerable to Malcolm seizing control again, so after the attack, Ocean had plucked out his father's remaining eye, cut out his tongue, and taken out his ears so that the man could never see, speak, or hear anything ever again.

Malcolm Kilpatrick became nothing more than a brutal reminder of the past.

Effie was *delighted.*

"My feet are killing me," Coby groaned as soon as we climbed inside the Bentley Mulsanne, this one a grand limo. She kicked off her white heels and wiggled her freshly pedicured toes at Ocean. She already knew not to point them my way. Wife or not, bestie or not, I didn't do feet. Ocean chivalrously took Coby's small foot in his hand and began massaging it. "Are we really spending our honeymoon on a yacht?" she asked him, then perked a brow. "Just how rich are you?"

I raised my brows in interest while Ocean laughed. "Rich enough to buy your own if you like," he offered smoothly.

Coby giggled, and then the two of us made eye contact. When I nodded, she pulled her foot from his grip and climbed into his lap. "We don't give a shit how much money you have. We just want you." Coby pulled his shirttail out of his pants and slowly began undoing the buttons.

"We'll be at the docks soon," Ocean weakly protested when she started dry-humping him. He responded by thrusting his hips up, fucking her back through their clothes.

"Then you better make us both come fast," I told him.

Ocean's heated gaze became even more intense when he saw I was already shedding my wedding dress. It was a short, tight, strapless, asymmetrical dress with a long side train.

It looked fucking fire on me, especially with my hips, which weren't as wide as before I started training with Abel, but I still had most of my curves, thank God. I was just a lot more toned now. My dress, however, had pissed Ocean off so much when he discovered just how tight it was around my middle that he cursed me out for twenty minutes straight.

Knowing he didn't get to fuck me in them often, I kept my heels on.

Coby climbed off Ocean's lap and knelt between his legs, loosening his belt buckle while Ocean's lips sought mine. I met him halfway for a kiss that was all tongue and very little inhibition.

It was the kind fueled by passion alone, without technique or thought. It was about leaving a mark and giving as much of yourself as possible while using only this small part of you.

Ocean groaned, and I knew Coby had him in her mouth now.

Breaking the kiss to watch, I snuck my hand between my thighs while Ocean was distracted by Coby's pink lips stretching to accommodate him. Our husband was palming the back of her head, and she was eagerly bobbing her head up and down in his lap, slowing here and there to take him deeper down her throat.

"God, wife," I moaned. My hips lifted from the seat as I played with my pussy. "You look so fucking sexy. You're going to make me come."

Unable to stand watching anymore, I climbed off the seat to join her.

In tune with one another, Coby released him with a pop, her brown eyes glossy and a long wet strand of saliva and pre-cum connecting them for half a second more before she wiped it away. I quickly replaced her mouth with my own, feeling his hands in my hair next as I deep-throated him.

"Goddamn," Ocean moaned. "Suck that dick, baby."

I heard the rustle of clothing, and then Coby returned. Back and forth, we took turns being choked by our man's dick. It was Coby's turn when Ocean finally lost control and came, spilling his load in her mouth.

Releasing him, she immediately turned to me, wrapping her arms around my neck and pressing her closed lips hard against mine until I parted them for Ocean's cum. I could feel some of the thick fluid transferring to my tongue as Coby kissed me deeply, and when we eventually pulled away, I held her gaze, and she held mine as we swallowed his cum.

"Fuck."

Coby and I looked over at Ocean and saw his hand stroking his dick. He was already hard again at the sight of us swapping his load. Releasing himself, Ocean carefully lifted me from the floor and gently laid me on the seat.

There was nothing soft or tender about what came next.

Ocean was between my thighs, throwing my legs over my shoulder and shoving inside me before I could even blink.

We held each other's gazes as I held onto the back of my legs, holding myself open for him as he served me nothing but long, hard dick. "Please," I choked out as he moved inside me. "Please, please, please…"

Just as I thought I'd go insane from all the pleasure, Coby was suddenly there to balance me out again, throwing her leg over my head. I released my legs to make room for her as she lowered herself onto my face.

I wasted no time licking my wife's sweet little pussy.

Below her, I was still being pounded into the seat by Ocean, who was fucking me even harder now. I couldn't see him anymore, but knew he was watching us.

"Oh, God, Huuuunter!" Coby's nails dug into the seat as she held herself above me. My tongue eagerly lapped at her pussy, not wanting to waste a single drop. The taste of her and Ocean together in my mouth was indescribable. Coby's pussy gushed as we came together, but I didn't take my mouth from her until she was forced away by Ocean.

I was too sated to do more than watch as he tossed her to the floor and mounted her. His hand was a vise grip on the back of Coby's neck when he lined up his dick, streaked with angry veins from behind. Coby's face was turned toward me, her soft cheek pressed to the floor, so I saw the anticipation on her face just before he pushed inside.

Pulling back, Ocean gave a sharp flex of his hips, entering her again and making Coby claw at the floor.

But there was no running from this.

I should know. I tried.

I never thought I could feel this way about anyone, and then Coby came along, followed by Ocean.

He held my wife and best friend still for the onslaught of pleasure he unleashed on her.

Suddenly, my fingers were buried in my pussy as I sat up to face them. The movement caught Ocean's attention, and the hunger in his eyes grew as he watched me play with my pussy. I already knew what he would say.

"What did I tell you about that?" he scolded me.

Pulling my fingers out to daringly tease my swollen clit, I held his stare. "But I want to squirt for you."

"Do it, and our wife won't get to come," he warned with a grunt.

Coby was no doubt tightening around him.

My toes curled against the seat as I felt another orgasm rise. I didn't want Coby to be punished, but I wasn't sure I could stop it. The two of them were addicting to watch.

Watching Ocean and Coby fuck had quickly become my favorite pastime. Even when I closed my eyes, the sounds they made as they dug inside her pushed me closer to the edge.

"Oh fuck!" I cried when my clit began to throb. My ass clenched while my thighs widened even more as I rubbed furiously at the little bundle of nerves. "Yes, yes, fuck her good…don't stop…oh, God…"

Dammit.

I was going to come.

"Hunter, please!" Coby choked out when she realized how close

I'd let myself get to the edge. She was close, too, but I knew Ocean finishing inside her was what she wanted most of all.

I growled in frustration and snatched my hand away just in time.

Ocean pulled out, and my heart stopped. I thought I pushed him too far until he flipped Coby on her back and entered her again.

I sagged against the seat.

"You gonna have my baby?" I heard him ask her as he slowed his pace to stare into her eyes.

As predicted, those words sent Coby over the edge.

She threw her head back and came, her orgasm triggering Ocean's, who told her how much he loved and needed her as he flooded her pussy. "There you go, *mo aingeal*. Take it all, sweet thing." There was so much cum that when he finally pulled out, his seed began spilling out of Coby, so he promptly scooped it up and pushed it back in with two fingers while kissing and whispering sweet nothings to her.

I wasn't aware of my hand moving until it rested on my growing belly.

I knew, most of all, that Coby was having mixed feelings about me being pregnant.

She was excited to be an aunt, but had understood more than ever how it had felt to watch them get married, with me stuck on the sidelines—even if it had been a sham wedding.

To everyone who didn't matter, only she was his wife. Only our inner circle knew the truth. I held that knowledge close to my heart because the truth was all that mattered. I was theirs, and they were mine.

Irrevocably.

Forever.

And now, we are having a baby.

Ocean pulled away from her, his long dick semi-hard and covered in our juices when he rolled onto his back next to her. His eyelids were low when he looked across the small space at me, his hand reaching for his dick and slowly stroking the length back to life.

No words were needed when I went to him.

He was fully hard by the time I squatted with one hand on my thigh to steady me inside the moving limo and my other hand around his dick. Lining up my pussy with his long pole, I slowly seated myself.

"All the way down," he ordered when I started to feel full half-way down.

I gave him a cutting look, and he gave me one right back.

"You can do it, bestie," Coby sleepily mumbled with her eyes closed.

Knowing Ocean wasn't playing, I sank lower until my fat, round ass met his solid thighs, and every inch of him was buried inside of me. We both moaned at the feeling. "Like that?"

He gave my ass a slap, making it wobble. "Hell yeah."

Planting my hands on his chest and keeping my heeled feet on the ground, I slowly began bouncing on his dick, loving the feel of our skin slapping together with each downstroke.

Coby had regained her energy and sat up to suckle at my sore nipples. The bite of pain mixed with pleasure made me clench around Ocean, who let out a tortured groan.

"Coby, sweetheart," Ocean pleaded when she kept teasing my nipples, and my pussy consequently strangled his dick tighter and tighter.

"Fuck, this dick feels so good," I moaned as I bounced harder and faster. Coby's mouth traveled to my neck, and I turned my head, our lips and tongues tangling immediately. "God, I love you," I whispered between kisses. "Thank you for being my family."

We'd always said 'I love you' before as friends, but it had taken on a different meaning now. One that we couldn't hide from.

Coby broke the kiss and stared into my eyes, her gaze hopeful as she searched mine. A moment later, a huge grin broke out on her face. "Ride or fucking die, bestie. I love you, too."

With Coby's help, I rode our husband until I came. Sensing that Ocean was about to erupt, I slapped my wife's ass and climbed off our man's dick. "Go get it, bestie."

I wanted Coby to have as much of his cum as she needed until her belly was round and full like mine. Ocean was already sitting up and reaching for her when she mounted him while I curled up next to them and tried not to fall asleep.

Our collective baby was wearing me out already.

EPILOGUE

OCEAN

Seven years later, in their hideaway home…

"YOU TASTE HER, DON'T YOU?" HUNTER'S MOUTH WAS full, so she couldn't respond, but her hand moving faster inside her leggings told me she did. "Yeah, you do. Our greedy little wife made a mess before she ditched me. Be a good girl and clean it up for me, baby."

Hunter shivered and nodded while I forced another inch of my dick down her throat, fucking her mouth without restraint.

Goddamn.

I could feel my nut rising when my office door burst open.

I looked over my shoulder and swore viciously, hurriedly slipping my dick out of my wife's mouth and back into my sweats as soon as I saw a small form running full speed for my desk.

"Aye, little girl! Stop right there!"

"Oooooh!" my worrisome daughter said, stopping in her tracks after hearing me cursing up a storm. "Daddy said bad words again. I'm telling Mama Coby. She gon' get you."

"Nevaeh."

Hearing her mother's voice but not seeing her, our six-year-old daughter frowned before inching closer like she thought something would jump out at her from behind the curtains.

She was distrustful and stubborn, just like her damn mama.

And too smart for her own good, which is why I shot Hunter an annoyed look. Nevaeh had already been on her way back out the door. Hunter had just given her a reason to stay.

Explaining to our daughter why she had two moms and a dad had been hard enough. I wasn't ready to explain what mommies and daddies did when they loved each other. Realizing her mistake, my wife quickly swiped a hand over her mouth, and I helped her wobble to her feet, rubbing my hand over her swollen belly where my son grew.

Abel was still grumbling over me knocking her up since he'd trained Hunter a little too well. It had only made sense to make her his second in command. It also meant he got more time off, even though I didn't know why he needed it. Motherfucker didn't know how to relax if someone slapped him with the instructions.

"You okay, Vengeance?"

"Perfect."

I couldn't help feeling up that incredible ass as I leaned down to kiss her. "Tell me you love me."

She reached up, her heart and gaze open as her soft hand stroked my beard. "I love you, Ocean."

I never got tired of hearing it.

Every time felt like the first, which had happened the night I almost lost them both. I had been apologizing for not being there when she blurted out that she loved me. It was the moment I learned what it felt like to be weak in the knees.

"I love you too."

Nevaeh paused after seeing her mother get up from behind the desk, her long pigtails swaying when she cocked her head and put her little hands on her hips like she was the parent. "Mama… what were you doing down there?" she yelled like she was appalled.

"I was looking for something," Hunter answered sternly, letting our daughter know the subject was closed. "What did your father tell you about knocking?"

Nevaeh suddenly started looking around guiltily and shrugged.

"Little girl…"

Just as Hunter was about to lay into her, Coby walked in carrying our son. Nevaeh immediately ran to her and wrapped her arms around her waist with a fake ass pout. "Mama Coby, they're being mean again. And daddy cursed."

"Snitch." I ran over and tickled Nevaeh's stomach, making her giggle and beg for mercy until she couldn't take it anymore.

She ran to hide behind Hunter.

Taking the baby from Coby, my wife smirked at the dirty look I gave her.

Coby knew what she'd done—using me to get off and then leaving me hanging with a hard dick because the little cockblocker in my hands started crying.

I lifted my son and kissed his fat cheek.

My kids were growing too fast for my liking. I need time to slow down. I needed more moments like this with them.

I worked way too fucking much, but my wives were patient with me.

Most of the time.

"You're going to make this up to me tonight," I warned Coby in a low tone. "And I don't want to hear shit about you being sleepy or wanting a back rub first."

Coby smiled and leaned in to kiss me, giving my dick a surreptitious squeeze while Nevaeh was distracted with rubbing her mother's belly and talking to her new little brother. "I sent Hunter to find you. You didn't come?"

I shook my head.

"Aww, you poor thing," she cooed, stroking my dick through my sweats. It gave an excited jerk under her palm.

"Shit, girl. I fucking love you," I blurted.

"I love you too, hubby." I pulled Coby closer for another kiss, and Adonis immediately latched onto her hair and yanked. "Ow!"

He already had a fucking death grip at only a few months old.

After freeing his mother, I carried our son over to the sofa.

Sitting, I stared at him as I always did, wondering what his future held. Unlike my father, I made a vow to let him follow his own path.

My son stared back and suddenly smiled as if he could see right through to my heart.

Did he find me worthy?

Did he feel how much I loved him?

Did he know how terrified he made me?

I had these same questions when Nevaeh was born, and she still scared the shit out of me. I was afraid that I'd screw them up—that I'd turn cold and cruel like my father had been.

May he rest in shit.

Asshole finally up and died a year after I turned him into a stump.

Adonis babbled emphatically while bouncing on his legs as if he'd read my mind and agreed.

"Yeah, fuck him," I secretly whispered to my son.

Adonis screeched and bounced even harder.

It was a blessing that he'd never known his grandfather.

Unfortunately, he'd never know his grandmother either.

My mom died a year ago while Coby was pregnant with our second child. The first time she'd gotten pregnant was shortly after she and Hunter were married, but she suffered a miscarriage. It had nearly broken us all, but none more than Coby. We helped each other through it, but Coby had been so crushed that she refused to try again, out of fear that it would happen again. And then, after one reckless weekend in Greece, our baby boy was born.

He'd shown up and restored her faith in fate.

Now, Adonis was only a few months old, and Coby was already pregnant again. It was my first time knocking her and Hunter up together, and I admit… I've been walking around like my nuts were full of magic ever since.

Nevaeh ran over and climbed onto the sofa next to me. Hunter and Coby snuck out while Nev told me about her new teacher, Mrs. Harris, who was nice, and how she wasn't talking to her little friend Prudence anymore because her dad said I was a bad man.

"Are you bad, daddy?"

For a moment, I was stuck between the truth and a lie.

I knew the day would come when my daughter would come to understand our way of life, but I wasn't ready for that dose of reality yet. I wanted to keep being her hero.

"What do you think?" I asked.

"No way! You're nice to my brother, my mommies, and me. You watch Doc McStuffins with me and make the best chocolate milk."

I smiled down at her while I quietly wrestled with indecision once more. "I have done bad things, baby girl. My job... it isn't a nice one. But I want you to know that I love you, and I would never hurt you or your brother."

"I know, daddy. I've been bad sometimes, too. I ate two cookies yesterday when Mama Coby said I could only have one, and I knew I was supposed to knock first, but I just forgot."

I said a silent prayer that she'd stay this innocent forever. "That's okay. We'll just keep it between us."

Nevaeh exhaled as if relieved to have lifted that burden off her shoulders. She rested her head against my arm and sighed again. "I don't care what Prudence says. You're the best dad ever. She's stupid anyway, and her hair is ugly."

I swear to fucking God, I'd never felt taller.

Coco's old cranky ass, who I hadn't noticed napping in the corner, growled as if he agreed. It was more likely that he wanted us to shut up already.

"Yeah, she sounds like a fucking hater," I agreed. Nevaeh giggled, and I perked a brow. "You're not going to tell Mama Coby that I cursed?"

She shook her head without lifting it from my arm. "Not this time, daddy."

"Thanks, baby girl. Let's go see what your mommies are up to."

Adonis just babbled and drooled while Nevaeh took my hand. The three of us left the room, my daughter talking my ear off while we traveled through Glamis in search of Hunter and Coby.

Turn the page for a teeny, tiny bonus chapter.

BONUS CHAPTER

OCEAN

THERE WAS A MAN IN MY OFFICE WITH HIS FUCKING FEET ON my desk.

The room was too dark to see much, but it was the pungent aroma of weed that had given him away. The intruder didn't react when I hit the lights or flinch when I promptly placed a gun to his head.

I would be impressed if that were easy to do.

The stranger with a death wish was obviously expecting me.

"How was your honeymoon?" my uninvited guest greeted calmly. "I heard Tahiti is nice this time of year. Or was it Bora Bora?"

"Both," I said, recognizing the younger man's voice from the phone call I'd received a week ago. "I heard you were in prison."

"They let me out for good behavior."

"Hmm." I pulled out my phone with my other hand and texted Abel to lock down the place, then Hunter with instructions to get herself and Coby somewhere safe until I came for them.

"That's not necessary," the intruder said without turning around. "I'm here for answers as promised."

"So, is this a friendly visit or an unfortunate one?" I asked after receiving replies from both of them and slipping my phone back into my pocket.

The man cocked his head slightly to the side but still made no move to let me see his face when he said, "I thought I was clear. That depends on you."

"And if I don't have the answers you want?" I lowered my gun and pushed his feet off my desk before sitting in my chair on the other side.

At last, I was face-to-face with the man who once ruled Chicago.

Angeles Knight.

I heard he'd given up his seat for love.

Suppressing a yawn and feeling a headache on the rise, it was all I could do not to check my watch.

Maybe I should have done that.

If I had given up my birthright like Angel, I could be in bed right now, curled up with my wives. Instead, I'm dealing with this shit.

"Then I'll leave the same way I came," he swore.

"And I'm supposed to believe you came alone?"

Angel's lips tilted, but no amusement could be found in his dark gaze. "Of course not."

"I hope you've warned whoever's sneaking around my house not to piss off my wife. Her trigger finger is itchier than mine."

"Funny. I thought there were two."

Unwilling to give the former Knight intel that he might not already have, I ignored his bait and changed the subject. "Why are you here?"

Angel's expression suddenly darkened, his voice taking on a hard edge when he spoke. "You know why."

He moved fast, slamming a worn photo on the desk. There were three people in the shot—Angel, another White man with sandy blond hair, and a much younger version of my former associate.

His black-and-blond-streaked hair was longer, but his green eyes were familiar as they stared into the camera.

Kellan.

It was all I could do not to snatch the picture from the desk for a closer look. Instead, I sat back in my chair, feigning indifference.

"Where is he?" Angel bit out.

I shrugged as if I hadn't combed every inch of the city looking for the man after he disappeared. I didn't know if the man sitting across from me was a friend or foe of Kellan's, but either way, there was only one reason he didn't tell Angel where he was going.

Kellan didn't want to be found.

As much as it killed me, I was hellbent on respecting that. It was the least I could do after he risked his life protecting Hunter and Coby. He'd gotten what he wanted when he killed Michael Black, which meant he could have easily slipped away before the carnage.

"I wouldn't know," I answered. "He didn't exactly give me two weeks' notice before taking off." It was the truth, though I could tell Angel didn't believe me. "Until you showed up here, I assumed he went home."

Kellan had come to Black Veil to kill Black, his father, for what the pimp did to his mother when he was a child. I couldn't fucking blame him, and neither could Hunter. It was the reason Hunter hadn't killed him that night. She'd even been moved enough to let him take her beloved Deborah.

Angel shook his head before shoving tanned fingers through his dark hair. His gaze turned bleak as worry began to overshadow his anger.

I sighed. "Go home, Angel. Be with your woman and son. Enjoy your freedom. You were away from them for three years. Kellan will let us know when he's ready to be found."

"Z."

"Bless you."

Angel rolled his eyes and then shot to his feet, snatching the picture from the desk and pocketing it. "His name is Zachariah Ellis. His real family calls him Z." I looked away, my teeth clenched so hard that my headache immediately became a migraine. A moment later, I heard Angel sigh. "Kellan is his middle name."

I relaxed.

At least, it hadn't all been a lie.

"I'll let you know if I hear something," I offered reluctantly.

If Kellan—Z—ever decided to come home, which one would he return to? I had hoped it would be here in Black Veil, but now I wasn't so sure. Maybe he'd return to Chicago.

Angel obviously cared deeply for Zachariah/Kellan—enough to risk coming here, breaking into my home, and pissing off my wives.

Angel nodded at my offer but didn't promise the same before walking out.

Custody battles were always ugly like that.

In case you're wondering about this little crossover, Angel is the anti-hero from the Stolen duet, and Kellan/Zachariah is his best friend and a side character in Angel and Mian's story. The Kellan and Michael Black plot line served no real purpose other than giving my long-time readers a chance to see Z again. Hope you don't mind. They've been waiting eight years for his spin-off. >.<

ACKNOWLEDGMENTS

To everyone who read the original serial in 2023, thank you so much for showing me that there is an audience for Ocean, Hunter, and Coby's story, and I hope that you loved them just as much a second time around. Sometimes, I like to step off the beaten path and do something that scares me. Thanks for keeping me company. Best. Readers. Ever. xoxo

ABOUT THE AUTHOR

B.B. Reid is a bestselling author of several romances, including *Crucible*, the imaginative retelling of Goldilocks. She's most known for her dark, diverse, and contemporary romances but began her career writing new adult. B.B. currently resides in Atlanta with Ivan, her moody tuxedo cat. When she's not being a nomad, she enjoys gaming, white chocolate mocha, home decor, and retail therapy.